The Unexpected Daughter

Sheryl Parbhoo

The Unexpected Daughter

Editing, writer's coaching, and project management:
Wayne South Smith
www.waynesouthsmith.com

Cover design:
Mark Sandlin

Cover production design:
Laura Nalesnik

Author photo:
Kelly Weaver

Interior page design:
Jason Orr
Jera Publishing

ISBN: 978-0-9982310-0-6

For my mother, Jean Bryant, and my mother-in-law, Sarlaben Parbhoo, who both taught me the meaning of a mother's love.

Chapter 1

Jenny

Jenny opened her eyes and licked her parched lips, but her tongue scoured the surface instead of soothing it. Her lips stuck to her teeth as she closed them, and no matter how much she rolled her tongue around inside her mouth, the damage of sleeping with her mouth gaping open all night had been done. Wincing at the sharp glow peeking through the blinds on the window, she lay still as the crisp lines of the slats blurred in and out of focus. Her hair fanned out on the pillow, and the scent of white tea and ginger shampoo radiated from the strands baking in the morning light.

When her heavy eyelids fully opened, she surveyed the sleek black dresser with several square bottles of cologne lined across the top, all in a perfect color spectrum from darkest glass to a pale blue tinted one on the end that glinted in the light. In the corner sat a chair with a pair of black slacks and a man's dress shirt neatly folded across the leather seat cushion. Shiny black dress shoes lined up straight, touching each other between the chair legs. A twisted thong draped over a shoe, and it was then that she saw her cocktail dress crumpled inside out on the floor. Afraid, she looked at herself and saw the sateen sheet snaked around her torso with one of her breasts lying exposed. With a tug of the sheet, she covered her chest and stayed on her side facing the window. Vodka still swam through her veins, and she tried to squeeze out some recollection of where she was and why she was nude. Suddenly, neurons began to fire and electricity lit up her skin from the weight of a wiry-haired arm draped across her waist and the tickle of breath on her exposed neck.

Oh, shit, Jenny!

A ripple tickled her back as her inner voice squealed.

Roshan is right here. Naked. Oh...my...God!

Like plucking fish from an iced-over lake, she tried to extract snippets of the last twenty four hours from the holes opening up in her thawing consciousness. Okay...walking across the stage, diploma finally in hand. Tasseled mortarboards raining on her head. Yes, that's it...adjusting the front of her strapless dress... her friend Marissa yanking her by the hand into the restaurant. Okay, and clinking champagne glasses, classmates calling each other doctor over and over, trying out the title for size.

"Doctor Jenkins, would you like me to fetch you a new drink?" Roshan had whispered into the baby hairs at the nape of her neck.

"Why, yes, Doctor Desai. Thank you." She had turned her face to his and whispered back.

Yes, that's where all of this began.

Pinned still under the weight of his limp arm, she listened to the in and out of breaths on her neck, resisting the urge to rub the tickle away.

Play dead until you figure this out, Jenny.

So, she lay there, eyes squeezed shut against the beating in her head, and continued to pluck more moments out of her defrosting brain, playing like scenes from a movie.

She and Marissa arrived at the door to the ballroom guarded by a sign reading "Welcome Graduating Class of 2005, School of Dentistry." Inside, dimly lit crystal chandeliers cast a golden glow on the people waiting at the bar. In the middle stood their friend Jay, a tiny man with a big personality, a female student, and Roshan towering over them.

"There are Jay and Roshan over there," Marissa pointed. "See? In the line for drinks?"

Jay saw them and waved. Roshan turned around and half-hugged Marissa, then Jenny. His hand lingered around her waist for a few seconds longer than usual.

"Marissa and Jenny," Jay said. "You know Whitney, right? From upstairs in oral surgery with me?"

Whitney shook Jenny and Marissa's hands. "Nice to see you both."

They'd reached the front of the line, and Jay said, "Okay, Whitney, Marissa, order a drink." Jenny turned to Roshan.

He was already looking down at her. "Your usual Cosmo?"

"Of course! You and Cosmos have been my best friends for four years. Why stop now?"

"Right. And I'll never abandon my old friend Jack...or you either." As the others drifted away to mingle, he turned to the bartender. "One Cosmo with an extra—"

"I'll order for myself, Roshan—"

He grinned at her but continued her order. "—with an extra lime twist. Jack and Coke for me. Light on the Coke." He placed the short glass in her hands.

"I'm going to miss our study sessions together," she said.

"Yeah, me too. I'll miss seeing you in your sweats, peering over at me from behind your horn-rimmed glasses under those God awful fluorescent lights in the library."

"Yeah...and those sketches you did of me. You spent more time drawing me than you did studying."

"It's fun drawing you. You're funny looking." He stuck his tongue out at her. She punched him. "But, no more time for that silliness. Time for us to have real jobs."

As they stepped over to their friends, Jenny's fingers tingled as they accidentally brushed up against his hand.

Jay raised his glass. "Here's to my little cousin's class of 2005. Wishing you all the best in life as you schmucks make your mark on the grills of unsuspecting patients all over the country."

"Here, here!"

And the drinking began.

After her four drinks, she'd stopped counting. Jenny's forehead pounded now with regret, annoyed that she let herself, the child of two addictive parents, get so out of control. As she lay there, she listened to his soft breath and inhaled his musky cologne and man scent.

With the second drink, their fingers had entwined when they danced under the glow on the dance floor.

She turned her head softly toward Roshan now, stealthily shifting onto her back. His arm slid across her belly, and he mumbled.

With the third drink muffling her inner voice's screams to stop drinking, she and Roshan huddled in a corner outside the ballroom, his body pressed against hers, just talking. After the final swallow of her fourth—or was it her fifth?—her inner voice was silent. Roshan turned over his keys to Jay. They tumbled into the backseat of Jay's car.

Marissa's voice echoed in her mind, "Why don't you two get a room?"

Then there was the mingling of vodka and Jack on their lips. Their giggles and Jenny's "shush!" as they entered their apartment building, making their way down the first floor hall to Roshan's apartment. Then, the taste of sweat on his lips as she pulled him to her gently by the hair. His hand slid around her waist to pull her inside. The door shut behind them.

Now, she watched Roshan's face, still again, eyes moving under their lids. Her stomach turned in mild panic, hoping he would rouse, at the same time hoping he would keep sleeping. She needed more time to think. She lay her arm gingerly across his. She liked the contrast of hers, with its soft blond hairs, lying against his sinewy bicep. She couldn't resist the urge to run her fingertips across the top of his hand. He shuddered and opened his eyes, nestling his head further into his pillow. A smile spread across his face as he squinted and blinked, focusing on her face.

Time to face the music now, Jenny.

He lifted his head close to hers. "Well, good morning." He squinted and dropped his head back again. "Why didn't I shut those blinds yesterday?"

She giggled nervously. "Good morning to you too…I'll close them."

She twisted her torso around, spooling the sheet around her, and dropped her legs off the bed toward the window, but Roshan tugged the edge of the sheet, and she slowly fell back toward him.

Okay. He's not screaming and running from the premises. This is a good sign

She placed her head back beside his arms, and he shielded his face with his hand.

But now what?

He propped himself up on his elbow and looked around at her clothes heaped on the floor next to his folded clothes. He rubbed his palm across his lopsided hair, then his bloodshot eyes, and let out a puff.

"Well, it seems we have a situation on our hands, don't we?"

How do I blow this off? Or do I blow this off? Is he going to blow this off?

"Uh, yeah. We do. Look, Roshan—"

"Just look at that mess you made with your clothes. And a thong in my new shoe?"

"Yeah, well, I don't really remember how that got there."

"I do." He plopped himself onto his back and stared up at the ceiling. "I remember very well." He looked at her with a shadow of embarrassment crossing his face, and she felt her cheeks flush.

"You must not have had as much as me."

"No, I did. But, I'm bigger than you, and I've built up more of an alcohol tolerance than you. I get more practice."

She shuddered, flashing back to images of her dad on their sofa snoring with a beer in his hand. "I hope you don't have any drunks in your family. It's catching, you know."

He blinked and put on a cheesy smile. "Nope. I'm golden."

She thought his smile was a little too practiced, but didn't say anything. It was none of her business.

"Okay, okay. Who am I to judge?" The weight of an elephant's foot crushed her forehead as she tried to turn her head toward the clothes in the corner. "God, you took the time to fold your clothes?"

"Of course. Why wouldn't I?"

She looked into his eyes for any hint of jest, but he was serious.

"I knew you had obsessive compulsive tendencies in the clinic, but wow, this has opened up a whole new side of your personality to me." She playfully smacked him on the shoulder and dropped her hand softly onto his bare skin. In their four years of friendship, she had never been invited to his apartment. They would share a drink, maybe two, at a pub after exams. Occasionally, a group of friends would have dinners at the barbecue joint down the street where he ordered salads and bread after study sessions, and increasingly in the last few months, it became just the two of them. But when time came to go home, he was always a gentleman and walked her to her apartment door. Despite the intense heart fluttering she felt when they hugged goodbye, he never hinted at any other intentions with her.

He grinned sheepishly. "I was raised with order around me. There's a lot about me that you don't know."

Her hand felt awkward lying there. The air between them felt cooler to the touch suddenly, and she felt their friendship wall plant itself back between them. Despite herself, her eyes were drawn to the almond shape of his eyes, the black drape of eyelashes around them, and the curve of his mouth. She wanted to brush away the shaggy wisps of hair that hung in his eye, but kept her hand still.

"That makes two of us." She pulled her hand back and lay flat on her back. Her head throbbed. She fixed her eyes on the brass ceiling light above, but she could feel his intense gaze and knew for a slice of a moment his guard was down. What it would feel like to wrap her naked legs around him. To breathe in his breath. Snippets of last night didn't satisfy her desire for him, but she knew it would have to. This could never happen again.

A hammering spread through her head, and she grimaced.

"You okay? Need some Advil?" His warm breath tickled her face as he kissed her temple gingerly.

"Yes, please, that would be wonderful." Even her whisper was now painful. Lifting her half-shut eyes, she caught a glimpse of him rolling off the bed, and embarrassment tingled her stomach. Her eyes stored the image of his bare, tan back and tight behind securely in her mind, and she closed them to seal in the image. She heard him quickly step around the bed and slide on his boxer shorts, and not until the medicine cabinet opened and closed with a thud did she look again.

Dishes clattered in the kitchen, cups clunked together, water ran, and finally the pills rattled out of the bottle. Roshan sat on the edge of the bed beside her.

She pulled the silky sheet up to her neck as she sat up and swallowed two pills, praying for some quick relief. She pulled the sheet up higher and tucked it over her shoulders. "Thanks," then added, "Um, I need to get dressed. But, oh God, I need a few more minutes for my head."

"Why don't we get something to eat? Soak up the alcohol in your stomach." He gently put his hand on her shoulder, the way he did with strangers when he talked.

Good, we're moving on from last night.

She nodded, willing to try anything. He placed one of his clean tee shirts and a pair of pajama bottoms on the bed next to her and walked away so she could dress in privacy. Jenny gingerly placed each arm and her head into the shirt and cautiously stepped into the pants. Acutely aware of how disheveled she must look, she pulled her blonde wispy hair back into a ponytail and knotted it with a section of hair to keep it out of her face. When she looked up, there was Roshan leaning on the bedroom doorway, holding a piece of toast, watching her with a sympathetic grin.

He placed the corner of the toast to her mouth and said, "Nibble. You need food in your stomach."

Gratefully, she chewed a piece and let him lift her arm to lead her to the kitchen table.

"You don't even know how beautiful you are, do you?"

Her stomach fluttered at his spoken thought. She wondered how she must look at that moment: mascara smeared down her face, bags under her eyes. He saw beauty in that?

"It's really too bad I won't be able to see you again. Not like this."

He was right. This was a drunken, wild mistake. Nothing more.

In the kitchen, Roshan pulled some stainless steel storage bowls from the refrigerator and sat them on the counter. Jenny peeked inside the nearly empty refrigerator. After years of watching him eat lettuce, tomatoes and cheese on a bun at Burger King, she knew he was vegetarian. At that moment, she hoped he cheated a little and would have something familiar. In high school, she'd get breakfast at the all-night diner by her house after the few times she went drinking with friends, and she wished for some of that right now.

Disappointed, but ravenous, she asked, "What...do...you...eat at home?"

He laughed. "Not bacon and eggs, if that's what you're looking for." He pulled her over to him at the counter and slid the lid off of a bowl, exposing some type of fluffy yellow food, peppered with poppy and cumin seeds. It resembled a greenish Thanksgiving turkey stuffing. But, without the turkey, undoubtedly. "It's called *gora no lot.* Taste it."

"What's in it?" Her stomach was churning so hard, even the strong unfamiliar smell made her curious.

"Don't ask. Just try."

After warming the food in the microwave, he scooped a heap of it onto a paper plate and spooned a small morsel into her mouth slowly. She felt his eyes on her as she chewed slowly. With each chew, the gingery, cumin aroma filled her nose and throat, taking her by surprise. She chewed more because the mingling of the spices and heat in her mouth exploded. "Mmmm. That's so good." She grabbed the spoon out of his hand and helped herself to another spoonful. Suddenly her eyes started to water, and she had to clear her throat. "Hmmm, but really spicy. You eat spicy hot food for breakfast?"

"Nothing says good morning like some masala spices with your coffee and green chili in each bite."

"Oooh, I guess not. But, I'm used to bland in the morning. You know, buttered toast, scrambled eggs. They kind of ease you into the day. This is like…wow!" She scooped yet another spoonful into her mouth.

"We call this *tikku*. It means spicy. And if it ain't *tikku*, it ain't worth eating."

"Spoken like a true Indian southerner," she muffled as she chewed. "How do you make this?"

"No idea. My mum or some aunts cook for me and Jay every weekend. Mum drives with Jay's mum, my Monisha Auntie, from Atlanta about once a month to see me, and they do prayers with my aunts at the temple. She stays at my aunt's house—well she's more of a family friend really—and they cook all weekend long for me and Jay. We were raised on this food, and the mums know we need some flavor America doesn't have. Plus," he elbowed her gently in the arm as she chewed, "it's their job to keep us from converting to the evil ways of getting burgers and chicken nuggets at a drive through."

"Or, any other evils, I bet." Winking, she puckered her lips exaggeratedly for a second, then they both self-consciously laughed it off.

She remembered seeing him a few months before in the clinic the morning after he said a lot of family members had flown in from California, his eyes drooping with exhaustion.

"Wild weekend? We missed you at the Cantina after classes. Where'd you and Jay disappear to?"

"Family time." He pulled his patient's chart out of the bin. She waited for more explanation, but none came.

"Gee, you sound so excited."

"It gets old sometimes."

"I wouldn't know." She smiled wanly. "So was it a special occasion?"

"Yes."

"And...what was the occasion?"

"Just a get together." He looked depressed as he bit his lip.

Curious, she tried to pry more information from him, punctuating every word. "And...did it go well?"

"Sure." He rubbed his hand over his eyes. "I got engaged."

"You're engaged." Her words fell flat despite her efforts, and she picked up her heart from the floor and cheerily asked, "That's great! How long have you two been dating?" The wheels of her memory began turning as snippets of flirty glances over the past months and close conversations between them popped into her mind. Just how long, she wondered.

He didn't have the happy, enamored look of a guy who was engaged. "Priya and I never dated. It was kind of an arranged thing."

"Seriously?"

"As a heart attack. It's an Indian thing." With that, he turned and started toward his patient's cubicle.

Though his back to her made it obvious he wanted the conversation to end, she pried.

"Oh. Okay. Well, did everything go well, then?"

He'd only replied, "Aunts and uncles, food, ceremonies. The way it was supposed to go." He'd turned to look at his patient's chart, and the subject was over.

Priya. Her name was Priya. Over the next couple of months, he'd never shown her a picture of this Priya. She was a faceless entity with only a name.

"Yeah. American food, American women. You're all the devil." His eyes sparkled and he leaned in close to her now, but pulled back reluctantly.

"As long as I've known you, I had no idea you didn't cook for yourself."

"My mother does it because it keeps me a vegetarian. And her food is kind of her hugs. And, yeah, well, what she doesn't know won't hurt her. Besides, it's how she shows her love."

"You're very lucky. I was raised on the evil ways of cheeseburger Happy Meals. I've told you before, right? My mom wasn't around much. And my dad couldn't cook at all." She felt her eyes go foggy with the memory, but perked up and smiled up at him. "If I had a dollar for every Happy Meal toy I ever got, I would be set for life! But, alas, education had to be the ticket for me to riches."

"You had more toys than me."

"What? No happy meal toys? You're kidding."

"Nope. Not a one."

She shook her head. "I'd trade those for home cooked food anyway. I barely know what my mom looks like anymore, much less if she's learned to cook or not. Your mom loves you. That's better than toys."

"Don't be fooled. It comes with a lot of strings." He covered his mouth and nose and pretended to suffocate himself. Pretending to gasp for breath, he listed, "She manages my food, so she can check up on me. It's been just me and her for a long time, and her life is all about me. Sometimes I fantasize about eating a hamburger in front of her and watching her reaction, but I'd never really do that. I've never been able to stand to see her cry."

They finished their breakfast in silence, leaning against the Formica countertop and staring at the floor.

"Are you going to tell Priya about this?"

"Hell no," he answered without pause. "I may not love her, but don't want to hurt her either. She's flying in from L.A. today for the graduation party, and with all the people around, I wouldn't have the chance to talk to her alone anyway. Besides, we are not married yet."

"I feel like a scumbag." She looked him in the eyes as she spoke and squeezed her hand into a ball against the counter, resisting the urge to touch him. "I think it is her business. I'm the other woman. Even if it was for a night."

Am I an "other woman?" I don't think he even likes his fiancé. Does that count?

"Don't feel bad." He laid his hand on her shoulder. "We were both into this, but I'm the one who is the dirtbag." His fingers caressed her shoulder through the cotton shirt. "You will always be my best friend. We all have our crosses to bear." He removed his hand and diverted his eyes. "That's why we need to stay friends. I need a reminder of this."

"I, for one, will never get married or have kids. My mom left my dad when I was little and my dad, well, isn't in an exactly normal marriage now." She paused, not sure if she should go on, but then spat out the truth. "He married a girl much younger than him."

His widened eyes made her self-conscious.

"Creepy, huh? And now, your enthusiasm over spending the rest of your life with someone is just the nail in the coffin for my desire to marry."

He shook his head and slid his hand to the nape of her neck, looking her in the eye. The sadness and longing made her look away. His hand slipped away from her neck and down to his side.

No good can come of this.

"So, friends, right?" he asked, hand extended.

They shook hands, and Roshan pulled her into a hug. He kissed her on the cheek, and she pulled back to look him in the eye. He leaned in close to her and brushed his lips against hers, but she pulled away. Her back bumped into the bowl of food balanced on the edge of the counter, spilling the green fluff all over the floor.

"I'm sorry. Your mum would kill me." She reached for a paper towel, but he stopped her hand.

"No. I'll get it. This was my fault."

Nodding, she headed toward the bathroom. "I'd better freshen up and get out of here."

She saw him standing in the kitchen, a wad of paper towels clenched in a fist, watching her leave. When the bathroom door shut behind her, she heard a loud thud that shook the walls. She opened the door and peeked out. "Are you okay?"

He was standing in a field of food on the floor, some still sprinkled on the tops of his feet, and holding his hand tight. In front of him, a hole in the wall gaped open, and white powder covered the trash can that sat beneath it. He didn't look at her. "I'm fine." He placed his powdery white hand under the faucet and ran water over it until it was rinsed off.

She quietly shut the bathroom door again and left him alone. A few moments later as the roar of the vacuum cleaner numbed her head, she blocked out his hurt look. In the mirror, she surveyed her messy hair and face, wondering again how Roshan could see beauty in her right now. She bent over the sink and splashed warm water on her cheeks, and with drips falling on the vanity top, wiped herself dry. Her face was brighter and fresher, and the smeared mascara was gone. Perhaps he had seen past the mess to how she really looked right now. She brushed her hair with his brush. Her long, blond hairs wove their way into the bristles and tangled with his wavy, black ones. She set it on the sink, not wanting to untangle them but to leave him with a little reminder of her.

The vacuum noise ceased, and all she heard was the sound of a spray bottle sputtering cleaning spray around the kitchen. With a dab of his toothpaste on her finger, she rubbed her teeth and swished. She looked and smelled like a new person, except for the sagging pajama bottoms and tee shirt she wore. Afraid of what kind of mood she would meet in the kitchen, she opened the door. A fresh bleach smell was in the air, and Roshan was on hands and knees, rubbing vigorously with a paper towel.

"Let me help." She lowered herself to the floor and took the bleach bottle out his hand.

"I can do this, Jenny. I have a bit of OCD as you know. Let me just get this. My way."

"No. I made the mess. I'm helping."

He grabbed the spray bottle from her hand, held it out of her reach, a small smile stretching across his mouth. Relieved at his lightened mood, she grabbed for the bottle again, but he got up and ran into the other room, holding it above his head. She dropped her paper towels on the linoleum floor and ran after him.

"You know you can't reach. You can't stop me from doing this myself."

"You can't stop me from helping you. I clean up my own messes." She jumped up and tried to grab the bottle, but he was so tall, she stumbled and fell into him.

A jingling sound came from outside the front door, and they stopped. He looked at her, handed her the bottle, and stepped quickly to the door. The lock in the door clunked, stopped, and clunked again, and the door opened a crack. Jenny froze in place, confused, with the bottle balanced delicately on the tips of her fingers. Roshan glanced at her, and as he turned his head toward the door, it opened wider, revealing a tall woman in a pink and turquoise sari. She said something in another language and thrust a cardboard box in Roshan's direction. He lunged to catch it, and his arms flexed under its weight.

"Mummy." He smiled and smoothly laid the box on the kitchen counter, obviously careful to walk between her and the living room, giving her a tentative hug.

"*Kemcho, dikra,*" the woman said, pulling him closer.

His mother!

Jenny held her breath, and looked for an escape route. The living room door led out onto the balcony, and the only other door was the one that led to the corridor next to them. Besides, she was braless with no panties in a tee shirt and huge pajamas pants, and barefoot. She wasn't going anywhere.

The kitchen opened to the living room through a breakfast bar that divided the two rooms. She saw Roshan standing next to his mom, who nearly reached his height, strategically placing himself between her and Jenny's direction. She could see his mother's face peek in and out around his frame, her black rimmed eyes focused on putting away containers in cabinets and the refrigerator. The jingle of the bangles on her wrists crowded out the sound of their voices, so Jenny didn't even try to make out any English words that might have been spoken. Jenny was surprised to see that a stud in her nose glinted of gold as brightly as her bangle covered wrists. Though she wore a different color today, Jenny recognized her glint from the crowd of family around Roshan at their graduation ceremony. She was the thin older woman by his side in every picture, the one who towered over the other women around them, beaming down with pride. Her thick wavy hair was tied loosely and fell lazily in different shade of bronze down her back, unlike the other women her age whose undyed salt and pepper hair was pulled back tightly in oiled braids. Her black almond eyes had only small crinkles at the corners and added drama to her face. She was striking. But, the striking beauty drained from her face when she put her last dish down and cupped Roshan's cheeks in her hands. His tried to block Jenny from view, but Esha spotted her anyway.

Jenny tried to slide to the side of the room, but Esha looked head on at Jenny.

"Roshan," the woman whispered, perfectly still, only her lips moving, as if she'd seen a snake and didn't want it to see her.

"Mummy," he turned to look at Jenny and then stumbled into the living room to stand in front of Jenny.

His mother said nothing but did not drop her stare.

"Mummy, um, this is my friend Jenny. She graduated with me." His accent suddenly changed to choppy and fast, with rolled "r's" and random foreign words dropped in the middle that Jenny couldn't follow. Shakily ushering Jenny toward the kitchen, he rambled, sounding like a different person. "Jenny, this is my mum, Esha."

Wishing she could squeeze under the door and disappear, she forced herself to cheerily extend her hand to Esha. But Esha's arms remained at her sides.

"Hello." Jenny's voice landed into silence. She let her hand drop softly to her sides and tried not to look into Esha's eyes or at Roshan. She fingered the soft seam on the side of her pants leg and waited for Roshan to do something. Anything.

"Mummy, what...are...you doing here now?" His English rolled out gravelly and slowly now. "I told you I'd come to Auntie's house by three this afternoon to get ready for the party." The muscles in his jaw protruded like stone, and his Adam's apple bobbed up and down slowly as he swallowed hard. Esha replied curtly in their language, and nodded toward Jenny.

"English, Mummy. We're not in our house now."

Instead, Esha silently pointed at the kitchen, then brought her fingers to her pursed lips.

"I already had food. From the batch you brought two days ago, my God! Couldn't this have waited?"

Esha bobbed her head to the side, turned to the refrigerator, and silently continued putting away food containers, carefully placing each item with label facing forward, stainless steel containers on the bottom shelf, and glassware on the top.

Despite the distance between them, Jenny felt the hardening of Roshan's form and sensed an impending explosion. She tapped his forearm, and whispered to him, "I'll go now."

He didn't move.

Esha put away the last container, closed the refrigerator, and turned to the floor beside the trash can. Jenny's wad of paper towels lay on the sparkling floor where she'd laid it before chasing Roshan just moments ago. Esha swiftly picked them up, pushed the pedal opening the aluminum can, dropped the paper towels into the black liner, and looked Jenny square in the eye as the lid slammed shut.

In perfect English, eyes still fixed on Jenny, Esha said, "Roshan, you need to take out the trash."

Jenny's jaw dropped but she held Esha's eyes fixed on her own while all feeling drained from her face.

How dare this woman?

Jenny's hands squeezed into fists at her side, and she fought the off-color words rising in her throat.

Esha tapped the top of the can and said, "Roshan, now. Or maybe I do it myself." She glared at him, nodding her head in Jenny's direction.

Shaking all over, Jenny looked to Roshan, waiting for him to defend her.

He shifted from one foot to the other. He looked at Jenny, and then at Esha…and said nothing.

Jenny froze in disbelief for a moment until Esha sighed dramatically and, without speaking, turned her back to both of them and opened the refrigerator.

Roshan moved toward Jenny and silently mouthed, "I'm sorry."

She couldn't stand him or his mother or being in his apartment for another second. She grabbed her purse from the couch where she had tossed it last night, snatched up her pumps, and pushed past him as she walked to the door.

"Jenny, wait…"

She ignored him as she wobbled barefooted through the door, nearly tripping over his long pajama pants she was still wearing. She was several doors away, her head pounding so much she wanted to stop, when he caught up with her. She didn't look at him and willed herself to walk faster.

Falling in rhythm beside her, they slowed down in the dimly lit corridor to the elevator.

Jenny felt naked wearing his loose pants and T-shirt without a bra or the thong that still lay in a heap on display in his bedroom. Feeling lucky that her walk of shame would only be as far as two floors up, she held her breath, afraid to let it out, lest unwanted words from her upbringing should escape. The unbroken silence in the air between them hung thick enough to touch.

Roshan, in an attempt to chip away at the awkwardness, finally spoke. Forcing a chuckle, he asked, "Gee, do you think my mum was pissed?"

"Well, gee, it was hard for me to tell," Jenny replied curtly. "Is 'trash' one of the only English words she knows?"

Acutely aware of the itchy feeling of her unwashed skin, she was eager to be home, to stand under scalding water, and to let the steam clear her mind. Finally stopping in front of the double doors, staring at the floor, she extended her hand to push the "up" button, unwilling to look at him. But before she could depress it, Roshan brushed her hand down gingerly, then pulled his hand back quickly.

At his touch, her insides turned over, half butterflies fluttering around, half vodka threatening to rise. Part of her wanted to take his hand and let her weight fall onto him, the other part wanted to get as far away from him and his crazy mother as possible. She pictured the woman's stare, still feeling the unfamiliar smack of being judged a whore. She'd never had a one night stand before this, much less been discovered by a guy's old-world mommy wearing her baby's pajamas the morning after.

And then the picture of Roshan standing there, impotent, in front of his mother infuriated her.

Why do I wish this wasn't a one night stand?

She allowed herself to look up at him, confused about letting herself, but stared silently.

Roshan peered down into her face, his dark eyes moving from her eyes to her mouth as if searching for something. He looked just as disheveled as she did, but carried it off well. His hair was tousled in dark waves from the bed, really no different from the sexy, messy look he wore by day. The Polo he had thrown on didn't match his shorts. Any other day, she knew he would never set foot in public looking like this, even in the hallway. His breath still hinted sweet of Jack and Coke.

In another attempt to break the ice between them, he laughed, "I really think the icing on the cake was that you were wearing my clothes. I could tell by the look on her face."

What? Was he just using me to get back at his mother for something?

"Yeah! That was icing alright. Just priceless." She glared at him, feeling angrier by the second. "I have parental baggage too, ya know. But I have the guts to speak up for myself, and I sure don't sleep with a man to get a rise out of my family."

But, oh, what a rise she would have gotten out of her dad this morning. Had the tables been turned, and she and Roshan had been discovered by him, well…there would be no standing around staring at each other. Her dad would have made sure of that.

Visibly taken aback, Roshan looked around them as if he were expecting someone to come out of an apartment at any time. Jenny looked over his shoulder in the direction of his apartment, and without her contacts in, all she could see was a blur that looked like a head leaning slowly out of his door, pause for a moment, then pull back inside.

That woman is spying on us!

She looked back at Roshan and tried to focus on what he was saying.

"No, no. I don't want you to think that…I just wanted you to know I hate the way she is sometimes. I…I've lived with her smothering me with love and rules. Now that school is done," he touched her hair, "and I've been thinking about this happening, about us happening, and I don't want to care what she says. And I don't want you to either." He brushed his fingers on her cheek, but she pulled back from his touch.

"This is too much. I have to get home." Finally, she pushed the elevator button, then repeatedly hit it over and over and over again before banging it with her palm. When it opened, she quickly stepped inside, willing the doors to shut fast. Upon turning around to face him, her eyes locked on his, and the angry pounding in her head subsided just a bit, and she fought the urge to escape the box and stay before the doors closed.

Chapter 2

Roshan

She was gone. He would give them both time to digest things and call her in the afternoon. But right now, Roshan had some business to take care of. Sucking in his breath, he marched back into the apartment and locked the door behind him. Fury and embarrassment lodged in his throat. He approached his mother, glaring. She was at the sink rewashing his dishes from the drying rack.

"Mummy," he yelled. "You should not have come..." Realizing what she was washing, he asked loudly, "What are you *doing?* Those are clean!"

Cringing ever so slightly, but standing firm, she kept her eyes on the water flowing from the tap as she answered in Gujarati.

"There were spots. I am washing them properly."

"Oh my God!" He yelled in English, slamming his fist down onto the Formica countertop next to the sink. "You should not have come here this morning!"

"I have a right to visit my own son, Roshan. I'm so proud of you and wanted to bring you something extra special this morning. See in the brown bowl over there." She directed him with her head toward the refrigerator. "I had no way of knowing you would have, ahem, company." She squirted dish liquid onto the sponge with a splat.

He waited, sensing she might cry, and composed himself.

Trickling water onto a glass. Soap. Rinse. Upside down on the rack. He tapped his foot on the linoleum, realizing no tears were coming from her.

"You really need to dry these with a clean towel. Drip dry leaves spots." She reached for another clean glass off the rack, but Roshan grabbed her wrist tightly. She stood there, glass in hand, staring at his knuckles wrapped around her slender wrist, silent, motionless. Roshan knew years of experience had taught her to wait patiently for his fury—and his father's before him—to pass.

"Will you please speak English? We are not in India." Disgusted with himself, he gently released her hand and tried to ignore the white prints that remained. "This is my apartment, Mummy." His voice softened. "This is my life. My business."

"*Dikra*," her words rolled out in Gujarati, "I am your mother. If you have to hide things from me, you shouldn't be doing them. Your business is my business. It is the whole family's business."

He knew it was true. She was his mother and she had raised him with good morals, to uphold family ways. So, why was he doing this?

His eyes twitched as hers burned a hole in him. Holding a dripping glass, she walked over to him, letting soap puddle at their feet, and peered hard into his eyes. He darted his eyes away.

"Look at me, *dikra*." Her voice was unexpectedly soft, and he swallowed his fear to meet her eyes. "Have you been drinking?" She leaned in and sniffed. "Don't answer. I smell it."

It was then that a veil of tears misted her eyes, causing a chain reaction to his own. Her eyes searched his from side to side, reducing him to the same little boy who broke his mum's favorite vase with a baseball bat like it was yesterday.

"Mummy. I'm fine. Just a few last night to celebrate."

She looked down at the suds dripping off her toes and went back to the sink. Soap. Rinse. Dry.

"I don't drink a lot." He lied, desperate to repair the look on her face. She wouldn't look at him, and he was torn between running out the door and saying "fuck you" to the whole thing, and touching her feet and asking for forgiveness. He added, "I'm not him, Mummy. I stop whenever I want."

Flinging the dish towel over her shoulder, she turned to him. "Now your business is Priya's business too. So stop whenever you can, and please make it now."

"Priya," he repeated flatly. Roshan massaged his forehead and closed his eyes. "Yes, Mummy. How can I forget her?" He turned his back to her and walked into the bedroom.

He fluffed his pillow, smoothed the pillowcase, and pulled taught the twisted sheets and bedspread, making sure to tuck them in tightly under the edge of the mattress. Finally, feeling order, he stretched out across the bed. He lay there listening to the clanking of dishes in the kitchen and inhaled Jenny's lingering perfume on her pillow.

Priya. The name violated the intimacy of Jenny's scent, but he mouthed it silently. The rolled "r" was sandpaper on his tongue. Just a few months ago, he had sat next to her in the country club hall of his uncle's neighborhood celebrating their engagement. He'd watched the gray winter sky loom over them outside the window and tried not to shudder in the winter draft in the room. Their potential match had been chosen by their families, their marriage endorsed by their horoscopes, the day chosen by their families, but had his opinion been asked on the matter, the occasion would not have happened until spring…if it had to happen at all. Getting engaged to anyone was not on his list of fun things to do, but aunts and uncles had put on the pressure, and he caved to please them and his mum. Priya was a nice enough girl, and the happily anxious look on his mum's face after he took Priya out to dinner cinched his decision to go ahead with the engagement and tuck away the many portraits of Jenny he scratched out on notebook paper over the last couple of years.

Priya's long, thick hair draped over her shoulders, and she nervously avoided eye contact with him. The lavender tie he wore, purchased by his mother, complemented the expensive sheer green and purple sari that draped around her slight frame, finishing in heavy pleats on her shoulder. Her wrists were stacked with jingling bangles of gold and purple, and her heavy earrings swung wide whenever she turned her head. She could weigh no more than 95 pounds, and he had wondered how such a child-like body could carry the weight of so much clothing and jewelry.

The day began with his side of the family lining up at the door to greet her family as they entered the club house before seating the crowd to watch the short ceremony with the priest. After prayers with one another, some handfuls of rice thrown in a small fire, sipping water on cue from the priest, and an exchange of coconuts between her parents and his of which he had no idea the purpose, the blessings, eating, and photographs began. He had yet to present her with the diamond solitaire that his mother and aunties had helped him pick out, and he was really in no hurry to do so, though he knew it had to be done soon after the ceremony. A stark contrast to the proposals made by his American buddies to their fiancés who planned on romantic picnics or surprise rings in glasses of champagne, this engagement was formal and public. A privilege for all of their family members to participate in. To celebrate. To mark their stamps of approval on the match. But, placing the engagement ring on his wife-to-be's finger was not something he was willing to perform for the world.

During the party, he and Priya made their way together down the line of people to be blessed and congratulated. In unison, the couple placed their palms together and greeted with *Namaste* each *Ba, Dada*, aunt and uncle, and their parents. *Namaste.* Bend down. Touch their feet. Receive a gentle hand on the head and an envelope with cash, always an amount plus one dollar for good luck, then on down the receiving line.

A huge meal and many, many thank you's to guests later, he and Priya had been left truly alone for only the second time since their first meeting while the women cleaned up.

"So, back to L.A., huh?" He had tried to make small talk to break the tension. She looked at him, but still avoided eye contact. Her tiny frame dressed up in such formal clothes looked odd to him. She looked like a child playing dress up, he thought.

"Yes. I have finals. Then I have to get ready for hospital rotations next month." There had been a whisper of exhaustion in her voice.

"This was bad timing for you. It's too bad all the old people couldn't break from tradition this once and have the engagement at the bride's place instead of the groom's hometown." He looked back at all of the women scurrying around inside the hall, cleaning up like a troop of worker ants. He imagined her merging among them in future years, and felt sorry for her. Their bangles jingling, dishes clattering, and voices gossiping were a shrill chorus in his head. Priya shook her head.

"There'll be no breaking tradition in my family. My dad has always seen to that. He took us to his village in India every summer as kids to drill our traditions into us. And, I guess now I am pretty glad."

"Hmmm. Not me. This engagement was not about us. It's for everyone else. What good did all of this pomp and circumstance do for you and me? Look how jet-lagged you are."

He leaned in closer to her and awkwardly put his arm around her shoulder, hesitant to relax it. He looked back at the women cleaning to make sure none saw. She leaned into him stiffly and he tentatively squeezed her in an attempt to comfort her.

"It's okay because I like being with my family. I'm proud of this. And my kids will be too."

"*Your* kids?"

As if slashed by his words, she reluctantly look him in the eye.

Grabbing her abruptly with sarcasm, he instructed her, "Being a traditionalist, keep in mind who's the head of the household here. I'll have some say in this." The harshness in his voice faintly echoing his father's voice trapped in the recesses of his mind, and he shuddered angrily within himself. That voice needed to stay buried.

Her mouth tightened into a straight line. "Of course." She turned to look out into the garden. "But, don't you think it's important, hypothetically speaking, for kids to have a dad who is an example in the house, you know, to teach them as a leader?" Quietly, she added, "I mean, I know you're about your dad. So maybe you just missed out on—"

He knew his dad would come up. He always did.

"I didn't miss anything. I had my Uncle Pete….after he got out of India. He's a great dad, treated me just like he did Jay. And I had Mum and everyone else to teach me plenty. They never let up teaching me, as a matter of fact. So, we need to make sure our kids turn out better than me, right?" His neck clenched in a spasm.

"No. No, that's not what…" Priya looked around her to see if anyone was listening to Roshan's biting voice. "I'm sorry. To be honest, if it were left up to me, I don't even know if I'd have kids at all."

"Don't have any then."

She watched his face with surprise, and he detected a hint of amusement. "Yes, I suppose so. We'll see. But, I am going to get my residency done. Then, maybe. Your mom will be there to take care of the kids when—if—we have any."

His dad's mum, Ba, in India had taken care of him while his mum worked around the house or shopped during the day. He remembered one morning during rainy season while nestled in the folds of long sari fabric on her lap, he told her all about a picture book he had made at school. The window was open, and the smell of earth and leaves misted the room, moistening the paper in his hands under the spray of the downpour outside until his shrunken Dada had come in, humphed at them as he shut the window, and padded away in bare feet to his room.

Roshan loved the smells of outside because Ba loved the smells of outside and pouted when Dada left the room. She couldn't walk so well anymore to go outside with him, and this was supposed to be their pretend time outside together.

"Don't pout, *dikra*. It's not fitting for a young man."

"I wanted the window open." He crossed his arms in front of him and growled. Ba smoothed back his hair and kissed him on the forehead.

"No, no, *dikra*, don't be naughty. We'll have our window time again. Why don't you show me your book and then go draw me another one with your cricket field and the garden in our neighbor's yard? I hear they have a huge mango tree in their courtyard now."

She praised his art in her slow and grainy old person voice, telling him how happy his pictures made him. That warm voice and soft hands. "Ba, I want to be a drawer when I grow up."

"Sure, sure, my little one. There will time for drawing. Your daddy is a wonderful painter. You can do that too."

When Daddy came home at night happy with purples and blacks and greens on his hands, Roshan loved to jump into his arms, hoping the colors would rub off on his clothes, even if Mummy would shout him for it, though it never did. He had never seen his daddy's pictures, because Ba and Mummy said they sold so fast, but he imagined they were full of dragons and knights and gods with lots of arms and faces like monkeys or elephants, like he saw other places all around him. He hoped he could paint that good someday, just like his daddy.

"I want to draw pictures in books. Like this polar bear here. See?" His chubby finger covered the bear's head.

"Oh, little one, that's nice. So nice. You'll make a wonderful illustrator." Her words rung in his memory as it shifted to the words of his Ma, his mum's mum, whom he met for the first time after they left India. She had a stiff white braid down her back and always wore the same white sari—boring—because she was a widow. He was older then, and when she tried to pull him to her lap, her bony knees dug into him, and the clock couldn't tick fast enough until he could get off. Her voice was crackly, and when he told her he wanted to be an illustrator when he grew up, she would tell him, "Ah, you can draw, *dikra*, sure. But, you'll make an even better doctor. You want money, no?"

Roshan thought about that. Money could buy a lot of toys, but the needles, like he'd gotten in his arm at the doctor last time, were like little swords. He never wanted to do that to people.

The tightness in his neck softened. He glanced at Priya. "Okay. We have plenty of time. Table this for now."

"Yes. I was accepted to Johns Hopkins. And I hope to get a residency there after med school."

A load lifted from his shoulders, and he felt a tinge of guilt. "Oh. I guess we have a long time until we cross bridges."

"My mom and dad didn't live together for two years after they were married. He sent for her here after he settled. We can do it too. It'll give us time to...get used to things."

Jay swung open the doors to the hall and yelled out.
Thank God.

"Come on, you love birds. Time to go. Priya, your dad is looking for you. All good things must come to an end. *Chaal*, let's go." He clapped his hands.

Grateful for the intrusion, Roshan turned to her awkwardly. "Have a good flight."

Their bodies did not touch as they hugged goodbye.

"Thanks. I will," she said, lingering like she wanted a first kiss. "I'll be back for your graduation in a few months. Then you'll be the doctor I want to marry." She giggled like a simple-minded school girl, and he flinched with annoyance, wondering how she could be so driven in her career, yet sound like a child. She had pretty hazel eyes fringed in thick lashes, very pretty and young, and despite her immature personality, he wondered what her petite frame, what her petite breasts underneath all of that pomp and embroidery, would feel like. He had never slept with an Indian girl. Oh, no, that was a no-no. He had not even slept with that many white girls either, though he liked to put on a big gigolo show for people. One of his buddies in high school knocked up his girlfriend, and that was all of the evidence he needed to keep his business in his pants most of the time. Dating wasn't tolerated in his family, and certainly illegitimate, casteless babies wouldn't be either.

The engagement night ended there with another goodbye, and Roshan drove home with his cousins and mum in his car, screeching around corners like it was a getaway car.

Now that graduation was done, and his mum was in the other room fuming, he lay there on his bed, the memory of Jenny's breasts against his chest when they hugged in the kitchen this morning thrusting him back into the present. Her strawberry blonde hair tickling his nose. Her swagger when she entered a room.

Lying on his stomach on the bed now, the pain of the present squeezed his chest. Mother in the kitchen. Jenny up two floors in her apartment, probably planning to never see him again. He swelled again with anger, got up and yelled into the kitchen from the doorway.

"You were so rude to Jenny. Horrible. How dare you treat anyone like that?"

"How dare I?" she retorted, wiping her hands on a towel and stepping toward the room. "How dare she be here? A white girl. She doesn't belong here." She put her two fingers together, tapping hard on her head. "Use your brains. What's your last name?"

He looked at her as if she were dumb and said nothing.

Louder, she asked again, "What's your last name?" She would not drop this until he answered.

"Desai."

"Exactly. Desai is a Gujarati name, right? What is Priya's last name?"

"Patel." He knew where she was going with this and wanted to cover her mouth but let her vent.

"Gujarati name. Desai and Patel—both Gujarati. Two Gujarati families. What do you know about this Jenny's family? What does Jenkins mean? Who are her people?" Before he could answer, she spat, "Nothing! I don't know her parents! I don't know her religion. Do you?"

"No, Mummy. But, it doesn't have to matter—"

She put her hand up to stop him. "Just go out somewhere else and sow you oats and be done with it. But don't you dare bring it home to your family. You of all people should know that."

Sickened, but not surprised, he replied, "Are you saying 'Don't shit where you eat.' Like Daddy did?"

Her face paled. He had crossed the unspoken line.

He could take no more today. He threw his hands up and stormed to the door of the bathroom. "I am going to shower now. Lock the door behind you."

Esha lowered her head and shook it slowly. When she got to the door, she raised her shoulders and heaved a deep breath.

"Be at uncle's house by three o'clock. Your family and your fiancé will be there. For *you*. For *your* graduation. Do not disappoint."

She let herself out, and the apartment door and the bathroom door slammed in unison.

Don't disappoint. All I've done in my life is to not disappoint.

Maybe it was time for him to worry about disappointing himself for a change. But, at what cost?

Later, he emerged through a cloud of steam from the bathroom and walked nude into his bedroom, scrubbing his hair dry with a towel as he went. He shook his head and shaped the waves into place, and draped the towel lightly over the end of his bed to dry. After grabbing a pair of pressed jeans and a starched button-down shirt from his dry-cleaning bag, he tousled a gel-covered hand through his wavy hair and grabbed his car keys. He picked up his racquetball racquet from a corner and slammed the door behind him. His muscles ached. His brain ached. He needed to get his blood pumping on a court and clear his mind.

Once behind the wheel of his old, dinged-up Toyota, feeling the jar of every pothole and hump in the road, nausea set in. Frustration, longing, and the after-taste of last night's liquor burned in his throat. He decided that puking on the racquetball court might really ruin his less than stellar day, so he cut in front of an approaching minivan and sped onto the next entrance to the interstate. With a heavy thrust of the accelerator, he smoothly glided over the broken white line of the approach lane and placed himself in the flow of traffic. Once his speed had climbed to eighty five miles per hour, despite the sputtering engine, the road evened out and his stomach settled. He fumbled with the loose radio dial and finally got it on a good station before sinking into the worn driver's seat. The road shined like an oil slick in the sun, and he tried to catch up with a Mercedes ahead of him. He wanted to see the face of the driver. And pass him.

Roshan mashed the gas hard. He pulled up parallel to the car and looked at the driver. A blond, muscle-jawed business man glanced at him through mirrored sunglasses. A moment later, his grin disappeared, leaving Roshan a view of the car's taillights, getting tinier in the distance. He mashed the gas again, but the speed sputtered, and he had to slow down. This car—the frugal, sensible ride his mum had insisted he buy—was going to be history.

After manually cranking down the window and letting the wind whip onto his face, he turned on the CD player. A lady's high-pitched voice sang Hindi to whining sitar, and he ejected the CD. Not in the mood for even his favorite movie soundtrack, he popped a Nirvana CD into the player and blasted *Come as You Are*. Kurt Cobain's raspy words inspired his decision even more, invited him to be himself. Freedom tingled through his limbs with the sunshine beating in on his skin, pouring in through the sunroof. He amazed himself at how great he sounded singing along with Kurt Cobain, and by the looks of himself in the rearview mirror, he could have the personality to make it in music, but then he came alongside a car full of teenage boys who started pointing at him and laughing. A little embarrassed, but not put off, he rolled up his windows and pretended he didn't notice them, still singing along.

Where would he go? Anywhere he wanted. Anywhere at all. Fighting the urge to turn around and head back to the apartment building, straight to the third floor, he cruised. Driving as far away from his mum, he cruised.

Faster and faster. Reaching one hundred miles per hour. One hundred and five, undaunted by the rattling. Euphoria engulfed him.

He was finally in control of himself. He wouldn't be afraid anymore. And he knew what he wanted at that moment. For only himself. The yoke around his neck loosened. Others could dictate who he married, where and how he lived. But they could never take away his soul. He'd never pleased his family, he'd never pleased his dad. He was his own man and would damn well enjoy it.

Three exits later, he merged into traffic on Car Dealer Row. The road was lined with car glinting dealerships on each side. Honda, Chevrolet, Toyota and Hyundai. Seas of cars gleamed in the sun, hot and inviting. But he made a beeline for the BMW lot, craving speed. An engine to be proud of. A child's giddy laughter erupted from him.

A tall, lanky middle aged man clad in a black polo shirt with the dealership's name embroidered on left breast pocket slickly moved in on the car before Roshan had even pulled the key out of the ignition. Ready to cash in on the credit worthiness his new career could afford him, he shook the salesman's hand through the open car door window and grinned from ear to ear.

Two hours later, he sped off the lot behind the wheel of a cobalt blue BMW 328i convertible. The color had just called to him, like the night sky he watched sometimes when he wished he could float away into it, into the mosaic of stars, like falling into a painting. Top down, tires screeching, he wove in and out of cars too fast for the other drivers to react. With intense horse power under his foot, he headed for the interstate with nothing but speed on his mind.

Wherever he was going, it would be his way.

Chapter 3

Jenny

Jenny sat in the afternoon sun on her deck with the cellphone in her hand, listening to Bryan's voicemail greeting. Not wanting to leave a tearful message, she ended the call and decided to send him a text. No emotions, just letters. No worries.

She wondered where he was. They'd had many talks about how stressful his new job was and how he worried it was ruining his relationship with Craig. She'd commiserated, but not empathized. Bryan had always been the one to let emotions get ahold of him. But, work was her life. Work was her ticket. And, unlike Bryan's romantic dreams of life with Craig, her flirtation with Roshan had always been safe. Like two countries with firm borders. Until today.

Why couldn't he be there now? He was the closest thing to family that she wanted at her dental school graduation. Life was so unfair. With tears in her eyes, she remembered their college graduation: their iron grip of fake diploma rolls and each other through rented gowns, her kiss on his damp cheek, and the specter of their dads grinding cigarette butts on the pavement by the exit. Tammy, with dullness like a used up, frayed dishtowel on her face, pulled her dad with her and pushed her little sister Brianna in a stroller to them, raising her cigarette hand up so as not to burn them in her embrace. Bryan's dad hovered by the door. Over Tammy's spaghetti strapped shoulder, she glimpsed Bryan's moist gaze in the direction of the door. She followed his eyes and saw his dad lift his hand in a subtle salute and nod at Bryan, before turning his back and disappearing out into the day.

Bryan turned to hug some political science friends that Jenny didn't know, and she was left with Tammy, her stroller, and her dad hovering beside her. When her dad hugged her, the Marlboro box in the front pocket of his white, short-sleeved button up shirt crunched, and he pulled back into another family walking behind him. He stumbled back just a step and into the path of the mother whose ankle turned in the high heels she wore.

"Excuse me." She stated, annoyed, as she'd leaned into a row of seats to balance. Her leather handbag dropped to the floor. Dad had put his hand on the small of her back and bent to retrieve it. He spoke too closely when he handed it to her.

"Excuse me." This time her voice was repulsed, and she pulled her head away, almost hopping away into her husband's open arm, which was waiting to pull her up toward him.

"Watch out, buddy."

They walked away, pulling each other tighter, whispering loudly.

"Did you smell that guy? He stunk like a bar floor."

"How'd that whole group get in to a college graduation? Unbelievable."

Bryan returned and grabbed Jenny's hand through the gown. Moments later, they drove away together, leaving her dirty little family at the door of the auditorium. Bryan turned the wheel hard, and they squealed away from the lot. Unable to resist looking back, she glimpsed Bryan's father, leaning against his glossy black truck, taking long drags on his smoke, and watching them disappear.

Shaking off that memory, she tapped out a text on the tiny push buttons on the keyboard.

Jenny
Hey. Call me. Missed U yesterday.
Lots 2 talk @! "Dr. Jenkins" :)

Sounds good-spirited, right?
Not thirty seconds later, a response chirped.

Bryan
So busy! Sorry! Miss u 2.
Have surprise 4 U. <3

A surprise? Was he going to announce his promotion? No wonder he was too busy for her.
Okay, Jen. Stop the pity party. Text him back!

Jenny
Yay. Love surprises. Can't wait 2 hear all about it.

The doorbell rang and the phone vibrated in her hand. The caller ID displayed Bryan James. Excited, she answered as she stomped annoyed to the door.

"Hey!" her voice was a little too loud into the phone.

"Hey, chicky. Whoa, I'm not deaf! How are you?"

"Good." She answered more softly. Pausing for a moment, she put her hand on the doorknob. "Sorry, Bryan, hang on a second. Someone's at the door. Let me get rid of them."

"Okay, sure."

She pulled open the door and nearly dropped her phone. There was Bryan, flowers in hand, grinning from ear to ear.

"Oh...my...God!" She grabbed him and squeezed him so hard he feigned choking. "Oh my God," she said again, pulling him and slamming the door. "You're here."

"I'm here." He handed her the flowers and kissed her on the cheek. "Happy graduation, Brainiac."

She pulled him to the couch without speaking and playfully pushed him onto the seat. He watched her with amused eyes as she sat, and she folded her legs under her, facing him.

"You're here."

"Yep, honey. I'm here."

"Your hair is a mess."

"Thanks. You look like shit yourself. Do you know how easy it is to get lost here? After I parked my rental car in the garage at the corner, I walked in circles until I finally asked somebody for help. This is downtown? There are no signs anywhere?" He lifted a tendril of wiry frizzing hair and smirked, questioningly. "And you, Miss Perfect, what's your excuse?"

"Um, hey. You want a Coke?"

"You're evading, but yes. Have any Diet?"

She nodded and went to retrieve a can from the refrigerator. "Right, no sugar for Schwarzenegger. I remember. Atlanta is good, then?" She handed him his Diet Coke and sat down again. "I mean, it must be, since you're so busy these days."

"Atlanta is great. Craig is great." He squinted his eyes and frowned. "So, what're you not telling me?"

Despite the urgency she'd felt to spill it all to him just five minutes ago, her jaw shook at the thought of doing it now.

"Oh, nothing. The graduation went smoothly. I am thrilled to have the paper in my hand now. I went with some friends to the Peabody Hotel for the official banquet." She hesitated to tell him anymore. Explaining aloud her situation seemed suddenly scary, embarrassing to her. "I should take you today. It's really pretty—"

"And then...?" he probed, ignoring her.

"And then, what?"

"And then what happened?" He pointed at her droopy hair and face. "The circles under your eyes, the un-Jen stringy hair. Which friends did you hang with at the banquet, and exactly what happened to cause this disheveling?"

"I went with Marissa, you know, my New York friend? And Jay, you haven't met him yet. He's an oral surgery resident. Actually my friend Roshan's cousin. Remember him? He was there too."

Bryan smiled sheepishly at her and asked, "Oh, really. This is the tall, dark, and handsome study buddy, scientist and artist extrodinaire, who has been replacing me in your life." He poked her ribs.

"Hey. You're one to talk about replacing someone. 'Oh Craig, I love Craig.'" She pretended to stick her finger down her throat.

"Touché. Okay, so back to your dirt. Then, did you guys go party afterward, or did you take your boring-self back to bed like always."

"Unfortunately, I had a few too many after dinner..."

He glared at her; she had violated their pact to never drink.

"...but then I did go to bed. But, I...uh...didn't come home though." She watched at him sideways, waiting.

"Oh. My. God. You? Did you and Roshan finally do the nasty?" His face lit up. He placed himself square in front of her and tugged at her arm for more information.

"Um, yeah." Her face blushed into a smile. She wanted to keep the smile, yet she was dying to tell him the whole dilemma. Somehow, telling him over the phone would've been easier.

"Congratulations!" he play-slapped her on the arm and probed her for more information. "I'm pretty pissed off that you of all people were drinking, but you get a pass this time. Well, do tell...any gory details to share?"

Jenny just sat there, looking at him, halfway smiling. Feeling like they were in college again, she was ready to spill it. All but the drinking part. She hated disappointing her best friend.

He stared at her quizzically, then she finally said, "Okay, yes. It's a little trashy, but, let me tell you—" Her stomach growled. Hunger and nerves. "Hey, before we get into the good stuff...I'm starving. You want to go grab some lunch and continue this over a bite?" She relished the annoyed look in his eyes. "I haven't eaten lunch yet." She jumped up, and he looked up at her, mouth pursed and one eyebrow cocked up to one side.

"Really, Jen? You're going to do this to me?"

"Do what? I'm hungry. And I still have a headache. I can't take Advil on an empty stomach."

"Hungover, huh? Serves you right." He stood up and stared at her hard, a dark flash flickered across his face, then disappeared. He hugged her. "Fine, let's go eat."

"I need pizza."

"No pizza. If you're going to torture me after traveling all this way to see you," he lifted his huge hand to his brow dramatically and smoothed his still windblown hair, "you're at least going to take me somewhere with food that won't kill me. What have you got around here that's vegan?"

She furrowed her brow and glared at him.

"Okay, how about vegetarian?"

Still, her face did not change.

"Okay, fine, is there anywhere I can get a piece of grilled salmon and a bottled water?"

Pulling her damp hair back with a hairband, she grabbed her purse and keys, and linked her arm around his. "Absolutely." She steered him to the door. "I know just the place. They have great burgers too."

He stuck his tongue out as if gagging, and the door shut loudly behind them.

A blanket of sunshine covered them on the busy cafe patio, and Jenny wished she had put on sunscreen before coming. Even a short time in the sun would mean a lobster look for days.

"Pretty day." She picked wind-blown pieces of hair off of her face and sipped a soda. The bubbles soothed her stomach.

Bryan sat motionless and stared at her, smirking. "So why the down face?"

Touching his lips to the rim of a water glass, Bryan looked at her dead on. Silent, like The Terminator, the way he stared through his sunglasses.

She froze, her skittish tongue too thick to say any more.

A pair of middle aged women carrying shopping bags walked past them on the sidewalk and stared at him in tandem. The short one with a sassy bob haircut whispered into the ear of her bohemian companion, and they giggled. Bryan nodded and smiled. The bohemian one smiled back and flipped her long free hair away from her face.

"I love your shirt." She paused slightly in mid-stride. "Aqua is my favorite color."

"Thanks." He smiled coyly again at the woman. "Mine too. It matches your eyes, I see."

"You're so mean." Jenny whispered to him and smacked his knee under the table.

"Have a great day, ladies." His voice melted out of him, and the two women swaggered slowly away. As they turned the corner, the bohemian woman turned her head, tucked her hair behind her ear, and locked her eyes on him until they were gone.

He turned back to Jenny, snickering

"You're such a tease. We'd better order fast. Those women may come back and stalk us. What'll you do then?"

"Show them this picture of me and Craig at the beach last month."

He pulled it up on his phone. They stood in front of the surf. Both wore only swim trunks, and Craig's arm was draped softly around Bryan's shoulder. Their tilted heads touched. Jealousy pinged her stomach. They looked so happy.

"So, here we are. Talk to me."

She didn't want to have raccoon-eye tan lines on her face, so she removed her sunglasses, only to have to squint to the point of near blindness. She was happy she couldn't see him, because it would be easier to talk.

"It's simple. We got drunk. We had sex. I woke up naked in his bed." She hung her head and tapped the stem of her water glass nervously. She sighed deeply, only then aware that she'd been holding her breath at the thought of what had happened after that.

"Ooh. Great. So what's your problem? Other than the fact that you're the child of addicts and shouldn't ever drink. Ever. But, you got laid. You pined away for this guy for a long time, right? Why so glum?"

"His mom let herself into the apartment wearing a sari and a big fat diamond in her nose," she enunciated "wearing" like it was a thing of bewilderment, "and I…was wearing his pajamas."

Bryan held up his hand in front of his open mouth and gasped, "OH NO! What happened?"

"She called me 'trash.' Told Roshan to get rid of me."

"That old bitch." His own inner trailer park attitude came out when he was mad, but it shifted quickly. "Well, what would you expect? I've asked my friend Raj at work about this and I told you Indians can't fraternize with us. And he is engaged, for God's sake. What should his mother think?"

Jenny rolled her eyes, "You're right."

"Did he tell her off?"

"No, not really. He kind of blew her off, but never came out and told her she was out of line. I wonder if he really thought she was out of line. And I get the feeling that they keep all of their dirty laundry under wraps. Have to sort of keep up appearances, ya know?"

"Mmm, mmm. If that had been my mother, God bless her bigoted soul, I would've gone all crazy on her."

"Well, apparently that is against the sacred code of ethics for Indians." Her slow drawl rounded out the words with a twang. "They are a different breed from us down-home folk. They don't associate with the likes of us crackers from down in Jaw-ja."

"So, okay, his mom hates you. What does Roshan say about all this?"

"Not much. He says he is not like her. And he has said so many times before that he hates being engaged to this Priya in California. But I had to have time to think. I'm so confused."

"Don't forget you have your Jaw-ja clan to contend with." He squeezed one eye shut and pretended to shoot a rifle at a black man passing by on the sidewalk. Mimicking her redneck drawl, he said, "Your daddy would probably say 'Ain't no brown people gonna defile one of our girls.'"

They laughed.

"And then there's my mom. She'd probably screech 'Jesus will send you to the depths of a fiery hell with a heathen like him.' After putting down her pill of the day, that is."

"Jen, who cares about your mom? Are you never going to get over trying to please the woman? You have seen her how many times in the last ten years?"

"Four."

"And what does she want when you've seen her?"

"To convince me she's clean. And to save my eternal soul."

"And then what happens when you refuse both?"

"She goes back to her Jesus freak friends and forgets about me again." Gritting her teeth, she adds, "and when Jesus can't get her high enough, she starts using. Every time."

"Okay, then. You really like this guy?"

"Yeah, I do."

"Then forget her. Forget the clan. Forget the foreigners. Go with it. See what happens a little. I took a chance with Craig. And my dad—MY dad—will let us both in his house now. He and Craig actually talk cars together."

"I know. I get it. You two are very happy. But, what about the California fiancé?" Her cellphone chimed with a text message, but she didn't flip it open to answer. Whoever it was could wait.

"Okay." He leaned in and numbered off his fingers.

"One, he hates being engaged to her. Two, he spends all his time with you and slept with you. Not her. Three, you're a phenomenal woman." He lifted his glass. "You are beautiful and smart and going to be the best damn dentist Atlanta has ever seen. Listen to me for once and love yourself girl. Then others will love you too."

She looked around at the other diners and smiled back at an older couple who looked on. She loved herself when she was with Roshan, albeit not so much after last night. She clinked her soda glass to his water glass. "Cheers."

"And the fourth thing. Sometimes people break the family mold. Neither one of us had a good start, but we did it. Why can't he?"

Jenny sipped from her straw and then wolfed down a hunk of bread. Oh, how good that felt in her queasy stomach. She smiled, contemplating. She needed this, and Bryan was the only person alive who could give it to her.

"Now that I have imparted my grand wisdom to you, I need to use the little boys' room. Ask the waiter for another water for me, will you? With extra lemon."

Nodding, she reached into her purse and flipped open her phone. There was a text from Roshan.

Roshan

Want 2 show u something. R u home?

Should I text him back? Oh, what the hell. I can handle him.

Jenny

Not now. What is it?

Roshan

Nope. U have 2 c it. Want to c u.

Jenny

@ Corner Bistro on Poplar with BFF. Want 2 c u 2.

"Hey, what did I miss?" Bryan asked as she slid back into his seat.

"He texted me. Wants to show me something. And said he wants to see me."

"And what did you tell him?"

"Nothing yet. Besides, you just got here..."

"Well, I still need to check into my hotel. Why don't you take me back to my rental and I'll drive to the hotel. Then you and Roshan can show each other 'things'...Lord knows you've been pent up long enough to have plenty to show him. We can meet back up for dinner. Sound good?"

"Yes, sounds good."

Bryan grabbed her hand and said, "Do this girl. What do you have to lose?"

Right. I feel real with him. What do I have to lose?

They paid the bill and walked out onto the sidewalk toward Jenny's car. They stood and chatted for a few minutes about the colorful people walking by, dreadlock-pants-falling-off-guy, twin eighteen year old girls with matching tramp stamps just above their thongs peeking out of their jeans, and the old lady in the antique store who looked like Mrs. Brown, the wacko who lived on their street growing up.

Jenny's back was to the street, but Bryan had a full view of traffic. The car that was parked at the curb behind her pulled out and moments later, a dark blue convertible slid into the space. Roshan sat behind the steering wheel, looking at Jenny's back with a grin. Mid-sentence, Bryan nodded in the car's direction.

"There's a very hot brown guy in a convertible behind you."

She turned around and saw Roshan's huge smile beneath his mirrored sunglasses.

"Hey! What are you doing here?"

"I wanted to show you my new toy." He nodded to Bryan hesitantly, "Hey, man. How ya doin'?"

Sensing that Roshan was none too pleased to see her with another man, she quickly said, "Roshan, this is my best friend growing up, Bryan. We grew up together in the sticks. Bryan, this is Roshan." Jenny had scarcely mentioned anything to Roshan about her humble beginnings and was happy to know that he was meeting the best person possible from her old world instead of all the rest of the baggage she carried.

Roshan got out of the car and shook Bryan's hand in an "I'm-more-manly-than-you" way. Bryan discreetly looked him up and down, sizing him up, protective of Jenny as always. Roshan stared back, nostrils flaring slightly. Bryan took a step closer to Jenny, and Roshan cleared his throat, flashing Jenny a quizzical look.

Turning her attention to Roshan, she said, "You bought a car. Wow. Today? Why?"

"Well, I needed a little diversion." He moved a little closer to her.

"Looks like you got the car you've been always talking about. Congratulations."

Roshan glanced at Bryan who looked on with curiosity at the woman coming toward them who wore her Chihuahua in a baby carrier on her chest. Jenny moved a little closer to Roshan, wanting to reach out to his hand, but resisted. She looked at Bryan, who was now focused on them with a mild grin on his face.

"So, you're *the* Roshan. I've heard a lot about you today."

"Oh, you have?" Roshan glanced in Jenny's direction. "All good, I hope?"

"So far, yes."

"I'm sorry, what was your name again? Ryan?"

"Bryan."

"Right. Sorry, man. What brings you all the way here from Albany, Georgia? Memphis is pretty far away from, where is that, the middle of the state?"

"I'm in Atlanta now, in-house attorney for an airline." His chest puffed noticeably. "I came for my girl's graduation." Bryan grabbed her hand and kissed it.

Jenny cringed. She knew Bryan was relishing every moment of this.

Roshan peered at Jenny, eyebrows raised. "Your girl? Oh, okay. So, you two have known each other a long time. What, did you like, date in middle school or something?"

"Well, let's just say we spent a lot of time together over the years. She'll always be my girl." Jenny dug her fingernails into Bryan's palm, and he smirked at her. Roshan's jaw hardened, and he turned toward Jenny. Speaking to her, he asked, "Do you guys want to go for a drink down at Joe's Place? I've got a couple hours to kill before I have to go to my party."

Jenny looked at Bryan, pleading with her eyes to not scold her, then said, "Oh, thanks, no drinking for me today. I still feel like hell. Besides we are just heading back to my apartment to get Bryan's car. He's going to check in to his hotel. I'll have to—"

"Jen," Bryan tugged her keys out of her hand and said, "give me those and I'll drive your car back to your place to get my car. You two go. Get a drink." He hugged Jenny quickly, and shook Roshan's hand. "Bring my girl back soon." As he slipped off down the sidewalk, he put his hand to his ear and mouthed "call me."

Roshan took Jenny by the hand and ushered her into the seat of the convertible. They took off smoothly into traffic, and Jenny relished the wind in her long hair.

"Nice wheels." She ran her fingers along the supple leather of her seat. "What gives? Where's the clunker?"

"Ditched it. Time to let go of the old. Enter a new chapter." He looked at her and grinned. There went the butterflies again for her. "And I want to get there fast!" He stepped on the accelerator and took a sharp right onto a side street. Jenny looked at the street sign whizzing past confused.

"Where are we going? Joe's Place is that way?"

"We aren't going to Joe's Place. I am taking you down to our bench by the river."

Her heart leapt despite herself. She loved looking at the water and the riverboats going up and down the waterway. The ride down to the Mississippi River was a short one, and they bumped around the historic cobblestone river landing next to the water's edge in no time.

Wasn't he afraid of messing up the suspension on his new toy?

The Hernando-Desoto Bridge connecting Arkansas with Memphis hovered on the horizon. Roshan grabbed her hand and led her from the car to the river's edge. This was a place that they had come several times in the past few months to escape the pressures of the clinic and exams. The two of them would wrap up their study sessions with Jay and slip off together to this spot. It was there that Jenny learned the first little kernels about Roshan's Indian life and they had many heated conversations about whether a woman should be the only cook in the family. Why wouldn't Roshan help cook dinner with his wife someday? And change diapers? She had punched him in the shoulder more than once when he swore he'd never change a diaper or do a 2 a.m. feeding with his future kids. But, she could never stay mad at him, chauvinist or not. The twinkle in his eyes somehow made her doubt how serious he was about the whole thing. And after all, he wouldn't be her problem anyway. She would never get married.

Jenny kept her past to herself, and she adamantly defended her feminist stance. She had ranted playfully to him over and over about how Gloria Steinem had paved the way for her generation to have lives, to have their own rights and privileges, and not have to wait on the men in their lives as if they were servants. But Roshan explained to her that many of the women in his family were professionals, but they valued their family just as much as themselves. Everyone worked for the good of their family in his culture. Careful never to divulge her own family's culture of neglect and abuse, she instead named successful women in the world whom she was certain never did a dish in their lives. They always ended in a stalemate.

They sat silently on their bench and watched the flow of water in front of them. The bridge loomed over them in the distance, and a barge was making its way down river in the other direction. The one o'clock sun beat down on their heads, but they breeze tickled their hair and clothes, cooling them enough to be comfortable.

"You're going to burn," Roshan stated, breaking the silence.

"Yep, I will. Give me fifteen more minutes, and I'll be a lobster."

"I am going to turn black. So, I guess we will be an interesting pair soon."

"Pair? Us? A pair of what?" she laughed. "A pair of idiots is what we are." She paused, "At least I am."

"We are not idiots. You are not an idiot." He grabbed her hand and pulled it to him. They continued staring out into the water. "Last night was not stupid."

"Well, you aren't the one in my position. I feel like trash now. I slept with a guy who I know is engaged, albeit to a practical stranger, and met his mother the morning after wearing his pajamas. Not such a good moment for me." She placed his hand firmly back onto his own leg and patted it down. "But I can't stop thinking about you." She knew his eyes were on her, but she forced her eyes to fixate on a boat passing by. She could make out the outline of the captain through the window on the bridge. Skinny guy in a hat.

"I can't stop thinking about you either." He picked up her hand again and held it when she shrugged back. "Before I got you, I drove around town, even contemplating just keeping on the road out of town to get away from this party tonight, the front I have to put up my family, but I couldn't do it. I kept thinking about my mom, and I can't do it to her. But the biggest reason I came back was because of you. I wanted to come back to you."

"Me? How can you come back for me when half of yourself is all about your family? You can't have both." She paused. "Obviously, after my meeting with the mother."

"I know, but we are both moving to Atlanta. I will have a little freedom to breathe, just like I can breathe when we're together. Besides, I'll be building my business. Doing my own thing."

"How? You will be living with your mother! I'll never understand a grown man doing that."

"Well, it's what I have to do. It's what we do. But she doesn't control everything. I will be able to come and go as I please."

"Until Priya moves in after your wedding."

"Yeah. Her…I am not sure if I am going to go through with it." He waited for her reaction.

"Because of me?" She felt suddenly scared and excited at the same time. Was this what she bargained for? Commitment has never been in her plans, and now this? She pictured her father loading up his magnum and pointing it at the two of them with Esha looking on laughing.

What do I really want?

"No, not because of you. Because of me."

Jenny had no idea what he meant by that. How many times had they discussed over books or drinks how deep his obligations to his family and culture ran? How many times had they compared American and Indian families? He emphasized that Indians were always there for each other, unlike Americans who would up and leave their parents after college and stick them in nursing homes in their golden years. She had defended her culture, stating that Americans had independence, were autonomous, and were the masters of their own destinies. Though she never revealed more than a snippet of her own background to him, she held herself up as an example of a self-made person, unfettered by unwanted family baggage. Though she secretly had as much baggage as he did, she was able to keep hers more or less a secret, while his ties were public and all around him at all times.

He began slowly, "I don't know why. I just don't think I can do it. I have my mother to contend with, and I don't want another woman just like her in my life doing the same things." He paused, then began to list, "If I don't want to eat, I want to be left alone. I don't want to be asked five hundred times if I'm sure I don't want just a little bite of food! If I don't want to attend a community gathering, if I don't feel like watching everyone gossip about everyone else in the room, I don't want to be guilted into going! And I just want to put my own underwear into the washing machine!" He sighed deeply and turned to Jenny, leaning in to her face, his breath warming her lips. "And I want to be excited when I walk into the room and see my wife's face. Like I do with you."

He pulled out a piece of paper folded into a square from his pocket and held it up for her to see, looking like a little boy showing her a hidden treasure of marbles. He let her touch the softened edges, and the creases were nearly transparent from frequent opening and closing. Her face covered the middle of the page, the curves of her profile marked and smudged in perfect shading.

"I drew this during our first class together. See how short your hair was?"

"You've been carrying this around for four years?"

He nodded, caressing the shaded graphite lines of the face. "I think I captured the light in your eyes. I recognized it the moment we met, like I've known that light before somehow, and have been looking for it ever since. Does that sound weird?" He slipped it from her finger tips, folding it gently, then put it away.

No, it wasn't weird. It's real, .Too real

She held her breath and looked at his lips to avoid his gaze. She pulled away from him and stood up from the bench. Face afire, stomach boiling, she ran away from the bench toward the river's edge, stumbling on the cobblestones as she went. She heard his feet hitting the stones behind her.

"Where...?" Stumble, trip, thunk. "...are you going?"

She stopped and looked back at him. He was plowing toward her with such force that when he tipped the toe of his shoe into the crack between two uneven cobblestones, he flew forward, arms flailing in the air, his knees catching the brunt of the impact. She ran toward him.

He moaned quietly and fell from all fours to his side, holding his knees, crying out on pain. When his shoulder made contact with the rounded corner of a cobblestone, he cried out again, trying to reach to his shoulder to rub away the pain. Jenny crouched down gingerly beside him, careful not to put her knees down to the ground.

"Oh, Roshan! Are you okay?" She hovered her hand just above his body, not sure if touching him would help or hurt the situation.

"Yeah, yeah." He rasped, growling under his breath as he righted himself and put weight on his legs. "I'm good. I'm fine." He brushed himself off, straightened his shirt, and looked around to see if anyone had watched his mishap. Of course, there was a man with three young children and a group of skateboarding teenagers looking on, fixated on the entertainment he was providing.

Jenny extended her hand to him, and he took it, accepting her help to help him hobble back to the car. Holding her hand out for the keys, he reluctantly plopped them from his fingers, and she got into the driver's seat and cranked the car. The purr of the engine was so mellow, barely audible. She watched Roshan close his eyes and smile.

"Aah, she's smooth, huh?"

"Yes, the car is very nice. Now, where to? Home?"

"Yeah. I need ice."

She put the gear shift into drive and glided off the cobblestones onto the pavement, heading toward their apartment building a few miles away. After hitting all the red lights in their path, both silently looking ahead at the road, they arrived in the parking garage under the building. She helped him out of the car, into the elevator, and they stared at the inside of the double sliding doors, ears full of easy listening music. At his floor, she put her arm around his waist and let him lean on her a bit as they made their way to his door. When they arrived, he leaned his weight against the door frame and pulled her chin up so he could look in her eyes.

"Thanks," he said. "I meant what I said earlier."

Ignoring him, she took his key and opened the door, allowing him to slip into the apartment clumsily. His arm wrapped around her waist, and as she helped him to the couch, he held her tight to him. She wriggled from him and went to the door and slammed it shut. She stepped into the tiny kitchen where her humiliation had opened her day just a few hours ago, the wound opening up new and raw again, just to find an ice pack and a dishtowel. She returned, saw his satisfied grin and turned her eyes to his feet, thrusting the ice pack in his direction.

"You can't do this to me." Her voice resonated louder than she intended, but she was really angry. "You have this fiancé. You have this...this mother! And you tell me I excite you when I walk in the room?"

She stood facing him, her arm outstretched, hands fanned out wide, shaking.

"I just don't know what to do here, Roshan."

She sat down close enough to him for her leg to touch his and sighed.

"Jen, there is really nothing to do. I am just telling you how I feel. You let me be real. But I don't know what to do either. My mom, my family. I am the only son. I have duties. But, sometimes I hate it. I really hate it." Her face softened and he looked her in the eye. "There's so much about me that you don't know. This is so complicated."

"Ya think?" She turned away from him, shirking her leg away from his. "You may have your baggage, but so do I. I know I have not really told you much about my family, but let's just say they are not to open to brown people, as they would call you. They are not exactly worldly." She sat up straight and added, "But unlike you, I have spent my life trying to get away from and becoming better than my beginnings."

"Well, I can't do that."

"I know that." She looked him in the eye, somehow wishing to see something different while in love with his devotion at the same time.

Sorrow filled her belly, and she leaned in to lay her head on his shoulder. She felt like she was losing her best friend. But, he lifted her face and kissed her. A goodbye kiss. Their lips barely brushed against one another, but as soon as they touched, she felt that ping of excitement that she had felt for him every time their hands brushed each other, every time they gave each other lingering friendly hugs when hanging out, the same ping she felt when she woke up that morning entangled with him in his bed.

She pressed her lips harder to his, opening her mouth, inviting him in. He responded in turn and slid his hand behind her neck, fingers buried in her hair, tickling her now alive skin. She placed both of her palms on his cheeks, holding onto him, feeling him in her grasp. He leaned into her, pushing her gently backward, and pressed himself into her body as she tilted her head back and let him kiss her exposed neck. Time stood still, and they lingered in each other's arms, bodies heating up more and more. He moaned quietly and rearranged his legs to the side to take the pressure off of his bruised knees. Breathing heavily, he began to run his hands over her hips, her belly, and under her blouse, finding her breasts. She moaned and pressed herself into his hands, her own hands exploring his body.

Lips locked, they stood up, knocking the ice pack to the floor. Once inside the bedroom, he pushed her onto the bed and undressed her. As he began to pull his tee shirt up over his head, a banging on the apartment door stopped him.

"Shit. What time is it?" he asked himself, looking at his watch.

"What's up? Your party tonight?" Jay's deep voice penetrated the door. "Dude, *bhai*, open up!"

Leaving her on the bed looking up at him, he pulled his shirt back on and motioned for her to do the same. Shutting the bedroom door softly, he went to the outside door and let his cousin in.

Jay, walked in wearing a white oxford shirt with a purple and black paisley necktie. He spun his keychain around on his index finger and rushed into the room. Expensive aftershave burned her nose.

"Dude, come on. Your mom sent me to fetch you. You need to hurry and get dressed! Do I need to pick out your clothes or something?" He barged in through the closed bedroom door, but backed up covering his eyes quickly to Jenny, who was stepping into her panties. "Whoa!" Backing out the door, he grinned at Roshan, then called, "Hey, Jen. Um, how are you feeling today?"

Her cheeks caught fire when he flipped his hand up off his eyes for a second.

Did he just wink at me?

"Good," she said self-consciously.

Pulling Jay toward the front door, he slapped him on the back and said, "Man, let me get dressed. I'm running a little…late."

Jenny cracked the door and saw his big smile. Jay punched him on the shoulder and playfully whispered loud enough for Jenny to hear him, "Way to go, dude!"

"Shut up, man! Get outta here. Go on. I'll be down at the car in a few minutes."

Jay left as Roshan moved into the bedroom and grabbed a shirt and tie that were hanging pressed and ready on the closet doorknob. After throwing the clothes on, spritzing himself with cologne, and running a comb through his smooth, glossy hair, he grabbed Jenny by the waist and kissed her.

"Wish me luck at this party. I'll text you later. We need to talk more." He brushed away a wisp of hair that was stuck to her mouth

"Yeah. Okay. Text me." She sat down on the bed still in her panties and looked up at him. She had a lot to think about. She couldn't wait to get back to Bryan and talk. Her stomach suddenly felt queasy again, but she didn't think it was still a hangover. She swooned a bit and Roshan limped slightly toward her.

"You okay?" he asked.

"Yeah. I'm good. Just a little nauseous. A little hungry. I didn't really eat at the restaurant with Bryan."

"Well, why don't you grab a bite to eat from the fridge? I have to run now, but help yourself. I don't want you passing out."

She nodded and said, "Thanks. I will."

He grabbed her quickly and planted a heavy kiss on her lips. Waving goodbye, he opened the bedroom door again, and he was gone. She sat on the bed for a few moments and looked around the room. The pillows, the blankets, the sheets smelled of Roshan's cologne and invited her in again. She knew she needed to leave, but right now, this was the place she wanted to be. She rested her head on the pillow and inhaled for a moment. Then she got up, finished dressing, and went into the kitchen looking for a snack. Her stomach growled at the thought of the curry and cumin flavors that she could still taste from the morning. She was ready to move on to more new things. Maybe ready to move on to something new with Roshan.

Am I insane?

When she closed the microwave, she noticed a small picture propped against the backsplash on the counter. She picked it up and felt its weight in her hand as she turned it over. Enclosed in the hand-painted black frame, was a crisp line drawing of a smiling little boy holding hands with a dark-haired mom with a red mark on her forehead and in the part of her hair. On the left was a smiling watercolored sun that reminded Jenny of a Monet she once saw in art appreciation class 101 in college next to a poem or prayer written in childlike, yet elegant letters, which she assumed to be in their language. The bottom corner was signed in a cheerful, slightly childish slant, "To my Mummy, Love your little son Roshan." Stuck to the glass was a pink Post-it note that read, "You drew for me on Mother's Day at age 10. Keep remembering to pray this prayer. God knows you."

His mother had been there again today. The woman had let herself into the apartment.

Move on with Roshan? Not with that mother of his in the picture. No way.

Chapter 4

Esha

Chopping up cilantro into fine feathery bits soothed Esha's mind. Her fingertips, which had short, neatly trimmed nails, were covered in the green speckles of the herb, and the knife in her hand worked efficiently. She was already dressed for the graduation party, and her armful of thin gold bangles clanked as she worked, adding to the vibration of chit chat, dishes, and pots clapping together, and doors opening and closing as children came and went from the kitchen.

"Eshabhabhi, take this extra bunch of cilantro," said Ashmi, her bhabhi, her sister-in-law, in Gujarati, who was next to her at the counter, plopping the moist bunch down onto Esha's cutting board with her plump hand.

Women bustled around them in the spacious kitchen, chattering only in Gujarati when they were together, filling steaming foil pans to the brim with rice dishes dotted with cloves and cinnamon sticks and curries sloshing around fenugreek bobbing on top. As with all big occasions, families pulled together today to cook a spread fit for an army, and today Ashmi's kitchen was headquarters for the crew of seasoned cooks with a mission to feed at least one hundred people.

Ashmi's kitchen was usually the headquarters because of its size. Its cherry cabinets and expansive island with hardy granite countertops provided plenty of work space for the many cooks. It opened to a breakfast area next to a tall picture window where a long white table with brass trim sat, perfect for assembling and packing up dishes for transportation to the hall. Today, nine ladies chopped and stirred and fried while their husband's sat on overstuffed leather sofas in the TV room, watching football with bowls of spicy seasoned popcorn in hand.

Esha's baby brother Arun, Ashmi's husband, sat in the recliner nearest the TV, yelling so loud at each play that his spilled popcorn all over the carpet around him. Esha tried not to watch his spoiled antics as she worked, but he sat there like a raja in the vaulted room, and when he gestured impatiently to Ashmi for a glass of water, Esha's skin pricked in annoyance. Ashmi served him immediately and returned next to Esha.

Ashmi was in charge of rinsing and draining the vegetables, and washing and peeling the potatoes. Though only thirty, her tight voice always commanded with every word, and had bristled Esha's skin from the moment they met. Her bhabhi's taut personality mismatched her soft loose body, and as the two worked Esha glanced at the doughy flesh exposed at Ashmi's middle not covered by her sari.

With a body like yours, you should have more sense than to dress like a young girl. Wrap your sari tighter next time.

Esha smiled, though, and kept chopping as Ashmi rambled on about her new chunky 22 carat gold earrings and bangles she had just bought on her latest long stay in India.

"Do you just love this new sari?" she motioned to the gold and black fabric wrapped around her from shoulder to toe. Esha didn't even look up from her cilantro again, remaining silent. "My father has such good connections in Ahmedabad. It's amazing the high quality of things we can get when we go there."

Esha felt Ashmi's expectant eyes on her, but scooped a handful of the chopped herbs into a bowl, mouth closed. Envy gripped her, but she stopped herself because she would never serve a husband or father again, no matter how many heavy silk saris they could buy her.

"Esha, you should come next time...we would find you something...new."

Esha felt the surveying gaze in Ashmi's voice.

"Oh, I'm sorry, bhabhi," Ashmi abruptly said, "I forgot." And she walked away, pretending to busy herself with a stack of roti bread on the stove behind them.

You did not forget. When have I ever been back to India since you've known me? You know very well why I don't go.

"*Kemcho*, everyone!"

Esha sighed with relief when a middle aged woman dressed in a black and red trimmed sari appeared.

"Sorry I am late!" she gushed in English like a character on a TV show. Sweeping into the room with a gust of perfume around her, she spotted Esha at the sink and rushed over, but was intercepted.

"Monisha! Finally!" announced Ashmi in exasperated Gujarati.

With a flip of her curls, she turned from Ashmi and eyed Esha and her green fingers.

"Oh! You are going to get your sari wet, Esha. Give me the knife. I'll chop."

Esha was good-naturedly bumped away from the sink by her best friend. The whirlwind had arrived.

Esha smiled, "*Kemcho*. Hi. Where have you been?" she asked her sister-in-law in Gujarati. She felt like she would explode over the events of the morning and wanted to drop the words into Monisha's ears immediately. But oh no, this was neither the time nor the place. Absolutely no whisper of Roshan's deeds could be breathed with all of the women around. The rumor mill in their community was relentless.

"At the hall, managing the decorations. The tables are ready finally. I had the kids help me sprinkle confetti on the tables and a couple dads brought all of the young guys to move chairs."

Leaning into Monisha's ear, she whispered, "I have to talk to you. About Roshan."

Monisha, with her fingers now covered in green speckles, nonchalantly nodded and whispered back, "Sure. Let's go in a few minutes and take a drive to the hall. We can leave everyone else here to handle the food." Then a little bit louder than conversational volume, Monisha said to Esha, "Bhabhi, when we are done here, let's go check on the cake at the hall."

Wrapping up the kitchen chores, Monisha and Esha waved goodbye quickly to their fellow women and got into Monisha's car. They headed across town to the local community center where the graduation festivities were shaping up.

Once in the car with the door shut, Esha slapped the dashboard and spouted, "Roshan is up to no good again."

"*Are baap re*, oh my gosh, what? Tell me, bhabhi, what's going on?"

"I took breakfast to him this morning and found him with a white girl in his apartment!"

Monisha laughed and said, "Is that all?" She reached out to touch Esha's hand, which shook in fury now that she was talking about the subject. "Bhabhi, you know how he is. He had a white girl girlfriend before. In high school, remember?"

"I know. But he was a good boy back then when I found out. He stopped seeing her and started focusing on his schoolwork more. But now, he seems so, so…belligerent. So independent. So angry."

"Maybe it's because of the engagement. A lot of our boys rebel a little when they get engaged. He will settle down once he and Priya are married. Until then, let him be a man."

Esha's skin prickled at the thought, but she sighed, resigned, and looked out the window at the houses and trees that whooshed past them. Monisha was a fast driver, even on residential streets. She had learned to drive in India. The rules of the road there were optional, and her old habits hadn't died, even after more than two decades in the U.S.

She looked over at Monisha, who was growling under her breath, riding the bumper of the car in front of her. Monisha, her dear friend for so many years, the doctor who saved lives was a tough woman who still reminded Esha of their short time together in boarding school, and being alone with Monisha anytime made her feel like a teenager. She could open up to Monisha about things that no one else could hear and would get a genuine response, whether she wanted to hear it or not.

Monisha was the beautiful rebel Esha never could be. Always aware of Indian rules of etiquette and responsibility, she bent the rules enough to enjoy herself just outside the confines of an Indian woman's life.

When Esha was a young wife in India, only weeks after Monisha's departure from school and Esha's quick, but elaborate, wedding, her life changed drastically. For several years, when Esha was home chopping vegetables and grinding flour for roti, she received Monisha's monthly letters about life in the U.S. with the chain restaurants she went to, the long hours studying in medical school followed by drinks out with fellow interns, and the support of her husband. Esha had worshipped her older brother Prakhar as being the best brother a girl could have. Monisha's marriage to him was bittersweet yet happy for Esha as she, too, was beginning a new life with a man, yet one older and much more traditional than her.

Taking her baby brother Arun with them, Esha's parents had followed Prakhar and Monisha to the U.S. where Prakhar became known as Pete. Her parents lived with them, raised Arun through engineering school, and practically raised their grandson Jay. They lived the grandparents' dream, and Esha always felt abandoned.

Esha was, after all, a daughter, and daughters become more a part of the husband's family after marriage. On those lonely nights after finishing her work and putting Roshan to bed, she sometimes cried with Monisha's letters in her hands until her husband came home. Quickly, she would stash them away for her next private fantasy time.

She was a battered mess, alone in a husband's village house, thousands of miles away, with a child to protect. But, she dared not to write the pain of her bruises in her letters to the U.S. She was sure her husband would read them, and she knew better than to provoke him. That knowledge came quickly when he turned from an attentive husband to an intolerant, drunk monster. All she could do was slip away from her husband's drunken snores out of bed, open the window, and silently scream to the universe that her family could hear her, that God could hear her. And then, she would slip back under the sheet, always keeping her head down for her son, for herself.

Instinctively her mind jumped to her last night in his house, and, as Monisha's car sped ahead, she pressed her belly. God had heard her screams. Prakhar had somehow heard her screams. Family friends had been keeping an eye on her and secretly contacted him that she needed help. In India, divorce did not come easily, and the strongest male member of her family needed to come take her safely. And that is what he did.

She turned to her sister-in-law. "Monishabhabhi, Roshan was so angry. Angry like his father. I have only seen this in him a few times. I saw his father's fire in his eyes. It's as if my husband was back." She shuddered just at his mention. She would never speak his name though.

"Well, Esha, what's the worst thing that can happen? That he marries her?"

"Bite your tongue!" She slapped her hands on the dashboard as they pulled up in the parking lot of the community center. Esha fumed that Monisha would even suggest that as a possibility.

Monisha turned to her. "Relax. If you push him too far, he just might marry a white girl."

Esha gritted her teeth.

"Just relax and let him have his fun. Don't worry about the talk. Everyone else's sons are all doing the same thing."

"Bhabhi, how can you be so cavalier? This is my Roshan you are talking about here, not some cousin's kid to be gossiped about. People will talk about us, of all people, after our, my, past."

"Roshan hasn't done anything yet. He is engaged to a good girl from a good family. He is a good hearted boy, and you raised him right."

"Yes, I did raise him right! But he has done something, and now I don't even know why I told you this…you think good things fall in people's laps like they have for you. My life has not been so—"

At that moment, Jay spotted their car and made his way over to open their doors, first helping and hugging his mum and then Esha.

"Auntie," he addressed Esha, "there is a problem with the cake. You need to come see it."

"Okay, *bhai*. But, where's Roshan? Didn't you find him?"

Jay and Roshan were cousin-brothers to the highest power, living as brothers and best friends. When Pete had come and pulled Esha and Roshan from their prison home in India, he had taken them into his home with Monisha and Jay. Esha and Pete's mother was still alive for a short time after. Esha's brother was a strong man both physically and mentally. He had helped raise Roshan along with Jay, and the two boys shared a room until they left for college. Esha knew Jay was the reason Roshan went to dental school. After years of filling countless sketch books with portraits so real they seemed to breathe of everyone he met and ignoring Esha's nagging to study harder in science, he made her the happiest mother when he lovingly placed his artwork in boxes in the attic and declared his biology major freshman year at college. His auntie and uncle were doctors, Jay was two years ahead of him and would study to be a doctor. It made sense for Roshan to do the same. No one makes money doodling in this country, she told him over and over. You need a serious career, she would tell him, though the bigger reason she forbade art for him went unsaid between them: his father.

"Um, yes." He cleared his throat. "I got Roshan from his apartment. But, he took his car, said he'd catch up with me. And when we pulled onto the interstate, he…disappeared."

"Disappeared?" Esha's cheeks burned. "Did you call him? Where would he go?"

"He's not answering."

Esha looked at Monisha's eyes, who shook her head slightly. "Come, come. Let's go in the hall, Esha. He'll be here." Esha let herself be led by the elbow by Monisha into the building.

Steeling herself as they entered the room full of people helping with set up, she tried to convince herself Roshan will get here. She straightened the pleats on her sari, pulled her shoulders back, and made her way to the cake table.

The time was already half past one. All of the guests would be there in two hours. Things had to be perfect, and there was no time to play around.

Although the party officially started at three o'clock, it wasn't until nearly four o'clock that a steady stream of guests flowed in through the open double doors.

Jay walked over to a group of people chatting with Esha near the door and slapped a young man on the shoulder. "Good you guys could make it. Only one hour late. But, you're still running ahead of Indian Standard Time."

The group chuckled, and the young man turned toward Esha and asked, "Speaking of Indian Standard Time, where's our guest of honor, Auntie? Is he taking time to get pretty like he did in high school?"

Esha cringed inside but shook her head nonchalantly. Roshan's reputation was of a pretty boy among his friends, especially after the hours he spent gelling his hair before leaving the house as a teenager while his buddies always yelled up the stairs for the girl to hurry up. But she repeated the stock answer she had used for years now since Roshan had started drinking more. "He's been held up for a bit. A bit under the weather, actually, but he's on his way."

The young man, whom Esha had known since a child when he and Roshan played Frisbee in the front yard after school, gave Jay a sideways look and a smirk. But when he saw that Esha noticed, he straightened his shoulders and said formally, "I hope he feels better soon, Auntie. I look forward to seeing him tonight."

Esha nodded with a smile and walked away, pretending to go greet other guests, but really had to look away from the knowing look on the man's face. She heard him whisper a little too loudly to his friends, "Yeah. Under the weather. That's Roshan. Always under the weather on party day." The muffled laughter ground in her ears. A hand lay on her trembling shoulder, and Jay stopped her from behind, and whispered, "He just called me. He's on his way." Relief rolled down her body. Now, she just had to wait a little longer. Of course he wouldn't disappoint her. He really was her good boy. Why had she worried?

Thirty minutes later, Roshan had not arrived. People continued to arrive, naturally separating inside the doorway, women gathering toward one another near the crowded food tables, men standing around in clusters, talking business. As she mingled with her friends, Esha enjoyed breathing in an aura of curry and friend food, an aura that smelled like home. The women smelled of perfumes and the scent of mothballs clinging to their saris, fresh out of storage, and she swore she could smell her mother's ghost there beside her. Children trotted around, tiny girls danced their chubby little dances to the high-pitched crooning of Bollywood soundtracks blaring out of the huge speakers, while little boys dressed in white collared shirts and bow ties ran around tagging each other under and around tables. A growing group of preteen boys hovered over the shoulder of the one boy lucky enough to be allowed to bring his Nintendo DS to the party.

Next to their table, some young men, clouded in an atmosphere of nose burning cologne, stood against the wall, hands in pockets, talking coolly to each other. One short boy punched his chunky friend's shoulder next to him, when they caught him staring at a girl in a saffron and black *salwar kameez*, a long gown-like dress with pants underneath, talking with a group of friends near the stage. Her hair draped over one shoulder, and as she glanced at the chunky boy for just an instant, she flipped it to the side where her scarf was pinned to her shoulder. Esha overheard short boy growl, "Dude, she's my sister. Gross."

The rhythm of *tabla* drums in Bollywood soundtracks music pulsated around the room above the bustling voices, and Esha wondered how anyone could have a conversation like this. She had to lean her ear into people's faces to hear anything. All the while, she pictured dance scenes from the Bollywood movies—there were so many—and she fought the urge to go on the dance floor and move. She had been such a good dancer when she was younger and loved dancing at *garbas* with her friends. They would dance for hours to music by live musicians with *tablas* and *sitars*, spinning and clicking their wooden *dandiya* sticks as they moved in perfect sync with one another. She loved the skirts she got to wear to *garbas*. They were brightly colored with tiny mirrors embroidered on, and they sparkled so beautifully. Oh, how she loved the way her skirts flowed around her as she danced. She felt so free back then. But, she was here in a sari now, stiffly awaiting her son's arrival, and dancing to this canned music just wouldn't be the same.

Esha hovered near the entrance, greeting each guest with a smile, a *Namaste* with palms pressed together at her heart for elderly arrivals, and then a hug, inviting them in. All the while, her eyes scanned the parking lot, searching for Roshan's worn out Toyota. Her smile began to crack as time went on and he didn't show.

As she was hugging an elderly woman dressed in a white sari with a single silver braid down her back, a blast of rap music lit up her ears, followed by the revving of an engine peeling around the corner into the parking lot. Then, a car appeared with brakes screeching into the handicapped space closest to the building. Trying to remain calm, she released the woman and stepped outside. The convertible had tinted windows that made it impossible to see the driver. As the door opened, Jay stepped from behind her and made his way to the car. Slapping the hand of the driver, whose arm was all that she could see above the door, "Man, that car is sweet!"

"I know, *bhai*. I can't believe she is mine." Roshan stood up and ran his hand across the grey leather seat and the side of the door sensuously.

Esha felt awkward seeing her son this way. He might as well have been caressing that Jenny in front of people. And this car is his? But how? He wore a starched white shirt and black slacks, and his hair was combed smooth and shiny. He was clean shaven, and his face gleamed behind mirrored sunglasses. The picture of success and of perfection. He looked like a young Amitabh Bachchan, straight out of *Kasme Vaade*, her favorite movie as a teen. She'd daydreamed of marrying the famous actor, and the only consolation to her during her wedding at age sixteen, was that after the curtain dropped between them during the ceremony, and she saw him for the first time, her new husband, looked a little like Amitabh. And now her son looked the part of movie star. Just as she quickly found out that her husband's looks never betrayed his true soul, she knew that Roshan's looks covered his own struggles. She watched him stiffly, silently, as the two boys—yes, she still thought of them as boys—hovered around the car for a few minutes, drawing a crowd of young men who were arriving for the party.

Inside the hall, the speakers from the stage screeched a moment and Vipul, the self-appointed emcee of the party, spoke into the microphone. Esha watched him while keeping tabs on Roshan in the parking lot out of the corner of her eye through the outside door. Something about him didn't seem quite right.

"Welcome, everyone. Welcome. Although we are still waiting on the guest of honor, please mingle and enjoy the music from the soundtrack of *Sajaan*. We have a great playlist that I, the master of song, have compiled for my great friend Roshan. And for later, when we younger folks are left, I have an awesome rap playlist. I hope our friend gets here soon to enjoy the night with us!" Vipul made his selection on the Ipod docked by the speakers and danced off the stage, clapping and waving with the music, encouraging the small children in front of him to dance. Jingling and squealing, two toddler girls joined hands with each other and allowed themselves to be led to the dance floor by preteen cousins and sisters who demonstrated a mix of dance class moves and Bollywood moves they had seen on TV.

She turned her attention back to the men outside at the car as there was a lull in the guests arriving. Her cellphone was in her handbag, but she knew that Priya and her brother would be arriving soon with her uncle, who also lived in Memphis. Their flight had been late, and they'd called an hour before to say Priya needed time to dress for the occasion, and they would be at the party within the hour.

Catching Roshan's eye finally, she motioned her head toward the building discreetly as another family came to the door to be greeted.

"*Kemcho, bhai*," she greeted her friend's husband. "Oh, how are you?" She shot another glance back at Roshan then back to the husband as she gushed, "Oh, so nice to you came all the way from Florida. How's your mom? The boys? I saw a picture of them. They are grown so big!" Ushering the man in the door, she decided to be more aggressive with Roshan to get him inside. Guests were waiting, and she was getting embarrassed by the looks so many guests were casting in Roshan's direction, smirking as they entered the building. Finally making eye contact with him, she tapped her watch and raised her eyebrows. He nodded, closed the car door gingerly, and began to step sloppily onto the curb. His foot slipped, and Jay caught his arm.

"Dude, you okay?"

"Oh, yeah. I'm good. Oh, forgot something." He smiled a devilish grin and unlocked the car with the remote and a beep. Reaching into the passenger seat, he pulled out a silver flask and slipped it into his pocket. To Jay, he laughed and said, patting his bulging pocket, "For a little more added fun tonight."

Jay replied, "Dude, really? You stopped at a liquor store? Come on, not tonight."

Roshan shrugged and walked on.

"Okay, bro. I'll be good."

Esha saw the whole thing, and anger and embarrassment mingled in the juices of her stomach, threatening to come up at that moment. Among all of these people, he would bring alcohol? He was like his father in so many ways now. And everyone in the community would never let her—or him—or any of their close relations live it down. How could he do this to her? And himself?

Approaching Esha, Roshan, surrounded by his pack of buddies, reached out to his mother in an exaggerated motion of love, giving her an uncharacteristically huge hug, breathing Jack Daniels into her ear.

"Mummy, hi," he slurred ever so slightly. "I'm here." He raised his hands in the air to greet everyone around him. To his friends, he said, "Let's go party!"

As they walked in the door, Roshan pulled back a little and stepped up to his mother. Placing his hand on her shoulder, he whispered in her ear, "By the way, Mummy. How do you like my new car? I traded in the old garbage heap for a sweet ride, huh? I'm sure someone out there will swipe up the old one, though. Oh, and thought you'd like to know...there's some more garbage at the apartment. It's like they say: 'one man's trash is another man's treasure.'"

He patted her quickly and walked away, leaving Esha stunned beneath her plastic smile. Could her Roshan have actually just said that to her?

"Hello," she had to sing to the next guest. "Welcome, welcome. Please come in." The acid in her stomach swirled around overpowering the threat of tears in her eyes, and she fought the need to run into the bathroom. If this ever got out, this party would be the last event ever where she could show her face.

Chapter 5

Roshan

Guilt mixed with booze in a toxic whirlpool of emotion inside Roshan as he walked away from his mum and politely broke through the guests at the door to the hall. Yes, guilt circulated through his veins that moment, but he knew it would never go away no matter what he did. The pounding music drowned out the guilt as he limped in, his knee still throbbing from his cobblestone fall, and guests began to cheer for his arrival. A hand pulled his shoulder back gently. He turned, expecting a buddy, but it was his mum standing beside him with a frozen grin on her face. Aware of the eyes on them, Roshan froze his smile as well and asked her in a ventriloquist's voice, "What are you doing, Mummy?"

She straightened his collar and ran her hand across his cheek. They were the center of attention. A woman's voice nearby cooed to a friend, "Aww, mum and son. She's so proud." Roshan smiled artfully down at his mum and put on his best son face. Even drunk, he knew the part by heart.

"My *dikra*, you're not only my son, you're a doctor now. What I always knew you could be. Never forget how proud I am." She projected her voice just slightly as a stage actor would, and Roshan slightly felt the urge to gag. Either the Jack or the moment spun his head, and he floated his hands up to his mum's shoulders and pulled her to a hug. The crowd erupted in "awws."

As they pulled apart, Roshan allowed himself to be surrounded by guests. He never looked back at his mum for the rest of the night. He loved her and couldn't stand to see the hurt look in her eyes.

He shook hands, hugged, and high-fived people he called uncle and auntie, and kids he called brother and sister. Surrounded by buddies, Roshan made his way into the crowd inside the hall and began limping. He patted men on the shoulders, women got hugs, and he high fived the children. When asked what happened to his leg, he evaded answering, leaving room for whispers and speculations to course around the room.

At least a hundred people were there, mostly family or close family friends. All Gujarati. All with connections a generation or two ago with the same villages in India. Roshan had known the uncle with the round belly sitting at a table with all men since Roshan's first year in preschool. His wife, who was stirring pans of rice at the buffet table, had helped his grandparents when they were alive by babysitting him while his mum tutored their Indian community's children in Gujarati.

The guys who crowded around one guy holding an iPhone, groaning about football scores, had been his buddies growing up. Raj came here in high school from London and still had a British accent. Minesh, the guy holding the iPhone, still sported the slicked back hairstyle and guttural South African accent of his former home in the Indian neighborhood outside of Johannesburg. He flew back so often to visit his family, some of whom Roshan was related to, that he never had a chance to acquire a southern twang.

Jay was the only guy in their group that had been born in the states, and being roommates growing up, he and Roshan sounded and dressed alike. They wore Polos from middle school and worked hard to spill out southernism outside of the house as teens. But among these guys in their Indian home life, Roshan and Jay were always a solid part of this group. It didn't matter when in the world their grandparents left their same few villages in the Indian state of Gujarat in indentured servitude or if they were among the lucky to start new businesses in territories of the British Empire generations ago, the Gujarati blood in the veins of their now British and South African families, along with families fresh from India like Roshan's, flowed toward the same Gods, the same vegetarian curries made by mothers who grew up together, and the same pickup cricket and soccer games in front yards as their progenitures did. And so these boys grew up this way, still adhered to one another, as men of a darker shade of brown than the fair faces of the Southerners around them.

Roshan loved history in school because he could sketch scenes instead of taking notes, of wars and people sailing across oceans, and when they got to the history of the British Empire in tenth grade, he sketched an entire notebook of his ancestors boarding ships and working fields in *kurtas* and saris, eager to settle in new worlds. Most became indentured servants in British colonies, some left India to become small business owners, so they could educate their children into doctors and executives where caste had no reach. But his people always found a way to keep the threads of culture in tact wherever they lived, for better or worse, like Roshan.

As the slugs of Jack Daniels from his drive over really began to kick in, he got louder and happier as famous Bollywood party songs and delicious curry smells filled his senses. His drunken state was just barely tolerated by judgmental aunties, though, and he laughed out loud each time clusters of aunties formed gossip circles of pointing fingers and bobbing heads of disgust in his direction. More than once, he saw his mum turn on her heel when she saw the lips wagging around her.

He knew the social impact of his actions, and he was sorry to publicly embarrass her. All of his childhood, she had chided him, "*Dikra*, you and me have to work harder to earn respect than anyone else does. What's ours stays ours in here." She would place her hand on his heart each time. "Outside you and me, always smile and be good, and people will accept us."

But during one of their talks when he was a high school senior, he pulled her hand from his chest and walked away, yelling at her, "My heart will explode, Mummy. Hands off from now on!"

After that, his father invaded his dreams. Roshan would dream he was in his room. He would wake reeking of liquor like his father and get up to look in the bathroom mirror, only to see his father's face staring back at him. Slivers of mirror sliced his fist as they collided, and he would turn to see his father lying on the floor in blood. Next to him, little Roshan, a tiny child holding a plastic gun, just looked at him, helpless and cold. Roshan would then startle awake, face down on his pillow, knuckles aching, and ready to vomit. It was then he started wearing too much cologne, just in case others could smell the phantom liquor on his breath. The real drinking began in college, and his breath turned a real sour sweet each weekend. He was grateful his mum was back in Atlanta as he was able to hide it well from her. And now his gut hurt at the thought of the mix of Priya and Jenny and his mum, and the only thing he knew could dull the ache was another shot, which had become the only salve for perpetually oozing wound of guilt on his soul.

And no matter how much he was to blame for what he was doing to his mum and about to do to Priya, he knew that Mum and Priya would be the objects of blame. They were women, and in many eyes, a woman was the root of all problems. Men could almost get away with murder or adultery, and nosy, gossipy old people would find a way to blame his mum or wife. Women were the bearers of a man's sins.

An unexpected surge of affection for Priya and his mum overcame him. *Stop this now! Idiot, help them save face. No more shots!*

Priya still had not shown up with her parents from the airport, and he wanted to enjoy the music and snacks from the buffet without fresh booze sloshing around in him as he mingled. His mum had fried his favorite samosas, and he carried a handful of them around as he talked. His head cleared with each swallow of the crushed pea-filled pastries.

Everyone sat at banquet tables and watched some of his sweet little cousins gathered onstage to perform their dance numbers they had learned in their Indian dance lessons. They struck perfect poses. They were a ball of hip-shaking frenzy and jingling anklets, true to the choreography, mouthing the lyrics with sass.

The thing he loved most about being Indian was the dancing which was done at most functions around, his favorite being the yearly Diwali festival celebration. Last year, he had dressed in the traditional outfit with a scarf around his head, and performed a number with his fellow male cousins and friends. This was something he did not share with his friends in the white world because he knew full well that just as real men didn't eat quiche in the white world, neither do they dance barefooted in long pajamas and click sticks in a circle with other people.

The food spread was amazing and he devoured two plates. In between plates, he got up and danced with the crowd to a song from the soundtrack of the Bollywood movie, *Bazigaar*. One of his favorites, he knew the words by heart to most of the songs and often blasted it in his car in between tracks of Led Zeppelin and Queen.

After finishing up a song on the dance floor, he decided to text Jenny. Although he was immersed in his party, his thoughts kept going back to her.

Roshan
Thinking of u. Feeling better?

A few moments later, his phone vibrated in his pocket.

Jenny
Yes. Thx. Thinking of u 2. How's party?

Roshan
Fun. Wish I could show u how 2 party Indian-style. Someday.

Jenny
Call when u leave.

He stepped away from a group of people and leaned against the buffet table, phone in hand. He couldn't help but smile as he read the texts. He couldn't wait to call her, and now he wanted to leave.

He bent his arm to slip the phone into his back pocket and his elbow bumped into a stomach behind him. Warm breath puffed into his ear, and Ashmi auntie squeaked into his ear, "Oh, sorry *bhai*. Didn't mean to sneak up on you."

"Auntie, you okay?" He turned to her and rubbed her shoulder lightly. "So sorry! I didn't know you were there."

How long was she there?

"*Bhai*, it's okay. I'm okay. I was just checking the *papadums* in the pan here." She quickly shuffled the spicy crackers around in the aluminum pan, and said, "Ah. Good. Enough."

Did she read my texts over my shoulder?

She leaned into him and asked softly, "You not having fun, *bhai*?"

He was confused. "Yes. Why do you ask?"

She smiled coyly. "Well..." She paused and nodded toward his pocket where his phone was. "You were texting someone. Thought maybe you were bored here."

Shaking his head, he said quickly, "Nope. Not bored. Having a great time. Just texting a friend from school to tell him about the party. He wants to get together later."

"Oh. That's so nice." Her voice pitched with insincerity. She patted him on the shoulder and turned him toward the doors gently. "Priya's here! Keep your phone in your pocket, and go greet your pretty fiancé! I'm sure your *friend* Jenny can wait for you to call *him* later."

Priya stood with her parents at the door. She wore a long paisley dress and had her hair pulled into a low ponytail that draped to the side over her shoulder. Being only the fourth time he had seen her ever, it was actually the first time he had seen her in American clothes.

She looked great, he thought. Very pretty, but still oh so young. He imagined that the high school boys in the room would be turning their heads at the sight of her. Though she was twenty three, she looked more like she belonged with them than with him, a guy who at the ripe old age of twenty seven, was already sporting greying temples. It ran in his family and made the men look distinguished beyond their years. He and Priya were an odd couple.

To be courteous and to keep up appearances, he tried not to limp as he made his way through the crowd to her, where she met up with several women her age and hugged them tightly. They giggled and quickly dispersed, and he gave her a short, impersonal hug. He was still sweating from the dance floor and hoped he didn't offend her nose. He saw his mum out of the corner of his eye staring at him as he released her, grinning smugly at the sight.

"I'm glad you could make it back to town for this!" He said to Priya and her parents. "Seems like just yesterday you all were here for the engagement. How was the flight?" he asked her father directly. No matter what happened he wanted her father to know he respected him and was a respectable human being.

"Fine, *bhai.* A little turbulence, but fine. Priya and her mum," he nodded at his wife and daughter, "got a little nervous, but you know how women are." He smiled jokingly and patted Roshan on the arm.

"I saw you break a sweat during the worst of it, dear," said Anjuli, Priya's mum, in a British accent, prodding him back. "Don't listen to my husband, Roshan, *bhai,* we women in this family are stronger than we look. You will soon find out with my Priya." She leaned into him and gave him a tight hug. "You two, go mingle with friends. Priya, go eat something. I am going to find your mum."

Her dad rubbed his hands together. "And I am going to find my friends. I've got some business to discuss with your uncle. A great opportunity had just opened up in a hotel deal."

"Have you eaten, Roshan?" she asked. She was a true Indian woman. First and foremost concerned with her man's stomach before she herself can eat.

"Yes, I have eaten. You?"

"Not yet. I'm starving." She put her palm on her tiny belly, and Roshan wondered if she ever ate.

"Would you like me to sit with you while you eat?" he asked, flashing a Bollywood smile.

"Sure. That would be nice." She smiled and touched his hand.

His kind gestures obviously were making her warm up to him more than she had before at the engagement. He was afraid he would be leading her on though and began to think twice about his kindness tactic. Then she reached up and adjusted his tie and gave him a satisfied look. His skin crawled. At that moment, his phone vibrated in his pocket again. "Excuse me, Priya." He couldn't wait to step away from her.

Jay
Dude. What r u doing? Need to talk. Meet me out back.

Several women young women Priya's age rushed upon them, swarming Priya with hugs. Priya was from California, but just like Roshan's buddies, her friends were from all over too. He excused himself, and with a curt, sullen glance at him, Priya went on to the buffet with the ladies.

At the long tables set up with food trays, Jay stood in the back, beckoning him out the door. "Man, what the fuck are you doing?"

"What do you mean?"

"You have to ask! You and Jenny have had your thing cooking for months, you nail her, but now you are buddy, buddy with Priya. You just playing the field with Jen?"

"Dude, I don't know. I just don't know."

"You know you can't be with her, man! Why don't you just let this thing with her go and do the right thing. By Priya. And by your mom."

"Like you did?"

"Yeah, exactly. That Jewish girl I saw for a while in college…it was fun, but it couldn't last. And I love Hema now. It grows after a while. I'm happy. It's all good."

"I just don't think I can do this. Priya reminds me of my mum so much. I'm to the point where I don't care what my reputation is. I just want to live my own life."

"Yeah, and have you thought about what happens if you stay with Jenny? Are you willing to be an outcast? And your mom too? With your guys' baggage, you need to work doubly hard for your mom."

Roshan knew he was right.

"Besides, Jenny could never be a part of our family. Ever."

"I know. But breaking things off with Priya really has nothing to do with Jenny. I just don't want her. I don't want to marry my mom."

"Man, you are messed up."

Jay shook his head, slapped Roshan on the shoulder, and walked back inside the building.

Roshan stared out into the wooded area behind the building, listening to the music filtering outside, enjoying the calm cool spring air. He loved being outside, but his grueling schedule in school all his life, over the last twenty years had scarcely allowed him to enjoy peaceful times outside. He spent hours of his life that he would never get back sitting at a desk in a dimly lit room under the watchful eye of the house nurse and doctors and overachieving cousin, while he dreamed of sitting in piles of pine straw and sketching the burnt colors of leaves in the fall. By the time he arrived at college, he had all but forgotten the feel of the breeze on his cheeks, and after the first day of classes, he sat in the courtyard by his dorm to do his homework. All because he could. And when he brazenly took an art class sophomore year instead of the extra biology class his uncle recommended, he sat in that courtyard sketching every morning with his new oil pastels he'd gotten from the university store. It was worth the countless reprimanding phone calls his mum made every week. But, the reality of medical school set in two years later, and he had to give the outside world up for four years. Fluorescent light became the only light he lived under.

Now, feeling the fresh breeze against his cheeks, his head cleared of the alcohol, and he weighed his life, trying to balance his wishes from his duties. He was a good son. He had to prove to his mum, to his uncle, to his community that he was not his father, that he would redeem his family from his father's actions. He loved his mum, had been raised to honor her before anything or anyone else, and he loved his culture, his community. They were home to him.

He noticed an anthill about a foot tall a few feet away. He felt like one of the ants marching around in regimented order to serve their society. But, right there, in the dusk of the night, with the expanse of the sky, the woods, the freeing breeze around him, he longed to run away, to escape into freedom, to be himself, to think of himself, to find peace in himself. He could see the open door but was afraid to leave, yet also afraid to stay.

Jenny. The last few months he had grown to want to be around her all the time. The attraction he felt to her was indescribable, both physically and emotionally. She represented the freedom he craved, but also the rebel in him. If he pursued his relationship with her, would he—or she— ever be happy? He could be responsible for making every one he loved miserable. And what was she holding back from him. He knew very little about her own family. There was more to this story than he knew, and he wasn't sure that he wanted to know. It was odd to him that she rarely saw or mentioned her family. How could that be? And what did that mean?

All he knew right then was that he had to go back into the party and face Priya. It wasn't fair to her that he was ready to fly the coop; her life was in the balance too. He had to be frank and honest with her, and let the chips fall where they may. His karma was connected to hers, and they had a connection somehow to each other from a former life, but it was not up to him whether it ended now or not. It was up to her.

He also knew he had a connection to Jenny that was just as strong. Their paths had crossed for some reason that was planned before he even met her. Perhaps they had known each other in a past life, and that is why he couldn't explain his feelings for her. One night before board exams a couple of weeks ago when they sat with their fried brains reviewing notes in Starbucks, Jenny asked him what he was in his past life.

"No idea. Maybe a horse?"

"A horse? Why do you think that?"

"Well, I'm a vegetarian. Horses eat grass. And I'm a stallion. 'Nuff said." He winked at her.

She leaned in closer. "Then what was I?"

"You were, hmmm, let me think. You were a medieval princess who rode me." He grinned at her and went in for the kill. "But, you never rode side saddle. I remember that."

"Oh my God, Rosh. You're horrible! Your fiancé has got her hands full with you." Something in her look told him she didn't really mean Priya. "Now, get to work!"

She leaned into him and pretended to push him off his chair, but lingered on him a few moments. He didn't want her to move. But, she straightened up and exaggeratedly put her glasses on and stared at her book.

Perhaps he just wanted to justify his desires. Either way, he had to make a change. He had to make a move. He couldn't live this way any longer. He kicked the ant hill and watched the ants scurry around to pick up the pieces of their home before he turned and went back inside.

The festivities were winding down. Ladies were moving pans from the buffet table to the small kitchen, no doubt packaging food up in doggy bags to take home. The crowd had thinned out, and most of the old people and families with small kids were fading out the doors. The music volume was softer. Roshan began to say goodbye to his buddies and finally had a chance to ask Priya if she wanted to go grab a dessert or a drink with him alone. She pulled herself away from the clean-up duty with the other women, took her purse, and left with him.

His mum watched her and Roshan got out the door with a nod and a smile at Monisha auntie, who nudged her with approval at the sight of the couple together.

Once in the car, Roshan spoke little to Priya.

"Drink or dessert?" he asked in a friendly way. His conscience felt like a thousand pound bag of sand on his chest.

"I don't drink, so dessert would be good," she replied, her hair whipping around her face in the wind. "This is a beautiful car, Roshan. But can we put the top up? My hair is coming undone."

Roshan, annoyed but ever the gentleman, pressed the button on the dashboard, and in a few seconds, they were encased inside.

In the restaurant parking lot, Priya stopped him from going any further before she could straighten his tie.

"Your hair is kind of messy too," she said, motioning to her own head. "You could, you know, fix it a little before we go inside?"

Tempted to mess it up even more and thrust his head in her face, his own vanity won out, and he smoothed it down. Inside they were seated at a table near the bar. Roshan longed for a drink, but wanted to keep a clear head here, to stay focused and resolved. And to make sure he said only the right things. He knew when he drank that he tended to get too outspoken, and this was not the time or the place to speak too much of his true feelings. He needed to be delicate.

"What would you like? Brownie ala mode? Chocolate cake?" he asked her, avoiding her eyes.

"It all has eggs in it. We can't really eat any of this. Maybe we should go to your uncle's house. I could make you something sweet. More our food." Pausing, she added, "I tend to stay away from restaurants anyway. You never know if meat things are touching your food in the kitchen." She suddenly looked up at him and asked, "You are a vegetarian, aren't you?"

Roshan knew the correct answer was yes. Like her, he was raised to eat no food with eggs or meat in it, or drink alcohol for that matter, but in the last few years away from family more and more, he had branched out into eating eggs and, of course, drinking. He had even fallen in love with extra crispy Kentucky Fried Chicken, but kept that at a minimum out of guilt, as if his aunties or mum might smell the special recipe seasonings on his breath at any time.

"No," he said simply. The look of disapproval on her face stung him a bit. But he told himself he had better get used to it. He deliberately ordered a drink from the bar, though he planned to drink only a few sips. He wanted to show Priya the real him. Perhaps it would make her feel less badly about what he was about to do.

She looked away from him, and her eyes narrowed a bit as she focused on the light fixture above them. "Oh. Okay."

The waiter brought her water and his rocks glass filled with amber colored bourbon and coke. Again, she looked away and inhaled deeply as if she were fighting back words.

"Do you want a sip?" he asked, ready to get into the bad-boy role for her. This could really work, he thought.

"No. I told you. I don't drink."

He took a big gulp and looked directly at her. She was so tiny and delicate, but judging by the look on her face, she was capable of big anger. Much like his mum. He decided to try to make small talk to edge his errant ways into the conversation.

"Too bad. You should've seen us last night. Three sheets to the wind. We had a blast."

"Oh, who were you with?"

He knew she was probably trying to find out which friends he drinks with so that she could keep him out of their reach once they were married. "Jay," he said, then paused and smiled. "And Marissa. And Jenny."

"Who are Marissa and Jenny?"

"Marissa is mine and Jay's friend from my class. New York chick… wicked sense of humor. And Jenny is another person in my class. She and I are…good friends."

"Oh. Is that right?" She shifted in her seat and looked around as if she were afraid someone might hear their conversation. "Weird, kinda sounds like a double date."

Roshan cringed.

"Does Hema know?"

"Hema is in London visiting a cousin. And Jay went home early…without Marissa, thank you very much. It was no double date." He tapped his fingers on the table and looked all around them, "But, let's not share this, okay?"

Priya looked confused and angry. "And this Jenny. She is your friend?"

"Yes. My friend." He paused waiting for his words to sink in. They both knew that having a female white friend, regardless of whether he was sleeping with her or not, was taboo.

"How close are you?"

"Very. Priya, you need to know that I am not the kind of guy to follow the straight and narrow." He sucked in air for courage and dove right in. "I am going to do what I want to do. Drink, eat meat, choose my friends, and I don't go to the temple. You just need to know that."

Her fingertips tapped on the tabletop. Then she swirled her finger around in the condensed water that collected at the base of her water glass. But she was silent.

Swallowing hard, he kept going. "I am not sure if I am marriage material really. I am not exactly a good guy like I was made out to be before the engagement."

She nodded her head, and her eyes moistened slightly. But her eyes fixed on the tiny puddle of water below her finger.

He continued, softening his voice, switching to a more sensitive tone. The sight of her face brought out the guilt in him, and he knew he had to finish this. "I've been doing a lot of thinking, Priya. I am not the guy for you. You are devout. You come from a good family with a good reputation. You know my family's, um, history. It's not as good as your family's. I think I will just bring you disappointment."

She breathed deeply and looked him in the eye, placing her hands neatly in her lap. "Okay, I see. You are not the guy for me. Uh-huh." She leaned in to him and sliced him with her eyes. "And you didn't know this before you agreed to see me at my auntie's house. Before we got engaged?"

She didn't seem so tiny to him anymore as her rage inflated her.

"I knew, Priya. But I was trying to do the right thing. Be the good son. Ya know?"

"Yes, I know. Well, I'm trying to be a good daughter too. Do you think I wanted to get married now? I am about to start my residency! I don't want to be cooking for a husband after working 36 hour shifts! But, I am being a good daughter!" She slapped her hand on the table and tears slipped down her cheeks.

"You can blame this on me, you know. Tell your parents it is my fault."

"Oh, and that will make a difference? You know as well as I do that I'm the one who will look bad here. The first thing my mum will ask is what I did to run you off."

"You can tell her it is because I am seeing someone else."

"Well, you are. So it will be the truth." She thrust herself forward across the table. Roshan leaned back instinctively.

"Yes." The truth, finally out in the open, sounded strange to him. Yes, he was seeing someone.

Am I really seeing her? Or did I see her, past tense?

Priya lowered herself back down and looked around the restaurant. He was relieved. She pulled her purse into her lap and said, "Please pay for your drink and take me back to my auntie's house. My parents will be waiting for me."

He did as he was told, calling the waiter over for the tab. As he was signing the credit card slip, she stood up and said, "My uncles warned us about your family. But my mum said no, you were different." Priya smoothed down her skirt and flipped her loose ponytail behind her shoulder.

He looked up, ready to accept his punishment.

"You're a cheating alcoholic," she said venomously. "People warned us about your family. I'm like my dad and give people the benefit of the doubt too much. But, I guess you are like your father, like everyone said you would be."

The words slapped him with a sting that he knew would last for a very long time. Yes, he was like his father. The dreams would never let him forget. Now he craved that drink and poured it down his throat, his eyes fixed on hers.

After a silent ride to her auntie's house, he parked the car in front and killed the engine.

"You will not do this to me, Roshan. My reputation will be ruined." She turned to him and clenched his shirt sleeves. "My brother is one year younger than me. My parents are already looking for a girl for him. If we break this engagement, it'll be hard for him to find somebody." She squeezed her nails into his biceps. "Your reputation will rub off onto my family even more if we split."

The look of fire in her eyes singed his own building anger. He thought of his mum and the look on her face when she saw Jenny in his apartment. He thought of the things he heard some people say about her when he was growing up when they didn't think he could hear: "Worthless." "Bad luck." "Never deserves another husband." His beautiful young mum who must be so lonely in the blackness of her room each night. And when he looked into Priya's smoldering eyes, he decided he couldn't let that fire be extinguished by his actions. He grabbed her hands from his sleeves and held them to his chest. She looked at him in surprise, and he pulled her to him in a hard kiss. She held stiff for a moment but let herself go in his hands. They pushed and pulled each other in angry and purposeful kisses until both of their lips were chapped red. He let her go and said simply, "We will get married."

Without a word, she nodded and exited the car into the darkness under the trees in her auntie's front yard.

He pulled the car away from the curb slowly and stopped a few blocks away. He pulled out his phone and texted Jenny.

Roshan
Party over. U home?

Seconds later,

Jenny
Yes. 8 with Bryan. He left! U come over! :)

Putting the car in gear, his tires burned rubber as he pulled away from the curb. He put the top down and shook his head in the wind. The cool air caressed his face, and he felt the vast expanse of sky above him. His shoulders felt lighter, but his stomach was in knots.

What am I doing?

Chapter 6

Jenny

Jenny stood in front of her open closet and huffed. It was midnight, her muscles ached from exhaustion, and her eyes burned. Bryan was back at his hotel. Her belly was full from the huge dinner she had scarfed down in front of him, and she wanted to curl up under her covers and sleep. But, she couldn't do it. Roshan was on his way over.

She brushed a thick tuft of hair out of her face and began to pull clothes off of hangers and throw them into "keep" and "donate" piles to prepare for her move to Atlanta. She needed something to occupy her while she waited.

The floor was quickly littered with dying sweatshirts and sweaters, and she surveyed her life in piles. The "donate" pile heaped over in two mounds of stretched and faded study sweats and cheap jeans, along with some ratty sneakers and comfort flats she had worn out during clinical rotations. She pulled a handful of old panties and socks from a drawer and threw them in as well. Out with the old. And now, in with the new.

The "keep" pile was not really a pile. It was just enough fabric to cover her body for a few days until she could shop in Atlanta for her new job.

A nice pair of jeans, a pair of dress slacks, some nice tops. All she needed for now and less to pay to move.

A late night talk show was droning on the TV, and she was glad for the distraction. Nerves about her residency started gripping her. This was the end of the line for schooling and the beginning of performance. Her whole life of work led her here, and if she didn't perform, she was screwed. But she would do it. Looking at the things she was shedding and the tiny amount of things she was bringing along, she knew she had nothing to lose. And still everything to prove.

Her mother had made that clear very early on.

Wanda was a drug addict. Her father was a construction worker and traveled a lot for jobs. Days went by when Jenny had to walk past her lying on the couch strung out, stinking of dirty hair and sweat. But when her fix wore out, Jenny took her rants silently. Fingers dug into her arms each time, and her mom shrieked how worthless a daughter Jenny was. Finally, one day her teacher saw the bruises on her skinny arms, and thanks to children's services, she found herself sleeping in a foster bed until her father got home. Five days later, she got to fall into his arms, letting him squeeze her until she couldn't breathe. His familiar whiskey-smoky-daddy-musk comforted her. It was the smell of hugs and warm fast food dinners and bedtime stories. Daddy took a job close to home, and her mom hopped from rehab to jail and back again, and then disappeared. That's when Jenny stopped calling Wanda "Mom," and vowed to be everything Wanda wasn't.

Roshan knocked at the door as she dropped a brown cable knit sweater into the donation pile to open the door. Roshan walked through the door looking ruffled. Jenny pulled him by the hand to the sofa, and he pulled her to him in a kiss.

"How was it?" she asked.

"Fine. What are you up to?"

"Cleaning out closets. I only have this weekend to get packed up for the move. Movers come on Wednesday, and I have to start work the next Monday."

"I'll help." He clapped his hands together and asked, "Where do I start?"

His enthusiasm shocked her and made her smile. She knew no one else who was ever that eager to help her with anything.

The burning question in her mind was to ask what had happened with Priya. But she didn't. She felt like it wasn't her business. She had a definite sense of boundaries with Roshan. What went on across that cultural fence was his business, and she couldn't interfere. Just like he couldn't understand or change anything she dealt with concerning her family.

He retrieved some plastic garbage bags from her kitchen and began helping her stuff piles of discarded clothing into them.

"What are you going to do with these? Take them to Goodwill?"

"No way. Goodwill sells them. I am sending them to some people who really need them." She paused and added, "To my family."

Puzzled, Roshan looked at her as she avoided his gaze. He wanted to ask more details, but she didn't offer any further.

Jenny stood up and said, "I'm thirsty. How about a soda?"

He nodded, and she left the room to get some sodas out of the refrigerator. She so wanted to tell him more about herself.

You can't tell, Jenny. Don't be stupid.

She came back into the bedroom to find Roshan holding a framed picture of her. He had found it in a box that had been pulled from the closet and sat half opened. It had been propped on her dresser behind some knickknacks, but he must have zeroed in on it. The picture was of her and Bryan with Bryan's mom, and they were wearing their graduation caps and gowns. They stood in front of a tiny house in need of repair. Jenny's hair was long with pink and purple steaks though it.

"Wow, that's you?" He held up the picture to her, and she came and took it away quickly, burying it under a pillow.

"Um, yeah. That's me."

He pulled the picture out again. "Wow, you really went through a phase in high school."

"You have no idea."

"Where was this picture taken? Was this your house?"

"No, it was Bryan's house. Mine was just like it, just with cardboard in the broken window and my dad's old mustang rusting in the driveway. My house wasn't exactly picture worthy."

Okay, the info's seeping out. I'll see how he handles it.

"Oh, okay. Do you have any pictures of your family?"

She paused, took a deep breath, and changed the subject, asking, "So, what went down at your party tonight?" She wanted to see where they stood before she could bring herself to reveal anything further.

Roshan sat her down on the bed and looked her in the eye.

"I went for a drink with Priya and tried to explain to her that I wanted to break it off with her." He paused and then looked away. "But I couldn't do it."

Jenny felt like a hand had slapped her across the face, but disappointment was so familiar to her that she rebounded in less than a second, hardening her chest to the news. She took the picture from Roshan and put it back in its spot on her dresser.

"Okay. I see," she said. "I didn't think you would be able to do it anyway." Despite her disappointment, she felt a little relief wash over her. She could picture her father putting his shotgun down. Her insides were a swirl of emotions crashing into one another, and she stared hard at Roshan.

He sat down on the edge of her bed and stared back.

"So, I guess we are just going to stay friends now, huh?" she stated, patting his hand that rested on his knee. She laughed, "It was silly for us to even talk about being together. It is really for the best anyway."

"Yeah, I guess it just wasn't meant to be. My family could never accept you. It just can't happen."

"Well, neither could mine. What little family I do have anyway."

They looked in each other's eyes, and Jenny tried to see what was going on behind his amber eyes. Was he feeling as torn as she was? As disappointed? As relieved?

"We can be friends, can't we?" he asked.

"How? Do you want to go out on double dates with your wife and my boyfriends? Are you kidding? That's stupid." She paused a moment and added, "This has got to end. I won't be able to stand to be around you anymore, and you don't need me in your tight little Indian world anyway." Her voice began to sound more acid, as if her anger and disappointment were overpowering the sadness and love she suppressed inside her.

"We can be friends until the wedding. I don't even know when that will be. And Priya may not even move to Atlanta if she gets a residency somewhere else. That's a lot of wasted time for us to not be in each other's lives. Look, Jenny, I really care about you. In another life, if the circumstances were different, I would get down on my knee and ask you to marry me someday. I want to be around you. This sucks. But if I can't actually be with you, I want to be around you."

"How do you think that will work Roshan? We can see each other at dental conventions and continuing education courses. We can meet sometimes after work for drinks. Then what? Every time I see you, I will remember what we could have had. What we couldn't have. Ever since I met you four years ago, every time I have looked in your eyes, whether you have been talking to someone or studying or looking straight at me, I have wanted you to hold me. I have wanted you to make love to me. When you do things for me, like bringing me Gatorade at 3 a.m. when I'm puking from a stomach virus I caught from my patients, or even when you stayed up all night helping me not fail pharmacology, I have fought showing it, but I want you. I feel this pull to you that I can't understand, and I don't want to fight." She pulled her hands from him, balled them into fists, and pushed them into the bed. "So, I can't see you. I can't be your friend."

"You're right. I know." He grabbed her fists and pulled them to his chest. She let him hold her wrists as if his hands were handcuffs. "I am drawn to you too. There's something about you that makes me feel like I'm home. It's in your eyes. It's like I've been looking for you since before I can remember. I want to make you feel as happy as that makes me. I can't stand it if we just never see each other again."

"Well, if you want to make me happy, just stay away from me." The hurt look in his eyes made her want to cry, but she held firm with her words. "It's best if we go our separate ways when we get to Atlanta. My apartment is an hour away from yours and your mom's house anyway. It's a big city. There's plenty of room there for both of us."

He stared at her for a while letting her words sink in.

She got up off the bed and resumed pulling clothes off the hangers in her closet. She ripped. She yanked. She jerked them onto the floor in a pile, venting her anger on the clothes. After a few minutes of watching this, he stood and walked toward the door.

"I'll go ahead and leave then."

She stopped and said, "That's best." She walked over to him and gave him a peck on the cheek. The warmth of his skin made her want to kiss his lips, but she resisted. He turned his mouth toward her, and she turned away, lightly pushing his chest away from her. "Go," she whispered, tears in her eyes, her anger giving way to sadness.

They stood for what seemed like minutes with their eyes locked, neither of them wanting to pull apart, but both knew there was nothing to say or do.

Jenny's cellphone rang and broke the moment. She didn't recognize the number. And who would be calling her at two in the morning? "Hello?"

"Jenny?"

The voice was an older woman's voice. A tingle went down her back. It couldn't be. "Yes?"

"This is your mother."

Jenny nearly dropped the phone. Forgetting that Roshan was standing in the doorway watching her, she leaned against the wall of the bedroom and stopped breathing for a moment.

"Wanda." She sucked in her breath again.

How dare she call me? I need to hang up right now.

"Jenny, I am calling about your father. He is in the hospital. In a bad way."

"What? How did you get my number? How do you know? Why are you the one calling me?"

The woman's voice was soft and rough like sugary sand, but her words were short. "I got your number from your daddy a few years ago. Ain't never had the guts to use it before, but I figured now's the time. Tammy told me to call. She's too wrung out to talk."

Jenny tried to soak in the surreal. The woman who gave birth to her—she'd never call her a mother—was on the line, breathing words into the phone, real and alive. And her poor daddy, she just talked to him. How? What happened?

"What's wrong with him?"

"Well, the cop was just at the hospital when I got here, and he says to me, he says, 'Ma'am, this man was so drunk he should'a been dead from alcohol poisoning. It's a miracle he could even sit upright enough to drive into that telephone pole.' And I says to him, 'Well, officer, that ain't nothin' new. He's always been so drunk, I don't know how he kept nothin' upright enough to even father three kids.'" She chuckled.

Daddy's a drunk and doesn't deserve to die. But, you, Wanda, maybe...

Wanda cleared a wet mess out of her throat and stopped laughing. "I just thought you should know, doll baby. You best be gettin' here soon. No tellins' what's gonna happen in the next few hours." The touch of sympathy in Wanda's voice brought up an echo of her voice from long ago when she had once kissed Jenny's skinned knee as a tiny girl. That was before the men with little packages started coming around the house, leaving her mommy passed out on the couch.

She hated this woman, but wanted to say something else to keep her on the line.

"I graduated from dental school," she blurted out.

"I know."

Jenny had not exchanged a call or letter with her mother in at least five years. And she knew that her father and mother did not speak. Maybe she knew that Jenny had been in dental school, but how could she have known about the graduation?

"How did you know?"

"Your daddy called me a couple weeks ago. Just outta the blue, ya know. He said he figured I outta know since you're my daughter and all." Her breath rasped in Jenny's ear for a moment, then she blurted, "I was there." Her voice was matter-of-fact. There was no emotion in it at all.

Jenny slid down the wall and looked at Roshan who, sensing the gravity of the phone call, had sat down on the bed while she talked and waited.

"You were there?"

She was in town yesterday. This is creepy.

"Yeah. I drove home right after. Now, come on down here. Quick. I gotta go."

Just like that, the call was over. Jenny absentmindedly dropped the phone on the bed.

"That was my mom," she said, looking at the phone as if trying to solve a puzzle.

"Is everything okay?"

"No. My dad is in the hospital, may be dying."

"Oh my God, you need to get there. Is your mom with him at the hospital?"

Jenny sat there. "Yeah, they've been divorced since I was eight, so I don't know why. I haven't seen her in years. And I'm glad about that."

"Years? Really? Your own mom?"

"Yeah. She now calls me to tell me my dad hit a telephone poll and... that she was at our graduation. Oh my God, what the hell is going on here, Roshan?"

Chapter 7

Roshan

"Are you okay?" he asked her.

"I...I don't know."

She got up and started to wad clothes into a duffle bag, looking to him like a wild animal, picking stuff off of piles, reshuffling with no plan. Lift, shake, wad, shove. He resisted the urge to grab her by the shoulders.

"I have to call Bryan. Maybe he can drive me home and drive back to Atlanta afterward."

Roshan handed her cellphone to her.

"Hey, Bryan. Oh my God, my daddy's been in an accident." Tears streamed down her face as she turned her back to Roshan and shut the bathroom door. He tried to suppress his hurt feelings that her hushed voice and sobs are for Bryan and not him. Kind of feeling like an intruder, he listened, just able to make out the conversation.

"You're already at the airport? Oh, Okay. Yeah. No, it's okay. I was hoping I could have caught you in time to maybe drive me back home. But...no, no...I'll be fine."

Roshan could tell by the pitch of her voice that she was in shock. He couldn't let her be alone. Or drive all the way to South Georgia at night on her own. He couldn't let her fly home alone. At the sound of her phone hitting the tile floor, he moved in quickly to go hold her, but just as he reached for the door handle, she opened the door and stared blankly at him. He led her to the bed by the elbow.

"Maybe I could fly to Atlanta tonight and rent a car to drive the rest of the way." She dug her nails into her knees and heaved a sigh. "But, I don't even really have enough money to fly right now."

Roshan pulled her chin up and cupped her cheeks. "Jenny. Hold on. By the time you get a flight and get to the airport, you could be halfway there if I drive you." She looked around her room with blank eyes again. He saw she was in no state to make decisions. Roshan stood up and commanded. "Come. Get packed. I'm taking you."

She looked up at him in shock and shook her head. "No, no. I don't want you to."

"I am driving you. It doesn't matter what you want right now. It's what you need. Get your things together, and let's get in the car."

He stood her up gently and handed her the duffle bag. "Pack quickly. I'll grab my things now, and then we'll head out of town."

"Roshan, no. You can't come with me."

"Yes. I can." He was not going to take no for an answer.

At that moment, he loved her and had to take care of her. She needed him and it felt good.

"My family...my dad...won't want you there. They're not exactly tolerant of anyone with brown skin."

"Okay, fine. Then I don't have to go into the hospital with you. I just want to make sure you get there in one piece." He paused and ran his hand along her arm, giving her a pat on her shoulder. Keeping a platonic distance from her was killing him. "I am your friend, Jenny. This is what friends do."

She looked into his eyes, held his gaze for a moment, and looked away with a weak smile. Her shoulders relaxed under his hand. "Okay, then, friends. Take me home."

Relieved, he stood her up. "Pack. I'll run downstairs and be right back."

He returned in five minutes, asking her if she was ready. She nodded. Ushering her out the door, he said, "Everything will be okay, Jenny. I'll be with you." He hoped that his words meant as much to her as they did to him. He would be there. No one could stop him from doing that.

They took elevator to the parking garage, and as they exited the parking area into the moonlit night and the car negotiated the curves elegantly, he steeled himself for what he had to tell her.

"So, we should make good time at this hour. I'll get you there fast. But, I just need one minute to swing by my uncle's place and let them know where I am. No one there is answering the phone. They'll worry." He paused for her reaction, but when met with only silence, he went on. "Plus, my mom is heading back to Atlanta in the morning, and I won't see her until my move in a couple weeks. I was supposed to go there for lunch with the family tomorrow, so I really have to talk to them all before I leave."

She looked at him like he had to be joking. "Will Priya be there?" Her lower lip trembled.

Oh God, I want to grab her right now.

"No, I hope not. She's staying at her aunt's house and flying back to L.A. tomorrow. We said our goodbye tonight anyway." His lips still ached from Priya's hard kisses in the car just a couple of hours ago.

After barreling through the dark streets to get back to his aunt's house, he left the car running and rushed inside. Almost as quickly as he'd packed, he returned, put the car in gear, and drove toward the interstate.

Once cruising, Jenny broke the silence. "You and Priya have a strange relationship. What kind of marriage is that going to be for you?" She looked away out the window.

He wondered how to respond to that. Should he say "comfortable?" Should he say "angry?" But as he pictured his life with Priya, he stated, "Correct. It will be the correct marriage for me."

"But how can you live without love?"

Her eyes shifted to him, and he could feel her eyes beside him. Taking his eyes off the road for a moment, he looked back at her and smiled. A single tear ran down her cheek, and he wiped it away with his free hand

Are these tears over her dad, or us?

Headlights coming from behind came closer and nearly blinded him in the rearview mirror for a moment, and after he shifted lanes to get out of the way, he pressed the cruise control button and leaned back into the seat with his hand extended to her. She took his hand in hers and held it loosely on the center console. He noticed she checked for texts on her phone and waited until she put the phone face down in her lap before continuing.

"There will be love. Love takes many forms. I love my mom, I love my family. I'm sure I'll love Priya." But his guts felt like they were being torn out of his belly having to talk to Jenny about this. Of course, learning to love a wife after a marriage was what he had been raised to expect. Now, he wanted to say he loved Jenny. But he just couldn't do it.

I can never say it. Ever.

She shook her head and caressed his cheek. "That's so sad, Roshan." She dropped her hand back onto her lap and stared back out the window at the stars, fidgeting with her phone nervously.

He knew sadness in his life; he worked with it though. Channeled it into schoolwork, good grades, and extracurriculars. Into building an academic resume to get him into the school of his family's choice. Into becoming what his mum wanted him to become. He was a doctor now. He would try become be a good one and smother voices from the past that sometimes still breathed in his ear. Sadness was for the weak. Feelings were made for burying.

But Jenny made him feel like he didn't have to pretend anymore. And he liked it. She was a spark in his life that finally gave him strength to breathe. Her distress and grief over her father's accident, her bewilderment over her mother's call, made her look small, fragile. Her tiny fingers shook holding the tissues at her eyes. It was all he could do not to grab her and hold her, to be her strength. The sight of her, even in pain like she was at the moment, made him want to breathe in her presence. She was there. She was honest. She was real.

And he wasn't sure how he could bring himself to not have that breath in his life.

It really was sad. But he was strong and would have to dig a hole deep enough for all of his feelings, the place where they belonged.

Chapter 8

Jenny

Her eyes burned as they opened to the burnished gray sunrise outside the car window. With one foot still in dream world, she lazily reconnected with her physical body. Her neck cried out in a cramp from its position on the headrest, but she made herself smooth back the disheveled hair that dropped around her cheeks. The slowing of the car's engine and the turning corners had wrestled her from her sleep and her heart began to beat fast.

"Hey," Roshan said.

"Hey. How long did I sleep?"

"About three hours. You're not much of a navigator."

She yawned and said, "Sorry. That's what maps are for."

She was upright now, watching familiar buildings around them and knew that they were close to the regional hospital. It was small, and still two hours away from her hometown, but it was the best people had down there in the middle-of-nothing-ville of her childhood.

"Turn at the next light." She wanted to tell him to turn the car around and take her home. The thought of being back in this town made her nauseous. She hadn't been back since beginning dental school.

Fifteen minutes later, Roshan pulled the car into a narrow spot next to a banged up pickup truck with a bed full of drywall and ladders under the low ceiling of the hospital parking deck. Jenny sat motionless and looked at him.

"This is it." She inhaled deeply and pulled her purse close to her chest, preparing to hoist herself out of the car. Her body felt like a rock with magma swirling around in her core.

"Yep." He covered her hand with his and intertwined his fingers with hers.

She wanted to recoil; the line had been drawn between them last night. A rational decision had been made between them, and she shouldn't let her messy life and the soft warmth of his hand cloud up her brain. But she allowed his fingers to grip her gently.

"So, the million dollar question right now, Jen, is do you want me to stay in the car? Or do you want me to go in with you?"

She looked long into his eyes and wanted him to be by her side. Instead, she said, "You can't come."

She slipped her fingers out of his and avoided looking at his face as she slid out the door. She closed it softly, leaving it just ajar, and the luxury car closed the door the rest of the way with a whoosh of air. She looked around her in the dark, spotted a glowing exit sign with a sign underneath it that directed her to the elevators, and made her way around the car toward it. Her feet were asleep, and with each step her blood pumped faster and faster until she nearly felt like she was going to reach the same target heart rate she sought on the treadmill.

As she approached the fluorescent glow of the elevator bank, she couldn't help but turn back and look at Roshan. Though she didn't have her glasses on, she was able to see his face through the tinted windows. There he sat, inside his new car that even gleamed in the oily, sooty air of the parking deck, watching her. She felt uncomfortable by how protected she felt by the hold of his stare, as she disappeared into the opened elevator.

Near the key pad inside, a small sign indicated the hospital lobby level with a star. The double doors slid closed, cutting her off from Roshan and swallowing her into a different dimension. She felt like Dorothy being taken into a new world, only the world she was leaving was Technicolor, and the one she would land in was merely black and white. She already wore the ruby slippers, and she knew she would have to protect herself from those who would want to rip them out from underneath her.

Once on the intensive care floor, sickly silence stifled her breathing, and she felt as if she would die to just from taking in the air. A black woman wearing scrubs passed closely in front of her, directing an orderly coming around the corner pushing a bed on wheels toward a set of gray double doors marked "staff only." She pushed the large circular button on the wall, and the doors swung open, swallowing the nurse, the orderly and the tiny old woman nestled inside white sheets and faded blankets on the bed. Jenny faced the ward's reception desk, alone and nauseous.

"May I help you?" the fat woman behind the desk asked her.

"Um, hello. Yes, I am here to visit Bill Jenkins."

The woman moved her chubby fingers deftly across the keyboard in front of her, eyes on the computer monitor the whole time and asked, "Are you family?"

"I'm his daughter."

"Have a seat, and I will let a nurse know you are here."

She sat in one of the dirty mauve and green upholstered chairs that lined the walls of the small waiting room and looked around at the other occupants. In one corner of the room was a Hispanic family gathered together in conversation. A middle-aged woman with short black hair spoke softly in the ear of a younger woman, whose eyes swelled and looked on the verge of overflowing. Directly across from her sat a man in a white short-sleeved collared shirt and dark green slacks pulled up past his waist. The age spots on his face were an array of shapes that looked as if they could be fitted together like a puzzle, given a few more years of skin sagging and meeting together in papery folds. His head, covered in slack, gray hair with a dull orange tinge, drooped down nearly to his chest, and his large jointed hands rested on his thighs. Jenny watched him for what seemed like several minutes, imagining that he was here for a sick wife, worrying about her death, wondering when his would come.

He raised his head suddenly and smiled in her direction. Circles surrounded his eyes, but their blue sparkled displayed the fire still lit inside him.

She nodded politely and looked away, embarrassed at being caught staring.

The man stood up and straightened his back, turning toward the window behind him and breathed in the filtered light that shown onto his face. He then shuffled over to a water cooler in the corner near Jenny's seat and poured himself a Dixie cup of water. He looked over at her and told her, "You sure are a pretty thang. You remind me of my granddaughter."

"Thank you," she responded a little self-consciously.

He continued as he shuffled back to his chair, "Yep. She's a beauty. Looks just like my wife did at her age." The man gently lowered himself to the chair and let out a breath. "Whew," he said shakily as a slosh of cold water spilled out of the paper cup and onto his pants leg. He sat there for several moments with his hands up, the cup slightly tilted and looked at the dark splotch on his thigh, his reflexes too aged and joints too locked to allow him to jump up.

Jenny scanned the room for anything absorbent to soak up the water for him and found a box of tissues. She stepped up, grabbed a wad of them, and handed them to the man. "Here, Sir. Maybe these will help some."

He extended one hand to clutch the wad, and the tremor of his hand nearly prevented him from grasping. He was able to finally clutch his crooked fingers around half of the wad, letting several others flutter to the blue carpet, resting between the toe of his brown loafer and the tip of Jenny's Nike.

"Thank you, young lady." He said shakily as he blotted at the cold splotch on his thigh.

"You're welcome," she said, walking backward to her seat.

"My wife will be so tickled at me," he snickered. "She always gets so tickled when I'm clumsy. Says I ain't changed a bit since we met up in high school. She always laughs that her daddy told her not to marry me because I'm so darn clumsy. He said, what kinda mechanic is this boy gonna be when he cain't hold nothing in his hands? He said I'd be dropping wrenches on my feet and breaking toes all day long." Squeezing the ball of damp tissues in his fist, he looked up at the door to the intensive care unit and paused. "I guess nothin's changed."

"Are you here visiting your wife?" Jenny asked, tilting her head in the direction of the door.

"Nah. She's in a nursing home. I get to see her about once a week, when my granddaughter drives me. No. I'm here waitin' to see my son. My granddaughter's daddy. Heart attack."

"I'm so sorry. How old is he?"

"Sixty three. Smoker. He's a police officer."

"I'm sorry." She said again. She thought of her daddy in the bed, maybe next to the room of this police officer. Sixty-three is too young to be in here, but her daddy was only forty-three. He was 18 when he and Wanda had her. He was way too young to be in here.

"My daddy is here. He was in a car accident."

"Drunk driver hit 'em? We got a big problem here these days with drunk drivers. My son," his eyes looked in the distance and he cleared his throat, "he talks about it all the time how many drunks he arrests coming from those bars downtown."

She shifted her feet and glanced back at the desk.

"Ain't enough people with Jesus in their lives these days. Used to be when I was young, ever'body went to church, and drinking, well, we only snuck beer once in a while when we was out in the field."

"Yeah, it was a drunk driver," was all she could say.

"Do you live around here?" He asked.

"No sir. I live in Atlanta." It may not be true yet, but it felt good knowing it would be in a week.

"Oh, Atlanta! Ooh, I been up to the Atlanta Motor Speedway with my son a few times! That place is somethin' else. Love the races, though." He tapped his cheek and added, "You know, there's some good churches there too. You belong to one?"

Beginning to get a little impatient, she glance at the desk and said, "No, sir. No I don't." She pictured Wanda the last time she saw her with her big wooden cross around her neck and brand new bible in her hand when she stood outside of her rusted Datsun. She literally thumped the cover as she lectured Jenny about finding Jesus before she went off to college and got caught up in drugs and alcohol and the gay lifestyle of "that friend Bryan of yours."

"No, sir, I don't belong to a church."

Hell, no. Not with people like Wanda there.

"Excuse me for a second," she said to the old man. Her legs were getting antsy, and she looked toward the reception desk for the fat woman. She had left her post, so Jenny stood up and walked over to the counter and waited for her. After several minutes, the woman came and slid in behind her desk, cackling at a joke as the voice of her coworker trailed behind the door.

"May I help you?" she asked as if she had never seen Jenny before.

"Yes. I've been sitting here for quite a while, and no one has come to get me to see Mr. Jenkins. Would you please let them know again that I am here?"

"They know you are here," she said flatly and examined something caught under her curly, index finger nail. "Only one visitor at a time is allowed. Fifteen minutes at a time. There is someone with him now. When they are done, the nurse will come get you." Digging the royal blue tip of her thumbnail under the index fingernail, she clicked the two together and a speck flew across the desk, landing near her coffee cup. The woman said through pursed lips and looked at Jenny, "Have a seat," then blew the debris off into the air, and turned back to her keyboard.

As she passed by the old man's seat toward her own, she wondered who was back there already with her father. Probably Tammy. Of course. For the first time since tenth grade, Jenny actually wanted to talk to her, to find out more details about her dad's situation. All she knew was the information Wanda had given her, and she's unreliable with everything. She tapped her fingers on her knees as she sat in the chair.

"You'll be here a while," said the old man.

Jenny looked at him and rolled her eyes in the direction of the desk.

He snickered. "I've been here off and on for three days, and I've only gotten to see my son maybe twice a day. They're strict about their visitor policy. When there ain't no other visitors, they's always this test or that test they's doing, and you cain't go back."

"I suppose you and your granddaughter have to split up your time with him, huh?" she asked, watching the door.

"Nah, it's just me. She picks me up and drops me off. But she don't come up."

Curious, but afraid to get too personal, Jenny didn't ask why.

He offered, "Her daddy don't want her."

"That's terrible. Do they not have a good relationship?"

"They did." He paused and looked sadly toward the window. "She loves her daddy. But she don't live a Christian lifestyle. She got caught up with a girl. Her daddy said 'get out.'"

Jenny immediately thought of Bryan and the night his father found out through his brother that Bryan had been messing around with a boy that had been visiting a family in the neighborhood over the summer. She had been asleep when a stick hit her window, their childhood signal to meet him at the park. She walked right out the front door, her father snoring on the couch with the TV on, and ran to the park in her night shirt and a pair of shorts underneath. When she found Bryan, he was perched inside the enclosure at the top of the metal slide with a cigarette between split lips, wiping his swollen, red eyes with the sleeve of his shirt. Without speaking, they got up and walked out of the neighborhood down dark roads that whole night, planning their escape. By morning, reality had set in, and they had to go back home and get ready for school. They both knew that school bus, taking them to where they could learn enough to go to college, was their only real ticket out. She wondered what it was like for the police officer's daughter to not be able to go home.

The clock was still ticking, and still no one had emerged from the back to get her. "It sounds like you are okay with her?"

"Well, I don't like it. No, I don't. But, I don't care what nobody else thinks either. And that's my son's problem. He worries about that. Me, nah. Everybody I worried about is dead or a vegetable now, so don't matter to me. She's still the little girl I plopped on my lap when she was little. And Jesus knows that."

Her eyes started to burn when she heard that, and she picked up a gossip magazine to take her mind off of his words. She smiled benignly and focused her attention on a spread about celebrities without makeup caught buying milk. As she was regulating her thoughts and trying to tell the difference between the big-breasted blond celebrity that was divorcing her husband and the one is featured in the photo spread with her new twins that were delivered by a surrogate, a familiar voice at the open door to the ICU near the reception desk made her look up.

"Jenny?"

Standing at the propped open door was a petite woman with bags under heavily-lined eyes smiling wanly. She pushed frizzy hair behind her ear, revealing tattoos of words behind her ear and a blue and pink flower that disappeared into the neck of her blouse.

"Tammy," Jenny called out in breathy words, waving her hand in the air from her chair in the waiting room as if the woman wouldn't see her or know who she was. She wondered if the bags under Tammy's eyes were from being married to her drunk and crazy father with three kids, or if it was just from worry right now about her dad. She was much thinner than Jenny had remembered, though, and even looking disheveled, she had new strength in her posture.

Tammy kept the door to the ICU ward open with an elbow and a warning signal beeped loudly, but the receptionist was too focused on correcting typos caused by her curly nails to look up.

"Jenny, you're here." She stared in amazement as Jenny stood up from her chair and came to the door.

"Yeah. I'm here. Didn't expect to see me?"

The elderly man nearby rasped softly at them, roused from his nap. "Ladies, would you mind going in and shutting the door? That darned noise is going to disturb patients, and you know they need rest."

Jenny nodded and smiled at the man and walked to the door.

"Come on back. Let's go talk in the room. Quick," she whispered, glaring at the receptionist. "They ain't as strict as they say."

When they got to her dad's curtained off room, they stopped and stood silently. Beeps and the sound of oxygen flowing all around them was all she could hear.

"Actually I didn't think you'd come," Tammy said quietly.

"Why didn't you call me? Why'd you have Wanda call me?"

"I didn't think you'd come."

"And Wanda being the one to call me was supposed to make me want to? He's my daddy. Of course I'd come."

"Well, you didn't call us when Jaden was born, so I didn't..." Jaden, the youngest of her three half-siblings was born the previous summer. Jenny had not even known that Tammy was pregnant again until her father called her to ask for money when Tammy was in the hospital with the baby. She didn't have any to give him at the time, and he ended their phone conversation abruptly, without any more details about the baby.

"You thought I didn't care."

"Yeah. I thought you didn't want no part of us no more."

You're right. But I'm not that cold.

She really didn't ever want to see her dad with his creepily-young wife and kids. It made her skin crawl to think about how they lived, paycheck to paycheck, her dad drinking their grocery money away. She visited once when their oldest was three, and he ran around the house only in a dirty diaper. When she asked Tammy why she didn't change him, Tammy had looked directly at her dad and said, "'Cause we have no money right now to buy diapers."

It was true; they didn't fit in with the picture of her new world. She didn't want to come visit the new baby for fear of dragging a piece of that life, the old rejections, back with her like lint on her clothes. She thought about Roshan in the parking garage and was glad he wouldn't come in to this dusty, dirty past of hers. But now she just kept her mouth closed with Tammy.

Tears spilled out of the corners of her eyes.

"Hey, don't worry about it." Tammy leaned in, squeezed her in a hug, and held her for a few moments.

"You look good, by the way," Jenny commented, wiping her eyes on her sleeve. "Your hair. It's cute short."

Tammy's brown hair was cut in a chin-length bob, a far cry from the eggplant colored straight style she had sported last time they met, and on her nose was a tiny little patch covering the hole where her nose ring used to be.

"Thanks. I'm going to nursing assistant school now."

"Good for you." Jenny raised her voice too much in her surprise and she instinctively pulled the room curtain closed tighter. Her daddy was in there, probably a pulp, and she wasn't ready to go in. She motioned for them to move away toward the bathroom.

"Thanks. I know it ain't nothing compared to dental school. But it's something."

"What does Daddy think of this? He didn't say anything about it when I talked to him yesterday." Jenny could hear the old South Georgia drawl creep back into her voice, pronouncing Daddy as "Diddy" and cringed inside herself.

You can take the girl out of the trailer park...

Tammy grabbed her hand softly as if they were the closest of friends and gave her a maternal look. "Jenny, your dad and me are splittin' up. I'm movin' on."

Surprisingly saddened by memories of her childhood, Jenny knew it was his drinking and his laziness. "Daddy doesn't mean any harm, Tammy. He really loves you and the kids. He just doesn't know better."

"He's a drunk." Tammy stated as if the words had never been spoken by anyone before. "I gotta move on."

A nurse brushed by them and bumped Jenny's arm with her clipboard. The nurse looked as haggard as Tammy, and Jenny was glad she had decided against medicine in favor of dentistry. You couldn't beat the hours.

Tammy started to cry. Jenny pulled her into the bathroom door and handed her a wad of toilet tissue from a stall.

"We had a fight about him drinkin' away the money that was for the kids' clothes he was gonna give me. I called him names. He called me names. He left for Johnny's Bar where he always goes to hang out with his scummy buddies. The cops called me at one in the morning to tell me he wrapped his truck around a tree off route 41."

Suddenly, Jenny looked in the mirror at herself with Tammy, and the absurdity of the picture overwhelmed her as guilt pulled her under water. But the guilt was not from not spending time with her family or not helping her dad more somehow, but from remorse at her lack of empathy for any of them. What kind of person was she?

I'm the kind who survives, that's what kind.

"The receptionist told me someone is with him right now. Has anyone else been here to visit him yet?" Jenny asked.

"Yep. Matter of fact, your mom went in as soon as I came out here."

"Wanda? You're joking."

"I was leaving yesterday right after they brought him in, and she came into the waiting room. She didn't say nothing to me. Just sat there. I knew who she was, and I ain't afraid of her or nothing. She looked better than pictures I seen of her. Her hair's all fixed and everything. Her eyes looked, you know, clear. So, I says to her, 'Bill's hurt real bad.' And she says to me, 'I know.' And I wanted to ask her how she knew he was here, but I didn't. So, I say to her, 'You wanna go back there?'"

Tammy now sighed and stood straight, wiping her nose with shredded tissue, finally over her crying jag. A toilet flushed inside bathroom stall, and the door handle jiggled.

"She says yeah, and I says okay. Because, you know, she was married to him. It ain't right that I say no. It's not like she ever bothered me or nothing like that."

They watched a woman, smelling of a burnt wood, come out and walk toward another ICU room. Her skin was smeared with black, and she held her red and blistered arm close to her, as she disappeared into the room.

"So, I ask for a nurse and tell her to let your mom back there. I say she's his sister so they'd let her go. I guess it's all right. I'm not gonna be with him no more, so she don't threaten me."

Jenny just stood there watching Tammy, hearing her words, but the words sounded like they were coming from the end of a long hallway, echoing through her brain over and over again. What the hell? She hadn't heard her mother's voice in five years before last night, hadn't seen her face in years, and all of a sudden she is around and concerned about everyone?

"Maybe she's cleaned up again. Aren't we lucky?" Jenny said dryly. But what could be her motive? Does she feel like trying to save her heathen cast off? As angry as she was, a tiny piece of her was still eager to see Wanda. Does she have gray hair or wrinkles? Does her blonde hair still fly away with static in the winter?

Exhaustion like she felt now always brought Wanda back to her mind when her defenses were lowest. During dental school, Jenny would often lay in bed at night worn out after long days of classes and patients and studying, in the space between awake and asleep, between her adult self and the scared child-self inside her and open the door to the room where she kept her Mommy. She would picture her mommy's face when she once wiped chocolate off of her mouth. Her green eyes were so pretty, and she smiled so softly when she took the wooden Fudgsicle stick out of Jenny's hand to toss it in the trash can. She didn't yell at her then about making messes. Her hands were so big compared to Jenny's chubby fist, and this made her feel so cozy when they held her. But, during those nights in bed when the image of the tender mommy morphed into the glassy, bloodshot mommy that came soon afterward, she'd shut the mental door and turn on her iPod to lull herself to sleep.

"I need to go in there now, Tammy."

"Good luck."

Jenny sucked in as much air as her lungs could hold and ducked in the curtain. What she wouldn't give to have Roshan hold her hand right now.

Leaning against the bedrail gently, she looked down at her father's face. His eyes were closed and he was breathing softly as though he were peacefully asleep in his own bed at home. An oxygen mask covered his nose, but the bloated, purple swelling on his left cheek and eye were obvious. From the looks of it, his zygomatic arch, his cheekbone, and his mandible were fractured. She had seen injuries like this in her clinical rotations in school and knew his teeth may be shattered as well.

He was prone on his back and one arm bent across his abdomen, taped up with a bulky plastic IV that connected to a bag full of saline hanging from the curly bar on a stand beside him. His other hand lay straight by his side, and Jenny lay her hand on top of it.

"He's in a bad way, Jenny."

The voice scratched from the corner of the room of the room hidden by the door, and Jenny's heart jumped. She glanced up and saw Wanda's silhouette coming toward her, taking firmer form as she entered more light. She was a tall woman, like Jenny, and her arms swayed as she sauntered closer.

Glancing up at her mother, fury flushed Jenny's head, feeling as if a stranger were seeing her naked. She had known Wanda was in there, but she still felt violated by her presence during this moment. Her father's hand twitched at her touch, and his eyes opened slightly. He turned his head toward her and within a few moments, he focused on her face enough to speak.

"Jenny. Hey." His voice was wispy, and he licked his lips.

"Daddy. Hey." She held his hand tighter and waited to see if he continued.

"I...am a little messed up." He turned his lips up in a sluggish smile and grimaced.

"Yeah, Daddy. I know." She didn't want to encourage him to talk too much so she patted his hand and said, "You rest now." Her words were not necessary because his eyes closed before she finished her short sentence.

"He's been in and out since I've been here." Her mother's gravelly voice invaded the quiet softly from her spot across the room. She sounds like a man, Jenny thought. Probably three packs a day these days.

"Why are you here?" Jenny asked without emotion.

Evading Jenny's glare, she replied, "I guess I just needed to see him. I don't really know why."

"It's been years. Now you come see him?" Her voice went up in volume slightly, and she had to take a deep breath to silence herself. "And you came to see me?"

Wanda's lipstick, obviously hastily applied, feathered into a million tiny wrinkles around her mouth, and her hair hung in crunchy wet-look curls down past her shoulders. At forty five, Wanda wore her lifestyle like battle scars on her skin. She could be eighty years old, but for once, her eyes were clear just like Tammy had said.

"I guess I feel bad."

"Bad about what? Do you feel bad about putting shit in your veins when you should have been putting food on the table for me? Do you feel bad about leaving us that way?" Her hands gripped the bedrail and shook so much she feared they would shake right off of her arms. Her father began to rouse again but did not open his eyes. She shakily put her hand back on his, and he squeezed.

"Yeah. I guess." Wanda reached out her hand toward his arm. "You wouldn't understand. I've been through rough times. I ain't been real good to the people around me, but it was the drugs made me sick. My soul was sick."

Jenny snickered and looked around the room, vibrating her leg impatiently, waiting for her to be done speaking.

"But, I walk with Jesus now."

"Yeah. You've told me before. Good for you. I sure wish Jesus had been around for me when I was a kid. I'm glad you found him. Again." Her voice was thick and bitter with sarcasm, and she was torn between telling Wanda to leave and wanting to keep her there to bleed her anger out on her. "Where was Jesus for Daddy when you left us? And how about me? Where was Jesus when I had to eat left over fries from wadded up McDonald's bags in the garbage because you were half dead on the couch?" She realized she wouldn't be able to stop herself and, after patting her father's wrapped up leg, pointed outside the room for Wanda to join her there. Once outside, she continued down the hall and, summoning all of her courage, shot her arm out in the direction of the waiting room, an order for Wanda to follow.

The Hispanic family was still in their group, chatting in Spanish with each other and the mother of the teenager looked up briefly at her. The old man was sitting in his chair next to a young woman with a tattoo on her neck and hair pulled back in a ponytail. Tammy was reading a *People* magazine and texting at the same time, and the receptionist was hard at work again excavating under her nails. Both looked up at Wanda and Jenny in surprise and watched unabashedly. Without regard what dirty laundry the strangers would hear, she began.

"Does your Jesus forgive you for treating your child like she wasn't wanted?"

The receptionist stopped typing, and the room fell silent. Even the baby stopped cooing.

"You weren't wanted. I was fourteen when I got knocked up with you. How could I want that?"

The woman's words speared her through the chest. She had always known it was true, though. Jenny looked at her elderly acquaintance with his arm wrapped around his granddaughter and the Hispanic mom patting her baby on the back softly, and she felt cheated more than ever in her life.

"Then why did you come to Memphis? Why were you at the graduation?"

"Like I said. Jesus wanted me to. I got to make amends." She leaned toward Jenny and lifted her hand as if she might touch Jenny but pulled it back. "I guess I am proud that the daughter I made could do so much. I just wanted to see it for myself." She paused and looked at the reception desk, eyes unfocused. "I must not be all bad after all, if I could give birth to you."

Jenny rolled her eyes and spewed, "Don't you dare be proud of me, Wanda. Oh, you are the reason I made myself what I am. But it's because I am going to be as different from the sorry sack of nothing that you always were to me. But, if I were you, I wouldn't be proud of that."

The old man and his granddaughter looked up at them uncomfortably. The old man squeezed her tight and turned his eyes to watch the TV mounted on the wall.

Jenny waved apologetically in the direction of the spectators and walked out of the room to the exit stairs, letting the door slam behind her. Bounding down the steps two at a time, wanting to get as far away as quickly as possible, she descended the five floors to the lobby level without noticing she was getting out of breath. Once out in the lobby, she look around her, not sure of where to go, of what to think. She contemplated sprinting out the double sliding door and down the street to nowhere when she spotted Roshan seated on a sofa near the door. He was sipping coffee and on the phone when he looked up and smiled at the sight of her. Suddenly a calm began to wash over her, and she walked over to him and sat down. He was speaking in Gujarati, probably with his mother, and she understood nothing but the tone of the conversation. And she was glad. All she wanted was to get as far away from herself and this world she was in right now, and the mystery of his words comforted her.

She slid onto the seat next to him and instinctively sank into him as his arm wrapped her close. In mid-sentence, he leaned over and kissed her forehead, and for the moment, she forgot they were just friends. His voice vibrated her head as he talked, and her eyes closed until she heard him say, "Okay, uncle. *Ov ja*, goodbye."

He breathed heavily and cupped her cheek. "That was my uncle. My mom is not doing so well right now. He said she hasn't gotten out of bed since I left." He straightened up and pulled back from Jenny to look at her. "But the important thing now is how did it go? You okay?"

From the opening sliding doors, a gust of wind hit them as someone exited into the piercing morning sun.

"It was fine." She said no more. There was no way she would sully him with this garbage. Her garbage.

"Don't want to talk about it yet, I take it?"

She shook her head and dropped it to his shoulder, absently glancing at a figure moving toward the sliding door as it opened. The woman paused, did a double take, and stopped facing Jenny and Roshan. It was Tammy.

Tammy looked from Jenny to Roshan, and then back at Jenny quizzically.

Jenny lifted her head and smiled and nearly stood up to introduce the two, after all, if any of them down here would understand, it would be Tammy, who was making her own way in the world now. But, as Jenny leaned forward to rise, Tammy shook her head, and said "shit" under her breath and turned to walk out the doors.

"Someone you know?" Roshan laughed it off.

"No. Not really. Just someone I talked to a little upstairs."

Over the next two days, Jenny came to the hospital for short visits. She and Roshan stayed at a motel near the hospital owned by some friends of friends of his family. She was happy to slide past the peering owners' eyes in the motel office straight to her room, and have dinners with Roshan, then retreat back to her room, alone, to mull over her life. Each morning she stood vigil for an hour over her dad until Tammy would arrive, colder to her now, and then Jenny would go meet Roshan in the coffee shop downstairs. Tammy never said a word about Roshan.

"Aren't you sick of being here with me yet?" Jenny pulled back the foil top on a creamer cup, splattering her hand with cold white droplets. The hot shower this morning woke her up, but she was bone tired. A nurse carrying a coffee with no lid bumped past Jenny's chair on the way to the creamer station, and she couldn't even jump at the thought that hot coffee might spill on her back.

"Honestly, no. I'm glad for the down time before I move back to Atlanta, and I'm actually enjoying people watching. I've never been in a town like this before." With a wink, he opened a magazine he'd been carrying and revealed a sheet of paper spread thickly with a scattering of the charcoal gray lines of faces, some of whom she recognized from the room.

She shook her head. "You're so weird."

An elderly man in a white coat sat in the table next to them reading the paper and shot a look at Roshan over his reading glasses before shaking a page out to straighten it and going back to his own business.

Roshan's hair was still wet and neatly styled, and he smelled of cologne. Jenny wearily wondered which part of the color spectrum of bottles on his dresser it was from.

She watched Roshan sip his coffee and glanced around the room at the clean-cut, white, doctors, both black and white nurses and visitors, all in various states of exhaustion around them.

"Plus, I'm getting to spend some time with my Uncle Pete's friends at their motel."

"You have an Uncle Pete?" Jenny mused.

"Yes, Pete. It's easier than Prakhar for people to remember. Anyway, my Uncle Pete is Jay's dad, my mom's big brother. He and this guy know each other from school in India, and I'm hearing some good stories about them as teenagers. I always knew my uncle was wild, but wow. He was crazy in the seventies."

"Crazy how?" She was beginning to like hearing about his family. They seemed like nice people, and his stories were a great way to avoid spilling her own. "Like, he was a partier?"

Roshan shook his head, "Oh, no way. He's too religious for that. No, he was fearless. He traveled a lot before college and climbed Mount Everest, hang glided, got a black belt. He never listened to anybody telling him what to do, and when he fell in love with my Monisha Auntie, which was bad because they had really strict arranged marriages in that day, he convinced her to run away with him, and they moved to the U.S. He's so awesome. He's not only a doctor, but for a long time ran a self-defense gym and could kick the asses of American guys twice his size.

"That's pretty cool. But how did he stay in the good graces of your straight-laced family?"

Roshan squinted in thought. "He was kind of a maverick, but people love him. He'd give anyone the shirt off his back. And he visited us in India when I was a kid. My mom needed help." His eyes got distant and he sniffed, cutting himself short. "So, he came and got me and my mom, and he kind of raised me, because my dad, um, didn't come with us."

Jenny knew his dad was dead but never asked details. That must be when it happened. "Is that when your dad passed away?"

Roshan's face scrunched up, and he looked at his watch. "Yeah. Yeah, it was. But, enough about me. How is your dad doing?" He picked up a sticky coffee stirrer with a napkin and tossed it toward the trashcan, but it fell a foot away from the target. "Oh, no points."

Jenny had never pushed him before, but she knew the veneer of nonchalance on his face covered pain, and she wanted to be there. "Roshan," she grabbed his hand and scooted closer to him. "How did your dad die?"

He gulped and looked at the speckled tile floor and squeezed her hand. "We don't talk about it."

"It looks like you might need to talk about it."

"No. I've gotten this far without doing it. Just like you. Some things don't need to get out."

"Roshan, come on."

He looked square at her. "I'll spill if you spill. It goes both ways."

A young man with a baseball cap leading his wife and two kids pushed past Roshan's chair on the way to order, bumping it as Roshan was sipping his coffee. "Sorry, man," the guy said sloppily, his bottom lip bulging. He slurped to keep the dip packet tucked in below his teeth and tipped his hat. Roshan nodded and went back to his coffee as the family walked behind him, and Jenny hoped he wouldn't see the man nod over in their direction and mouth to his wife, "A-rab."

She felt like a cornered animal and fought the instinct to flee but forced herself to agree. "You go first." They would probably never see each other again after they got to Atlanta. It would be fine.

"Okay." He stood up and walked to the outside window facing a courtyard dotted with benches and patches of purple streaked pansies, blowing in the morning wind. "It's going to rain." She came up behind him and put her hand on his back.

"Yep."

"It rained a lot in India, I kind of remember. Typhoon season sucked. I had to stay inside all the time and listen to my dad yell at my mum. I was only four when we got out of there, but I remember crying under my covers at night when he came home." He placed his hands flat on the glass and leaned in. "But, I didn't cry when we left the house that last night."

"What happened?" she whispered into his back, touching her forehead to him.

"My dad was a drunk and hurt my mom sometimes. The last time was really bad, and she stayed in bed a lot after that, and that made my dad madder."

Jenny's stomach clenched as she listened. "And?"

"And my sister died because of him..."

Jenny bolted upright. "Oh—" She didn't know he ever had a sister.

"And Uncle Pete killed him."

He turned to face her; he looked like a different person.

"Mum had written him a letter, and he came to help us. So," he held up his hands and looked around and said, "Here I am now, I'm twenty seven with a southern accent in po-dunk Jaw-ja with you. Your turn."

The well-practiced smile on his face gave her goosebumps.

Jenny turned away and became overwhelmed by the image of a young Esha lying so bruised in her bed she couldn't get up, and then she flashed back to her own mother, lying half-alive in her own filth on the couch. But, the sister, a soul that had not existed to her before now and didn't exist to anyone anymore, didn't flesh out in her mind.

Jenny pursed her mouth together to keep from asking,

How did she die because of her own father?

She turned back to him, the pain passing between them, and she blurted, "You know obviously that my dad's a drunk. But he's a sweet drunk." Feeling braver than ever, she kept going, counting on her fingers. "One, my mom is a drug addict and left me to paw through food in garbage like a dog when I was little. Two, I lived in foster homes for a while. Three, my dad slept with my best girlfriend when we were fifteen and married her. That's who saw us the other night in the hospital lobby." She had never even spoken those words to anyone, not even Bryan, but he was a part of her history, and she never needed to. But, now it was out there, real, hard on her tongue. It felt good. "And I am…better…than that."

They locked eyes, letting the pain pull them together. Then slowly they both turned back to the glass and pressed their foreheads on the cold surface, leaving cloudy imprints blooming from the spots.

Roshan laughed. "So, a hamburger and a French fry walk into a bar. The bartender says, 'Sorry, we don't serve food here.'"

Jenny is boggled. "Huh? What does that have to do with this, Roshan?"

Is this crazy guy losing touch with reality?

"Absolutely nothing. I'm hungry." He pulled her hand and took his keys out his pocket. "Let's go get breakfast."

When they sat in the car, she couldn't take her eyes off of him as he put the car in gear and drove them to the restaurant. He never looked at her, but tapped his fingers on the steering wheel to the beat of the Rolling Stones.

Wow. Over just like that, and we are moving on.

At the sticky, greasy Biscuit Hut around the corner, she ate an entire stack of pancakes and a bowl of grits with extra butter, more than she had since arriving at the hospital. Roshan picked up the bacon off his plate, put it on hers, sopped up the grease on his plate with a napkin, and scooted over the over-done French toast to the middle. When she handed Roshan the sticky blue syrup bottle across the table, he softly said, "Thanks."

And she knew he wasn't talking about the syrup.

They asked no more questions of each other for the two days they were there. Not a word was spoken about their conversation again. Not a word was spoken about Tammy discovering Roshan. They talked about plans for their new practices in Atlanta, and he schooled her in the night-life and attractions of the city. Lost in the prospect of her new life, she would watch his mouth move when he told her about Virginia Highlands, Buckhead, Stone Mountain, and the vast expanse of the city. The way his face lit up when he talked about his home city made her heart wish she could be like him. To have a place to call his home with fond memories and family ties.

"You have no idea how lucky you are, Roshan." She said on more than one occasion during his stories. He would smirk and keep talking while blades of envy sliced her skin from the inside.

Atlanta would be the absolute perfect place for her to blend in, lose herself in work, and forge a new life. She didn't need anyone to make her happy. She had let herself believe that she and Roshan could have some-thing. She had mistakenly let herself feel for him, even though she really knew better. And maybe, deep down inside, she wanted him because she knew she couldn't have him. She told herself it just the sex talking So far in life, she had not just gotten by, but succeeded despite being alone, and she looked forward to more of the same. Jenny felt free to head back to Memphis to wrap up, get the hell out of Dodge, and become one with the world of Atlanta.

The last night of their stay in the city, her father had been moved to a room outside of the ICU, and Jenny said goodbye to him as he lay in his bed. She had no idea how long his recovery would be, but she had to get back and start her new job. He had V.A. benefits, though, and would get some assistance, and Tammy had agreed to stay with him for a while longer. Jenny tearfully promised her daddy with a kiss on the forehead that she would come back soon after she settled in, and even told herself she would bring his kids something when she came.

It was Wednesday morning, and Roshan met her outside of her room, holding his duffle bag. He was unshaven and had a rough sexiness about him that made Jenny long for him.

"You ready?" he asked as he tried to pull her bag from her shoulder to carry it.

"Let's go," Jenny said, keeping a hold of the strap on her shoulder and stepping past him.

He relented and followed her, touching his hand to her elbow.

"I've got it, Roshan. I'm a big girl." Her words came out harsher than she intended and she stopped and turned toward him for a moment. "I'm sorry. I didn't mean to be bitchy." She hugged him and kissed his cheek, and then walked toward the elevator. They spoke about the weather and predicted how long it would take them to get back to Memphis in the day time if they met rush hour on the way.

Once in the parking lot, Roshan pushed the button on his car key and the lights on the car blinked as the doors unlocked. He remotely opened the trunk, and they tossed their things inside. When the trunk was closed, Jenny grabbed the keys out of his hand.

"I'll drive."

Taken by surprise and thinking she was joking, Roshan pulled the keys back and laughed. "Oh, no, you don't. You get some rest, and I'll drive. It's been a long couple of days for you." He rounded the side of the car with her trailing him close behind.

"No, Roshan, I'm serious," she said, wrapping her hand around his hand that clutched the key. "I want to drive. I'm good now. I'm tougher than you think, you know. I can handle a lot." Smiling, she opened his fist and said, "Now give me those keys," as she pulled them through his fingers and slipped into the driver's seat before he could react.

She settled into the seat, adjusting the angle of the seat and the mirrors as she watched him walk in front of the car to get into the passenger seat. The look on his face made her laugh. He looked lost and slumped down ever so slightly.

"You're not used to this, are you…not being in charge?"

"Hmmpf."

"Well, buckle up and relax. I'm tired of being the passenger." She twisted her head and right arm around as she backed the car out of the parking space.

The ease of the gas pedal and the feel of her hand sliding across the leather steering wheel gave her chills.

When she glided the car north onto the interstate, her heart jumped at the open expanse of road ahead. She floored the gas, feeling like they were flying into the orange sunrise on the horizon.

"Ooh, this is so nice, Roshan. I'll have to buy one of these when I get to Atlanta. I don't want to give this up."

"Um, maybe you should slow down just a bit, my dear. There are state troopers everywhere."

She playfully patted his hand. "It's okay. I've got this under control now."

When the speed approached eighty-five miles per hour, she sighed, turned on the cruise control and leaned back into the soft black leather.

Roshan was staring at her with a smile. "You do have it under control now. Good for you." He turned on the CD player. "Want to hear some Lynyrd Skynyrd?"

"Sure. Perfect." She tapped her fingers on the wheel to *Free Bird* and let the flat fields outside blur by into the past.

Chapter 9

Roshan

The leaves on the trees outside of the great room picture window in his and his mum's new house wriggled limply in the light September wind. The lines of the leaves were crispy red and orange and yellow, and the sun shone through their branches. His hands were pressed against the pane, leaving a white glow on the shiny new glass, and he knew his mum would scold him like she did when he was a kid. His finger traced the outlines of the shapes on the glass as he gladly soaked in the warmth of the radiating sun. He missed the summer. He had spent it moving out of his apartment in Memphis and sliding awkwardly into an old dentist's practice where he was hired to work. The best part of his work days were neither the patients nor the new friendships with staff he won over quickly with a grin, but the feel of the humid Atlanta breeze on his face when he rolled down the windows of his car at six o'clock every evening, reminding him that he really was alive.

He had also spent the past summer months trying to forget Jenny, and after two months of no contact, here he was, in the eye of the prep tornado for his and Priya's wedding. He turned away from the imaginary still life he had drawn on the window, feeling chilled. In the dining room a couple of his mum's friends gossiped as they scraped scissors across ribbons to curl them around wedding gifts to Priya. There, bundles were opened on the table and saris folded neatly waiting to go into their wrapping. A set of chunky 22 karat gold jewelry sat open in its case on a cabinet, a traditional gift for the bride from her new in-laws. Not only had he finally spent $20,000 on her diamond ring, but his mum had picked out an outrageously expensive set of bangles, necklace and earrings for her. His mum and he had very little money before he finished dental school, and he panicked at the thought of his newly earned dollars flying out the window for this occasion.

Damn glad I didn't go to art school after all.

The women shuffled back to their work stations, cooking sweets and wrapping gift packages for the bride's family. In the kitchen, dishes clattered and ladies' voices chattered. He had been banned from the kitchen after his Mum had been forced to slap his hand out of the pan of sweets for the third time. He was tired of wandering through the kitchen full of wedding treats he could not touch and female conversation he cared not to hear.

He faced a carefully laid out wardrobe of wedding clothes for him on the old cream leather sofa upon which he and his buddies had parked on in front of the TV in their old house so many times in high school. It was out of place in the gargantuan room under the vaulted ceilings, its edges comfortably worn with memories of wrestling and fits of fists pounding over time. He could still hear himself and his buddies' crackling pubescent voices yelling "Goooooaaaaalllll!" with the announcers as his mum brought them bowls of popcorn to munch.

He wanted to sink into the cushions, but barely an inch of cushion was open under the expanse of *kurta* suits and jeweled *mojari* wedding shoes. Monisha Auntie, still on the phone, whisked over toward him and mouthed to the clothes, "Look, look." He loved his auntie and mustered a smile for her.

She rolled her eyes at Roshan and nearly yelled into the phone as she lifted the sleeve of a shimmering red *kurta* jacket toward him. "Well, tell the attending that she is my patient and he is not to order any other tests like that without consulting with me first." She flipped the phone shut and reached up to hug his neck.

She said in Gujarati, "*Bhai*, come, come. You must decide. The red one with shimmers to match Priya's sari or the cream colored one? Decide. Are you a trendy kind of guy or traditional?"

They looked at each other and burst into laughter.

He said, "If that's how I make the decision, then how about a *kurta* with Andy Garcia's face on it? That'll scream 'Roshan' for sure."

She slapped him on the back and, lifting up the red one to his shoulders, said, "Oh, *bhai*. You have a lot to learn. You're marrying into a straight-laced family. Keep that 'Roshan' under wraps at the ceremonies." She motioned for him to hold the long jacket up in front of him and stood back.

He felt like a child, but seeing her happy made him happy. He knew his mum would be in any moment put the pressure on, and damper the mood with the tragic aura she carried with her at all times.

The jacket was above knee length on him and made of an iridescent silk with hints of red, orange, and green, depending on the angle you looked at it. From the collar down the front buttons stretched an elaborate expanse of golden brocade that he assumed matched the one on Priya's wedding sari. After all, she and her parents had picked both out on their shopping trip to India. They had brought another one—choice number 2—a cream-colored, less flashy suit, but also with the swirling encrusted brocade along its edges. He supposed her parents brought it in case he was a more traditional dresser. That assumption made him chuckle.

A Bollywood DVD played on the TV, and he split his attention between the beautiful girls dancing in unison to snappy club beats with Hindi lyrics, his flip phone screen, and Auntie Monisha's Gujarati chatter.

"That one, Auntie." He pointed at the red one. "I might as well look the part if I'm doing this in the first place."

"Okay, good. That's a nice one." Monisha picked up the jacket and held it up to his shoulders again. "Come, Eshaben," she called into the kitchen, "Come, all of you ladies. Stop cooking for a second and come see!" A few moments later, his mum and two other aunties came into the room in a flurry of excitement, drying their hands.

"Ooh, nice, Roshan," cooed his Suriksha Auntie as she draped her towel over her shoulder.

His mum came from behind the women and beamed. "Good choice, Roshan," Esha said in a proud voice. "My son," she hugged and smiled at him, squeezing his cheeks for the group of ladies to see, "he has chosen the exact style that Priya wanted for him."

Of course I did Mum. Was it ever really a choice?

Esha reached up and patted him on his hair. "Good taste."

"Mummy, it's the one you've had hanging on my bedroom door for a month now." He looked at the women around them and laughed softly. "Every time I put it in my closet with the other one, it appears back on my door when I get home from work."

The group chuckled, and she bobbed her head slyly at them, winking. She took the jacket from Monisha and held it up for him to slip his arms into the sleeves and shrug it onto his shoulders. All the women in the room stood there, singing a chorus of oohs and aahs at him while his mum and Monisha Auntie playfully spun him around in a circle.

This was the first time he had worn Indian clothes since he was a teenager, having forgone such uncool fashion statements for three piece suits as he got older. The jacket was made out of heavy silk fabric and hung down to mid shin length. The inside seam of the sleeve itched his arm. So unlike the soft cotton of the scrubs he wore at work. The weight of the gold threaded embroidery at the neck, the sleeves, and the hem pulled down the garment into a perfectly straight smooth look. He could see his faint reflection in the window and didn't recognize himself.

"You look so handsome." Monisha Auntie admired him as she pulled him to a stop in his spin. He stood heads above each off the women, and he felt like a giant amidst a crowd of little people.

Thanks, Auntie" He hugged her and leaned over to hug his waiting Mum too. "Shoo, now everybody. Fashion show is over."

Roshan peeled the jacket off and lay it down back on the sofa. His mother picked it back up again and shook it gently to remove creases that threatened it. He smoothed his fingers through his hair to calm any unruly strands that might get away. He may have his father's face, but he certainly had his mum's thick hair. The women always commented jealously about her pretty curls, and right now, with it hanging loosely around her face, she looked happy. Somehow younger. He was glad.

"We need to get this pressed. Or maybe we should wait until we get to the hotel in Los Angeles?" Mum turned abruptly to Monisha Auntie and began debating the pros and cons of pressing all of the saris, Punjabis and other ceremonial clothing that their entire wedding party might need in L.A. That meant planning perfection for all of his cousin-sisters and cousin-brothers that would be flying in from all over the world, because eleven of them would be in different portions of the many pre-wedding ceremonies and the wedding itself. Unlike in western cultures, the *jaan*—groom's side—had the place of honor in a wedding. They were the ones receiving a new daughter and would be showered with gifts by her family. The *jaan* must look the part, of course, his mum kept saying.

She knows best about everything.

His mum was so happy to be receiving her new daughter. He was warming to the idea that his mum should be happy and finally have a family she could be proud of. The thought of Priya moving in with them after the honeymoon and seeing the two of them in the kitchen together cooking for him felt kind of nice. His mum would teach her family recipes, and they would surely get along well keeping the house together, as much as Priya could be there while working long hours at the hospital. And as long as Priya remembered it was his mum's house first, the two women would probably be fine. They could run the house and leave him alone.

His heart skipped a beat when Jenny's face flashed in his mind out of nowhere. He whispered to her inside his head, as he often did at night.

And that, my dear, is why we could never be together.

Roshan walked away from the decision makers. The wedding details held no interest for him. He would be there. That was all that mattered. Whatever he was told to wear, he would wear. Whichever elderly relatives' feet he was supposed to touch for a blessing, he would bend down and touch. He would lead Priya around the fire on the stage seven times with a smile on his face as he had been told to do. He stepped back over to the window again and watched a cardinal land on a branch. His phone vibrated in his pocket. Anxious to chat with anyone but the women here, he expectantly pulled it out.

Priya
Hi. I know we can't talk b4 ceremony.
I'm excited. C U in 2 days in LA!

He read the text and proceeded to flip it shut and slip it into his pocket. It was his new cellphone and lived up to its slim name fitting snugly in his jeans pocket, so he could keep it with him all the time. It was always in the back of his mind that Jenny might call. Then, rethinking his actions, he removed and opened it back up. He had to buck up and make this work.

Roshan
Me 2. Looking 4wrd 2 Cing U.

There, he thought. He was telling the truth. He was looking forward to seeing her. She had grown on him in the last couple of months. He was amazed at how a person can convince themselves to feel…love? Would he call it that? Maybe in a few years, but not now for certain.

I need to forget her so I can move on with my life. My wife.

He was definitely was looking forward to having all of this behind him, so his feelings could have a chance to grow into something. Anything.

Since getting back from Georgia with Jenny, wedding plans took off and life got crazy. Just last month, he half flown out to L.A. for Priya's 23rd birthday party. He and Jay had flown out on the same flight and stayed in a hotel despite Priya's family urging them to stay at one of her uncle's homes. It was a good thing that Priya's younger brother met them at the airport to take them to their hotel because he and Jay were three sheets to the wind by the time they landed, thanks to the little bottles of liquor available any time they rang for the flight attendants. Jay, steadier than Roshan, stumbled slightly into Roshan's shoulder as they walked through the crowd deplaning when Roshan's shoulder strap on his bag slipped down his shoulder, sending his duffel bag flying into the backside of a young woman beside him in the crowd. She looked around her, ready to growl at whoever it was that hit her, when she saw Roshan grinning apologetically at her as he stooped down to pick up his bag. He had noticed her short blonde hair in the seat ahead of him on the flight and was glad to get a chance to speak to her. When she turned around, he halfway hoped she would look like Jenny, but her round brown eyes and olive skin were a lovely surprise.

"Oh, sorry, miss. Please forgive me." He flashed his freshly whitened teeth at her. He knew the effect he usually had on women. Her face softened, and she nodded, "It's okay. Don't worry about it." As she turned back around in the direction of a middle-aged woman reaching out her arms to her, she glanced back at him with a smile. He reveled in the moment and stepped toward her on impulse, as if to get her number, when Jay grabbed him and turned him around to walk in the direction of the flow of traffic.

"Let this one go, buddy. We're here to see Priya...remember?"

He wouldn't have used the number anyway, he supposed. But he was still a single man and panicked at the thought of all of his freedoms being taken away in just a few weeks at the wedding. During weddings, the bride and groom are tied together at the wrist by a scarf uniting them for life, but he knew it would be a noose around his single life.

"Okay," Roshan relented and turned his head one more time in the girl's direction, only to find her walking away flanked by what looked like her parents and a teenage brother.

As the crowd thinned out, they spotted a spindly short Indian boy by the ticket counter, leaning against the corner of a wall, eyes on the round dial of his white iPod with earbuds in his ears. He was sliding his thumb around the dial looking for more music to blast into his eardrums when the two men got to him. They stealthily walked up behind him and Jay stood on one side of the boy's shoulder but tapped him on the other side. When the boy turned abruptly in the direction of the tap, Jay and Roshan grabbed him in mock attack on the other side. The boy jumped and pulled the earbuds out of his ears.

"Ha, ha. You guys got me." He shook his head and pushed Roshan's shoulder back, trying half-heartedly to knock him down.

"Hey, little Tushar," Roshan said in a brotherly way. "Was that any way to greet your future brother-in-law?"

The boy stood there in skinny black jeans and a black tee shirt, looking him up and down, and shaking his head after whiffing Roshan's vodka breath. "Alright. Whatever. Let's go."

"Now that's the attitude, Tushar!" Jay slapped his palm on the boy's back and lightly pushed him away from the wall, nudging him to start walking. Jay and Roshan knew exactly where baggage claim was located in LAX, having been to this airport, as well as many across the world, visiting family over his life in the US. Roshan and Jay shared two sets of cousins who lived less than a mile from Priya's family growing up, and they had stayed at their houses for weeks at a time over the summers in middle school and high school. It was at a pool party at a cousin's house before high school senior year that Roshan first met Priya.

The parents were all gone to a dinner function that bored the teens, and they had sneaked friends, both Indian and white alike, into the backyard pool with a few cases of beer. Tushar was in eighth grade at the time, and he was there with his sister Priya, who was 13 and in charge of her brother. Roshan was chugging a Budweiser and chatting up a cute girl with reddish spiral curled hair when Priya caught his eye from across the pool.

She was sitting on a chair with Tushar and glaring at Roshan more and more intensely with each drink from his bottle. She looked around at all of the teenagers in and on the edges of the pool, legs dangling in the water. He was doing the same. A couple of girls from their Indian circle were huddled together, looking like they were talking about the boys' antics. They sat on lounge chairs with their long pants rolled up to their calves, barefooted, exposing six inches of smooth brown skin. One girl wore a long-sleeved Indian top and looked uncomfortable. She stuck her finger under the edge of the itchy neckline and blew down inside it.

Some of the guys were in the water with swim trunks on, throwing a beach ball and body slamming each other under the water. Dressed in bikinis, a few fair-skinned and freckled female friends from school hovered on the steps, giggling and talking about the boys. But only he, Jay, and the redhead beside Roshan had beers in their hands. Alcohol, the ultimate forbidden fruit among most of their devoutly Hindu parents, was in his hand, and she watched him with disapproval, no doubt learned from her mother and her mother's friends, her grandmother, and her aunts.

He suddenly felt self-conscious about his bottle, as if his mum were watching, and put it down behind him on the marble pool deck.

"What's the matter?" the redhead asked.

"Nothing. I'm just done with my beer."

"Me too. Want to get another one for us?"

Roshan looked across at little Priya, who was looking like a mother ushering little Tushar into the house away from the rowdy sinful play.

The redhead looked hard at him, waiting for him to focus his attention on her again. She tilted her face toward his, and when Priya was safely inside the sliding glass doors, he brashly pulled her face to his and planted a kiss on her lips. She pulled back in surprise, touched her lips and smiled, leaning in to him again.

"Wait here. I'll get a couple of extra beers."

That day ended with the party dispersing just in enough time for the parents to get home and discover nothing more than a few cousins and friends swimming and drying off. The parents pretended not to notice the thick yeasty smell of beer on several of the boys' breath, and that the number of towels on the deck outnumbered the amount of kids actually at the pool. Priya never ratted them out, but she always gave him eat-shit looks whenever she saw him at weddings over the years.

Water and drinking always seemed to go hand in hand for him. Perhaps because water meant relaxation for him, and the best way to achieve that was through a good drink. He wondered if Priya would object to putting in a pool at the new house.

Once checked in to their hotel rooms, Roshan and Jay took Tushar down to the pool to get a drink.

"Why aren't you staying with us or at your uncle's house?" Tushar asked the older men. He was uncomfortably perched on the foot of a lounge chair, swirling a straw around inside his virgin daiquiri.

"Just wanted a little space. You know how stuffy these family things get."

"Yeah." Tushar admitted. "I know what you mean. I have to sleep with my little brother in his room while my mom's uncle and auntie were in town. They flew here from India last month for two weddings, one here in L.A. and one in San Diego, and it seems like they'll never leave." He took a swig of his drink and added, "I can't even bring friends over while they're here because they don't like loud noises, and all they do was sit in front of the TV watching old Hindi movies and interrogate me on what colleges I am applying to."

Jay stretched his arms above his head and tipped his glasses down as a full-figured young woman passed in front of them, her tattoo on her lower back exposed. Jay shook his head, grunted and added, "I know, Tushar. I get enough of the visitors at home too. My wife's parents are here all the time. So with my parents and her parents around, we get no privacy. With us tiptoeing around so much and Hema having to be in the kitchen all the time, it's a miracle we ever had enough privacy for her to pregnant."

"Because you're a real man, that's how." Roshan reached over and slapped him on the shoulder. "And you know you like it, having everybody around. Admit it. Never lifting a finger. Besides, your mom is cool. She doesn't care if you eat meat. Or drink. You're lucky that you can do what you want to do in your own home."

"Yeah. It'll be better when we move back to Atlanta after I'm done with oral surgery residency. Once Hema and I move in with my folks, her parents won't stay with us when they visit, and I'll be a able to relax a little. But I just have to get through the next couple of years."

Tushar leaned back on his chair and rested his hands on his lap, relaxed a bit.

Roshan added, "I wish your mom's coolness had rubbed off on my mom when they were kids. Once Priya and I get married and we are all settled into the house with Mom, I'm going to have to hide the liquor in a towel closet and have to sneak upstairs with my cokes to get a little splash. Priya is just like my mom—" He stopped himself short and looked at Tushar, embarrassed that he had said too much about his sister.

Tushar stared up at the sky and said, "Aw, she's okay, man. There's nothing wrong with being religious. My mom and dad don't eat meat or drink, and we turned out okay."

"Wouldn't hurt Roshan to stop it all, either." Jay mumbled from the corner of his mouth.

"Yeah, I know, Tushar." Roshan backtracked, glaring at Jay. "She's all good. She and my mom will get along great. And happy women make for a good home." Then he added, "But dude, sometimes it's hard. Sometimes a guy needs to do what he wants."

The sun's rays were burning Roshan's face, and he knew that even after an hour in the California sun, his face would be three shades darker than it was when they got off the plane. His buzz had worn off an hour ago, and he looked at the empty glass in his hand. He knew he had to be sober when they got to Priya's house, so he set the sweating rocks glass down on the tiled table next to his chair. He looked over at Jay, who was furiously tapping out texts on his flip phone with a smile on his face.

"Hema?"

"Yeah," he said as he pressed send and set the phone on his lap.

"Everything okay?"

"Yeah. She said the baby just kicked. First time."

"That's awesome." Roshan gave his foot a shove and teased, "You're gonna be a daddy. Another girl to wrap you around her finger."

"Well, if she's anything like her momma, I'm okay with that." Jay picked up his phone to check a new text from Hema. The look in his eyes became distant, and he disappeared from the conversation, lost in his electronic conversation with his wife.

Roshan felt a pang of envy. Looking at his watch, he sucked himself up and announced, "Boys. We need to get going. Duty calls."

That evening, Roshan found himself seated at a long dining table among Priya's male relatives and family friends. The dining room's vaulted ceiling and marble floors caused the clanging of the dishes coming from the kitchen, combined with the voices of eleven men discussing their business and education ventures, to echo so loudly that he had to concentrate on every word spoken to him. Especially when he was spoken to in Gujarati. He could understand perfectly, but he had made a decision in middle school that he would only speak English. So after years of disuse, his language skills had deteriorated to the point that he spoke in sentences that were 80 percent English, mixed with 20 percent Gujarati.

Dinner lasted for over an hour, with the women in and out of the kitchen, continually spooning more *daal*, more rice, more vegetables onto their plates, until each man leaned back in his chair patting his stomach. Roshan scarcely had time to speak to Priya except for a quick peck on the cheek and light hand squeeze, when she greeted him, Jay, and Tushar upon their arrival before she disappeared into the kitchen again. He thought it a little unfair that Priya was in the kitchen on her birthday, but judging from the chatter in there, she seemed happy with the ladies. As the men exited the dining room through the kitchen, he caught sight of her pulling new plates out of the cabinet. She came out of the kitchen with her mom and aunt, both of whom he liked. They both had razor sharp wits that kept him in stitches, and he wished they could have eaten together. But they were carrying the plates and fresh cutlery for themselves, ready to eat, now that the men were finished with their meal. His mum was back home finalizing plans for their trip back here to L.A. for the wedding and couldn't be here. She didn't have much of a sense of humor, so he was relieved.

From the time Roshan was a kid, he had always thought it was kind of unfair that he got to eat first before the girls, but being a hungry boy, he had never turned down a spot at the table. He wondered sometimes, though, how he would feel if his sister had lived and she had to look on from the kitchen while he got to gorge on whatever he wanted first. He was sure that his mum would have been that much of a stickler for tradition.

Priya wore a sequined but simple Punjabi, a long pajama-type dress with loose pants underneath. She looked up at him and smiled, and he noticed that the green outfit made her hazel eyes look greener than he remembered. Her hair was pulled up in a loose *chignon* and had new light brown highlights mixed in with her natural black color. Light brown wisps hung down over her gold hoop earrings and framed her face. She really looked beautiful.

After the women had eaten, it was birthday cake time. The entire crowd gathered in the cleaned up dining room around a huge white cake, and Priya stood in front of the cake being photographed as she blew out the candles. One by one, relatives and friends, beginning with her parents, fed her bites of cake as they got their picture taken. When Roshan's turn was up, he approached her, feeling surprisingly shy, and picked up the spoon. Aware of the eyes on him, he tried not to look her in the eye as he touched the frosting to her lips. It was a sensual act that he suddenly wished was private. When he was done, he stole a glance at her eyes, which were already looking around her, embarrassed. The crowd oohed, and one guy in the back whistled at them.

When the moment subsided and the crowd filtered away from the cake, he turned his back on Priya to walk away from the cake table. Her hand brushed slowly against his buttocks. Shocked, he turned his head back toward her, but she gently shoved his back and pushed him forward. "*Chaal*, let's go. You sit in the den. I'll bring you your cake." He grinned and let her push him a few steps more and then left the room.

Wow. She's not the little girl like I thought she was.

Their angry kisses in the car outside her auntie's house after his graduation had been in the dark, and his mind had not been on her. He had felt her to be only a child throwing a tantrum that night, not a woman. But, not anymore. He wanted to get her alone and finish what they had started in the front seat of his car.

Yes, things will be really good with us. As long as we don't talk to each other too much.

In his own living room now, looking out the window again, his heart ripped a bit when he thought of the finality of his marriage. He wanted someone he loved to talk to. He pulled up his saved text messages and searched for Jenny's name. The last text she had sent him, dated two months ago popped up.

Jenny
Thx so much 4 ur company at hospital.
Ur the best. Take care of urself.

He pulled up a grainy close-up pic of Jenny he had snapped one of their last study nights in school. She wore no makeup and had her glasses on. She was beautiful. He touched the tiny screen with a finger, then hit delete, and the picture was gone. He did the same with her number and went back into the kitchen with the ladies to forage for something spicy to bite into. He was starving.

The next few days passed in a blur. Wardrobes were decided and pressed, and then a plane ride, two days, and countless pre-wedding ceremonies later, Roshan stood in the center of a crowd of over eighty of his closest family, waiting for the drumming to begin. He wore a turban of red silk with a jewel and feather that matched his suit and Priya's sari. His slippers matched his clothing and curled up at the toes.

The women wore heavily decorated, brightly colored saris, and their heaviest twenty-two carat jewelry, and the men wore *kurtas*, less elaborate than his, but just as traditional. They were gathered in the lobby of a large hotel, with hotel guests on the sidelines, sitting on sofas and standing with cameras at the ready to capture the spectacular sight in front of them.

A large speaker began to play a Hindi song, and the drummer began his rhythm. Roshan, moved by the music, began to dance, not the way he did at clubs, but in the way he grew up dancing. Joyful, bouncing and spinning, feeling the spirit of the music. His family, the *jaan*, surrounded him, joined in the dancing, and they traveled as a group, slowly, smiling, toward the bride's party gathered outside the ballroom, waiting to accept his family and him. For thirty minutes they danced, one in their joy, one in their culture. Hotel guests marveled, called others over to watch, gathering on the sidelines of the parade.

When they finally arrived at the bridal party, they stopped with the music. His hands trembled from the attention and the austerity of the moment, and he tried to focus on some meaning. The huge crowd stood back and Priya's close family gathered around him with a priest, shutting out onlookers from their prayers. Her father ushered him up onto a small pedestal before which the priest lay of tray of items used in prayers: a small container of water, some raw cotton, and two small clay lamps tied together with decorative cotton. The priest made Sanskrit prayers as he took the raw cotton to Roshan's head down to his toes several times, like winding him up. When prayers were done, he stepped from the pedestal and crushed a clay lamp with his foot, signifying strength. The whole crowd applauded, and he swelled with joy, feeling strong about his decision and the new family wrapping around him.

After being escorted to the stage by Priya's large extended family, he removed his shoes before ascending. Immediately, as tradition had it, some of the Priya's small girl cousins snuck up and stole one of his shoes for ransom. The cat and mouse game would inevitably end with him paying dearly for his shoe back after the ceremony, but he was prepared with plenty of cash for the cute little thieves.

He seated himself in the gilded chair next to an empty one for the bride, and he was filled with the love from his family. Surrounding him were hundreds of people dressed like him, in the middle of a world of people wearing jeans and tee shirts who spoke the same language as him, and joyful in celebration with him.

By the time Priya's splendid procession deposited her by his side—with upswept hair decorated with flowers and gold, with armfuls of chunky gold bangles, with henna-decorated arms, hands and bare feet—he was one with the moment. He looked in her eyes, and though he did not know what lay ahead of them in their new life together, he felt he was home. At that moment, he was proud to be Indian and locked away his desires for something different, something his own. His here and now was with his family, and that was what he needed to remember always.

Off to the side of the stage sat the bride's parents and on the other side sat his mother and his father's brother, who took the place of his late father. Priya's mother tried to hide the tears rolling down her face, and her father sat up straight in his chair, his lips trembling. Esha wore a fixed smile on her face as she listened to the Brahmin priest begin his rituals and give directions to all involved, but Roshan noticed several times that she looked at him with the kind of sadness he had seen in her eyes when he was a child after bad nights with his father, or when he would happen upon her in his teenage years when she thought he was asleep, holding a bright yellow blanket as she tried to read a book or watch TV. He had thought she would be beaming ecstatically at this moment. Her eyes met his and she offered him a tiny smile, then looked off into the distance. He wondered what world she was traveling to, and why she wasn't here in this moment with him.

As he and Priya each walked around a fire many times, each time a vow for their commitment to each other, he tried to focus on watching Priya's feet, covered in elaborate henna designs, and not look at his mother. The ceremony went on for another hour, and Roshan immersed himself mind and body into the rituals of his ancestors as he joined this woman and her family for life.

This is the right thing, isn't it?

That evening he lay on his side in bed next to his wife in the honeymoon suite, caressing her body and kissing her neck. She lay against him, her head propped on her arm. The sensation of her erect nipples against his bare chest excited him. Her hair, so intricately upswept during the ceremony, now lay smooth and brushed out across the pillow and across her shoulder. He pulled the ends of her highlighted black hair up to his lips and brushed the tips of the hair across her shoulder. Her hair, thick and course, reminded him of his mother's when he was a child sitting on her lap, playing with her braid. He let Priya's hair flop gently to the bed behind her, unable to prevent himself from comparing it to Jenny's fine silk hair that he relished running his fingers through. In the dark, he caught himself pretending it was Jenny beside him but willed himself to stop.

Priya smelled of incense and hairspray, along with a familiar perfume that he couldn't put his finger on. Usually scents were loaded with memory for him, but this one he just couldn't pinpoint. He slipped his finger under the spaghetti strap on her teddy, breathed her in, her scent would exciting him. Her ran his hands up to the nape of her neck and pulled her to him, kissing her long and deep. Her hips responded with a thrust toward his, and her legs spread open, as she turned onto her back, pulling him on top of her.

Roshan rested his body weight on his elbows with eyes closed and thrust himself into her, losing himself in the sensations. Her fingers dug into the skin on his back, and she moaned louder and louder, but never seemed to reach a peak. He was fully focused on the end and did not open his eyes until he found his release, rolling off of her to lay beside her. He finally opened his eyes and saw she lay there with her hands clasped across her belly, staring up at the ceiling. She looked like a teenager, not a wife, and he recoiled inside.

"I'm sorry," he mumbled, awkwardly caressing her hands and covering her up with a sheet.

"It's okay. No really. It's fine."

"No, it's not. I guess we need to work on this, huh?" He stared in the dark up toward the ceiling.

"Yeah," she said, "This is the first time I've slept with someone I barely know."

Roshan was shocked. "Um, okay." He hadn't given any thought to her having a sex life before him.

She turned onto her side toward him and asked, "What? Did you think I've been waiting on you my whole life? I am human too."

"No, I never thought about it actually." Just like he had never thought of his mother having sex. The two women were in the same category as far as he was concerned.

"You had your Jenny. Yes, I know about her. I have my story too."

In shock, he lay next to her petite nude frame and tried to process the conversation, while the familiar scent filled his nose. Involuntarily, he nuzzled her neck, trying to place his finger on why the perfume excited him so much.

"You like my perfume?"

"Mmm, yes. I know it from somewhere…"

"Oh, well, your mum gave it to me." She paused and added, "she said she found a bottle of it under the seat of your car when you came home from a trip. She said you must've bought it for her, but she thought I'd like it more."

Jenny! Her cosmetic bag had spilled onto the floor on their trip home, and she had asked him if he ever found the bottle, but he never did.

"Um, yeah. I did buy that for her." He waited, lost in memory about the South Georgia trip and his last hours with Jenny.

"No, you didn't," Priya stated. "It's that Jenny's. The bottle was half empty. Jay told me about your last fling with her."

His throat closed with anger—at Jay, at his mother, at Priya. He had no privacy. His life was an open book for everyone to read. He couldn't even try to make a go at his wedding night without meddling. He couldn't swallow enough to speak and just wanted out of that room.

"I could tell how much you liked it. I can wear it from now on, if you'd like me to."

He was incensed. "What, and do you want me to wear your old boyfriend's boxers or something? Are you kidding me?"

Priya sat up, held the sheet in front of her bare breasts, and looked down at him laying there. "No. I'm not saying that. But, whatever it takes to make this work, okay? I'm not pining away for some lost love, but you are. I've seen that look in your eyes. But, we are a done deal. Okay? Both of our families are in this. Help me out here!"

He threw his legs out of the bed and stormed naked into the bathroom. Amidst his fury, he couldn't help but note to himself that just a few months ago, he had walked away bare-assed from Jenny lying in his bed. He shoved the heavy door shut and locked the doorknob. The marble vanity had a sparkled shine, and there was a Jacuzzi tub off to the side, sunken down into the floor. Two fluffy cotton robes hung on hooks on the wall with slippers set beneath them in the same fluffy cotton. His attaché case was perched on one side of the sink, and Priya's cosmetic bag lay open on the other side. He rummaged through her case, clanking and banging bottles together until he found what he was looking for at the bottom.

Like a claw a children's arcade game, his hand removed a glass bottle filled halfway with a golden pink liquid. The bottle, sculpted into the abstract shape of a woman's body, fit snugly in his hand as his fist closed around it. Before unlocking the door, he paused to hold the tip to his nose for just a moment. There she was before him...snorting when she laughed...blowing stray wisps of blonde from her eyes as she studied... whimpering in her sleep in the passenger seat next to him...writhing under his body, eyes locked on his...

He wrapped one of the robes around himself and unlocked the door. Blowing past Priya, who he saw by the glow of the bathroom light was in tears, he pulled the door open and left. A teenage boy, with a girl on his arm, were standing in front of a neighboring door, gazing into each other's eyes. Roshan whooshed past them, his fluffy robe flapping at his knees and barely covering the hair on his chest.

"Nice outfit, man." The boy laughed and pointed, showing his date.

Without looking back at them, Roshan tied the belt tighter around his waist, and padded down the hall barefooted. When he found the housekeeping door, he tried the knob and was rewarded with a large trash dumpster inside. He slammed the perfume bottle down into the dumpster and left it to sink into the refuse where it belonged.

Chapter 10

Jenny

"Good morning, Kimberly." Jenny waved her pinky finger over the coffee cup poised at her lips as she passed the Italian marble-topped front desk. With her other hand, she lugged a heavy laptop case while trying to balance a designer handbag on the same shoulder with an iPhone precariously clamped between her fingers.

"Hey, Doctor J," Kimberly said from behind the office front desk, rifling through patient forms to prepare for the day.

Jenny had ducked in through the private employee entrance around the corner from the waiting room. It was the entrance used by their celebrity clients, because it led from the private parking lot hidden on the side of the building by strategic landscaping. Realizing she had forgotten to lock her car, she teetered the coffee and handbag on top of the laptop case and fumbled with the key remote in her hand. Precariously extending the key toward the door, she pushed the little button several times until she heard the satisfying beep of her car horn. She wiped coffee dribbles from her wrist, clenched the keychain between her teeth, and plopped the load onto the the patient check out desk, sending the iPhone clunking to the carpet by Kimberly's chair. A tuft of hair fell out of the corner of her upswept hairdo, revealing a light sprinkle of gray at the roots, and she pinned it back with a grunt.

"Rough morning?" asked Kimberly, whose alabaster skin glowed fluorescent in the light of the computer monitor as she handed Jenny her phone.

"Yes!" Jenny growled at her hair as more and more escaped her grasp. "Traffic was horrific! I woke up late, had a million emails to answer, and dropped my phone by my feet in the car. And I still need to work on notes for my talk this afternoon. How much do we have on the books today?" She strained to lean over the counter at Kimberly's screen, but her junk was in the way.

"About twenty grand. It's your big implant case." Jenny's face lit up as Kimberly went on, leaning in to add in a hush, "We got the call from you-know-who's agent early this morning that she's ready for you to do her work. They're stopping shooting for a day so she can come in tomorrow, and she will only see you."

Jenny couldn't hide the smile that bloomed across her face. The actress was not only one of her favorite stars as a child, but she would no doubt prove to be another door opening into the celebrity circle she strived for her practice to cater to. The poor kid in her wanted to post on Facebook about this victory to let most of her colleagues, who were the bulk of her friends list, know that she too was their equal, just as much as her professionally photographed profile picture portrayed her image to be. She cringed sometimes when she logged in to her account, as often there were friend requests from people in her past who would undoubtedly see through her perfectly applied makeup, fresh blond highlights, and designer dress to the scrawny girl they knew with self-trimmed dim ash blonde hair and Goodwill jeans. She immediately declined each of those requests, blocking them completely to prevent them from tainting her cultivated web presence. Aloof and professional relationships suited her best. She had no trust in people; after all, people come and go. But, her career was constant, and that would never leave her. Caught in a moment counting those she already treated over the last ten years—singers, baseball players,

CEOs, and now actors here for the new film industry in Atlanta—the prospect of things she could do someday when she had made enough money carried her away, but she snapped to attention at Kimberly's voice.

"Your implant sedation case is already in the chair. Been there for thirty minutes. You'd better hurry."

Jenny huffed at her watch, waved at Kimberly, and disappeared into her office in the back. Within a few minutes, she emerged in her white coat, goggles ready on her head, and hair pulled tightly and securely back from her face. Michael, her usually absent partner, was there, leaning against the wall outside of her office, reading an email on his phone.

"Hey," she said as she walked swiftly past him, only half glancing in his direction. "What have you got this morning?" She gave him a quizzical look when she finally saw that he wore dress pants and a buttoned down shirt instead of scrubs.

He laughed at her and replied, "A class. I'm heading over to the dental convention to get a jump start on my weekend."

Jenny turned around to look at him as she arrived at the door to her patient's operatory and suddenly gave him a look of recognition.

Asshole thinks the seed money that started us up a decade ago is all he has to give?

"Oh! That's right. You're going downtown now while I produce the revenue." Her sarcasm was mitigated by her genuine smile as she poised to pull her mask over her mouth. "Okay, go ahead and take your class in blah-blah practice-management-something-or-the-other with all the rest of the guys who don't really work. I'm sure I'll find you in the bar at the Ritz with the staff after my work is all done."

"Geez, you are bitchy this morning. Nervous about presentation over there? That's this afternoon, right?" He patted her on the shoulder and gave her a thumbs up.

"Yeah." She softened. He was an asshole sometimes, but he had always been there to catch her while they built their way up in their practice. And he knew she had a short fuse. "Now go away. I have some bone to drill."

She shooed him away and quietly stepped over to Amanda, who was already attending the patient, where he lay in the dimly lit cubicle in the chair, already in twilight sleep, waiting for Jenny to transform his mouth. Soft music played and a pulse oxygen monitor beeped. She whispered "hello" to her assistant Amanda, who was already gloved with mask on ready to begin.

"'Morning, Dr. Jenkins. His x-rays are pulled up on the monitor. His wife is waiting in the lobby, and I told her *you* would personally go talk to her when he is finished." Amanda lifted her eyebrow as she spoke. "And I'll remind you this time." Amanda half-laughed.

"Good. If you don't, you'll have to buy me a drink tonight after the convention."

Jenny and Amanda took their positions at the patient's side and Jenny pulled down the light near the patient's mouth and angled it in the best way for her to see her working area. Getting down to business, she honed in on only the mouth and did not bother to see who the patient was. She knew his x-ray but not his face. He was forty seven, thin, on blood pressure meds, and into a legal settlement that was funding the restoration of his bombed-out mouth. Just the type of patient she liked if not a celebrity. Big cases like this excited her: the dollar signs. This case had perfect timing too. The closing on her house was coming up in a few days, and she also needed a last case study to present for more credentialing in even more professional organizations. In turn, this meant more "cha-ching." Her skin began to tingle as she extended her hand toward Amanda for the first instrument. She loved the challenge of surgeries; the money was simply the icing on the cake. She was in control of everything, and that was how she liked things. Always.

For the first hour into the surgery, things went smoothly. She had set several implants into the patient's top arch and was prepping for the rest when she ran into a problem that she couldn't overcome.

"Dr. J., look." Amanda was suctioning and Jenny heard the disguised urgency in her voice. "Lingual side of the tongue, Doctor."

"Yes" was all she said as she calmly jumped into action. During the process of the procedure, she had nicked the surface artery under the patient's tongue, and blood pulsated from the tiny wound. She took a deep breath to fight threatening panic in her, counted to three, and took control. She sutured the wound adeptly, and in no time, she was back to repairing the patient's teeth. But, her luck was wearing thin today, and her thin file broke off inside the tooth and she couldn't dig it out. Again, she didn't panic but stayed in control. Even when she turned over the possibility of a malpractice suit in her head in that moment, she convinced herself that she was in control and silently recited the mantra that had gotten her through her life so far.

I am always the strongest person in the room. Things don't happen to me. I make them happen.

"What are you wearing tonight?" Amanda asked as she pressed gauze rolls into the patient's mouth.

"Really, Amanda? Now?"

Must be a nice luxury to only have to worry about your wardrobe.

Amanda apologized, and Jenny pointed to the door.

"Get me Dr. Patel on the phone. I need an oral surgeon."

A moment later Amanda handed the phone to Jenny.

"Hey, Jay. It's Jen. I have a problem."

"Okay, lay it on me. I have about two hours 'til I leave for the convention."

She explained her difficulties with the case, after which he advised her to close him up and send the patient to see him on Monday. She trusted Jay's advice. He was the only surgeon that she referred to all these years that treated her patients the way she would. They had stayed friends even after she graduated from school and he stayed back to finish his oral surgery residency. She had been so glad when he had finally finished and moved here with his wife and new son a few years ago. But sometimes, when they talked about teeth, she wanted to ask about Roshan. They were cousins and both had the same eyes, and it was hard to control her urge to ask. But she always did.

"Thanks. Before we hang up…do you want to meet up for drinks tonight? I'm giving a talk around three o'clock, but I'm meeting my staff at the bar at the hotel afterward. We've got a supply rep lined up to buy us free drinks. I'd love to see you."

"Oh, you're a lecturer now? Moving up in the world, are we?"

Her head swelled a little bit with pride at the tone in his voice. She was getting respect. That and the money were all she needed.

"Sounds good," he said. "I'll have Hema with me. We're leaving the kids with my mum and making it a date weekend. I'm sure Hema will post pictures of us all. She's the love of my life, but that woman does love her selfies. Text me later. Now go take care of your patient."

"Yes sir. Looking forward to it."

In less than thirty minutes, Amanda had called the patient's wife back to speak with Jenny about his after care. The woman was in her early twenties and wore skinny jeans and a tight tee shirt with three-inch heels, and her overly made-up face was full of concern.

"Hi, I'm Doctor Jenkins…" Jenny extended her hand to shake the woman's hand. The woman kept her arms at her side and stared at Jenny. "Are you Mr…" she quickly cheated a look at the chart and continued, "Blackwell, yes, Blackwell's daughter?"

Amanda cleared her throat behind Jenny and elbowed her in the back.

"We met at his first and second appointment already." Shifting her weight from one foot to the other, she added through smacking gum, "And I'm his wife."

Feigning recognition, Jenny backtracked and apologized profusely. Trying to do damage control, she did her best to charm the wife as she explained the situation today, offering the woman a credit for a complimentary massage and paraffin hand dip from her office masseuse. This brightened the wife's attitude, and she walked out of the office with her woozy husband on her arm, looking happy as a clam.

"Wow, Doc. What happened there?"

"I let my nerves get the best of me, which are shot from stressing about my talk." Followed closely by Amanda, Jenny strode down the plush carpeted hall and into her office.

"Not that." Amanda said, leaning on the door frame with her arms crossed in front of her chest. "Mrs. Blackwell? Hello? You really pissed her off."

Jenny glared at her over her shoulder as she tossed her overnight bag onto the fashionably distressed wood desk, skewing some of her charts in the process. She unzipped the heavy silver zipper on the expensive leather bag and pulled out a neatly folded dress and another neatly folded outfit, laying them on top of the charts.

"I know. I just have a hard time remembering all the people on the fringe of a case."

She lifted a black spaghetti strap dress and let it drape over the edge of the desk.

"It may not be my place to say, but I think you kind of need to be more...more personable with people."

Jenny glanced sideways at her while she separated a pair of skinny jeans and a a gauzy black top and lay them next to the dress. "What do you think? Dress or pants?"

Letting out a frustrated sigh, Amanda surveyed the clothes. "What shoes are you wearing?"

"These." She pulled out a pair of black, strappy, blingy Jimmy Choos from the bag.

Jenny waved her hands across the desk top and smiled in anticipation.

"CFM shoes. I guess you won't be all business this weekend. And you wore the dress on that trip to Miami for the staff development weekend."

Jenny smiled slyly, "Yeah, and...it worked."

"Yes, you're right. You got what you wanted." She stepped over to finger the hem on the dress. "Is this a Monica Lewinsky dress?"

"Ha, Ha. Don't judge. Everyone is not so lucky to find a good one to have kids with."

"Doc. You could if you wanted to."

"No, that ship has sailed. Not interested. I am doing my own thing and quite well I might add. No need to rock the boat. Anyway," she held up a pair of skinny black jeans and a black long sleeve top with a bit of lace on the trim. "Better?"

"Yes, better. Doesn't say you are open for business, ya know what I mean?"

"Right. I'm going to relax and have fun with you guys."

She gathered her belongings together as Amanda and Kimberly closed up shop in the office. Jenny changed into a conservative skirt and top for her professional presentation, but added pizazz to the outfit with the black Jimmy Choos.

Every year at convention time, many dentists in the region and even more dental offices in town closed to attend the Southeast Dental Convention. There were continuing education sessions for all staff and doctors, plus expensive dinners and drinks, courtesy of slick equipment sales representatives to sweeten the days off. It was kind of a dental schmoozing free-for-all of ordering supplies, team building with staff, and meeting old and new colleagues, a who's who in the profession.

Jenny loaded her briefcase and laptop into the backseat of the Mercedes convertible and sped over to the convention center. Her hands were shaking at the thought of standing in front of a class of fifty to sixty dentists, all gathered there to learn something from her. She was ten years out of dental school, and although she had continuously been adding credentials to her name at lightning speed, she worried constantly if she would be taken seriously. Having given up on personal approval from the world, she desperately craved professional approval from her peers.

Five minutes before the class was to begin, she hooked up her laptop to the room's projection system and reviewed her clinical pictures for the PowerPoint presentation on the big screen. Her forehead was feeling moist, and she hoped her foundation didn't begin running. She rubbed her clammy hands together, then blew on them, as she busied herself on the computer, avoiding the expanse of the crowd filing into seats.

In the front row sat nondescript men and women, most of whom wore button down shirts and sport coats, prepared with their class agendas and pens. Murmured conversations filled the room as colleagues from the same dental schools, organizations, and social circles caught up with each other. This was the first time Jenny had attended the convention in a long time because she had taken advantage of the patient load, thus the income, during previous conventions when high-paying emergency patients had nowhere else to turn.

As the crowd settled to a hush, she looked across the sea of faces with eyes on her and swallowed her fear.

"Thank you for coming today," she announced, hoping that her nerves would calm soon. "Please, sit, there are a few spaces in the front row. I don't bite." The audience politely laughed. She didn't recognize any of the faces.

As she took a deep breath, she put on her game face and began her talk, eyes on the screen of her laptop to avoid the eyes that were all focused on her. A whisper distracted her from her laptop screen, and she looked up to see the double doors to the conference room crack open and a figure slipping into a seat at the back of the room. Jenny couldn't believe her eyes. It was Roshan.

He was dressed in a lavender button down shirt and a coordinating purplish tie. She paused speaking and a hush fell over the room. Some people, curious about the pause, turned to look to the back to see the commotion. Roshan whispered one last sentence into the phone and looked around him apologetically. He slipped the device into his pocket and turned toward the front, waving toward Jenny to continue, mouthing "sorry" to a lady next to him.

She couldn't believe he was here. Graying temples made him look older, and he had gained weight since she last saw him. By the look of the tight sleeves around his biceps, it was muscle weight. He grinned flirtingly at her, and she felt her face heat up. She was so fair, that she knew her cheeks would be crimson. Hoping her makeup was thick enough to cover her embarrassment, she continued her talk. She spoke for two hours, and they were the longest two hours of her life.

While she shook hands and passed out business cards to those who lingered after the presentation with questions, she couldn't take her eyes off of Roshan. He had stayed in his seat by the doors and watched her while he talked on the phone and answered texts, waiting. Once the final person exited the room, she walked in his direction at the same time that he got up and came toward her.

"Wow. Hello, stranger." She grabbed him lightly in a polite hug, careful not get too close. She already had butterflies.

"Hello. How've you been?" he asked warmly, sounding excited to see her.

"Great. You? You're married right?" She knew full well he was.

"Yeah. Almost 10 years. Priya and I got married right after dental school. You?"

Priya, right. How could I have forgotten that name?

"Oh no, not me!" She waved him off, as if shooing the idea away from her. "I'm not the marrying type."

"Yeah, I remember." They looked each other in the eye, neither knowing where to take the conversation from that point. Roshan broke the silence.

"So, you have an implant practice. That's great. I'm getting into them myself, but I'm not as dedicated as you, it looks like."

"Well, I'm sure you remember. I am my work. That's what I do."

"I remember." He held her gaze for a moment until she finally broke away.

"I guess I'd better get out of here. There is another seminar in this room soon."

He followed her to the podium, and she started to gather her things.

"Okay. Well, it was great to see you again." He reached out to shake her hand and said, "really, really good."

She let her hand linger in his for a second then pulled away. She had forgotten how his amber eyes gave her warm shivers.

He held the door open for her and followed behind her.

"Can I call you sometime? About dentistry, you know, practice stuff? It would be good to have an expert to ask questions of sometimes." He pulled out his phone, at the ready to enter her number.

"Sure." She felt okay about giving him her number. There was no harm in it. It was purely professional. Absolutely professional.

They both lingered, awkwardly looking at each other, neither knowing how to say goodbye. Jenny said she had to get to a meeting, and he agreed that he needed to go too. As she walked away, she felt a sudden sense of panic, of sadness that she might never see him again. Against her better judgement, she stopped in her tracks and spun around.

"Do you and your wife want to join us for drinks tonight? I'm meeting with my staff and a supply rep at eight o'clock." She really wanted to see his face again and didn't want to let the opportunity slip through her fingers. Even is his wife would be there. She added, "The rep might be able to hook you up with a good deal on supplies."

A sly grin took over Roshan's face, and he paused. Looking away, he thought it over for a moment, and then replied, "Yes. That will be great." He turned to leave and said over his shoulder, "But Priya won't be here. Her brother is getting married, and she's in L.A. helping her family get ready for the wedding. I'm sure you remember what I told you way back about my culture's formalities, don't you?"

She stood there, feet planted, shamefully allowing a tingling feeling to work its way up her spine. There's no harm in a drink, she muttered to herself as she headed in the other direction. "I'm sorry, Priya won't be here. I would have loved to have met her," she lied.

That evening, the group sat in plush leather chairs that they had scooted together around several low cocktail tables, chatting with sweating bottles of beer and an assortment of bar glasses in their hands. The crowd consisted of Amanda and Kimberly from her staff, Ethan the supply rep, Jenny, and two men from New Jersey who were visiting for the convention. Jenny sat with her long legs crossed and leaned back in her chair, scanning the other patrons of the hotel bar. Her skinny black jeans made her legs look longer and thinner, but they were so tight she longed to shed them for sweatpants. She sipped the tart lemon drop martini in her hand and absentmindedly contributed to the conversation when a comment was warranted.

"Looking for someone?" Ethan asked. He had been blatantly staring at her all evening, and she had tried to pretend she didn't notice. He was a good looking guy with piercing blue eyes that were framed by a fringe of blonde lashes. He had bragged about playing lacrosse in college and training for triathlons. Sort of the all-American guy. But that did not turn her on. Besides, most all-American guys would eventually want to settle down with an all-American woman. And settling down was not her style.

"Uh huh. I'm looking for a doc that I went to UT with. He's a really tall Indian guy. Do you see him anywhere?"

"Nope. But, I'm not really anxious to find him." Ethan looked at her, waiting for a reaction.

She ignored him.

Her second martini was half full and Roshan had still not arrived. By this time, only she, Ethan and Amanda remained, and they were nearly done with their drinks. Amanda, forgetting her husband at home for the moment, blatantly couldn't keep her eyes off of Ethan, while Ethan directed conversation toward Jenny. Things were getting awkward. She wished she had gotten Roshan's number at the same time she gave him hers. She decided to gulp down the last swallow of her drink and when she tipped the glass into her mouth, a pair of hands patted her on the shoulder from behind. Inhibitions at a low from the alcohol, she smiled big and stood up to greet Roshan.

He was striking with his black hair gelled back just a bit and the black Polo shirt he wore. As she hugged him, the crisp scent of his cologne excited her, taking her back in time a decade. It was the same cologne he wore in dental school. She felt his breath on her neck as he said hello.

Oh my God. Oh my God.

"You made it." She grabbed his hand and let it linger as she introduced him to Ethan and Amanda. Amanda shook his hand drunkenly, and Ethan stiffly did the same.

"Sorry I'm late." He motioned for the cocktail waitress to come over to him. "Some family issues came up."

"It's okay, Doctor Patel." Amanda piped in. "But, I'm going to have to get up to the room. I have an early class tomorrow." She got up and tripped over the coffee table, adding in Jenny's direction, "My doc won't let me hear the end of it if I miss it. Gotta be the best!" She stepped between Ethan and Roshan's feet around the table toward the steps to the hotel lobby and stumbled again. Roshan and Ethan both jumped up and held her so she wouldn't fall. Jenny, torn between staying at the bar and helping her friend, forced herself to do the right thing and announce that she had to see Amanda to the room they would be sharing.

"I'll help you," Ethan offered, staying out of his seat.

"No, thanks. I've got it." She didn't want to be left alone with him in the hallway after putting Amanda to bed. Speaking to both men, she offered, "You two talk shop. Roshan, Ethan can help you out a lot. I'll be back down in a little while." Jenny saw that Ethan glared in Roshan's direction, but Roshan was looking at her. She hoped that Kimberly was up in the room already so that she could take over with Amanda and Jenny wouldn't miss this opportunity to catch up with Roshan.

"Okay, sure." Ethan relented, his eyes trailing Jenny as she disappeared around the corner to the elevators with Amanda on her arm. She was happy to see that Roshan relaxed back into his chair. He looked like he was there to stay.

After depositing her wobbly charge into Kimberly's care, Jenny felt a surge of excitement and willed the elevator to hurry down to the hotel lobby.

As she approached the empty bar, her heart sank. Had Roshan given up on her? She still didn't have his number. He might be gone for good. The bartender nodded to her and must have noticed her disappointment because he pointed over to the figure at the end of the bar. Roshan sat facing the bar, spinning a beer around in his hand and watching the TV mounted on the wall behind the bar. When he saw the bartender motion toward him, he turned to Jenny as she approached with a genuine smile.

"Hey." She tried not to sound too excited to be there, face to face, finally. "Where is Ethan?"

"He gave me his card right after you left and said he was going up to his room. I guess he could tell we wanted to talk alone."

Jenny was relieved. "Good," she said as she slid onto the barstool beside him. Her shoulder touched his as she settled onto her seat, and she tried to fight how good it felt to be so close to him.

He is someone's husband.

She ordered water, needing to clear her head from the martinis of the night. She wanted a clear head so she wouldn't say anything to him she would regret.

They begin to trade stories of the past decade, going over professional goals and accomplishments. Both skirted around anything too personal until Roshan asked about her father.

"He passed away. A couple years after the trip you drove me on to see him after graduation." She gulped down the sorrow that sometimes threatened to show itself, but she strong-armed it back down inside where it belonged.

Strong.

"Oh, Jen, I'm so sorry to hear that. I know that you loved him despite your feelings about your family."

She nodded in gratitude. "Yeah, I'm still not too proud of how they think, but I actually see my mom from time to time now."

"Your mom? Wow. I thought you guys—"

"She's kind of shaping up. Goes longer and longer between relapses each time. We'll never be good, but something in me wants to have a mom in some way. So, I keep it to visits back home, and then I leave it behind when I come back to the city."

"That's great. I'm happy for you. That trip we took when your dad had his accident really made me worry about you. And then you dropped off the radar. Jay mentioned your practice a few times but never really brought up how you were."

That was probably best.

She focused her attention on her drink, afraid to look him in the eyes, for fear of connected too much with him. He reached over and touched her hand, and she froze, trying to ignore how she wanted to share with him. To redirect the conversation, she asked, "So, how's married life?"

He shook his head. "Married life is married life. Good, I guess. We live with my mum. Priya works at Emory. Don't see much of her between both of our jobs."

"Any kids?"

"No, oh no. Two people have to be together long enough to make that happen."

She hesitated, wanting to know more but didn't want to get more personal than he was willing to go. She really wanted to know what living a full Indian life was like for him. "How does it work, living with your wife and your mom? Is that weird?"

"Not really. Mum takes care of the house, and Priya and I bring home the money. It's how I was raised, so it's no big deal."

"I don't think I could ever get married myself. And your story makes me want it even less." Without really thinking, she leaned in to his shoulders and asked, "Are you happy?"

He leaned away from her, his eyes on the TV, and sighed. "Happy? What's happy, really? I am content, I guess. I'm living a good life, the way I was raised to do it."

"Do you and Priya love each other?" She began to feel such a tug at her heart for him.

"We love each other, just not like you would like to think of love. Our families get along, we take care of my mum, and we are a team, I guess. My culture is set up around teams, I guess you could say. And the heads of the team don't always fall in love. But, it's all good for me. I can't be a loner."

"But it sounds like you are alone anyway, Roshan."

"It doesn't matter, really. I was happy with a girl once, but love doesn't always get you anywhere."

Jenny stopped swirling the ice in her drink and looked at him, shocked. He had spoken about the elephant in the room. He looked back with a nervous grin, but leaned back as if he expected her to smack him.

"Love, huh?" She was eager to put the love topic to rest. Her discomfort was growing by the second. "You're right, my friend. I've loved a lot of people, people in my family," she stopped herself from saying "you," and instead finished, "But, love has never gotten me anywhere."

He raised his glass to her and she tapped it. "Cheers."

Jenny went on. Because of the liquor, her words started spilling from her. "We're not so different, you know. You may have people around you all the time, but you're alone too. You accept loneliness so you won't be rejected. And I run away from people so they can't leave me."

She saw the bartender out of the corner of her eye watching them while he emptied out nut bowls into the trash and wiped the bar counter off. There was no one else left in the bar but them.

She searched Roshan's eyes, pitying him, pitying herself, and wanting him at the same time.

"Sounds like life kind of sucks for both of us," he said.

"Yeah. Kind of. If only..." she placed her hand on top of his next to his beer.

"Right." He replied, not taking his eyes off of hers. "If only."

He leaned into her and brushed his lips softly against hers then pulled away, surveying her for a reaction. For a moment, they watched each other, waiting.

"Last call." The bartender stated politely in their direction as he switched on the overhead lights.

The moment broken, she stood up and looked at her watch. "Well, um, yeah. I guess it is late, huh?"

He stood slowly as well, and they awkwardly faced each other.

"Yeah. Late. Right." He read the receipt and lay down a fifty dollar bill, thanking the bartender.

The walk to the elevator was excruciating for her. They were silent but close enough to touch with each step. When the elevator closed, she couldn't ignore the awkwardness or her feelings. She turned toward him and pulled his collar gently toward her, reaching her face up to his. Her lips met his slowly, tentatively, afraid of how he would react. His lips responded by opening, and his tongue met hers. Sinking into him, the four walls of the elevator disappeared, and all she knew was him.

The *ding* that they had arrived at the fifth floor interrupted the reverie. Heads together, they watched the doors part down the middle and show them the red carpeted hallway in front of them.

"Your floor," Roshan said.

"Yeah. My floor." She ran her lips across his cheek and breathed in his ear, her move encouraged by the tickle of his palm up the small of her back.

She did not move toward the open door. He did not push the open door button on the wall. Bodies pressed together, they both watched the doors close shut again. Neither spoke, but Roshan smiled at her with a smoldering look in his eyes. The arrival bell for the twelfth floor sounded, and the door opened. This time, both of them stepped out, and Jenny let herself be led down the corridor.

What am I doing?

What fuzziness she had felt over the evening from her drinks was gone now thanks to the water. She had no excuse for what she was about to do. They entered his darkened room, and Roshan shut the door behind her, leaving the light off. His hands covered her all over at once, and she pressed herself harder and harder into his body, desperate to feel him, to confirm his presence.

Pulling back, she asked him breathlessly, "Are you sure?"

Without a word, he began to undress her.

Bypassing her shirt, his large hands peeled the skinny jeans from her hips, and he bent down on his knees to slide them all the way down her thighs, her calves, and her feet through the tight bottom cuffs. She stood there beside the bed, looking down at him on the floor level. In the twinkling city lights reflecting from the window from the open curtains, she could see him. He looked up at her and rose slowly, running his hands along her bare legs as he moved. Her skin tingled, and she had the urge to throw herself on top of him on the bed. But his hands, still slow and steady, caressed her body, over her silk panties, fingertips up her back, then stopping at the nape of her neck. He pulled her face to him and kissed her in a long, sensuous kiss, whispering, "I missed you."

She couldn't respond for fear of killing the moment. She didn't want to think about what they were doing. All she could focus on was the overwhelming desire to feel his naked body against hers and have him inside her. Now. Their arms and legs intertwined in a fluid dance of heat, and painful desire ended in the cries and shudders that had waited for years to be released.

Hours later, Jenny woke with her head on his shoulder and her arm wrapped around him, the familiar feel of his wiry chest hair on her skin and listening to the regular sounds of his breath gave her déjà vu. The curtain was still open, and the bright moonlight cast an unearthly glow on his face as she watched him sleep. They had been through this once before, and she knew how it would end.

But unlike the last time, she had learned how to bury her feelings and protect herself from pain. Being close to him felt so right, and she knew she would not let herself want more. His scent on her skin, the fresh memory of his body on top of hers, was all she needed. She needed nothing else. And no one else but herself.

She felt around on the floor for her clothes quietly, and once dressed, picked up his iPhone, hoping he didn't have a security code set up. With one finger, she silenced her own phone, and then dialed her number from his. Her screen lit up with his number, and she canceled the call on his, slipping her phone into her purse. In a second, she walked away from the carefully shut room door and clutched the phone to her chest in the hallway. She had his number again. And she would make sure she used it again. On her terms.

Chapter 11

Esha

"Give, Priya. I'll put those bowls away." Esha took a stack of bowls out of her daughter-in-law's hands and made a beeline for the upper cabinet where they belonged. The theme song from her favorite crime show played from the sitting room off the kitchen, and she was getting anxious to watch it. Rarely did she stay up this late for TV, but lately the plots had hooked her and she looked forward to it each week. And she needed the diversion from her thoughts. Today had been a rough day.

Priya picked up their two plates from the kitchen table and put them in the sink. A splash of soapy water spattered onto her pale green scrub pants, but she seemed not to notice. Her eyes were focused out into the darkness outside the large window above the sink. An outside light was glowing, and moths and other large insects threw themselves at the light, sometimes missing and throwing themselves onto the glass.

Esha noticed Priya's face was blank as she stood still with her hands in the water. Esha had caught glimpses of her doing that a lot lately and had the urge to fill the silence.

"Shoo, shoo. You are getting your clothes wet. Away. I'll clean." She good naturedly pushed Priya aside with her hands and then led her out

167 •

of the kitchen. "Go. Throw those clothes in the washing. I get to them in the morning."

Rubbing her eyes, Priya just said, "It's okay. They got worse on them at the hospital than water. I'm fine. Let me help finish up."

The poor girl's eyes are hollow. What has Roshan done?

Esha shook her head and shooed her away again. "You are exhausted. Rest." Her heart broke when Priya looked at the clock worried. "Roshan will be home soon, my dear. He told me he had a dinner with somebody, a man named Ethan, I think, about clinic things. I'm sure he won't be long."

She was a good liar. Roshan had not told her where he was, but dear Priya couldn't know that. Sometimes, many times, lies were easier than the truth.

She had learned that from the moment she and Roshan landed at the airport from India with her brother, and they were greeted at the gate by a circle of loving relatives. "So glad you are here and safe now," they had said. "Your husband won't dare to come after you here," they said. "What did you he do when you left?" they asked. Esha's response was simply, "Nothing." It was the truth because they left him on the floor in a pool of blood, and he could do nothing.

She shuddered and shook the image from her. It would never go away. But she could pretend it never happened.

"It's okay. I'm exhausted. I think I'll go up and soak in the bath. "Priya rubbed her face with both hands and smoothed her short cropped hair away from her face.

"Are you feeling okay?" Esha asked.

"I've been nauseous the past couple of days. Just under the weather. But I'm fine"

"Nauseous?" Esha honed in on that word. Suddenly the idea of a pregnancy lifted her spirit. Today had been tough, but the slightest inking of a baby in the house changed her mood entirely. But with Roshan gone so much, how likely would it be?

Priya picked up on her look and quickly added, "A stomach bug. I had a patient last week with vomiting and diarrhea. We admitted her, but I think I picked it up."

Esha couldn't hide her disappointment, and Priya gave her a hug.

"Mummy, I don't want to hurt your feelings, but maybe you should get a job or do some volunteer work. You haven't worked since Roshan and I got married. That's ten years. You should, you know, keep busy." She pulled away and walked toward the staircase. "If you keep waiting for a baby, you're going to be bored for a very, very long time. My husband has to be here to make it happen. And look…" She held out her arms at the empty TV room. "…he's not here." Priya glanced at her watch as she stepped onto the first step. Esha couldn't muster any words to ease her daughter-in-law's pain, and both of them knew Roshan would not be home any time soon.

Despite her pity, Esha felt exposed. She had failed to hide her desire for a grandchild from Priya and was a little hurt by her condescending tone. What else that she tried to bury was really exposed?

She laughed off Priya's suggestion. "Mother's always wait for their son's to give them a grandchild."

Priya looked irritated and tired. "Well, there is more to life than having babies. Every day I see with my patients what can go wrong. I don't even know if I want to get pregnant. Is it even worth the risk?"

Esha stood there in the kitchen, feeling echoes of the kicks of the two babies she had grown in her belly. Simultaneous joy and grief filled her, and she looked defensively at Priya. She knew that Priya was aware of Esha's loss. And the unspoken events that caused it. That knowledge made the words sting that much more.

"Yes. It is."

Priya stood in the middle of the stairs and shot her a pitying look. "I guess women these days want more than babies and an absent husband."

"You think I don't want more than living alone with you and Roshan, watching the two of you so cold to one another? I want more for both of you. And for me."

Priya rubbed her eyes and exhaled her exhaustion, then disappeared up the stairs and into the dark hallway. Esha was left, staring after her.

"Put your scrubs in the laundry room, and I'll wash them tonight." Esha called in the best cheerful voice she could muster. She could not let on to Priya that she had struck a nerve. She was determined to maintain a veneer of contentment in this family. Even if the veneer was all that kept them together. This was all Esha had.

If you tell a lie often enough, doesn't it become the truth?

Esha, exhausted, longed to be able to lie down on her bed in her first floor master bedroom. Her knees hurt, and she was glad they had used an Indian architect for the house design. He had understood the needs of an Indian family. The house was laid out so that when grandchildren were running around the house with dolls and toy cars, there would be enough room for Roshan and Priya to sleep with the kids upstairs and for Esha to dote on them and still have her own privacy without having to climb stairs when she was old. She was only in her mid-fifties now, but by the ache in her joints already, it wouldn't be long before she was truly old.

When the last countertop was wiped, a covered container of *tikku* biryani rice was set out for Roshan, and the ending music from her show had stopped, she turned off all the lights on the main floor and got ready to retire to her room. She left the stove hood light on in the kitchen for Roshan, however, because she didn't want him stumbling around in the dark and possibly wake Priya when he got home.

In her room, she sat on her bed and picked up her iPhone to set the alarm for morning yoga. She loved technology. It was amazing. She had gone from living in a village in India with no telephone line or indoor toilet as a young newlywed to living in a sprawling home with travertine bathroom floors and owning a cellular phone that was a gateway to the entire world. When Roshan was growing up, she had worked as a Gujarati tutor after school, and parents would bring their kids to her from all over the metro Atlanta area after school and on weekends. It was a job that she loved dearly. She loved the kids, she loved sharing her language with them, and she loved the independence the money gave her and Roshan, meager as it was. But, in a way, her job had kept her in India even while in America. Safe, comfortable, but in the dark on outside things and people.

Maybe Priya was right. Maybe she should get a job. Get out of her cocoon of friends and cooking and doting on the two people in her life that mattered to her. She feared that her cocoon was about to split open, and maybe she needed to be ready to fly out before she got eaten.

She opened "The Google," to look "on the line" as she always said to the amusement of her son, and searched for volunteer work. She was glad the computer inside the phone could decipher what she entered, because her spelling in English was no good. The list that came up was long, and she clicked around, looking at pictures of happy volunteers holding kids and building houses for the poor. Money wasn't necessary for her anymore, so maybe she could help some poor children who could use an aging mom's help. The thought of going outside of her people, into the world of people who lived around her was terrifying, yet exhilarating. Or maybe she would just go back to Gujarati lessons.

Baby steps for me.

A text message from Monishabhabi interrupted her internet search.

Monisha
How you doing tonight? Forgot today is the anniversary.
Call if you need to talk.

Esha considered how she *was* doing tonight. For the first time since she left India—it had been so many years—she had forgotten the anniversary of her daughter's birth and death. Guilt invaded her every cell. She had been so focused on the worry over her living child, she had forgotten the one who slipped through her fingers unprotected by her own mother.

She would never forgive her dead husband for it. She was glad he was dead. And she would never forgive herself for making him angry. Eight months pregnant, she knew how he was. She should not have been so proud and just shut her mouth. In a way, she killed her own daughter. And God would judge her when he was ready.

But, she had to be strong, as always, even with Monisha. Any crack would cause the dam to break.

Esha
Good, Bhabhi. God is great. He takes care.

She pulled out a silk-trimmed baby blanket from the bottom drawer in her dresser and lay it out on her bed next to her pillow. The washed-out marigold-yellow fuzz on it had balled up over years of use, and the silk edges were frayed from her fingers caressing it every night as they tried to walk her into sleep. Eyes heavy, she readied herself for bed while her stories of the past and present bled together inside her. As happened so many nights at this time, she replayed that night, feeling the blow to her skin even now.

She had waited up all night for her husband. She still remembered that she had fixed his usual Thursday meal, *matter paneer* and rice, and it sat cold on the table next to his empty plate. He smelled of liquor and the same perfume as usual. Little Roshan lay in their bed, sweetly breathing on her pillow, and she shut the bedroom door. Something in her snapped. She was so young and just forgot her fear for that stupid moment. Fists clenched at her sides, her words spewed out and up to her husband's drunken ears.

"You shame me!" she had yelled at his glazed eyes as he leaned against the sofa. For that moment she transformed into the strong girl she always wanted to be, that Monisha had always told her she could be, and moved toward him with her finger pointed into his chest. He was tall and so good looking with the greying temples in his movie star-coiffed hair, but the liquor and her words had contorted his features into an unrecognizable beast.

"I hate you," she whimpered as the blow came at her. The crunch followed, then the nauseating flash of his foot against her huge belly. The flood of blood from between her legs as she lay on the floor, soaking her nightgown before the blackness came. As the nothingness swallowed her, she felt the small warm hands of her mother-in-law on her cheek and a shawl slip under her head. Her gentle whispers in Esha's ears that all would be okay, and then Esha blacked out.

Light filtered back into her head. She heard her own grunting with contractions, pushing. She listened to her own screams from above and then there was silence. She felt the weight of the cooling, soft bundle wrapped in its first and last satin-trimmed blanket, lifted from her arms. Minutes later, the blanket, folded neatly, was returned to her lap by her mother-in-law. Roshan stood in the doorway stunned and blurry eyed, and when his *Ba* shooed him gently away, he ducked under her arm and ran to Esha, placing his head on her chest. She held him tight, and covered both their shoulders with the marigold-yellow blanket.

But, that night was over long ago. It was her history, and she was sleepy now and remembered Priya's laundry load waiting for her upstairs. She left the blanket on the bed and went upstairs to fetch the clothes and throw them into the washer. Priya was in the bathroom with the bathtub water running, and Esha knocked quietly, "Hi, I'm here to pick up washing. Just letting you know." She got a muffled "okay" and went about her business.

As she began her routine, loading, drying and folding, her thoughts continued.

Roshan wouldn't come home. Later, Priya would snap. Her words would spew out. Then the two of them would retreat into their usual silence. Nothing lost, but nothing gained. Esha had lost, but she had also loved. The living and the dead. Was her need for him to be married to Priya worth his misery?

She didn't know another way. Her mother had taught her that life is not what you make of it, but what karma sets in your path. Everyone has their path set in front of them, and to stray would send one in a wrong direction, away from God. The path has been set for thousands of years, and the ancient prayers salved her soul. It was never up to us to decide for ourselves not to take the right path. If we did, it could take everyone we loved along for the ride to a place they didn't want to be.

Colored clothes in a pile, whites in another. She sorted, unwadded socks, and emptyied pockets. At the bottom of a pile, she found a pair of Roshan's khaki pants from the night before. He had come home after midnight, but Priya was on call and didn't know. Her hand slid into the front pocket and touched a stiff corner of something. At first she thought it would be a crisp hundred dollar bill, as she often found cash in his pockets. She recoiled when the pointed corner of a foil package jabbed underneath her fingernail. She sucked on her finger and then reached back inside to pull a square package with a circular ridge out.

In one hand she held the belt loop of his pants, in the other, a silver condom package, similar to the ones her husband kept in his bedside table, and often in his wallet. Who could he be using this thing with? Is *this* why Priya wasn't getting pregnant? It wouldn't be in his pocket if he was using them with her. Then who?

It doesn't really matter. It's not his wife.

She slipped it into the pocket of her robe and finished folding, unable to sleep until all chores were done. A necessary habit from her married days. When she was done, she turned on the light in one of the guest rooms and turned down the bed. She pulled an extra blanket out of the closet and placed it at the foot of the bed. Roshan always got cold at night.

She pulled the chain on the bedside lamp and stepped back into the hall. She knew he slept there most nights when Priya was home. She could tell by the wrinkles in the bedspread, and the pillows arranged differently from how she left them. Now she knew why.

She stepped lightly down the stairs and made a beeline into the garage to the trash cart. The chill of the March night hit her, and she squeezed her arms to herself. Letting go for a moment, with one swift movement, she lifted the lid and tossed the condom into a yogurt container on top of the trash and pushed it further in the rubbish. Shutting the lid, she went back into the house and into her room. The cool smooth sheets soothed her feet as she slipped them down under the covers. She checked the alarm setting on her phone so she could be up earlier than Roshan and Priya to have their breakfast ready and lunches packed.

Her eyes closed and the worn satin trim of the baby blanket that bunched up under her face absorbed her tears.

A few months later, autumn blew in, and Esha had found some joy tutoring a small group of busy primary school aged boys in Gujarati and spending time at Monisha's home. Monisha surrounded herself as much as possible with family and friends since Pete's passing from cancer several years earlier, and the home she now shared with Jay and Hema and their children was a warm, beautiful gathering place. After discovering Roshan's sinful pastime that night in the laundry, she had asked God to lead her on the right path, and meditated on it for hours on it every day before she fixed breakfast for Roshan and Priya when they were home. Priya had started working odd hours at the hospital and often Esha ate alone in the morning sun on her deck, staring at the garden and the high fence between them and their neighbor's house. The sunshine burnished the depression out of her. She wondered what life was like on the other side for the people she had never met, and she wondered what they would think of hers.

One morning, she stood up from the patio table, swallowed the last gulp of her chai, and dialed her sister-in-law Ashmi's number.

"Bhabhi, you want I give lessons to your boys?" she blurted out in English before even saying hello. Ashmi never spoke Gujarati anymore.

"Um, Esha. Good morning to you too." Ashmi's voice gritted with irritation and dragged out sleepily.

You were asleep. It's nine o'clock in the morning. Lazy woman.

"Good morning. Okay, you and my brother speak only English nowa-days. My nephews, they growing big, they needing to be learning Gujarati. They are forgetting who they are. I teach them." The boys, six and ten, had the cherubic cheeks of their father. He still had a baby face. And often acted like one, but his boys were sweet and always gave her big hugs when they met.

Ashmi yawned. "But, bhabhi, they are so busy. Raj plays travel baseball now and Nikhil is just starting karate four days a week. I don't think we have time. They both have taekwondo and piano lessons and—"

"I come on Sunday afternoons. They home then. Tell your friends to bring their boys too. All these young people need this."

"Bhabhi, hold on. Arun and I, we've decided it's best for the kids to speak only English right now. It helps them fit in more. They will test better in school, have more friends."

Esha was getting tired of speaking English now. She couldn't express her annoyance with enough precision without her Gujarati words. She replied in Gujarati. "No. Are you mad? My mother would scold my brother like a little brat for this if she were alive."

Ashmi sighed into the phone. "Eshabhabhi," she paused. "We take them to India every few years to visit my parents. But we live here. No. They don't have time."

Esha wanted to reach through the phone and drag her brother's irri-tating wife out her bed by the hair and shake her. Ashmi was younger. Esha knew better than her and her flaky little brother what was best for kids. And she loved those boys and wanted to play with them and get out of the house.

"I'll be there Sunday at four o'clock. Make sure you get the other boys there too."

And that was that. Now she spent time during the week planning fun activities and projects for the boys' lessons and brought Pyrex dishes full of sweets for the kids and fried samosas with her for the family when she came on Sundays. At first it was only her two nephews, but gradually she gained three more students, and the young parents often, with nostalgic faces, listened in on the Gujarati songs and rhymes they all played at the end.

It felt good to fill her time again. She had missed teaching kids. One of the boys, who came from across the city to the home for the lesson reminded Esha of Roshan. He was tall with gangly arms for his age, and though he wasn't handsome like Roshan had always been, his big sweet smile could charm her into calling on him first every time. She fought herself from pretending he was her grandson.

Diwali celebration time was coming, and she added sweets and snacks preparation to her days. Diwali was her favorite time of year because it was such an auspicious celebration of light triumphing over darkness, full of prayers and lighting *diya* lamps and putting aside petty daily problems to spend time with family and friends. This year, she felt especially hopeful and felt the light more than ever in her mind's eye during meditation. And she didn't really know why.

Monisha's house became food central for the season. One Sunday before Esha's Gujarati class, she joined Ashmi, Suriksha, and Hema's mum Neela, who was visiting from India, in Monisha's kitchen and concocted the most amazing sweets imaginable. Of course, Priya was working and couldn't be there, but Jay's wife Hema was at home with their three children. Jay, Hema and their children lived with Monisha and Pete in the traditional Indian way. Hema had quit her engineering job and was a stay-at-home mom now, but thank goodness for Monisha because they could evenly share the cooking and house duties together. Whenever Esha visited them when Monisha was not working, she and Hema always had a child on the hip or at their feet and something simmering on the stove. Hema's mother Neela, clad in a casual sari, was also in the house for three months now, having come from India for the birth of her third grandchild. The house sounded and smelled of happiness.

Sweets production became an assembly line that took over the kitchen and dining room for the entire afternoon. Blocks of *paneer* yogurt cheese sat on counters next to bags of sugar, flour, jars of pistachios, butter, and cardamom seeds. Scattered in the kitchen were spools of ribbon and rolls of colored plastic wrap and bright plastic trays for the treats to be packaged and delivered to loved ones.

Esha was in charge of mixing the dough for *paneer barfi,* her favorite dessert of all time. While she inhaled the sweet smells of the *paneer* cheese and sweet cream cooking together with rose water and cardamom mixing with it, she couldn't resist pilfering a spoonful of dough even before she spread the mixture into a pan to be cut into squares from each batch. She hoped no one noticed. As she spooned the fourth dough glob into her palm and rolled it into a neat ball, Ashmi commented to Esha from her station at the sink full of dirty pots as if she were scolding a child.

"Bhabhi, slow down. You'll get a tummy ache."

Esha smiled at her and popped the whole thing into her mouth. She muffled back in terrible English, "But it's only one time a year. Is okay." Her mood was so good, even Ashmi couldn't ruin it.

Hema came in holding her baby on the tail of her five year old daughter, who made a dash for a bowl of *gulab jamun* cake balls next to Monisha at the kitchen island that had not yet been soaked in sugar water.

"Jyoti, you come here right now." Hema's brown brow glistened from sweat, and she swatted the little girl's hand from the tray. The baby started a hungry squall, and little Jyoti pulled her hand to her stomach, pushing out her lower lip. Esha couldn't help herself.

"Oh, Mummy, don't shout me," she said in a child's voice and patted her grandniece's hair. "I'm just so hungry for some good sweets here." She cupped the girl's cheeks and looked at Hema with a mock childish grin. Jyoti looked up at her mother with round black eyes full of tears and corn niblet teeth grinning wide.

"Oh, Auntie. She hasn't had lunch yet. No sweets yet." She started to turn Jyoti around with her free hand, but Esha stopped Jyoti and handed her a half of a *gulab jamun* ball. "Okay, *dikra*, just half-half. Okay? When you eat your veggies, you come back, okay?"

Hema raised her eyebrows but smiled sweetly at Esha. Taking a deep breath, she said, "Eat, then go play. Let the Mummies cook." Jyoti shoved the cake piece in her small mouth and ran upstairs without looking back.

Monisha called from the dining room to Hema. "You sit with the baby, eh? I'll mind Jyoti's lunch. Go, honey, you're tired."

Hema's shoulders went slack with relief, and she went into the dining room to give Monisha a hug. "What would I do without you?"

Esha felt pangs of jealousy hit her as she watched the two women out of the corner of her eyes.

Monisha hugged her daughter-in-law with one arm while caressing the baby's head with the other. "Hey, what would I do without you? I wouldn't have this precious baby now, would I?"

Hema rubbed her eyes with her free hand and ran her fingers through her long, shiny black hair. She wore a loose fitting blouse embroidered around the edges that her parents had brought her from India when they came for the birth, and her soft belly slightly stretched it out. The baby was already three months old, but Esha imagined that with three kids, Hema didn't have much time to care for herself and get back in shape. "Okay, I'll go nap after the baby is fed."

Ashmi piped up. "Oh, if the baby won't sleep, you just give her to me. I'll keep her." She came over and clucked her tongue and cooed in a high pitched voice to make the baby smile.

"You'll have to fight me for her." Chimed Hema's mom from the kitchen. In a few moments, the food was forgotten and all the ladies huddled around Hema's bundle.

Esha hesitated but moved in too. Her heart fluttered at the thought of holding the baby girl and the sight of her grin and sparkling eyes inside. *So beautiful. Such a lucky little girl.*

Her heart ached. Her home echoed these days, and an unwelcomed picture of Roshan in a bed, maybe some hotel room, with some woman every other night made her furious. His lust was robbing her of this kind of beauty in her life.

Hema finally loosened herself from the little mob of mothers and disappeared upstairs to nurse and nap. A couple of hours later, Esha's joints and back ached as the women set trays of sweets to set on the counter and cool in the refrigerator. Ashmi and the others went home, leaving Esha, Monisha, and Hema's mom, in the kitchen. Monisha pulled out a stainless steel saucepan and ushered the others to the kitchen table. "Go, sit. We have some chai and relax now. Our turn."

Esha's knees hurt from the standing, but she said, "No, no. I'll help." Neela, much older and grayer than the other two, sat without hesitation and let her light gauzy sari draped over the back of the chair. Esha fetched the milk from the refrigerator and the sugar from the cupboard while Monisha boiled black tea leaves. She hated to sit and hated to idly chat with people she hardly knew. But, hey, she thought, small talk is a necessary evil. She couldn't let Hema's mother go back to London and share with her relatives how rude Esha was. That would be no good at all. Not after all Neela knew about her.

"Neela, how is the family back home?" She didn't know Hema's mother well, but she knew that Neela was from a town close to the village she lived in with her husband until her and Roshan's escape. Of course Neela knew the story—word travels fast when a man dies in his own home, and his wife and child disappear, only to reappear in America. People don't speak of such things. Ever. But they never forget.

"Good. Everyone is good. My youngest daughter, Sushila, is getting engaged next month. An engineer from Surat. His family is good. From my husband's village. Asked for Sushila after a cousin's wedding the uncle saw her at. Good match we have made."

Esha kept her eyes averted from Neela, but caught a sideways smirk from Monisha on her periphery. They had heard the rumors from another relative visiting months ago from India. Again, news travels fast.

Esha wanted to blurt, "They met in a club," but kept their knowledge under the rug where it belonged.

"Congratulations. That's wonderful."

"So, Roshan good? I hear his practice is doing very well." Neela shifted in her chair and leaned forward to accept the tea cup and saucer Monisha placed on the plastic placemat in front of her. She placed her hand by the cup as Monisha poured the milky tea into the cup. *"Bas,* enough. Thank you, *ben."*

"Oh yes, very well, indeed." She bobbed her head in acknowledgment, feeling herself revert more to her Indian mannerisms as she listened to Neela's fresh thick Indian accent. "My son, he's the best." She crossed her hands across her chest in a hug and sat down at the table too.

He really is the best. I just wish he could show it.

"Your daughter-in-law? She's a doctor, no?"

Esha smiled and lifted her proud shoulders as she nodded. "Yes, oh so dedicated. She's in practice with one other doctor. Indian boy. You know Kamalben in London? I think her son-in-law is related to your *babuji* somehow, way back.

Neela nodded her head and tilted to the side. "Ah, yes."

"Anyway, the partner is Kamalben's sister's daughter. Such hard working family. It's a very good partnership."

Neela dipped a biscuit in the tea and nodded in approval. Monisha and Esha both leaned back and relaxed in their chairs. Esha poured the hot tea into her saucer and waited for it to cool. She was too full of sweets already to have a biscuit, but thanked Neela for bringing them from India because it was hard to find that brand here, even in Indian grocery stores.

From upstairs, they heard a giggle from Jyoti, pattering steps through the ceiling, and a sweet baby crying out to nurse. "Jyoti, please now, it's time to take a bath. Into the bathroom, honey." The door shutting echoed down to the kitchen, and Neela hugged herself and looked at Monisha.

"We so lucky, *ben*, no? Good girls, we've been blessed with. I so wish I could see them more often. God willing, my son will marry in the next few years and give me some grandsons in India."

Monisha sipped her tea without a nod. Esha knew she hated old fashioned attitudes about sons, but as always, she was good at biting her tongue.

Neela tilted her head toward Esha. "When does your son plan to have children? Married ten years now, no? So long and nothing?"

Monisha interrupted quickly as the thick lump formed in Esha's throat. "Neelaben, you're finished with your tea. Would you please go check on Jyoti upstairs?"

"Of course, yes." Neela stood, and lingered her eyes with expectation on Esha.

Esha reached for a biscuit, pretending to choose just the right one on the plate. When Neela was safely out of earshot, Esha grasped Monisha's hand. "Thank you."

"No, thank you. Just getting rid of her. I've seen that look on your face today. I can tell you need to talk."

Esha gripped the table's edge. "He's cheating on Priya." The air electrified her as she heard herself form those the words for the first time.

Monisha dropped her head and plunked her cup into the saucer. "Oh, Roshan. Oh. What is he doing?"

Tears sprung to Esha's eyes. She bit into a biscuit without tasting it. Monisha went on. "Oh, *ben*. I'm so sorry. I was sure he had straightened out. It's been a decade. I know things are tense at your house, but I really never suspected our Roshan would do this." She pulled out her phone and began to text her son. "I'm going to have Jayesh talk some sense into him."

Esha pulled Monisha's hand from the phone. "No, *ben*. No. I think that will push him away more. He just seems so set on living his life his way. I don't think it will make a difference."

"Do you think they will divorce? You know, our young people are getting divorces these days. It's not like when we were young anymore."

She paused and put her hand on Esha's wet cheek. "It may be the best thing for everyone."

Esha cringed at hearing the words that had already been pinballing inside her head lately. Her heart ached for him. Why was he so unhappy?

"Maybe. But I just want to know what he is looking for. What's so wrong with the way we live? Priya is such a good girl." She dropped her head and heaved a sob. "And am I such a bad mom that he would do this to me?"

Monisha said, "Esha. *Ben*. Calm down. He's always been different. Strong minded. And think about what his life is like living with his father's ghost. He is a very good boy at heart. You know that. But, he is cut from the cloth that his past made him."

Esha inhaled deeply and swallowed.

Monisha continued. "None of this was your fault. Pete and I did what we could. And you did your best."

"I want to kill the woman who is doing this with him. Who does she think she is?"

"Maybe she loves him, *Ben*. Maybe he loves this mystery woman. Maybe he will get over her. Maybe not."

Esha crumpled her napkin at her nose and wiped. "But does he love me? I'm his mother. I was here first. What will people think of us if this gets out? Of me? 'Oh, poor Eshaben, with such a son. She had no chance to raise a son without a father. We all know what happened in India. But she should have stayed for her son. It was her duty.'" She stood and collected both tea cups and made her way to the sink.

Monisha went into the TV room and came back with a framed picture of Jay and Roshan, arms around each other at a *garba* when they were in the eighth or ninth grade, just on the cusp of becoming men.

"Look at these boys. His sparkling eyes. He looks like his father, yes. But, the sparkle is because of you."

"*Ben*, I can never accept this. I want my son to be okay. He's all I've ever had."

"He will be okay. And so will you. Whatever he does, it's his path, and now you need to find your own."

"But Priya…"

"There's nothing you can do about her reputation. People are going to talk. It's beyond you. Just keep faith in God, and Roshan will do the right thing. Whichever way that turns out to be."

Esha soaped up the cups and the saucepan and let the warm water run between her fingers. Routines soothed her. Monisha was right. She did need to find her own way, and she was starting with her lessons. That was a beginning.

"Yes, Monishaben, thank you. I will take care of myself and pray that Roshan stops this nonsense."

"Listen, how about you get out of the house more and volunteer at the hospital? They are always looking for people to staff the information desk in the women's center. It would be good for you."

"Okay," Esha gladly accepted the idea and planned to call in the morning to inquire. It would be really nice to meet some new people, away from all the stress in the family, who knew nothing of her or Roshan, or who wouldn't gossip to anyone.

Monisha hugged Esha's shoulders and took the picture frame back to the TV room. "I'm going to go up and check on the girls upstairs. Jyoti usually wants me to tuck her in for her nap."

Esha said, "Go, go. I'll see myself out. Have a good evening." She rinsed the dishes and placed them in the metal rack. The sudden urge to pick up one of the cups and fling it across the room overwhelmed her, and she had to step away.

And I will pray that God will make this woman, whoever she is, just disappears. Because if I ever see her, I may spit in her face.

She knew she had to get home and pray about this. Feeling so much anger over this scared her, and if she let it go to God, maybe she could move on.

Chapter 12

Jenny

Jenny followed Roshan out of the bubbling water of the Jacuzzi tub and pulled a towel off the towel bar. Hot and flushed, the cool air tingled her dripping skin, and instead of drying herself, she wrapped the towel around Roshan and pulled him to her. Her breasts were tender from Roshan's intensity in their lovemaking, but the sensation of them pressed against his hard chest turned her on again.

"Again, you rocked my world," she whispered and nuzzled his neck.

"Likewise," he laughed and reached around her waist to squeeze her rear end. He leaned away from her and bent down to the tub's edge to grab his glass of Merlot, taking a full swig. He picked up her glass from the tub as well, and handed it to her. "To our secret one year anniversary."

They clinked glasses and he sipped, but she only let the Merlot wet her lips. The bouquet, which she usually inhaled greedily, turned her stomach tonight. Roshan nuzzled her nose, looking deeply into her eyes. "I love you."

She hated every time he said those words, because she couldn't hold back her own feelings with him.

"I love you too." The words sliced through her, because it was so pointless to say them. It just made the reality of their lives hurt that much more. She pulled away and put her full glass of wine back on the side of the tub.

"Don't like it?" he asked.

"I do, just not in the mood, I guess." Her stomach had felt a little uneasy for a few days, and her appetite for the acidic taste of the wine didn't appeal to her.

"You feeling okay? You hardly ate dinner, either." His brows furrowed at her.

She pulled away and walked over to the tub to blow out a candle. She really didn't want to talk about it. He was always so concerned for her, it made her uncomfortable sometimes. She loved and hated his attention at the same time.

"Mmmhmm. I'm fine." She had to change the subject. She turned around and beckoned him to her with her index finger. His wavy hair, now turning salt and pepper, melding with the gray of his temples, dripped onto his smooth shoulder. Even at thirty seven, the rest of him still looked like a man in his twenties. He was still the young man she knew in school, which seemed like a lifetime ago. She pulled his hands to her and stood on her tiptoes to look into his eyes. "I love our little evenings together. Mondays, Tuesdays, and Fridays were never as exciting as this a year ago. If I hadn't finally gotten up the nerve to put on that lecture at the convention, I would've missed out on all this."

"*We* would've missed out on this. You woke me up, ya know."

Me too. But I will not say it, because you're going back home to her tonight, and I'll be left here to write up my treatment plans for tomorrow. They have to be good.

She let his eyes probe hers, letting herself get lost in his stare, if only for a moment. It was a good thing he couldn't read minds.

He backed her toward the tub, kissing her the whole time, but she stumbled slightly, knocking into her wine glass from the lip of the tub.

"Oh no," she squealed as she looked over at the side of the tub. Her glass tipped over onto a rolled up towel and dripped red streaks all over the marble surrounding of the tub. "Grab my glass!" He quickly picked it up, and she started blotting the wine from the marble.

"Crap. This is going to stain. So much for my beautiful imported marble." She huffed and threw the red soaked towel into the tub in disgust.

"It's just a small spot, Jen. No one will notice. Besides, whoever sees your bathroom? Just you and me...right?"

"Ha, ha. Yes, it's just you and me. But I'm thinking resale value. I'm only planning on being in this house for another year or so. I expect to make a chunk on this house and buy something closer to the city. The commute to the office is terrible."

"It'll be fine. Relax. It will only make maybe a few hundred dollars difference in an offer. What's the big deal?"

"Every penny counts to me. I've worked hard, and I'm getting all I can."

He wrapped his arm around her naked waist and tickled her, pulling her laughing into the bedroom, throwing her onto the king-sized bed. He pinned her down and refused to let her up. "Are you going to relax?" he demanded laughing. "Huh? Are you going to chill?"

"Yes, yes. Okay. I'm chilled."

He lay down beside her, and she caught her breath again.

"Why are you so uptight about money? You've got plenty."

She paused and stared up at the ceiling. "I got a missed call on my cell yesterday from my mom. She didn't leave a message. And I didn't call her back. She's emailed me a couple of times in the past month too. Telling me how well she's doing and asking to meet me just to talk. I've tried so hard all these years not think about her or my dad and his he had shotguns and cases of Pabst Blue Ribbon on hand when he was alive. It gives me the heebie-jeebies. He's gone, but she won't go away. When I'm reminded, I get a little panicky. Does that make sense?"

"Yeah. It does. You don't want to go back there. To your old life. I get it." He turned to her. "You don't. You're here. I'm here."

She smiled at him and jokingly said, "You're right. I've got everything I need. My work, my money…and you to service my every need on Mondays, Tuesdays, and Fridays."

He was silent, and she saw his Adam's apple bob with a gulp. Then he said, "Well, I hope I am more to you than that." He pulled back a little.

"Sure," she said. Propping herself on her arm and facing him, she was suddenly aware of the goosebumps on her chilling skin. "You are more to me. We've got a good thing here."

"Jenny, do you understand that you keep me sane? Being with you makes me feel. And all I want to do is take care of you. It kills me that I can't."

"You don't need to take care of me, Roshan. I do just fine by myself." She turned her face to his, hoping he wouldn't detect what a lie that was.

"You deserve to have someone take care of you sometimes. Let me in."

Her voice came out angrier than she intended. "You do take care of me. You buy me things. But I can buy them myself. You've brought me lunch at work, you take me on vacations. Hell, you've even done loads of laundry for me when you've been here. I love you for that, I love that you want to do for me. But you shouldn't do that. You're a good man and you have a wife who you are supposed to want to 'do' for." She sat up. "And I can't let you take care of me." She dropped back down to the bed. "And I don't know why you do it. Why this keeps you sane."

He whispered, "Because you let me be me. And that makes me want to do the same for you. "

She looked over at the framed sketch of the two of them cheek to cheek. Among the deep variations in charcoal shading on their features was an identical flash of something in both of their eyes, almost as if they were reflecting one flame. Was it shared love, or shared pain?

"You are so talented, and you should be you. I'll never understand how your family could dictate your life or why. If these people love you so much, why would they stop you from following your talent?"

"You're not a son. You don't have a family. You can never understand."

As usual, tension thickened the air between them.

"I do have a family, Roshan. And maybe I'm just stronger because I walked away from them and am taking care of myself."

A vein pulsed in his temple and he replied slowly "Or, maybe I'm stronger for staying with mine and taking care of them."

Why couldn't it have been me instead of them?

They laid there stiffly next to each other. The air conditioning vent blew air onto her bare body and goose bumps covered her. She wanted a blanket but was too angry to move. Roshan's phone vibrated, and he reached to the night stand to see it.

"It's my mum. Wondering if I'm coming home tonight." He lay it back down and sat beside Jenny, pulling a pillow into his lap. She was relieved by the barrier between each other's nakedness.

"Aren't you going to reply? Maybe you should go home tonight. You do have a wife and a mom waiting for you." She wondered a little forlornly what that must feel like.

He looked at her in a way that made her cringe. Tears were welling up in his eyes, and she was afraid of any emotion that may follow them. She had just wanted that night to be fun. Not this.

"I'm asking Priya for a divorce."

Jenny sat up and just stared at him in disbelief, her mouth hanging open. Feeling suddenly exposed and self-conscious, she turned and stood up, and put on the robe that hung from a hook on the door.

"Why?" was all she could think to say.

Hurt and surprised, he stared at her. "Because, after us...this...I realized I want more in my life."

"What...what...about your mom? What about all of your Indian-ness? What about you being the stronger one for staying with them all these years?"

"I can't live with Priya and my mom anymore. I am not like other Indian guys. I guess I'm defective. I feel suffocated with them. The only time I feel like I can catch my breath even a little when I'm around them is with a stiff drink, but when I'm with you, I can really breathe. I'm not strong anymore."

Jenny's head began to spin. The ever-present nagging nausea boiled in the pit of her stomach, and she sat down on a chair by the bed. She couldn't be close to him.

"Well, what are you saying here? Are you leaving her for me?" Anger boiled under her skin, and she got up and paced around the room, trying to not look at him, trying not to vomit.

Roshan stood up and pulled his boxers and pants on. "Yes." He crossed the room to her and tried to pull her to him, but she pulled back.

"Why are you messing this up? Why would you do this?" She glared at him, holding his hurt eyes locked on hers.

"I love you. I always have."

"Well, stop! We can never be like June and Ward Cleaver."

"No, but maybe we can make it work. You're helping me see I'm over trying to live my life for my family and all of the people who judge my every move. Look…" He pulled up an email from a college art program. "I won't ever do anything with this, but I found out about some adult art classes just around the corner. I want to be me, finally." He closed out the app and put the phone down. "My family, and all the other Gujaratis in town, can accept me and us. Or they won't. But I don't care anymore."

"You don't care? What about me? Do you think you can introduce me, the white girl who led you to quit your career, to your family? 'Uncle Patel, so-and-so auntie, this is my girlfriend Jenny. I cheated on Priya with her, dropped my profession, and now I want you to like her. Oh, and by the way, her mother was a junky and her father used to hang out with people in the KKK. You'll really like them. Good family.'" With every sarcastic word, he winced as if she were striking him.

"Then, I'll leave it all. I'll buy my own house. I'll distance myself from them all. I need to be away from them, and I need to be with you. I don't want to hide anymore. I want you to be my life."

"Look, Roshan. I know you feel this way about me. And I love you in my soul. But you will never get away from your family. Just like I can't. It doesn't work that way. I've been trying for years. Families haunt and linger. Some of them are like a bad smell that clings to you that can never wash off."

Jenny stood in front of him in a stance with her feet wide, her robe loosening and falling open. She felt hardened and pulled it back together, tying it tightly. Envisioning a look of repugnance on his mother's face if she ever laid eyes on Jenny again, she wanted to hurt Roshan now for loving her. "I've been through enough rejection in my life. I'm not about to ask more people to chew me up and spit me out." She softened a moment and looked into his eyes pleading. "Can't we just go back to the way we were ten minutes ago? We were perfect that way." She wrapped the robe around her tighter and waited.

He ran his fingers through his hair and rubbed his face, fixing his eyes on the wall in front of him. He sat on the bed, a statue with a blank face, nothing in his eyes. "No. I can't go back."

She stared at the floor where her pumps lay in a corner on their sides next to his perfectly lined-up loafers.

"And I can't...do...this."

They stared at each other then, challenging the other to cave in. He took her hand and squeezed it gently. She let it hang limp.

"I'm going to go now." Slipping on his clothes and placing his wallet in his pocket, he walked past her, pausing at the door. "You know how to get in touch with me if you change your mind."

Suddenly, concern for him overpowered her fury, and she called out, "Are you sober enough to drive?" She had been noticing he was drinking a lot more when they were together and was worried about both him and herself lately. Even before her stomach issues began, she had been weaning herself from so much drinking, feeling how easy it was becoming to slip into a problem, but he kept drinking.

"Yeah. I'm fine." He gave her a thumbs up and walked out and down the stairs.

She stood in the room staring at her mahogany poster bed and listened as the front door shut quietly. Tears flowed, and a growl grew in her throat. She heard the purring engine of his newest BMW, and then it roared, followed by the shriek of tires burning rubber on the road.

Anger and emptiness overwhelmed her, boiling up in her stomach. She nearly didn't make it to the toilet before her pain and her dinner erupted out of her gut. As she wiped her mouth with toilet paper with one hand and held her stringy wet hair out of her face with the other, she asked herself what she had done.

He was the only loving man in her life who really knew her.

And he's gone.

She gagged again and again until there was nothing left to come up. When she'd cleaned herself up and curled up in her bed, she needed to call someone to talk. Not Bryan. His happiness made her feel even emptier. She scrolled her finger down the contact list. There were numbers for equipment reps, specialists she referred patients to, and her employee's home numbers. The office staff were only casual friends, if you could even call that friendship at all. They all talked to each other about their husbands and kids, and how their mothers babysat their kids while they worked.

She had no friends. She had no mother to call. She had no one.

She crawled under the down-filled duvet her decorator had custom designed and squeezed her arms around herself. Gripping the phone in her hand, she suddenly remembered the missed call from her mother the day before and in a moment of desperation, pulled up the number and poised her finger to dial it. Instead, she pulled the duvet over her head and focused on the expensive raw silk on her skin.

As the numbness of sleep overtook her, the phone dropped from her hand, and she fell into blissful oblivion.

The next morning, her arms felt lifeless. After her shower she dried her hair, curled it, put on her makeup. The pit in her stomach pulsated, threatening to explode at any moment. But, breathing through her nose got her through the feeling, and two cups of coffee gave her extremities a surge of energy. She would be able to get through the day, she told herself. Before she left the office the day before, she had reviewed the schedule for today and knew there were a lot of procedures on the books. She knew she would have to make an extra effort to connect with the patients today because all she wanted to do was to crawl in a hole and cry.

She cranked up the radio talk show in the car on the way to the office, angrily cut people off, and cursed at stupid drivers in downtown traffic. The morning was mild and breezy, and she thought about putting the top down on the car, hoping to feel some comfort in the wind on her skin. She thought better of it when a driver, apparently disgusted with her rude driving, stopped abruptly in front of her and flipped her the bird, not allowing her to move forward while all the other cars on the highway inched along on both sides of them. Feeling safer in the confines of the closed car, she mouthed "sorry" to the driver and smiled apologetically to appease him, all the while hoping he would not get out of his car and come after her. She flipped her hair back and smiled a little flirtatiously, which had helped her get out of tickets in the past. Maybe it would work now. He finally relented, and she went about the rest of her drive using proper turn signals and avoiding eye contact with other drivers. She realized that the world didn't stop because her heart was broken, and she just had to get on with her day. Finally she turned on to one of the dozen Peachtree streets in the city and parked at her office building. Once inside, she told herself to suck it up and put on her poker face.

"Good morning, Doctor J," Amanda hummed as she rifled through sheets of insurance printouts on her front desk.

"Hey. Good morning," Jenny mumbled, avoiding eye contact as she made her way to the back to her private office. Even seeing other people was painful.

Amanda got on the phone and started talking in a motherly voice. "Honey, just calm down. It'll be okay. Missing the bus is not the end of the world. Daddy will take you to school on his way to work. Stop crying."

The tenderness in Amanda's voice tugged jealousy from inside Jenny. Before she shut the door, she paused and tortured herself to listen.

"Hey baby. Ashley missed the bus again. Thanks for being there for her...and me. I love you. Have a good day."

Jenny shut the door and sat at her desk with her face in her hands.

The nauseous pang swirled in her stomach again as Roshan flashed through her mind, threatening to send her to the bathroom, but it passed soon. She flipped her lab coat around her shoulders, sliding her arms into the sleeves, ready to tackle her patients. The black and white of clinical decisions, the exhilaration of sliding a scalpel into gums, and the vibration of her hand piece between her fingers would distract her. She would be in control again, and that energized her.

The morning went by in a blur until she took a water break a few hours later. Despite her focus on the work, the sad feeling in her stomach persisted. She needed to sit down for a moment and retreated to her office as her last patient before lunch waited for her in the chair.

"You okay?" Amanda asked, sympathy in her voice, as she peeked in to the office.

"Yeah." Jenny sucked in air as she leaned forward in her chair covering her mouth. She was holding her cellphone in her hand, focusing on reading the words on a Facebook message that had just pinged, anything to distract her mind.

Amanda approached her and asked, "Okay. You sure? By the way, my little boy is having a Mother's Day luncheon at his preschool, and I'd like to get over there for a couple hours. I don't know if you remembered me telling you about it last week. I hope that's okay?"

Already only half listening to Amanda, she completely tuned her voice out as she read the message that popped up, with a tiny profile picture of a woman with frizzy bangs in her face.

Wanda

Hi Jenny. It's Wanda. Your mom.

Going to a Bible study at a church near your office today.

Googled you to find out the address. Please say I can stop by.

Before Jenny could answer, she felt acidic coffee and water rush up her throat, she had to ran to the toilet in her private office bathroom. Amanda watched her from the bathroom door. Feeling better after emptying her liquid breakfast, she brushed her teeth and smoothed her lab coat without looking at Amanda.

"Okay, better. Time to get to work." She flashed a confident look at Amanda and strode shakily toward the door.

Amanda stopped her with a worried look. "You can get through this next one, doc. It's just a filling, you aren't going to lose it while you're in his mouth, are you?'

"No. I'm fine," she asserted with irritation while also aware of how green her face must look. Dismissing Amanda's skeptical look, she rounded the corner of the operatory. She hadn't even asked who the patient was. She pulled the file from the tray and looked at it as she entered. Before she read the name, she heard a man's voice.

"Hey, good looking." Bryan lay in the chair and beamed up at her. When he saw the swollen eyes and pale tone of her skin, he reached out from the chair and gave her a hug. "You okay, honey?" He grabbed her hand and held strong. His concern made her want to cry.

"Hey, you. Wow. I'm glad to see you." His happy glow warmed her cold lingering sadness. She missed Roshan already. She still kept her mouth shut. She couldn't let him pity her.

"I thought I'd surprise you. You're always working. I just figured finally getting a damn tooth filled is the only way I'll get to see you. That's how much I miss you!" He glanced at Amanda, who Jenny saw out of the corner of her eyes touch her stomach and mouth the word "sick" to him. As

Amanda nodded and politely slipped out of the room, he picked up her hand and asked her quietly, "What's going on, honey? Sick?"

Jenny's brick-strong façade collapsed, and her eyes welled with tears. Just the touch from her best friend dissolved her resolve. "Where do I start?" She looked him in the eye and tried to keep it together, but the tears fell. "It's over with Roshan," she whispered.

"Oh, I'm sorry, honey." Pausing, then going on. "You knew it had to eventually, didn't you?"

"I guess I'd hoped not."

"Really? You? What about our conversations about his family? Aren't you the girl who can tough it alone?"

She glared at him. He was the closest thing to a brother, and he was the only one she could let talk to her like that.

"I know I'm an ice queen."

"Well," the softness of his voice tempered his words, "like I told you, many, many times, you can't expect to keep people at arm's length and think they'll be happy with that. I only put up with you because I loved you before you really got fucked up." He nudged her arm, laughing softly, and she smiled.

"Thanks a lot." Her shoulders relaxed, and she looked him in the eye. "And to top it all off, I'm afraid. My mom keeps emailing me. Today she texted. She's found the office and wants to come see me. What do I do? Part of me wants to rip her hair out, but another part of me actually wants to see her. What's wrong with me?"

"Nothing. You're human. Whether you want to admit it or not. And my mom told me last time I called her that your mom is working in some church-based addiction recovery place here. Like a counselor or something. Sounds like she may have actually straightened up."

She looked at him like he was crazy.

He went on. "You need people, Jen. Roshan, your mom. Everyone is fucked up. So are you. Just let someone in. Even a little."

She began to wipe her tears and motioned for him to sit back in the chair. "You don't know what it's like to be so scared of people."

He didn't move, looking at her like she was an idiot and said, "You're right. I've had it easy the whole way. You think I wasn't afraid when I met Craig? You and I both come from the same stock, remember? Do you think you have the corner on the market for dysfunction? You're a white woman in love with an Indian man, okay? I'm a man in love with a man. Neither is exactly embraced by the world. But, life is scary. But you don't get anything out of it if you cower inside these walls here. Let someone in, will you?"

"Alright, enough about me. " She wiped her eyes and pushed him back in the chair. She was done talking. It was time to get back to her comfort zone. "Let's get on with this. Scared?" she smiled as she washed her hands and gloved up. She wanted control now. And this was the only to do it. Bryan looked over at her with feigned fright, squinting at the bright lamp shining in his face.

"Any last words?" She tried to sound light.

"Yeah," he laughed nervously. "Be gentle. I'm the only friend you've got right now."

"You're right, honey." She kissed him on the forehead, placed the nitrous oxide mask on his nose and got to work.

An hour later, when she hugged Bryan goodbye, he mumbled through his numb lips, "Come to our cocktail party this Saturday. Craig is cooking and I'm watching. It'll be good for you."

Craig came from the waiting room to pick up Bryan for a shopping date. He hugged Jenny too and told her that she'd better come to help him keep an eye on Bryan. "He'll probably be on painkillers and have a martini in his hand as usual. We may need some professional supervision," he whispered over Bryan's shoulder.

"Oh, he'll be fine! He's just a big chicken and won't be in that much pain. Just throw some Tylenol at him. But, I'll be there anyway."

She went back into the office to gather her things for her lunch break. She wouldn't be able to eat much of anything, but she could use the break. Maybe she would ask the staff to eat with her. At least it would be some company.

For the next few days, she worked intensely morning and afternoon, pushing for Amanda to put more patients on the books. She wanted no time to think. She paid for staff lunches just to have them with her and hear conversations to keep thoughts at bay. Later in the week, she had to lunch alone because everyone had errands to run during their breaks. As she walked through the front door of the office toward her car by herself, a squat woman caught her eye. Her back was to the door, and she was looking out at the traffic on the busy downtown street. She shifted from foot to foot and dragged on a cigarette nervously. Her blonde streaked red hair was styled in a bob, and she wore black slacks, a white sweater, and comfortable shoes. Not the typical image of her well-to-do patients.

The woman turned on a dime. When she made eye contact with Jenny, she smiled nervously and dropped her cigarette to the concrete, grinding it with her cheap shoe. "Hey," she said nervously, looking away from Jenny's face.

"Wanda?" Jenny was in shock at the sight of her mother in front of her. In the flesh.

"I'm sorry to just come here. I don't want to make you mad. I just…I just wanted to see you. Thinking maybe if you saw me, you'd see how good I'm doing for real this time."

Jenny's belly rumbled, hungry and sour from the morning, and her first reaction was to bolt to her car and get food before she vomited right there at Wanda's feet. Not this today of all days. The swirl of stress and unwelcome emotion stirred around in her stomach. But she stood still. Afraid to leave.

"You've certainly been persistent. I have to give you that." Jenny's voice was flat.

"I know. I'm sorry. Your dad gave me your email address years ago, but I guess it changed, huh? Thanks be to Jesus for Facebook messages, or I'd a never been able to talk to you. Before, your daddy died, when I seen him at the grocery store, he even says to me he was glad he seen me. He said to me I was looking good."

Jenny appraised her mother and had to agree. "Yeah. You do look good." Her hair was nicely colored, her makeup was more subtle than she'd ever worn it, and her conservative sweater covered her bust, which she had so garishly displayed in the past. "You look like a whole new person. I guess church work is good for you."

"Yeah. Yeah. It is. And it looks like being a doctor is really good for you. You're so beautiful. You always were. But look at this building. Look at your clothes. Is that your car out there?" she gestured to the Mercedes convertible that just chirped when Jenny pushed the button on her remote. Jenny's instinct was to lie and keep walking. Instead she just smiled and said nothing as she walked toward it, hoping to send Wanda a hint that she was in a hurry. "Well, baby doll, I'm glad to see you're doing good. That's what I always wished for."

Wanda stayed on the sidewalk and watched Jenny move close to her car. Droplets of rain began to splat on their heads, changing quickly to fast pelting drops.

"It was good to see you, Jenny." Wanda called from the sidewalk. She looked as it rained, holding her arms as if to protect herself from the water.

Jenny got into her car and backed up, ready to speed off away from this overloading day. But in her rearview mirror, she saw her mother hunker her head down against the rain and walk slowly toward the bus stop across the street. Feeling pity, and remembering Bryan's words, she pulled up beside Wanda and rolled down the passenger window. "Get in!"

The grateful look on Wanda's face softened Jenny's twenty-year old stance against her mother, but she felt at a complete loss of what to say once she jumped in to the car.

"Thanks."

"Sure. No problem." After a moment, as she merged into the slowing traffic, she thought to ask where she should drop her off.

"Oh, just at the MARTA station. That'll be fine. Thanks. I think I saw a small place where I'll grab a bite for lunch and head back to the home. I've got a big new group I'm working with today and really gotta get ready for it."

Acutely aware that the staff was probably having lunch and gossiping together somewhere, and Roshan was at his office across town and wouldn't be coming to her house tonight, or any other night anymore, she blurted out, "I'm going for lunch too. Maybe...do you...want to eat together?"

"Uh, yeah. Sure." Wanda smiled at the unexpected invitation.

Jenny didn't know why she said it, but there was no going back now. *Am I that lonely?*

"There's a little bistro on the corner down the road. Let's go there." She'd never been there before. Hopefully she wouldn't run into anyone she knew.

There was silence the rest of the ride until they entered the doors of the bistro.

After ordering, Jenny looked out the window at passersby with umbrellas, reflexively ready to duck if she saw a familiar face walk by.

She asked, "Where are you living?"

"I'm at an extended stay hotel right now. I'm looking for a one bedroom, but I can't find any place close to work that I can afford. Gotta save for a car, too."

Jenny drummed her fingers on the table and gritted her teeth as Wanda spoke. Grinding her teeth was a bad habit, and she tried to relax and be open to what her mother had to say.

Jenny took a sip of her water and looked at her mother. Unsure of where to take the conversation from this point, she commented on Wanda's hair style.

"It's nice. Different from the perm you had last time I saw you. And the reddish color is good. Makes you look younger."

"Thanks, Jenny. That's nice of you to say." Wanda looked around nervously and pulled her purse to her lap, resting her hands on it. Jenny noticed a small diamond ring on her left hand.

"Engaged?"

Smiling a bit shyly, Wanda said, "Yes. James. He's a peer counselor at the same mission I work at. He's a lot like me. Jesus saved him too."

"Oh," Jenny said, biting her tongue. Fellow peer counselor meant James was a recovering addict himself. "Good for you. When's the wedding?"

"No date. He's on probation right now, so we're gonna wait and see how things go with that." Wanda grabbed her cup of coffee right from the waitress's tray and took a big swig, glancing at the middle aged woman walking by, who wore skinny jeans with rhinestones on the back pockets and a tight sweater that displayed her perfect breasts. Wanda straightened her sweater and scratched her nose, then looked at Jenny with a smile. "How about you? Anyone special in your life?"

Although Jenny knew that this question would come, she still had to gulp down a lump in her throat before she answered. "No. No one."

"That's too bad. You're so beautiful and doing good. I'd a thought you'd have yourself another doctor or some lawyer begging you to marry him."

A slug hit Jenny's heart, and she had to look away before tears could form in her eyes. "Hmmm. That doesn't mean I'd want to marry him. I don't exactly come from a stable family. Maybe I'm just a little afraid to get into..."

Wanda finished the sentence for her. "Anything bad."

At that moment, Jenny spied Bryan across the street entering a baby store with Craig. Taken aback, she remarked to Wanda that she saw him.

"Really?" Wanda looked around with reserved excitement but turned back around when she didn't see him. "I haven't seen him since his daddy's funeral."

"You were there?" Jenny had sat behind Bryan at the service a few years back and did not have view of who else came in behind them.

"Yeah. In the back. I was afraid to say 'hey' to you. But I waited around outside until you left and then talked to Bryan and his mom. She's a good woman." A distant look came over her. "His mom and me used to be friends. We used to walk you and Bryan together in strollers when you was babies. But she was so much older than me. Kinda lost interest in hanging out with a fifteen year old complainin' about having a baby."

"So you found other friends?"

At those words, Wanda looked up at the ceiling and gulped. "Yeah. I did."

Jenny wanted to say so many things. She hated her and wanted her to know it. But, at the same time, she could handle no more feelings right now. She just shook her head and looked at the menu.

Wanda filled the silence. "You know, I have a better friend now. Jesus. He's been good to me and showed me how to be good to myself now."

"Good for you, Wanda." Jenny mustered a tinge of sincerity. "I've heard Jesus is one of the good guys."

"I don't want to get personal, but do you know Jesus?"

Jenny replied tersely, "Mmmhmm. I know who he is."

"Do you pray?"

"I used to. But I learned the only one who's going to make my wishes come true is me."

Wanda opened her mouth to respond, but Jenny put up her hand. Wanda backed off.

"I'm going to text Bryan and let him know we're here. Maybe he'll come say 'hi.'" Jenny was anxious to show Bryan that she was making an effort. And he was the only person she knew in the world that she would allow herself to be seen with her mother. As far as anyone else in her life was concerned, except for Roshan, she was an orphan. But then again, Roshan wasn't in her life anymore.

Over salad and soup, the two women chatted quietly about the weather and anything else they could come up with that meant nothing at all. Jenny's belly settled with the food. And she was able to feel slightly normal again. Right before Jenny placed the last forkful of Cobb salad into her mouth, Bryan appeared at their table with a crooked smile of welcome on his face, half of his mouth still slack from the Novocain. But his eyes looked happy and alert. He lay his hand on Wanda's shoulder and bent down to hug Jenny.

"Hi, Wanda. Good to see you. I heard you were living in town."

"Good to see you too, Bryan." She turned to the tall, slightly chubby red-headed man beside Bryan and held out her hand to him.

"I'm Wanda. Jenny's mom."

Craig shook her hand and said, "I've heard all about you. Nice to finally meet you."

"Well, I know what you've heard. But I hope to everyone forgets those stories these days." She laughed a gritty laugh and looked from Bryan to Craig. "So do you two work together?"

Bryan touched Craig's hand briefly and said matter-of-factly, "Wanda, Craig is my husband."

Wanda cleared her throat at the sight and shifted in her seat. "Oh."

An uncomfortable silence fell over the table, and Jenny spoke up. "Bryan, why were you guys going into that store? Are you...?"

"Yes! We just found out yesterday from the adoption attorney. We have the green light from China." He and Craig looked at each other with joy in their eyes. "It'll only be a few more months now."

"That's great!" Jenny exclaimed, forcing a happy song to her voice. The look on Bryan and Craig's faces changed from joy to sympathetic when they both seemed to realize she was still very much in mourning about Roshan and very lonely.

Jenny noticed that Wanda looked on the conversation, surveying Craig up and down, obviously ignoring what they were saying. Her nose turned up in disgust.

"Hey, Bryan, do you still go to a Southern Baptist church? I remember ya'll went to Poplar Street or Central Baptist years ago when you was growin' up. You still keeping Jesus close?"

Unphased, Bryan sighed, "No and yes, Wanda. Craig and I actually are members of a non-denominational congregation now. It's very welcoming. As you can expect, we looked for a church home with people who are tolerant and loving. You should come sometime."

"Hmm," she sniffed, then apparently realized how rude she was coming off, smiling politely. "I appreciate the offer, but I'm real happy with my little Bible-based church. All I'm concerned with is the Word. Don't matter to me what other people say God meant. If it's in writing, I don't argue with it."

Speechless, Bryan's mouth dropped open a bit, and he glanced at Craig, whose face said to Bryan to let just let it go.

Bryan turned to Jenny cheerily and said, "Hey, listen. I didn't get the chance to tell you in the office because I was so out of it, but this baby is the reason for the party we are having Saturday. Why don't you come celebrate with us? It may raise your spirits." He glanced at Wanda, as if he wasn't sure that she knew anything about Jenny's loss. "And Wanda, you come too." Jenny knew it was only a polite invitation, but still held her breath hoping the answer would be no. She was not disappointed.

"Thanks, Bryan. I don't drink. Besides, I got no car. I'm betting you don't live close enough to me for me to walk to. Do you and Jenny live near each other?"

Bryan started to answer, but Jenny cut him off. "Where is that waitress? I need the check. I have patients in ten minutes." There was no way she was going to let Wanda know where she lived. Baby steps in this thing.

Wanda seemed to take the hint and pulled out her wallet, tossing some wadded up bills onto the table, then embarrassed, smoothed them out.

"I'd better be going. Thanks for bringing me to lunch and keeping me dry. It looks like it's just misting now, so I'm going to head to catch the MARTA."

Jenny nodded as Bryan and Craig hugged Wanda softly. Wanda stood awkwardly by Jenny's side, and Jenny stayed still.

"Okay, then. It was good to see you," Wanda said. "I hope to do it again. Maybe soon?"

"Yeah. Maybe."

Bryan and Craig watched Wanda as she left. The waitress finally showed up with the check, and Jenny left more cash on the table.

"Shall we?" Bryan gestured toward the door.

"Yes, we shall." Jenny walked behind the two men. Craig extended his hand toward Bryan's but Bryan pulled his back and put his hand in his pocket. Craig's face hardened and Jenny felt like a fight may be coming on.

Bryan had always told her that he kept public displays of affection with Craig at a bare minimum which infuriated Craig. But Bryan was still afraid. He always told Jenny to be true to herself, but had a hard time with that philosophy himself. But at least he was happy with Craig when they were together. They had each other.

She wished she could have that with Roshan. She wished she were strong enough to take on his love at the promise that he could handle his family, and they could be together despite others. But she watched out the window as her mother walked down the street with her purse covering her against the rain. Maybe things could get better. If the person who'd hurt her most in her life could want her, then maybe there was hope that other people might also. Just maybe.

The next few mornings when she rose from bed, she fought hard to hold onto the dreams about Roshan lying next to her. But as clarity filled her, the familiar nausea of grief would overwhelm her and send her to the bathroom. By the fourth morning of this, she broke down and texted him. She just needed the physical release from all of it. If she could just see some words from him, perhaps she could eat again.

Jenny
Thinking of you. I miss you and
I'm sorry things turned out like this.

She waited with the phone in her hand for a response, but one never came.

She wanted to feel his skin next to hers again. She wanted to feel his breath on her neck. And most of all, she wanted to connect with him again, like they did when they stared into each other's eyes. Despite what she told herself—or him—their lovemaking wasn't just sex. It was intense, and sometimes careless and spontaneous, but all she wanted was to be with him. She wanted to feel him take care of her again.

Suddenly, a replay of a night six weeks ago weeks ago popped into her head. They had escaped for a weekend to Las Vegas under the guise of a continuing education course, and there was wine, there was an elevator with no one else in it. She wore a short skirt that night. So easy. He lifted her skirt and turned her around so her back was to him. With both palms spread on the wall in front of her, like a criminal being punished, she took all he had to give her. It was fast and fun, but she messed up taking her birth control pills on schedule during the trip. Picturing the calendar in her head it hit her that she was at the fertile time in her cycle then.

Oh, shit. I've been so stupid.

She threw on sweats and tennis shoes and ran to her car, speeding to the corner drugstore. "Oh shit, oh shit, oh shit," rolled out of her mouth the entire way until she checked out with a pregnancy test and ran to the back of the store toward the public restroom. When the second blue line on the stick lit up brightly, she held her breath so long she had to gasp for air. She picked up her cellphone shakily and dialed the office. She would not be seeing patients today.

On her way out of the bathroom, she tossed the stick into the trash can by the store, struggling to see through a fog. She needed to call Bryan but was too weak right now to bear his reprimands. She knew she and Roshan had screwed up badly, and Bryan would certainly tell her. And oh, God, could she keep this baby? How could someone like her possibly be a good mother? At the thought of mothers, the long ago vision of Esha in Roshan's apartment kitchen staring at her popped into her mind, and Wanda at lunch the other day, and sweat started beading on her brow.

She felt the sting of being unwanted by mothers. Could she bring a baby into this world knowing the same thing would happen to it? But, how could she not?

Suddenly she realized it was *her* baby. And it was Roshan's baby.

I want it.

Chapter 13

Roshan

Priya sat on the edge of the bed, staring at Roshan with hatred burning her eyes. "You. Want. A. Divorce," she stated, shaking her head.

He stood in front of her and rubbed his hands over his face, waiting.

"After eleven years, you decide you are not…happy." She got up and walked around the room, pacing and angrily repeating, "You are not happy. You want a divorce. Because *you* are not happy."

Her bloodshot eyes darted around the room, and he hoped they wouldn't land on him. She looked so tiny in her flowered night gown, and he wanted to pull her to him to comfort her. He cared about her enough to want to absorb some of the anger from her and wanted to breathe in the soft scent of her face cream one last time. But he was afraid of the anger already inside him that he couldn't quite explain, and he knew better than to take on more. He didn't know how it would come out. So, he just focused his eyes on the stitching across the floral quilt on their bed. One stitch was fraying, and he pulled it up between his fingers, waiting, hoping for the heat to subside.

He had known this moment would not be easy, but seeing the lines on her forehead and slits in her eyes as her face got more and more flushed was harder than he'd pictured in his mind on those long drives from Jenny's house late at night.

"Happiness? That's a novel concept, isn't it?" She stopped in her tracks and faced him, hands clenched in front of her. "In love? Were your parents in love? My parents don't even sleep in the same bed anymore. But they are married. They take care of each other I need them to be married. What would Tushar and I do if they weren't together? How would I choose one family over another?"

"Priya," he motioned toward her, but she flapped her arms in front of her to keep him away. He stopped, but said, "Priya, I care about you. Like a sister. But we don't have kids. And that's a good thing. There won't be any choosing."

She glared at him. "No choosing? What about your mum? She's been my mum for eleven years now. For better or worse. Our families are supposed to be one family, Roshan." She took a step toward him, eyes still focused upon him, then added very slowly, accentuated every word, "Remember when we first got married, that night on the beach, and you promised would always keep me from harm? You looked me in the eye and told me you loved me." She pointed two fingers at her own eyes and then his. "Liar." The word choked her, and she looked all over the room as if trying to find some kind of answers in the lamp shades or crystal chandelier hanging from the vaulted ceiling above their bed.

"I didn't lie. I tried to tell you—" He slapped his hand on the bed and spilled a little from his glass of Jack and Coke, soaking brown splotches into the fabric. Sitting the glass on the bedside table, he shook more drips off his hand, forming a blurred brown flower on the spread beside him.

"My parents gave me to you. There is no going back for me."

"Priya. We have nothing together. We have sex sometimes in the dark. We don't even see each other in the daylight."

Emotionless, she retorted, "You're never home when I am, Roshan." She looked him dead on and stated, "You're sleeping with someone."

Without moving, he said, "I want more. I feel myself becoming my dad. Anger at the smallest things here." He held a swig of the burning drink in his mouth for a moment, then swallowed hard. "Want more. I don't want to be him. We have no kids. Let's just end this before we tangle up more people into my problems."

She cackled. The anger boiling up in him at the sound of her bitter laugh scared him.

"So, it's not me, it's you."

He nodded and sipped from the Jack and Coke again. His liquid control. Or would he lose it? He leaned his back against the headboard and watched her, happily feeling his eyes droop and scalp tingle.

"Is she worth it?"

"She was."

"Was?"

"I'm not involved with her anymore."

"No? Then why a divorce? Why do this to me and your mum? What are you going to find away from me?"

"She made me feel free, Priya. And I don't want to lose that feeling."

Priya erupted, "You can't do it anymore?" She crawled onto the bed on all fours and set on him like a wild animal, her hot breath in his face. "I work long days and nights! I come home to my mother-in-law! When I'm home, I cook, I go visiting our friends, to your family's houses. I make excuses for you—even with your mum—when you are gone for prayers. I am the one who keeps your ties with your, with *our*, community! What about my life? Do you think I am happy sleeping in a cold bed? Do you think I am happy being married to your mum?"

"Shhh, Mum will hear you."

"Let her hear. There's no secrets anymore, right?"

Her stare dared him to move. Her bared teeth and sheer loathing in her eyes fueled a wild feeling inside him. No woman has ever talked to him like this. He wanted to slap her, to shut her up. He didn't want to hear her truth. And he didn't want his mum to hear it and hate him even more for it.

Carefully keeping his fists at his side, he slid away from her and walked around the room, pacing by the window, opening and closing the edge of the curtain as he looked out with his back to Priya. He wanted out of there. The fluttering bugs under the streetlight outside the house zoomed in and out, and he wanted to be out there alone in the still of the darkness, listening to the hush of the world.

Their door was shut, but he could hear the loud TV program turn off downstairs, and the shuffle of footsteps up the stairs outside of their room that stopped outside of the door.

Dammit, Mum, please just stay out of this.

"Tell your family it's my fault. Let them hate me," he whispered over his shoulder, eyes still fixed outside.

"Oh, they will. Your father's reputation preceded you. My uncle warned my dad about you. He should've listened." Priya stood and walked over to him and gently turned him to face her, placing her hands on his arms. "I guess it's not your fault."

He wasn't sure if her fury was deflated or she was luring him into a false calm. For a moment, he wanted to put his arms around her.

"You're right. Your dad should have listened. I am no good. I never have been. The apple doesn't fall far from the tree."

Catching him off guard, Priya pushed him backward into the window knocking the floor lamp next to it into the wall with a thump. She began to sob loudly into her hands, and he grabbed her by the arms.

"Shhhh. Please."

The door to the room opened slowly, and Esha appeared in her nightgown.

Roshan stood with the two women he was sworn to care for his whole life gawking at him in disbelief and heartbreak. All he could think to do was release Priya, grab his glass and down the whole thing without looking around the room. They all stood in silence as he swallowed, and for a blissful moment, he pretended it was just him and his drink in the room. His skin was comfortably buzzing finally, and his scalp was numbing. Just like he liked it. He looked into the bottom of his empty glass and laughed. "Oh well." He said to himself. "There's another bottle in my closet." Then he turned to the door and shuffled toward his mum. He put his arm around her and asked, "Did you know that, Mummy? I love you too much to keep the booze out. But, tonight, unfortunately, we're pulling out all of our skeletons."

Priya stood watching him, and he smelled her fury in the air. But, he didn't care. He couldn't care anymore.

Go ahead, please hate me. I deserve it.

"Roshan...you're a good boy. Don't do this." Esha reached up and ran her hand across his face and his hair just as she did when he was a child. He let her do it for a moment but grabbed her hands gently to stop them. Her eyes pleaded with him, and guilt swallowed his muddled mind, bringing tears to his eyes.

Priya snapped the moment in half. "Oh, it's done. He can go find a whore to shack up with. He wants freedom? Well, he'll have freedom from me, my family, and everyone who knows me once word gets out about his fling. Like father like son, they'll say. I'll be damned if I'm going to let society pin the blame on me for this!" She faced Esha and declared, "Mummy, I'm sorry. I have tried here. But, your son is the rubbish that people said he was. I'm so sorry for you."

"How dare you speak to me like that," Esha spat back.

"Why? Are you on my side? Will you be on my side when people gossip? He's your precious son." Priya's eyes glared red and swollen at both of them. "And you two belong together."

Roshan instinctively stepped in front of his mum, backing her out into the hall as if his body could protect her from words. "Do not speak to my mum like that."

"She's not anything to me anymore. And neither are you." Priya went to the door to the master bathroom and stood poised to shut the door.

"By the way, Roshan. Living with you lowlife must have rubbed off on me these last years. I can honestly say I never thought once about you last week when I was in bed with Chirag. He takes care of more than business at our office, he—"

Furious, he flew at Priya, fist held high. All he saw was blurred red as he hurled toward her, wanting nothing more than to shut that mouth. With terror on her face, she tried to slam the door before he could get to her, but he pushed it open, knocking her to the floor. Esha came up behind him and pulled him back, but his anger possessed him. He shoved her, and sent her stumbling backward. She cried out. That cry jerked him back into his body, and he suddenly looked in front of him.

On the floor, Priya crouched frozen on her hands and knees, shielding her head. Her long hair was a tangled mess, touching the floor in snarls across the black and white imported travertine marble tiles that they had so meticulously chosen when they built the house. His fingers clenched so hard his whole hand ached, and he turned around to find his mother.

She leaned against the wall with one hand on her chest and the other across her mouth. Her wrinkled eyes bored into him, pleading. He remembered how scared he was as a child when those same eyes looked up at his daddy, before his daddy's fists closed them.

He stepped into the bathroom and looked at himself in the mirror. His hair was the same, his clothes were the same, but his eyes were the eyes of a monster. They were the eyes of his father. Disgusted, he spun around several times inside the bathroom, ready to kill himself, ready to run, ready to hurt something. As he spun toward the glass shower door, the urge to punch something overwhelmed him, and he smashed his fist through the glass.

Priya and Esha covered their faces and ran shrieking in opposite directions.

Roshan's eardrums shattered with the echoes of screams and exploding glass, slicing into the skin and muscles in his hand and forearm, smashing all over the marble floor. He sat down and crossed his legs like he did in grammar school and stared at the blood pulsing out of him. A long, icicle-shaped shard stuck out of the top of his knuckle, and he left it there, enough of his medical wits about him told him he might bleed out if he pulled it out. He didn't move while he heard Priya call 911 or when his mum cautiously returned from another bathroom with towels to wrap around him. He heard her cry out in pain as she cut her foot when stepping into the bathroom to cover his arm, and he thought she smiled while caressing his hair until help came.

The last thing Roshan remembered before he blacked out was being strapped to a stretcher with his right arm secured to a board elevated above him. Priya's sobs faded into the background as the paramedics lifted the stretcher and awkwardly maneuvered him down the stairs and into the ambulance. His mum rode in the passenger seat with the driver, and he heard her soft sobbing prayers as the morphine mixed with the alcohol in his blood, carrying him away into nothingness as the frozen image of the shattered door that would never be put back together again faded.

The next afternoon he awakened from surgery and later found himself sitting up in the hospital bed, wearing only a loosely tied cotton gown, feeling foolish, ashamed, and depressed. The plastic tubing that dripped antibiotics into his vein had been annoying him, and he had the urge to pull it out. He fingered it occasionally, contemplating the scenario if he did. Free of the entanglement, he'd then be dripping blood again. He'd had enough of that.

He looked around the sparsely decorated room. The lights were dimmed, a vase of flowers sat on the table next to him, and a tray on the other side held his Styrofoam cup and the straw Esha had held to his lips to help him sip cranberry juice as he'd gradually come out of his medicated stupor. Fuzzy images of her and Monisha Auntie, talking in hushed voices, sometimes mouthing prayers with *mala* beads in hand, sitting in the chair and standing by his bed sometimes at night, sometimes in early morning light.

The TV was on but muted, and in the corner, covered by a white woven blanket, laid Jay reclined in a chair. His soft snores and the occasional sound of wheels rolling down the hall outside were the only sounds.

He slowly reached for his cellphone on the table beside his cup and began to scroll down his list of contacts. There were hundreds. With each one, he asked himself who he was to that person: business associate, colleague, employer. Mixed in between a couple of Johnsons and Smiths was a long list of Patels and Desais. Rima, Kishor, Anjeli, his aunties and uncles, and at least a dozen more. All family of some relation or another. At the Diwali celebrations he used to go to, he'd see Rima and Praful. Roshan had shown up in khakis and a polo and made small talk with them as they shimmered in their Indian clothes, immersed in the celebration of the Indian festival of lights and the subsequent new year. He knew their spouses' names and whose families they were close to, but he didn't know what they liked to eat for dinner or what kind of music they listened to. They were no one he could call here and now. The only person who would follow him now was Jay, his best friend, his cousin, his true brother. And he was already standing by him.

Jay's face was slack, and he looked as young as he did when they were in high school. Relaxed. He mumbled and moved to one side. Years ago, Roshan would've tossed something onto him—maybe aimed for his mouth—to rouse him, but now, as he watched his brother, he felt such shame that he just wanted to disappear and never be seen again.

He was bad. He had no wife, his mum and the rest of his family would no doubt kick him out of their lives. Why wouldn't they? He had no idea why Jay was here. How could he still be here for Roshan after what Roshan had done to Priya and his mum? Worst of all, he had no Jenny. He missed her. He needed her. He wanted her.

He had ignored her last text, and he wondered if she would speak to him again. With nothing left to lose in this life, he dialed her number.

"Hello? This is Dr. Jenkins." Her voice was slurred, thick, sleepy.

He looked at the clock. It was four thirteen in the morning. "It's me. Roshan."

"Oh. I didn't look at the caller ID. Wow. Why are you calling me? Now?"

"I just needed to hear you. Please don't hang up."

Silence.

"How have you been?" She sounded clearer now, coughing a little to clear her throat.

He sat straight up. The fact she didn't leave him hanging on a dead line perked him up, but what was there to say to her?

"Been better." He tried to sound jovial, but his voice crackled dry and short. "How about you?"

"Same," she said.

"It's been, what? Three weeks?" He didn't want to scare her off but wanted to tell her where he was.

"Yeah. Three hard weeks. I miss talking to you. A lot has been going on."

"Like what?" He wanted to let this become like things were before last week. It felt so good.

"Oh," she sounded distant. "Just some things. Like I met with Wanda."

Jay started to sit up because Roshan's whispers were too loud, but Roshan turned toward the other wall and hushed his voice to a tiny, breathless whisper.

"Wow. I guess that's good. Is it?"

"I don't know yet. Why are you whispering?"

He hesitated but couldn't lie. "Jay is here with me and I don't want to wake him up. I'm in the hospital."

"You're what? What happened?"

The alarm in her voice comforted Roshan. But shame overwhelmed him as he forced himself to answer. "I cut up my arm. Put it threw a glass door."

Her gasp on the other end of the line was followed by, "Oh my God. When? Why?"

"I …Jen, I can't talk about it."

"I'm coming over now."

Roshan heard rustling from Jay's chair and turned around to see him sitting straight up, his hair flattened on one side, listening intently. The sympathetic look on his face embarrassed Roshan, and he turned back around to whisper into the phone. "No, please don't come. I can't see anyone now."

"Why?" Panic filled her voice. "Roshan, talk to me."

Acutely aware that Jay was listening, he answered shortly, embarrassed. "I can't. Not now."

"Roshan, has Priya been there with you? Is she taking care of you?"

"Not exactly. It's complicated." He wanted to see her face so badly, but didn't deserve it.

"Roshan, if you don't tell me right now, I'm coming over there. Which hospital are you in?"

"Regional, but don't. I just wanted to hear your voice. I'm sorry I woke you." He was selfish dragging her back into his life. But he couldn't help wanting her to care.

"I'm coming now."

The line went dead, and he held his breath as he watched the screen go dark.

"Jen's coming," Jay stated and walked over to the sink to splash water on his face.

"Yes."

"Good. Maybe she can help you with whatever you need to get your shit together."

"I don't know, man. She dumped me, remember? She wanted out. Not me."

"She's coming to you, isn't she? Get a grip."

Roshan nodded, "Yeah. But I can't understand why you're here. After what I did."

"Because you're an idiot. And you need a wakeup call. My mum has already been getting calls from aunties and uncles from London and India about what happened. Your mum too. You are infamous, kind of an outlaw now. And you need someone to tell you like it is, you asshole. You're my *bhai*, and you're going to listen to me."

Roshan stared at his feet and clenched his good fist, listening.

"You fucked over your mum. You fucked over your wife. And now, they are the ones that have to live it down. You need to lay low and either pull yourself together and make amends, for your mum's sake, or you need to just get out of the picture and move on."

"How?"

"Figure out whatever it is you want and just do it. Quit dragging other people down with you. If you don't want to be married to Priya, fine. She's checked out anyway. If Jenny is what you want, then go get her. But, you've gotta make a decision about where your loyalties lie and get off the fence. We are your family, and we still care about keeping together, you included, and you pulling shit like this hurts all of us, too. You think my mum didn't scream when we got the call about you? Not to mention this makes us look bad to everyone. You're ruining your mum's life. Not to mention your own."

Roshan was speechless.

A drink would feel good right now.

He threw his legs over the side of the bed to try to stand up, but wobbled, and Jay rushed over to keep him from falling.

"Man, leave it to you to tell me like it is." He grabbed onto Jay's arm and asked him to lead him to the sink. "You're right."

He splashed some water on his face and brushed his teeth with his left arm, while Jay stood by his side in case his legs buckled. He looked in the mirror and watched his face scrunch in pain when he tried to raise his right arm.

"When I get home, if I can face her, I'm going to apologize to Priya. I know she will always hate me, but I have to do it."

"Man, her parents are at the house now packing her things. She'll be long gone before you get discharged. I heard they had an attorney drawing up divorce papers before their plane even landed at Hartsfield-Jackson. They're not wasting time."

There was a swift knock at the door, and a nurse entered.

"Hello, Mr. Desai. I'm Alisha, and I'm your nurse for the morning." She approached him and looked him up and down. "You're supposed to be in bed with that arm elevated, sir. Come on, let's get you set up."

He reluctantly allowed her and Jay to lead him back to the bed but when his head hit the pillow, he realized how light headed he really was. The shredded flesh under his bandage throbbed like it would explode. The nurse took his left wrist in her fingers for a pulse. "How's your pain?"

"About a six."

"Okay," she pushed a small paper cup toward him. "Here's two Percocet. It'll take the edge off."

She beckoned for Jay to get him a cup of water. "Are you the brother?"

Jay held a bent straw in a water cup to Roshan's lips as she took his blood pressure. "Yup. What other dude would be waiting on a guy like this?" Jay smacked him lightly on his good arm. "He's my little brother."

The nurse laughed politely at the irony of such a diminutive man being the elder to a younger Roshan's large stature, and looked at the chart. When she got to the bottom of the page, she raised her eyebrows at Roshan. "You really did a number on yourself."

"Thanks, I didn't know that." He didn't try to hide his annoyance. She was tiring him by the second.

"Hey. It'll be okay. You're darn lucky you it's only superficial damage. You could have lost the use of your hand." She arranged the pillows his bandaged arm rested upon as she talked. "I see a lot of things here. People do a lot of things to themselves to land in here. But the body is an amazing thing. It heals." She paused and added. "Just like the rest of us does."

Roshan looked away.

Leave me alone.

He had no interest in encouraging words from a stranger.

It wasn't long before the meds kicked in, and he was back in a drug-induced happy place. He tried to watch an infomercial on the TV to stay awake, waiting for Jenny to get there, but sleep kept pulling him under. He didn't know how long he had been in and out of watching the amazing chopper chop every fruit and vegetable known to man by an irritatingly chipper couple in aprons when a soft knock came from the door.

Jay turned off the TV and shook Roshan's foot through the blanket. "She's here, man."

Roshan nodded.

Jenny peeked in.

"Long time, no see, huh?" Jay said, bringing her in the room, giving her a polite hug before going out the door. "I'll just be in the waiting room. My aunt will be here in a couple hours for her shift, so—"

"I'll be gone by then. Don't worry."

Even with dark circles under her eyes, she looked beautiful, and Roshan couldn't have been happier to see anyone in his life than her at that moment. She came to his bedside and lay her hand on his head, looking at him from head to toe with tears springing to her eyes.

"I guess I'm a free man now." He began, but he couldn't look her in the eye.

"You did this over leaving Priya?"

"Yes," he answered softly, staring at the dark screen on the TV.

"I'm a free man now," he repeated, then added, "I guess I'm free to be an asshole by myself. That's what I deserve."

She sat on the edge of the bed and tipped his chin up to force him to look her in the eye. "Welcome to the lonely club." She touched the bandage on his arm and shook her head. "Oh, Roshan, honey, how did this happen?"

He looked away. How could he tell her he was a monster? "I got pissed off and put my arm through the shower door."

She pulled back and covered her mouth. He could tell she was holding her breath, waiting for more.

"Yeah, I told Priya I wanted out. Had too much to drink—" Looking up at her, he knew he should say it. "—as usual."

"Oh my God. You could have destroyed your arm. How could you work without an arm?"

He snickered. "Maybe no more drilling teeth could've been the bright side. I'm not good at it anyway." He laughed weakly and tried to lift his arm to look at it. "Yeah. I know. Not funny."

"No. Not funny. You think you could do your art without a hand either?"

Shaking his head, tears threatened to fall, and he wished he could sink his head into her arms. She was close enough he could smell the fabric softener on her T-shirt. The same one she always used. It comforted him.

She leaned over and kissed him on the cheek. "I'll help you get through this. I'll always be here for you if you need me, you know?"

"No, don't. I don't deserve it."

"Yes, you do. I've been doing a lot of thinking. Bryan has kind of checked out from me, and that hurts. Wanda has been messing with my head, it's all been crazy for me. I've been rethinking my life. You need me. I see that. I need you, but I just couldn't admit it. This is a big wake up call, to say the least."

She lay her head gently on his left shoulder, but he softly pushed her back up.

"I'm a bad guy. You don't need me. I need to get myself together first."

"I need you to do that." She looked him in the eye and squeezed his left hand and brushed her other hand across his bandages, then rested that hand on his chest. "I was so angry you were leaving Priya for me. I've been on my own all my life. You want me, and I let my guard down around you. That terrifies me." She heard his heart begin pounding faster against her ear. "What if I let you in and you leave?"

He ran his hand over the lumps in her ponytail. "What if you let me in and don't like what you get. What if you leave me?"

She lifted her face to his. "I honestly don't know. Your family could never accept me. Could you live with that?"

"Jenny, after what I've done, I don't know how they could accept me. You can't understand how much my mum depends on me. Booting Priya out disgraces my mum with everyone around her. I don't know what to do. I want out. Of everything. But I can never be out."

"Does that mean you don't want me in your life anymore?"

"No. Not at all. It means I don't know where I fit or you fit. Gotta figure out how to fix things with you by my side." He envisioned showing up at his Arun Uncle and Ashmi Auntie's house for a typical family Sunday brunch with Jenny and Mum together. They'd be like a leper trio. Just the thought of the looks Asmhi Auntie would give made his skin crawl. She probably wouldn't even speak to Jenny. And would pretend to be nice to his mum but gossip after they left. Jenny yawned into his hospital gown.

"All I can say is it's a blessing I don't have kids to ruin in this."

She stiffened against him and lifted her red lined face, sitting up. She rubbed one sleepy eye and wrung her hands together, avoiding his gaze.

He braced himself. "What's wrong?"

"Ah, you're actually not off the hook that easy."

He stiffened too and held his breath fearful of what he knew must be coming.

"I'm pregnant."

Blood rushed to his head and threatening to erupt. Happiness? Dread? Fear? Pressure? The feelings bled together inside him, like watercolors swirling around on paper, blending into one dark color soaking him to the core.

He pulled her to him and cradled her head on his shoulder, losing himself in the sensation of her weight on him. There were no words. He wanted another pain pill to send him back into oblivion. What kind of father would he be? It felt like he was pulling Jenny, his Mum, and now a baby into a whirlpool.

Maybe this could be my chance for redemption...

They lay like that for a long time, neither of them speaking. Roshan had no words. He just focused on the warmth of her skin and her breath on his shoulder, trying to put the rest away.

Chapter 14

Esha

"I can get you more cup of *chai*?" Esha asked Evelyn, the old woman nodding across the table from her.

The sunlight shone in the kitchen, mingling warmth with the sweet ginger in the air as the two women sipped their milky tea. She knew another one would make her jittery but was pouring more for herself anyway.

"Oh, bless your heart. Thank you, Esha." The woman pulled her sweater tighter in front of her and rubbed her shoulders. "This tea is so delicious. *Chai*, you called it? I guess I'm not too old to learn some new words."

Esha giggled a little at the way the word *chai* rolled out of Evelyn's mouth so slowly, ending the word with an "aahh" as if she were opening wide for the doctor.

"Yes. *Chai*," Esha repeated in one short breath with a smile. "We say quickly. *Chai*."

She loved chatting with her new friend in the afternoons. Helping the old lady made her feel more useful. "And you not old," Esha said. "Seventy nine is not old. My mother. She died at ninety three. You have long time in front of you."

"Oh, but I sure feel it. You can say that. You are a young thing. You said the other day that you're just over fifty, right?"

Esha nodded her head and poured more into Evelyn's cup. She tilted the saucepan over her tea cup into the strainer that caught the black grounds. A milk skin slid onto the strainer from the top of cooling drink and slithered down the side. Esha flipped it around and expertly deposited it into the saucepan. Evelyn waved her hand by the cup, "Thanks, good, thank you darlin."

"*Bas.*" Esha nodded her head politely and held her hand above the cup like she would around family.

"Excuse me?"

"We say *bas.* Means 'enough.' Another lesson for you. Say *bas* when you have enough *chai.*"

"Boss."

Esha patted the table amused. "Not 'boss' like at work. Say fast. *Bas!*"

Evelyn tried again, but laughed too. "I guess my drawl is just too set in its ways to learn anymore. Boss language lesson, honey."

"Okay, then, *bas.* Done. You learned a new word, though. See? Not too old."

Esha poured the rest of the tea into her own cup and sat back down.

"Mmmm. I love this gingery smell. So yummy. What all ingredients do you use?

"Black tea, boil, add milk, grate fresh ginger in the pot. And sugar. Better to be sweet, sweet."

"I bet my son would like this. He's always trying new ethnic foods up in New York."

"Then I make tomorrow. I pick him up from airport with you? I'm like, what you call...taxi for you now. Doctor's orders. I hear today." Embarrassed by her English, Esha cupped her ear, hoping with pantomime she could get her point across more effectively to Evelyn.

"Oh, honey. That would be so nice of you, but I can't ask you to do that. You've done so much for me in the last two weeks. You barely know me, and you've taken me to my doctor, the grocery store. If it weren't for you coming over to give me that UPS box that day, I'd never have known you. God must have been looking out for me."

"Ah, yes. God is great." Esha glanced up at the small framed prayer on the wall of the kitchen that Roshan had drawn as a child. She had given it to him years ago, and thank God she found it at the bottom of a moving box one day after moving to this big house. She had a gold and red Ganesha in the sitting room for morning prayers, but it was the prayer in her son's perfect childhood script that she usually turned to these days. She'd held his small hands so many nights before bed, repeating the *Gayatri Mantra* along with him, hearing God in his tiny voice:

> *Om Buhr, Bhuva, Swaha*
> *Om Tat Savitur Varenyam*
> *Bhargo Devasya Dheemahi*
> *Dhiyo Yonaha Prachodayat*

"I drive you tomorrow. No argue. You not good still."

Evelyn sipped the creamy tea. "Okay. Well, thank you so very much. Once my Rich gets here, he will take over. He's my sweet boy. Always a mama's boy, that one." Evelyn's eyes flickered behind the wrinkles like a new mom talking about her baby. "Even though he doesn't look like me."

"How does he look like?"

"Well," she leaned in and said carefully, "He's tall like his dad and has the most beautiful green eyes you've ever seen on a boy, and he's so smart. And funny too. Talk your ear off if you let him." She looked at her own arm, and laughed, "Looks like his daddy, certainly not like me." She paused looking at Esha, and leaned in further. "He's black." Esha thought she must have looked stunned and felt rude, because Evelyn explained, "See, his dad and I are from here in Georgia... met in the 50s at a museum. I was a student at Agnes Scott, and he was a student at Morehouse College. Way before Martin Luther King came along." Her eyes misted and she looked faraway. "Suffice it to say, honey, we couldn't be married down here, so we moved up to New York, and that's where we raised Rich." She clicked her fingernails on her cup and added in a bitter, sad voice, "My parents never spoke to me again. When he died, I retired here from teaching, because without him, I wanted to be home, even if I couldn't really go home. I do miss my boy, though."

Esha remembered Roshan's soft breath on her pillow after prayers those long ago nights. He used to be her mama's boy. At least she thought he was. Until that woman Jenny came along.

"What Rich does for job?"

"He's in sales. He's very good at it. Rich was always popular in school, charmed the girls. He can charm anyone into buying from him." She sipped her tea again with a faraway look in her eye and dabbed her mouth. "What about your son? Roshan, is it? He's a doctor?"

"Yes, dentist."

"I used to see him in his driveway washing his car before I got sick. Good looking boy. Always took his time polishing the outside, didn't he? And I used to see a really pretty little lady around here too sometimes. Always wearing hospital scrubs. Is that your daughter?"

Esha was careful to choose her words. She couldn't let her feelings show in her words. "My son. He working out some, um, problems. Most about work . But, soon he will come back." She took a sip of tea and it went down like a rock. "And girl you see…Priya…my daughter-in-law. Divorced now." She cut an imaginary string with scissor fingers to show the severing of the string that once joined them.

"Oh, honey, I'm sorry to hear that. Rich got divorced a few years ago too. But he's doing fine now. Don't worry. Your Roshan will be fine too."

Esha felt so at ease with Evelyn and wanted to tell her more. But she stopped herself. Family business stayed in the family, and there it wasn't really discussed either.

Evelyn looked around the kitchen and saw a framed picture of Roshan on a display shelf. "Is that him? He's handsome. I'd like to meet him sometime. Maybe introduce him to my granddaughter." Evelyn laughed, "She's a spitfire. Pretty, but has that New York attitude. She won't take nothing from any man."

"Oh, not sure." Esha hoped her surprised tone didn't offend Evelyn. We keep in ours, look for Indian girl for him soon. Ours, we keep to ourselves." Suddenly on edge, she stood and smoothed her clothes. "It help him let go of the not so good things in his life now." Esha pictured Jenny's face when she helped Roshan into the car leaving the hospital only a month ago. That woman had taken him from her exactly four weeks and three days ago, but it seemed like just yesterday that he was here in her kitchen eating her samosas on the rare occasion he was home on a Saturday morning.

She perked up when she looked at the clock. The *garba* was tonight! He was coming to get her!

"Maybe you meet him. He fetch me to take to a function tonight. Our community gives holiday dance. Our *Navrathi*. Very holy time."

"Isn't that nice? Do you go to a lot of holiday dances? I'm afraid I don't know anything about the Hindu religion."

"Used to. Not so much in the last year or two. I love to dance, was so good, even my age. But, not so much going on since...he moved out."

Her belly fluttered as she wondered if they would get looks when walking into the hall tonight. Perhaps people would keep mutterings discreet. His voice had been sounding better on the phone lately, so she was hopeful, more alive. And maybe they would get there and all of this business would disappear into the music and dancing. He loved to dance so much as a kid, and she loved to watch him join the circles with his friends. She hoped tonight they would blend in with everyone else amongst the music, and everyone would forget what happened. Like it used to be, but nothing will ever be what it used to be ever again.

She would be watching from the back of the room tonight. Just making small talk. No dancing for her, though she was always one of the best. Perhaps if she milled around people, asking after grandchildren and parents, and reminiscing about the old days, people would talk less about Roshan because she would be right there.

"His moving out must have been hard for you."

"Yes. It is. Our sons stay with us. So, yes, very hard."

They finished up the last sips of their tea, and Esha took both tea cups to the sink to wash, glancing nervously at the clock. Roshan would be picking her up soon. She could hardly wait. She had better get dressed soon.

"Evelyn, I know you still weak from our outing to the doctor. I have to ready myself for tonight. Would you like to sit here while I get ready? You can meet Roshan when he comes." Esha smiled thinking it would be so to see him without Jenny around.

"Sure. That would be so nice. What do you wear to these dances?"

"Not jeans." Esha looked down at her jeans, ruffled blouse and flat shoes. From the neck down, she could pass for an American mother. "No, I'll wear a sari. You know sari?"

"Yes. I've heard of them. Like a sarong?"

"Yes."

"I'd love to see you all dressed up."

Esha helped Evelyn up from her chair and walked her into the TV room. "I'll put on a program for you. If you need me, I will be in my room. Just over there." She pointed toward the hallway that led to her master suite.

Esha felt good to have a friend. Someone who was interested in her. Someone who doesn't care about reputation.

On both sides of the closet hung a rainbow of colors and patterns of shimmering outfits. There was a section with only Indian tops that would be worn with jeans or slacks, like the ones she wore to the hospital to volunteer today. There was a section for saris, each pressed and hung on hangers, ready for the next wedding or formal occasion. Some were light silk with small, simple borders and some were made of very heavy silk with elaborate gold or silver or embroidered edges. She had told Evelyn that she would wear one but decided against it. Tying the sari took a long time and focused attention to detail. Her heart was not in it today.

And she was so anxious, didn't think her hands could be steady enough to even fold sari pleats in her fingers properly. She stepped over in the closet to the Punjabi section.

Punjabis were the perfect garment for casual, family dinners. She fingered through one gold, then two different shades of green, her favorite color, but landed her hand on lavender sleeves trimmed in silver. She slipped into the loose cotton pants and tied the drawstring around her waist. She looked at herself in the mirror, topless, in her pants and sighed. Her belly rippled with the first softness of fat she had ever had in her life. She may be the mother of a thirty-seven year old man, but she felt like she should still be able to maintain her figure, even at 54. She did her yoga almost every morning after meditation and walked up the hills of her neighborhood with Monisha on weekends. At least she did before the last month had happened. But she did keep to her strict vegetarian diet, and that helped.

She pulled the long Punjabi top over her head and let it flow down her legs to her knees, glad for the loose modesty. She pulled the sleeves straight and made sure the hem of the long, shirt-like top hung straight just below her knee. Her mushy middle didn't matter anyway because she would be the only one to ever see herself nude in this life. Sometimes in the dead of night, she would awaken, often with the baby blanket in her hand, and long for the warm touch of someone against her. The silky, delicate touch of the baby she raised—and the baby she'd lost—were a ghostly memory on her skin, but she wished for something else, something she'd never had. Not the angry friction of her husband against her. Pretending not to want the gentle touch of a man disappeared and in the solitude in bed, and her inner longing exposed itself with raw clarity.

Looking at the watch again, she put the thought into the back of her mind. She was running out of time. She knew Roshan might be late this time. He was a changed man, and she didn't actually know who he would be when he arrived. She hoped he would be alone. Maybe she would have a chance to really talk to him. To find out what was going on with him. To find out what she could do to make things right for him. For her too.

Since Roshan's accident, Esha had seen him only a handful of times. And always with Jenny around. That woman hovered like a mother over her son! Esha was afraid of him, for him, and for herself. Jay would visit him and come report to her that he was well, but on the few occasions Esha could bring herself to go see him, Roshan was cold to her. He was staying at Jenny's house, and he was just different. It was very hard to set foot in the woman's house. He seemed to no longer be her son.

She had to remind herself that he hadn't been truly her son for a long time.

Running a brush through her black hair, she played back the first visit in her mind. Jay had opened the car door for her and led her to the front door of Jenny's house. It was an ostentatious townhouse for a single woman, in a suburb forty-five minutes away from where she and Roshan lived. But, it was very nice. Brown brick with a front door made of dark stained woods with scrolled bars across the glass in the center, identical to all of the other doors in the long line of doors in the building that no doubt belonged to people just like her, too proud of their money. God wanted people to shed worldly attachments. It's how she tried to live and how she raised Roshan. She had failed miserably as an example because she pushed him to succeed so hard that she pushed him away. Her doubt in his ability to resist temptations for attachments, women, houses, and cars made her even more sad for him over at that house with that woman.

God, give him strength to separate himself from it all.

Esha picked up her iPhone. No text or missed call from Roshan. Would he even be coming? Her mind flashed back to the look on Jenny's face when she'd opened the door to Esha that day. Had it been fear? Had her shaky smile been nervousness? Esha had forced a smile and said hello, and Jenny's face changed to a practiced smile, one that she presumably used for patients at work.

Now in her bathroom, she smoothed on some coffee-colored lipstick and replayed the visit like a movie in her mind. Jenny had shown Jay and Esha to the living room where Roshan sat on the sofa, watching a rugby game on CNN.

"*Kemcho, dikra,*" Esha had said softly, calling him her little boy in Gujarati. She waited for him to speak or move, but he just stared at the TV and nodded in their direction. After a moment, she'd gone to him and sat on the sofa near his feet, placing her hand lightly on his leg, which rested on the coffee table.

"Your arm? It's okay?" she'd asked, speaking in Gujarati the whole time. Jay sat in a chair near them and kept his eyes on the game. She continued, careful not to even mix in any English words as she spoke. Jenny hovered behind the sofa near them. Esha wanted to shoo her away like a fly. This conversation was not for her. Esha would not give her the satisfaction.

"Yeah, Mummy. It's okay." Replying in English, he looked at it and then back at the TV. "No permanent damage. I'll be back to root canals in no time." His eyes were dull and his face lifeless. Depressed.

She had seen the look in her own eyes before. The first time was after she'd given birth to her stillborn baby girl, those dull eyes had stared back at her from the bathroom mirror. After her mother-in-law had shut the door for Esha's privacy, she had stared at herself in the glass. Bruised and swollen, only one eye was fully open. That one eye had that same hollow look of a life sucked out. Perhaps it was destined to be a family trait.

Her heart ached, and she couldn't look at his face anymore. She didn't know what was worse: the look of a vacuumed soul or the boil of rage he'd shown her that night in the bathroom as he hovered over Priya.

"I brought you some *mug* and *roti*. Some mango *achar* too." Continuing to speak in Gujarati, she handed the bundle of glass dishes to Jay, and he in turn held them up to Jenny and asked her where he should set them.

"In the kitchen. I'll show you where. Come on."

When they'd both gone in the kitchen, Esha asked Roshan quietly, "Are you coming home? *Mara dikra*, my son, you must come home."

His silence made her uncomfortable and she went on, "Come, Roshan. Come home, *chaal*, let's go. I'll take care of you. You need someone—me—to take care of you."

He'd looked up and lifelessly replied, "No, Mummy. I don't need anyone to take care of me. Especially you. I can't go back to that house. Not after what I've done."

"Yes, you can. You will. *Chaal*. Come, now." She'd tilted her head toward the door and clapped her hands softly together. "Come."

"No, Mummy. I'm staying here. Jenny is helping me. She's working with my staff to get a temporary doc in my office to keep it afloat. I'm out for another eight weeks at least. She's handling things for me."

"Jayesh can handle things for you. Come on. We need you back."

Anger lit in his eyes, and he growled, "I don't want to go back. I want to be here. I can't be around the family now. I need to be here. No judgments here."

Jenny and Jay had reentered at that point and a hush fell on the room.

"I'm tired, Mummy," he said in English. "I'm going to nap."

She looked at his face, but his eyes were fixated on the TV screen.

He repeated, "I'm tired."

Esha looked at Jenny, who stood by the sofa with eyes cast out the window that looked out into the tall rustling trees outside. Her face was flushed.

"Okay." She stood and placed her hand on Roshan's face, caressing his cheek while pursing her lips and closing her eyes to hold back tears. She said in English clear enough for Jenny to understand the concern in her voice, "Eat some *mug*. Your favorite. With the *roti*. You'll feel good."

She cried softly on the way home and stared out the car window while Jay listened to the soundtrack from a Bollywood movie on his iPod. He respectfully did not look at her the whole way home.

Shaking off the threatening tears from the memory, Esha went to show Evelyn her outfit and wait for Roshan.

"Oh, my," Evelyn marveled from her spot on the white leather sofa. "You are beautiful."

"Thank you," Esha said, feeling good to hear another person compliment her.

Esha twirled around slowly in front of her friend. "I wear all the time when I live in India."

Esha heard the groan of the garage door open and walked over to the door nervously.

"Is that your son coming?"

Esha nodded and took a deep breath before opening the door with a happy smile on her face. Evelyn braced herself on the cushioned arm of the sofa and pushed herself up to stand and face the door. Esha smiled at her with expectant pride. She was happy to show off her son to someone who knew nothing of their family problems. Or of his actions. To Evelyn, Roshan would just be a handsome young dentist.

Esha couldn't believe her eyes. Roshan walked toward her, dressed in a *kurta* he must have borrowed from Jay, so he wouldn't have to come home. The long shirt hung down to his knees, and the sheen of the cream silk fabric shimmered even under the fluorescent light in the garage. His arm had only a small bandage on it and moved naturally as he walked. He had a slight smile on his face as he looked his mother straight in the eye. He looked alive again. He looked like her son again.

"Mummy, you ready?"

Just as she was about to usher him inside to meet Evelyn, Jenny rounded the corner of the house and entered the garage behind him.

Esha felt like her head would explode.

Jenny wore a green and gold embroidered Punjabi. Her blond hair was pulled back from her face, exposing her smooth skin and forehead. Between her eyebrows was stuck a green *bindi*, a sticker with a tiny sparkling gem, just like the red one Esha was wearing. As Jenny approached Roshan's side, Esha saw that the green of her eyes sparkled with the green of her clothes. She was stunning. Esha forced her mouth to close.

Why was she here? And where had she gotten those clothes?

Jenny could not go with them. The divorce settlement was not even done. Roshan was giving Priya all but the house to speed up the split for her, but still, papers had to be signed. He was still married until then.

"Hello," she managed to say in Jenny's direction without looking at her.

"Hello, Mrs. Desai." Jenny slipped her arm under Roshan's and looked up at him.

Esha thought she looked afraid.

"Jenny. You know how to *garba* dance? You know we're going to a dance?"

"I've told her all about it, Mummy."

Esha heard the clenching of his throat around his words. He obviously knew this was wrong.

"Yes, Mrs. Desai, I know. I can't do the dances, but it'll be interesting to learn about your culture more. Roshan explained what *Navrathi* is to me too."

"My Roshan is good dancer. The best. I hope you don't get lonely while he dances. You won't know our songs. You just watch."

"Oh, I'll be fine. I'm a big girl. I know Jay and several other doctors who Roshan said will be there. I'll have plenty of people to talk to."

And plenty of people to talk about you too.

"Mummy, are you ready?" Roshan's voice was impatient and curt. "The car is running."

Swallowing to moisten the inside of her dry mouth, Esha stepped inside the house and croaked, "You must meet my neighbor, she's new friend, Roshan." She turned toward Evelyn, who'd shuffled over to Esha's side. They both backed up to allow Roshan and Jenny to step inside the house. All four of them looked at each other. Speechless.

"Evelyn." She laid her hand on the old lady's shoulder and then on Roshan's. "My son, Roshan."

Evelyn extended her hand in a friendly, lady handshake. "Nice to meet you, Roshan. My, you are handsome as your picture."

Roshan gave an embarrassed grin and said thank you. Then there was silence again. Evelyn looked at Jenny, then Esha, then waited patiently. After an uncomfortable moment passed, Evelyn extended her hand toward Jenny.

"You are a pretty thing. Nice to meet you. And you are...?"

"Jenny," she replied, breathing a sigh of relief as she took Evelyn's hand. "Very nice to meet you, Evelyn." She looked at Esha and then back at Roshan.

Esha seethed.

"Well, Miss Jenny, your outfit is so pretty. Do you wear Indian clothes often?"

"No, ma'am. I just borrowed this from Roshan's cousin's wife. It's my first time."

"You should do it more often. It suits you." Evelyn patted her hand softly.

"Thank you," Jenny replied with gratitude in her voice.

Annoyed, Esha just wanted her out of there.

To Esha's further distaste, Roshan put his arm around Jenny's shoulder. "Miss Evelyn, it's been so nice to meet you. But, Mummy, we need to get going. Even by Indian Standard Time, we're late."

Esha turned to Evelyn. "Come, I walk you home." She took the older woman's elbow and started to lead her toward the door.

"No, Mummy, I'll help her. What kind of gentleman would I be if I didn't?"

She was so surprised by the cheer in his voice that it didn't dawn on her when she said "yes" that she would be left alone with Jenny. Too late to back out now. She waved to Evelyn and turned away from Jenny when Roshan walked the woman out the door.

She walked from room to room pretending to fluff pillows, straighten canisters on the kitchen counter, and look for her handbag. As she passed by the garage door where Jenny still stood silently, she couldn't help but watch her. Jenny had her phone out texting someone purposefully, her cheeks a darkening red.

She's nervous to be alone with me. Wonderful.

The *bindi* on Jenny's forehead was stuck much too high and was a bit crooked. Obviously Hema had donated the clothes but not supervised her dressing. She couldn't let her go to the *garba* looking like that. She would be humiliated enough and didn't need people talking about that. She lay her handbag on a chair and approached Jenny slowly. Jenny looked up from her phone startled, pulling back.

"I not bite you," Esha said, dripping with sarcasm. "Lean. Come. I must fix your *bindi*."

Jenny hesitantly leaned toward Esha, and she smelled of Dentyne and coconut. Esha had lotion that with the same scent that Roshan had given her for Mother's Day before all of this happened. She liked it then but would throw away the bottle when she got back to her bathroom. She peeled the sticker *bindi* off of Jenny's forehead and repositioned it, pressing harder than necessary to adhere it. The skin around it reddened slightly to Esha's pleasure, and she stepped back.

"Thank you, Mrs. Desai."

Jenny's politeness didn't matter to her. Esha locked her eyes on the woman's face.

"My son has problem."

Jenny titled her head expectantly. "Okay. Go on."

"You. You his problem."

Jenny's surprise pleased her.

"Excuse me?"

To Esha's delight, Jenny's voice pitched higher and the red in her cheeks blossomed a darker crimson. She wanted this woman to hurt like Jenny had hurt her and Priya.

"He not Indian now you came along."

Jenny started to speak, but Esha held up her palm to Jenny's face. "No. You listen." She pointed to her temple. "You stuck in him since school and now he throws away his life. Talking crazy for long time about quit his job and go to art school. Drink so much alone. For sure, I know is you." Esha felt herself out of breath trying to keep up with everything she wanted to say. "But, now listen. You wear these clothes. You keep him in your house. But you won't last. He wake up soon. Remember his real life. You remember that."

Jenny's face contorted, and she opened her mouth with teeth bared just as the garage door opened and Roshan stepped inside.

"Are we ready to—?" He stopped in his tracks at the sight of Esha and Jenny's faces.

Esha backed up and put on a smile, leaving Jenny with tears of fury in her eyes. Rolling Gujarati words off her tongue with great satisfaction, she stated, "Oh yes, *bhai*. All finished here. Ready to go!"

She walked over to pick up her handbag and checked to make sure her cellphone was inside. A text from Monisha was on the screen.

Monisha
Bringing Roshan? Be aware. Ashmi already talking.

Not surprised, she held up the phone and continued in Gujarati, "I'll wait for you at the car."

She placed herself in the front seat. Roshan gave her a "Are you kidding me?" look when he and Jenny got to the car, but Esha had to force back a smirk when Jenny held up her hand to him to let it go.

They arrived at the community center hall full of people dancing playfully in circles on the central floor to the swift-paced rhythms of fun *tablas* in the music. She looked down at her simple Punjabi, comparing it with envy to the fun *chaniya cholis* so many of the other women were wearing, especially younger ones. Spinning...sparkling...stepping...one, two, three, clap! Slow at first, then faster and fluid as the tiny mirrors on their flowing skirts created a swirl of colors, rotating in a circle, first one direction then switching in unison. The subtle fashion choice she made reflected her desire to blend in, not stand out like a peacock.

Longing to join in the fun with the changing rhythms of the music and the bright faces on the dancers, her fingers stayed clasped in front of her while she surveyed the room for familiar, and perhaps, welcoming faces. She hovered by the door for a few minutes, pretending to check her cellphone, after making it a point to pat both Roshan and Jenny on the shoulders and wish them a good time before they took off for a huddle of men they must both already know.

Monisha's face lit up across the room when she spotted Esha, who made a straight line toward her, careful to keep her eyes on Monisha and an expectant smile on her face, as if she were about to speak, so that no one would stop her along the way. Monisha's upper lip showed a thin bead of sweat, and her kiss on Esha's cheek left a trace of wetness.

"So, you made it!" Monisha said.

"I'm here."

Monisha looked her in the eye and through a wide smile, ordered Esha, "Put on a happy face. Have fun! Don't let sour people get you down."

Ashmi passed by and stopped with a surprised expression when she saw Esha. "Oh, bhabhi, I'm so glad you came! I was just talking to Suriksha over there and wondering if you would come."

If Esha didn't know better, she would think Ashmi were sincere, but Monisha's warning text about her made her very wary. She hugged her tight, and whispered, "Please, bhabhi, don't mention Roshan to people. I know people ask, but just say he's doing fine, okay?"

Ashmi looked hurt. "Bhabhi, you know I wouldn't say anything."

Okay, let's play pretend, if that's what you want.

Monisha clapped her hands at both and said, "Come ladies, enough serious talk. We're here to dance. But first, Esha, tell me how your new volunteering job at the hospital is going?"

Ashmi's face lit with surprise and Esha answered proudly, with determination to show Ashmi how well things were going in her life, whether it was a truth or a myth. Thanking Monisha with her eyes, she gushed about how good it felt to go the the hospital and meet new people, and that she even got to go to the nursery and hold babies sometimes.

"That's wonderful," Ahsmi said, and Esha sensed that just maybe a genuine thread of sincerity ran through her voice. "I know it will do you good!"

"Yes," Esha beamed while scanning the crowd, paying special attention to the women flowing off the dance floor for a rest. One woman, a second cousin named Anita, was not-so-discreetly looking over at Esha and talking to her friend as they sat down to drink some water. Trying to ignore it, she continued to talk to her bhabhis, until a clutch of women led by Anita made their way toward them.

At the same time that the women reached her, Roshan appeared behind Esha and said hello to all of the women, startling Esha who had no idea he was there. But where was Jenny?

"Aunties, hello, hello. How is everyone tonight?"

Polite responses made their rounds, and Anita looked on either side of her at the ladies with her, made an excuse to go see if help was needed with the food, and left with her followers, shaking her head, glancing back only once. To Esha's surprise, Ashmi even shook her head and turned back to them. "I was bracing for the worst."

"Mummy, why do you talk to her?" He leaned into her and gave Monisha a pleading look as if asking her to explain his mum's actions.

"She's my second cousin. You know that. What else am I to do?"

I can't just walk away, or people will know they've won.

Monisha bobbed her head and said, "It's okay, *bhai.* I'm here. I would stand up, you know me."

Ashmi chimed in, "Yeah, me too. I won't let people give your mum a hard time, just because of you and that woman."

The music was still going loud, but Ashmi's words dropped a bomb in between them all, detonating in Esha's ears, and she smacked her hand over her mouth, the color draining from her face.

"Oh, I'm so sorry, Ro—" Ashmi's eyes filled with tears, and Esha and Monisha both stared frozen at her in disbelief.

Roshan shifted from one foot to another, and sniffed a couple of times, but said nothing and instead of looking at Ashmi, scanned the crowd for Jenny.

Esha looked in the direction of his eyes, and spotted Jenny at a table nearby with Jay and a few other guys Roshan's age, laughing at something in conversation. Without one word, he walked away and joined Jenny and the crowd at the table.

Esha faced Ashmi, and Ashmi stared back in fear. "I'm sorry, bha—"

Esha put up her hand. "Stop. You spoke the truth. Stop saying sorry."

Constantly aware of Jenny and Roshan's whereabouts in the crowd, she monitored the glances from others in their direction. Jenny sat with the men, the doctors she knew, with curiosity on her face. At one point, Anita walked over to Roshan and Jenny in their group. Esha glided over subtly to a table nearby, busying herself with gathering some used plates and water cups so she could hear what was said.

Ashmi hugged Roshan. "So glad you're better, *bhai*." She regarded Jenny as if she were a strange object in front of her. She said nothing and went on to hug and greet the men in the group at the table, her chunky earring swaying into them as she hugged them. To all of the men, she said, "Come to the house for lunch sometime. It's been too long. I'll fix something extra special just to see you all more." She looked at Jenny again and then turned to Roshan, "You and Mum come too. I'll make your favorite peas *kachori*." Before Roshan spoke, Anita walked away to help another woman change out a dish of rice on the buffet table across the room. Jenny looked incredulous and Roshan's jaw clenched.

Esha was torn. She was glad Jenny wasn't acknowledged; she didn't deserve a welcome. But at the same time, she hated it for Roshan and could just imagine what Ashmi must be saying under her breath to her friend while holding up the tray and dumping the rice.

And despite herself, Esha did feel sorry for the girl. No one wants to be ignored. But Jenny was doing it to herself. She did not belong here.

The night went by without another incident, and Roshan drove them home. He dropped Jenny off first, and Esha got an ominous feeling when the two exchanged an intimate look as Jenny exited the car into the headlights.

Once alone on the road, Roshan came out and said, "When the divorce papers are signed, I'm marrying Jenny." His hands gripped the steering wheel, and his eyes stared straight ahead on the road.

Esha had to close her eyes because the whooshing by of trees and houses outside her window nauseated her as her brain and heart absorbed the news. She felt like she was in an elevator where the cable was severed and the box with her in it was crashing to the bottom floor. Her entire body racked with pain.

She remembered that night not long ago in the bathroom, holding him in her arms until the paramedics arrived. No words from her were going to make any difference, and she could not stir anything up in him.

"Roshan. *Bhai.*" She whispered and touched his hand on the wheel. His lips squeezed together, and she thought he looked like he would cry. "What are you doing?"

Where will he live? Will I always be alone in that house? Will I never have him again without that woman around?

"Mummy, I'm trying to be happy. She makes me happy."

"I didn't raise you like this, *bhai.* What did I do wrong?" Tears flowed, and she wiped her whole face with her palm, not caring about the makeup smearing in the dark.

"You didn't do anything wrong. You always say God puts us on a path. That we all have a connection, a debt to repay from another life. My connection is with her."

Esha couldn't swallow, couldn't talk.

What about my path? What did I do in a past life to deserve this?

They pulled up in her driveway, *his* driveway. "I'll walk you in, Mummy." He got out and came around to her door and opened it. She grabbed his outstretched hand and stood.

"No. You go," she replied softly. "I need to get used to being alone now." She pushed away his arm and walked to the door without looking back at him.

He didn't move until she was in the door, and he heard her lock it from the inside. His car sat in the driveway for a long time, and she watched from a crack in the window blinds. Finally he pulled out onto the street with a screech of tires, and she sat on the sofa in their—no—her TV room. Her eyes fixated on the shape of the fireplace across from her, and her mind swam in nothingness while the edges of the fireplace blurred in the dark until her mind was blank. The next thing she knew, her eyes opened into the morning light, and she lifted her head from the arm of the sofa.

The room felt cold, even with the hot rays of sunshine pouring in around her.

This is the life I worked so hard for?

She pulled herself up and started a pot of tea on the stove. There were lessons to be planned for the afternoon. There was washing to be done. That was that. She spied the prayer on the wall and looked away. She would go on, but the path she always thought she was on was unpaved now, and she wasn't sure how to pave it. The tea burned her lips, but she drank quickly and stood. Time to get to work on chores.

Chapter 15

Roshan

His head pounded in sync with the palpitations in his chest, but he couldn't take his eyes off of Jenny. She stood beside him watching, listening to the pastor's words, clutching her white long-stemmed lilies in front of her straight silk gown. The pastor's words muffled around in his head, but he kept smiling. Jenny smiled at him and turned back to face the pastor.

The cozy ballroom was half-filled his and Jenny's friends and family. "Friends" was a loose term, though, meaning mainly business colleagues, a couple of friends from college, employees from both of their practices, and Bryan and Craig. Seating had been tricky to plan, the subject of several tense conversations between Jenny and his mum, as both women refused to budge on tradition from their respective sides. His mum insisted that women and men be separated by gender, women on one side, men on the other, as most of their social events called for, while Jenny argued for seating guests on either side based on whether they were from the groom's side or the bride's side. Several earsplitting car rides home later from wedding planning visits at Esha's home, it was decided by a ref-eree—him—that since a limited sampling of his family would be invited anyway, and Jenny's family was pitifully small, guests would be ushered by Jay and Bryan to whichever seats were open.

Esha had already taken her place in the front row, and shifted in her seat to watch guests come in, looking nervous, fidgeting with the long red and green 22 karat gold earrings and choker, then smoothing over and over the burgundy sari fabric pleated over her shoulder. She was obviously out of her element, and Roshan pitied her more now than ever before because this was all becoming real.

The seating perplexed Ashmi Auntie and Arvind Uncle when Jay ushered them, along with Hema, to the second row next to his mum. Roshan had seen Hema smile sweetly at Jay and then whisper into Ashmi's ear before gently pushing her into the row after Arvind, who kept clearing his throat. Ashmi sat stiffly next to him, pleating her sari nervously on her lap and looking around like a wide-eyed child. Monisha Auntie soon joined Hema, Ashmi and Arvind in the second row. He was grateful he had this many family bless him with their attendance and nervously watched from the door as their guests filed in, his hands clasped in front of him counting the minutes until the ceremony could start. Near the time he was to go to the altar and wait for Jenny, Wanda and James showed up looking flustered. He himself led them through the rows of chairs where guests created a mosaic of black cocktail dresses and suits mixed with bright colored and shimmering saris, seating them on the front row next to his mum.

The minister stood in front of the assembly, facing the couple, whose backs were to the guests. Roshan was grateful for his soothing, rhythmic voice, because the thumping in his head was getting worse. This being the first time he'd ever heard a Baptist preacher speak, he was surprised by feeling stirred inside him by the words of Jesus Christ's love for everyone. But when he drilled in the message that only those born again in Christ would be saved, Roshan shut the door to his drawling voice. He groaned involuntarily and looked at Jenny sideways. She nudged his arm and urged him to be quiet with her eyes. She didn't agree with that school of thought either, and he had asked her why she wanted a Baptist preacher. She had justified, "It's just all I know. Even when you try, you can't always get away from your upbringing."

"Who here gives this woman to be married?"

Bryan stood up and stated, "I do."

Jenny gave him a look of thanks as he sat back down next to Craig, who held their sleeping daughter in his lap. Roshan loved that look of happiness in Jenny's eyes right now, and longed to see that again when she looked at him.

"Do you, Roshan, take this woman to have and to hold, in sickness and in health, 'til death do you part?"

He looked into Jenny's eyes and, with certainty in the moment, stated, "Yes. I do." He slipped the platinum band next to the three carat diamond already on her finger.

The preacher repeated the vows with Jenny, and she slipped his wedding band on to his left ring finger. When it slid past his last knuckle, she held his hand and gave him that look.

"You may kiss the bride."

The kiss was short.

So many eyes around him. On him. Judging him.

Roshan, clenching his teeth, flipped his internal switch and grinned from ear to ear as they walked back down the aisle toward the back of the ballroom. He squeezed Jenny's arm with his hand, and whispered to her, "We did it" with as much enthusiasm as he could muster.

"Yes. We did."

They disappeared through the double doors, leaving their guests watching in their seats. He looked into her eyes, searching. Did she want this? Could it really be true she wanted him and this was not just because of the baby?

"I love you, Roshan Desai." Jenny placed both palms on his cheeks and pulled him into a light kiss. "This is a good thing. We will be okay." She looked around and put his palm on her slightly round abdomen.

He pulled it away quickly, nervous that someone might have noticed. "I love you too, Mrs…Dr. Jenkins-Desai." They kissed again but the rocks rolling around inside his head made him pull back.

"Are you okay, honey?"

"Yeah, yeah." He put his hand on his head and pretended to shake off the pain. "Headache from nerves, I guess."

Fighting the urge to find a bar, Roshan whispered to her, touching her forehead gingerly to his. "I'm going to take care of you and our baby. Forever." He nuzzled her nose, and breathed her in. She was his home now, and in that moment, he vowed to himself to stop drinking and be the man she and their child would need.

Jenny squeezed his hands and kissed him, and as if reading his mind, said, "Thank you for that promise. And I promise the same to you. Now promise me one more thing: can we please both go forward from here, clean and healthy? For the baby?"

"Yes," he answered, hopeful, trying to stomp on the rising craving for a drink.

I can't give in.

She hugged him, and over her shoulder, he spied his college friend Beau filing out of the ballroom with his wife, conversing with others in the crowd. Beau was his lawyer and would try to find him, and right now, Roshan couldn't handle any questioning about the mishap he had caused at work. The pounding in his skull heightened as Beau approached, and he panicked, desperate for an escape route. Abruptly, he pulled from Jenny.

"I think I'll get a celebratory drink."

Looking at her belly, Jenny gasped.

"But only Coke for me," he lied. He shot his hand at her like a gun and winked. "Ginger ale for you?"

"Not now. I need to go change upstairs."

He was relieved by her peck on the cheek. Jenny needed to go up to their room to change into her Indian wedding dress. They were going to have a thirty minute refreshment break, and then reenter the ballroom to take part in a shortened Hindu ceremony at his mum's insistence. It was the least he could for her in the situation.

He went to the bar, holding up a finger for her to wait. Within thirty seconds, he was back by her side, rocks glass in hand, escorting her to the elevator. There was no sign of Beau, so he could relax for a few moments.

"Should I go up with you and help you get dressed?" He pulled his hips to hers subtly, while she looked around them at the swelling crowd. "Or maybe undressed?"

"Mmmm, Roshan, people are coming over here. And you know Hema and Monisha shopped with me for days for this sari and are coming up to help me get dressed in a second. I can't figure it out without them."

"Well, I don't know why you want to wear one for the ceremony in the first place."

"Really? Roshan, really?" Irritation gritted out of her throat, and she waved politely to a some friends exiting the hall toward the bar.

Her look of reprimand ruffled his fur, and he swallowed another swig of Jack. He wiped the moisture from his lips and kissed her on the cheek just as he saw Hema walking in their direction.

"I hope it's not for my mom, honey. You don't have to do this for them."

"I'm not doing this for them. Or you." She checked on Hema's progress, smiled at her, then just before Hema was in ear shot, Jenny whispered in his ear, "I'm going upstairs to put on a sari for our child. That's what people do. We do what's best for our kids." And slowly taking the empty glass from his hand and sniffing it, she added, "And I hope you will do the same." She stepped over to a bar table nearby and slid it onto the tablecloth.

He tried not to be angry. Not tonight. "I'm doing my best, Jen."

Hema interrupted before Jenny could answer. "Hey, ready to go up and get dressed?"

Roshan realized Hema looked prettier than he had seen her in a long time, having lost her baby weight, and her orange sari sparkled like her smile. She was the happiest person he knew and always made him smile, especially when she and Jay were together. They were both lucky people.

"*Bhai*, I hope you're good at unfastening safety pins later. Because this girl's going to be hooked up in safety pins tonight. When a woman is not used to wearing a sari, they are hard to keep together!"

Roshan smirked, wondering if Jenny's belly would be noticed. As he gave Jenny a quick peck on the cheek, he shuddered remembering his and Priya's wedding night. The idea that he would be sliding a sari off of Jenny tonight, the same way he did from Priya on their wedding night, made him a little nauseous. But the way things were looking between them, he may not have to worry about that later. He may be sleeping on the pull-out sofa in the suite.

He turned toward the wedding guests who were spilling out of the ballroom into the cocktail lounge area and steeled himself. The crowd was a who's who of dental specialist superstars, most of whom Jenny dealt with daily in her practice. In this one room there were enough to nearly staff a hospital, and every single one of them were important contacts for him. Lately, he had really had to work hard to keep himself together around patients, and it would be the same around these people who soon would see him for the failure in his profession that he was. He had started carrying gum with him everywhere he went for after-drink camouflage, which he needed most of the time now. He had to put on his poker face because the way his business was going these days, he was going to need all the help he could get.

On one side of the room, furthest away from the bar, was the small group of his family huddled in a crowd, chatting amongst themselves in Gujarati. His mum looked as if she smelled something putrid while staring around the room at the people carrying mixed drinks. The little enclave looked like a colorful island among the other guests. When he married Priya, they had at least one hundred guests who'd flown in from places overseas. Relatives don't miss a wedding, and often travel around the world to attend because of family obligations, but not in this case. Roshan's first wedding had merited that, but this wedding was one to miss, so only his aunts and uncles and Jay and Hema had been on the invitation list.

Monisha glided comfortably from circle to circle of people, leaving his mum with Ashmi, looking awkward and a bit sullen.

Roshan, anxious to appease his conscience for what he'd just done here, approached his aunt. "Monisha Auntie."

She opened her arms to him and patted his back as they hugged. "Roshan. Congratulations. I'm so happy for you." Whispering and turning so no family members could read her lips, she spoke under her breath, "Jenny is a beautiful woman. She seems to be a good person." She grabbed his hand and squeezed. "Be careful, *bhai*. Your mum will come around. So will others. But be careful what you do. With Jenny. With family..."

"Auntie, I don't care what family thinks anymore," he lied. "I'm just going to do—"

"Roshan, stop." She looked around and squeezed his hand harder. "You do care, or we wouldn't be here tonight." She paused, then added, "I mean, you be careful with yourself. You are the bridge between your new wife and your family. You know the cliché that issues become water under the bridge? Well, the bridge has to be standing for the water to pass under it. If the supports on the bridge buckle, then all of that water washes over it. You understand?" She patted him on the cheek like she would a little boy and looked at her watch. "Oh, dear. Hema and Jenny have been upstairs for a long time now. I'd better go help dressing the bride. Hema insisted on going up alone. Maybe she just wanted to talk alone with Jenny. I'm going to go get them. Jenny has another wedding to be in!"

She excused herself from Roshan, and he saw his mum watching the whole way as she walked until the elevator doors closed. Then his mum's smile got bigger, got faker, and she began to mingle among the crowd. He plastered the same kind of false confidence to his cheeks and threw himself into the host role around the room.

As Roshan crowd-hopped, threw back drinks, and schmoozed, he made his way to his mum. He figured he should speak to her at his wedding reception.

"Mummy." He hugged her. All at once, he hated her, he feared her, and he missed her. His eyes watered a tiny bit as he inhaled her perfume and felt the comfort of her hands on his back. For a second, he was a boy whose mummy was kissing his boo boo. It felt good. But a moment later, he saw himself the monster that he was, a bleeding coward standing over two women with terror in their eyes. He pulled back and averted his eyes.

"Roshan. Congratulations, son." She wiped at the edges of her eyes and took the glass of Coke that Roshan extended to her.

"Mummy." He struggled for words. "I love her."

"I know, *bhai*."

"You think I'm going to screw this up, don't you?"

Esha smiled her fake smile again, aware always that the guests were watching. She took a deep breath.

"No, Roshan. It's just all so…complicated."

Off to the side, he saw an elderly white woman wearing a stretchy satin pants suit walking toward them on the arm of a tall black man with greying temples in a sharp suit. He wondered if this was the neighbor his mum had mentioned.

"It's not complicated anymore, Mummy. It's done." Tingles tweaked his fingers as he said that.

"It's not done yet, son. We're not done with the wedding. Until we get blessings from the priest, it's not done. That's the least you can do for me after all of this."

The elderly woman arrived and touched Esha's arm. Esha turned toward her, a smile spreading across her face as she looked up at the man. Roshan didn't like the way she smiled at him or the way the man smiled at her, but the moment was gone in a flash, and he told himself his imagination was just running wild.

"Hi Evelyn," Esha said, adding, "hi Rich. This is my son, Roshan."

"It's very nice to see you again, Roshan," Evelyn said, reaching up toward Roshan and hugging him precariously, Rich's arm still steadying her. Rich extended his hand to Roshan and Roshan didn't like how tight the grip was.

Rich patted his mum's back and added, "I feel like I know you already after all of the stories your mom has told us." Roshan glanced at his mum, and she nodded, but at Rich, not him. He did not like this feeling he was getting here.

"Oh? Do you and my mum know each other well?" he looked questioningly at his mum.

She jumped in quickly, "Oh, Roshan, I've forgotten to tell you in all of this wedding business that I help Rich with taking Evelyn to her appointments and seeing to her at the house. We *all* love chatting about our kids sometimes *on the back deck*, don't we, Evelyn?"

She likes this dude!

Roshan covered up his distaste and politely stated, "Don't tell me which stories you heard."

"Don't worry. It's all good things. We know that you were soccer MVP in high school and that you graduated from dental school at the top of your class. Impressive."

"Oh, thanks, Mum." Roshan said to his mom playfully, secretly grateful to her for not telling this guy about his current disappointments for her.

"It was a beautiful ceremony. Jenny's dress is just gorgeous," Evelyn said. "My aunt made my wedding dress. But that was in the forties. We didn't have much of anything during the war. I bet she had that one custom made!" She gestured toward the saris worn by his aunts and added, "I can't wait to see her clothes for the next ceremony. These dresses are so exotic."

Rich looked at Esha over his mom's head with amusement at Evelyn's wonderment. Roshan wondered if Rich knew so much more about saris than his mom, and who was he to act like that with his mum?

Just then, Jenny made her entrance to the area flanked by Monisha and Hema. His heart jumped.

"If you'll excuse me, I'm going to go check on my bride."

"Roshan, it was nice to meet you. Beautiful wedding. I guess we'll be seeing more of each other after this."

Roshan stopped in his tracks. "Really?" he looked at his mum.

"I won't be going back to New York for a while. I took a leave to come help her. So, whenever you come over to visit your mom, I'm sure we catch each other in the backyard, like Esha and I do." He motioned toward Esha. "She's given me great advice on keeping mom's tomato plants alive."

His mum smiled shyly at Rich, and Roshan realized he had a real problem on his hands here.

Evelyn patted Esha's arm fondly. "Oh, look, her outfit is so pretty."

Roshan turned and saw Jenny in the middle of the room, surrounded by a small group of her female staff and colleagues, oohing and aaahing at the heavy gold embroidery across the deep red sari's border. Looking lost on the fringe of the group was Wanda dressed in a cotton dress with her permed hair pulled up in a banana clip. Her high platform pumps had laces that wrapped around her ankles which gleamed in the glow from the chandeliers, clashing with the beauty his new wife radiated. This reminded him of a shopping trip he and Jenny had taken a week before the wedding. T had passed by the window of a Payless Shoe Store, and Jenny had remarked about a pair of patent leather pumps with ankle laces in the window. "Probably the one-stop-shop for the streetwalkers on Cleveland Avenue." He bet she'd had no idea her own mom would be wearing those shoes to their wedding.

The women were fingering the sparkles on the trim of Jenny's sari as he quickly made his way over to her.

"May I steal my bride?" His headache was gone now, and the warm glow of relaxation was flowing through his veins

Wanda looked relieved and said, "I'm going out for a smoke."

Roshan steered Jenny back over to his mum, who was now talking to some of his office staff along with Rich and Evelyn.

Emboldened by his new relaxed mood, Roshan introduced Jenny to Rich and Evelyn, adding, "Doesn't she look beautiful?" She was the most beautiful woman in the world to him, aglow, her gold hair and the gold in the sari matching the glow of her cheeks, and he was now glad she had insisted on wearing the outfit after all.

Evelyn said, "Oh goodness, you're back. Yes, you are stunning dear. And your outfit is spectacular. You wear it well."

Esha added, "It is a nice sari, but our brides wear heavier saris for the weddings. And we paint henna on their hands and feet. It's tattoo art. Very beautiful." Looking at Jenny, she said sweetly, "But it's okay. You look nice."

She reached over and sniffed, fiddling with the folds of the pleats at Jenny's waist. The top edge of the long sari fabric had been painstakingly tucked into the waist of her drawstring petticoat, and at her belly button a large section had been expertly folded into perfect pleats, tucked in, and secured with a large safety pin before being wrapped across her body and pleated on her shoulder by Monisha. Even with the pin to secure the pleats to her petticoat, the whole lot had slackened and threatened to come loose.

Jenny's face bloomed scarlet.

Turning back to Evelyn and the others, Esha added, "Hard to wear our saris when don't know how, no?" Esha looked Jenny directly in the eye, inflaming Roshan's gut. "But, A for effort, yes?" As she chuckled, there was a nervous silence.

Roshan added, "I think she looks beautiful in everything she wears." Irritation replaced the pity he had been feeling for his mum.

Esha sniped, "Of course. So beautiful. But we should have shopped, you and me. Another, more better red. It look good on you. Something...not so too much for your color so...pale. This red...more for me. You know? More darker. More better." She clucked her tongue. "My fault. Would be better to help you."

Jenny turned her back and walked away.

Roshan began to boil and watched her stop for a moment to talk with James and Wanda, who held a rocks glass in a shaky hand, then move on to immerse herself in a crowd of colleagues on the other side of the room. He knew her well enough to know that work talk would calm her. It's where she wasn't a fish out of water. He turned to his mum, and as all but Rich began to slip away discreetly and quickly chat with others, Roshan stared her straight in the eye. The white hot anger in his eyes blurred his vision.

"So, saris only look good on dark-skinned people?"

"Son, I didn't mean that. It's just that they are made for us, not… other people."

"Other people? Us? She is an 'us,' mummy. Or, am I an 'other people' now?" He glared at Rich.

Why are you still here?

"Roshan," she pulled back from him, her social smile still on her face.

Roshan knew that Rich could sense the anger, knowing from his mum's "stories" what Roshan was capable of when his buttons were pushed. Rich stood close to Esha, but kept a steady eye on Roshan.

Esha continued. "I guess, I don't know which, *bhai*. Are you an 'other people' now? She's not an 'us.' Who is she to me? Your wife? Okay. Yes. But I don't know her. I don't live with her. I don't know her parents. Yes, saris are for Indians. I'm sorry you don't like it."

"So, what should our children wear, Mummy? Indian clothes? Or will they not be allowed? Does…it…matter?"

Rich laid a hand gently on Roshan's shoulder, and Roshan stared at his hand and then at Rich, resisting the urge to punch him for being there in a family discussion. Jenny had no place, but this guy did? What the hell was going on here?

"I pray we never have to answer that question."

Roshan flagged down the cocktail waitress, gulped some champagne, and said to Rich as he shrugged away his hand, "My mum had better come up with an answer to that question soon. Like in five months." And he walked away.

The rest of the evening slid by. The Hindu ceremony was nothing more than a few short prayers with the Brahmin priest, only a small flame in front of them instead of a fire to circle like he and Priya did in their wedding. Neither he nor Jenny understood the priests Sanskrit, handshakes, and clinking of glasses.

Beau caught Roshan in between chats despite his evasive tactics. "So, I've been trying to get ahold of you, buddy. I hate to do this to you now, but you've gotta meet with the other attorneys. You can't bury your head in the sand over this."

Roshan's eyes darted around him, and he said nothing.

Beau shook his head. "Come on, man. If you don't cooperate, this could become criminal. Do what you gotta do."

"Thanks, I'll take it into consideration." He pretended to catch the eye of another guest, "Look, nice talking to you, Beau. I've got to say hi to someone now. Go get another drink. Enjoy yourself."

Even though the wedding party was small, true to Indian style, they had the photographer get everyone in a picture with the bridal couple. Dozens with Jenny and him together in different poses, one with Esha and Roshan, one with Monisha Auntie and Esha and Roshan, another with him with his uncles, then with uncles and aunts, and so on. Smiling so hard his cheeks hurt, he reflected back to his first wedding. He was surprised his mum actually wanted to be in the pictures at all, but she did make sure she was at his side for every pose.

With the cutting of the cake, he smushed cake into Jenny's mouth. He had forewarned her that it was tradition in his family, and she graciously agreed to it as long as he promised no pictures and a towel for her close by. She wiped her mouth and returned the favor with bigger piece smashed into his mouth, and they laughed like they hadn't laughed in a long time.

In the dim lighting on the dance floor to the sound of their song, he took his bride firm under his hands for their first dance. They looked only at one another, and in that moment, he saw his future in her eyes. As the song ended, he felt a clarity he hadn't felt in months. His buzz had worn off, and he didn't care. His headache was over. In that moment, it was Jenny and him. Nothing but air between them.

"Let's get out of here," he whispered and pulled Jenny through the maze of the crowd. He pulled her to a corner of the ballroom and leaned into her in the dark. "I can't wait to get you upstairs." He breathed into her ear.

"Hold your horses, Tonto. We have to wait for our guests to leave." A guest caught her eye as he was leaving, and she playfully tried to slip away from Roshan to bid him goodbye.

But Roshan blocked her way and said, "I can't wait to get you away from all of this. These people. I can't breathe."

"Honey, we have guests. We need to get back to them. What will they think if we just leave?" she said with irritation in her voice. "We...I need to make a good impression here. Isn't that what this wedding was all about?"

Shaking his head and stepping aside, Roshan allowed her to pull him by the hand toward the man at the door. Saying nothing, he allowed himself to be led around the room to say goodbyes to departing guests. When only Esha, Wanda and James, Jay and Hema, and Evelyn and Rich were left, he lingered to the side of them, quiet. Hema' gave Roshan a quizzical look when Rich placed his hand on Esha's shoulder briefly to usher her toward the door. Roshan forced on his game face. He wasn't going to let any of them know how he felt. Not Hema, not Esha, and not this Rich, who apparently knew his mum so well.

Wrapping his arm around Jenny's waist, he pulled her to him and kissed her hard.

"Go, stallion!" Jay said, slapping him on the back. "Let's go people, the honeymooners need to get a room. "

"Jay, you taking Mum home?"

"Yes. Auntie, come. Let's go now. The valet has already pulled the car up."

Rich chimed in, "I'll give her a lift."

Jay and Roshan stared at the man, both of them motionless. Roshan would not have it.

"No, no. Jay will take her. Thanks anyway."

"Yes, I'll take her. Come, Auntie. Let's go."

Esha smiled at Rich and Evelyn, thanking them for coming, and after kissing both Roshan and Jenny perfunctorily, she followed Hema and Jay out the door into the night.

Rich shook his head slightly and smiled an irritated grin. "Well, congratulations, Dr. and Mrs. Desai. Goodnight." Evelyn hugged them both and let Rich lead her slowly and gently through the doors, his hand on her elbow, poised to catch her at any time.

Roshan and Jenny were left alone in the dim light as bus boys in white jackets entered and began clinking and clanging crystal and china into plastic tubs.

"We really did it," Jenny said, holding his hand to her belly.

"Yes. We did." He breathed deeply and kissed her as a tinge of joy and prick of panic swelled in his throat.

We did it.

Chapter 16

Esha

She locked the front door behind her and waved goodbye toward the fading headlights as they disappeared down her driveway and into the darkness. The dim light in the house gave her a shiver; she would probably never get used to living alone. She slipped off her gold pumps and hugged her chest all the way into the kitchen. The stove hood light was on, and her tin of black tea sat next to the cooktop.

It's too late for tea. I'll be up all night.

But since she wasn't a drinker, tea was her comfort. Besides, she told herself as she filled a sauce pan with water and placed it on the flame, she would not be able to sleep tonight anyway. There was no harm in having her tea.

The black tea boiled along with the water. She grated the ginger, poured in the milk, spooned plenty of sugar in, and mixed. The strainer was placed at the top of her tea cup, and she poured the creamy mixture into it, leaving a clump of black wet leaves behind. Grabbing a piece of *roti* to dunk into the tea, she walked toward the kitchen table to sit. Alone. To stew about the evening.

All around her was the night. The refrigerator hummed, the wall clock she'd gotten in India as a young bride ticked behind her, and, warmed only by the glow of the stove light, she allowed the night to hold her, feeling herself fading into the nothingness. There was nothing around her, she could see nothing, and she could feel nothing, until thoughts of Roshan's baby growing inside that woman began gnawing at her. This baby is a disaster.

God, why?

Jay had asked her several times to come stay with them at their house for a while. "You shouldn't be alone right now, Auntie. We want you to come. Come help with the kids. Jyoti loves you." But she couldn't. Wouldn't. Jay was like a son to her, no doubt. But he was still Monisha's son, not hers. She had so wanted to have a family like Monisha had with Jay and his family. She had even held out hope that Roshan and Jenny's marriage could end in divorce soon, giving him another opportunity to do marry in again, but a baby ruined that chance.

So there she sat alone, breathing in time with the tick-tock of the clock. She sat there for a while, eyes adjusting to the nothingness in front of her when she saw a light flicker on outside the back window. Peering outside, she saw that it was a flashlight shining around Evelyn's backyard, like prison searchlights searching for an escapee. There was a loud, "Hah! Get! Shoo!" and a shoe stomping on the wood planks of Evelyn's deck. It was Rich.

Though hesitant to rejoin the world, her curiosity got the better of her, and she carried her tea barefooted out onto the deck.

"It got away?" she asked across the shrubs that barely came to the height of either of their decks.

"I think so. That's the damn thing that's been eating my tomatoes!" His button down shirt was open several buttons at the top, the belt was gone from his dress slacks, and he was barefooted.

"What kind of animal you shooing?"

"A raccoon. They're sneaky and mean. I've been trying to scare him off for a week now, but he just keeps coming back." Rich took a deep breath and dropped the flashlight to his side. "How are you doing, Esha?"

She shrugged her shoulders and nodded, "Okay, fine. No problem." She was leaning up against the deck railing with the tea cup balanced on the ledge. Her gold bangles jingled against the wood each time she picked up the cup, but she said nothing more and continued to sip, avoiding his face and studying the grains of wood in the deck railing.

"I've never had to deal with raccoons before. Where I live in New York, the biggest rodent we deal with is rats. I guess they'd eat tomato plants too, if I'd had them. But, who has time for that in the city?" He stepped cautiously down the steps and shone his light under her deck, looking for any sign of movement.

"Thank you for having us at the ceremony. It really meant a lot to Mom." He stepped gingerly down onto the grass, then paused suddenly, bent over looking up under where Esha stood. She continued to sip her tea, amused with watching him.

She whispered, "You look like that cartoon man Roshan watched when he was small. Elmo Food, Fuss, something like that. Carried a gun. Chased a rabbit."

"Elmer Fudd," he replied, standing up, looking embarrassed. Esha was afraid she'd hurt his feelings, but then he said, *"I'm wooking fo' a waccoon, not a wabbit."*

Relieved, she relaxed a bit and put the cup to her lips against her smile.

At that moment, Rich lurched forward with a stick, shouting "Aaaah, get, get, get!" while banging so hard against her deck that she dropped her cup. The cup fell to the grass below her with a soft thump, and the tea splashed against Rich's pants leg beside it.

"Oh God. Are you okay?"

Rich stood there on one leg, fanning the hem of his pants away from his skin. "Ooh, ooh, that's hot stuff."

"So sorry," she said. "Come, come. Up here. I get you towel." She motioned for him to step up onto her deck and slipped into the kitchen. She picked up two dishtowels and ran one under cold water. She liked her *chai* hotter than most. He would need it cold.

When she stepped back outside, he was sitting on a step of the deck, rolling up the cuff of his pants. She handed him the wet towel.

"Put on the burned skin. It's cool. Burns need cool."

"Ah, that is better," he said and rested the towel on his ankle. He leaned back and handed her the empty cup he'd retrieved from the grass. "My mom has told me how hot your food is, but I thought she was talking about spices."

"Our food is spicy! My tea not spicy. Sweet. Very sweet. But must be hot, hot." She pulled up the towel and looked at his angry skin. "You've had?"

"No. Never have. I'm an iced tea drinker. Unsweetened. Only had green tea at Chinese restaurants. Yours smells very different."

"I make you some. You must try. You'll like."

"No, it's late, Esha. You don't have to do that."

Always eager to share her cooking with people—it was how she grew up, after all—she left him sitting on the step holding the wet towel to his leg and put more water on to boil. In less than five minutes, she had a steaming cup in her hand, bending over him on the steps to share with him.

"Thank you. You didn't get more for yourself."

"No problem. I don't need more caffeine." She wanted to say more, but stopped herself. She didn't really know this man, just the stories of him that Evelyn had told her in polite conversations.

Rich sipped cautiously from the cup and looked at her, "This is very tasty. Thank you." He sipped some more, as Esha glowed, and said, "You should give me the recipe for this. Mmmm."

"Your mom has tea already at home. I give some ginger too. You ask her. She can show you. Then you make *chai* for all of us."

"That doesn't surprise me. She talks about you all the time. For a lady who grew up with hamhocks and cornbread, she certainly has taken a liking to the spicy snack foods you bring over all the time. I've even had to hide some things from her because they aggravate her ulcer."

He removed the wet towel and pulled down the pant leg with one hand, still holding the cup in the other. His high cheekbones and blue eyes were proof that Evelyn was his mom, but Esha thought he must look more like his father. Trying hard to bury her attraction to him, she couldn't stop looking at his square jaw and dark hair. She continued to stand next to him as he sat on the step, uncomfortable with joining him. She looked out into the blackness in the yard and shivered. She was in back of her empty, monstrous house, outside, exposed. Nervous.

"I going to be a grandma. We say *Ba*. But I guess I be grandma here." Saying the words made it real, and she sat on one of the iron chairs at the table, the table set Priya had chosen but walked away from, satisfied with her quick cash settlement. Even after the fight and the venomous things Priya had said, Esha had been sad to see Priya leave with her bulging suitcases flanked by her brother and father, shutting the door behind them without a glance. The era was over, but Priya's mark still filled every corner of the house.

Rich had heard Roshan's announcement earlier, so this was not news to him. Congratulations. Right?" He looked up from his step questioningly.

She just looked at him as if he'd just said the stupidest thing in the world and smiled, shaking her head.

"Forgive me. So sorry. You don't know me well. I not supposed to say..." she cupped her chin in her palm and turned away from him, as a tear slipped down her cheek. Why was she doing this? Here? Now? His kind voice just made her feel safe.

"It's okay. It's fine. Sometimes it's easier to talk to people you don't know well. When I went through my divorce, I wouldn't talk to people for a long time, but when things got nasty between me and Olivia, then Jessica, our daughter got dragged into it, I ended up spilling my guts to a guy in a bar one night Strangers. They're just kind of a blank chalkboard to draw out all of your thoughts on, but then you can erase them as soon as they're out. And they don't hang around to remind you." He added, "Though I'll be here for a while…"

"Good point," she smiled. "I cannot speak to my family about these things. All too much. Back in India, no one does this. I do back then what my parents tell me to do. I marry young. He take me to his village. I do what I supposed to do. What I do wrong?"

"I don't know Roshan, and I don't know your situation, but maybe you didn't do anything wrong. Maybe he's supposed to be walking his own path? Just a thought."

"We don't make our own paths. We walk the same path with our family. And we don't pick people up along the side of the road."

"Well, if my parents had listened to everyone else back here in Georgia when they met, I wouldn't be here. So, I guess I'm not the person to sympathize with you."

"I'm so sorry. I didn't mean to offend you…"

"You didn't offend me." He sipped more tea and looked at her in a way that made her feel uncomfortably intimate with him, and she had to look away.

He sat for a moment on the step, peering under bushes toward the edge of the yard.

"I think I scared him off." He stood brushing off his slacks. "Thanks for the tea… *chai*," he added, smiling. "I'd better let you get back inside. You've had a long night."

She nodded and caught herself letting her eyes linger on his for too long. She took the tea cup from him and turned toward the house.

"I tell you if I see your 'waccoon' again." Her accent mangled the words, and he laughed.

"Thanks," he said, smiling over his shoulder. "I'll let Mom know I tasted the tea. She'll be happy."

Esha shut the door behind her and rubbed her face. Without looking at herself, she could feel the sagging of her eyes and cheeks from sheer exhaustion. In her bedroom as she unpinned the sari from her shoulder, letting pleats of fabric fall to the floor, she watched the picture of her husband staring at her from the dresser. He was a face whose name she never spoke any more. He stood there, his arm around a small Roshan in a possessive stance as he had in life. She'd always left the picture out for Roshan, who had lost a father, no matter how harsh his dad was. The man had never laid a hand on Roshan. He was a good father and sober during the days. There were even weekends when the two would play outside together and come back in for a snack, and Roshan would sit on his dad's lap while Daddy drank tea and he nibbled on a sweet biscuit. The bruises on her came at night and had been easy to hide from Roshan the next day. Roshan was small, but he sensed them anyway and became more protective over her around his daddy. Still, this was his father.

But tonight, it was time. She walked across the room and placed the framed picture face down on the top of the white and gold trimmed dresser.

She had nothing to lose anymore.

As she pulled her pillow off the bed to fluff it, her baby's satin-trimmed blanket fell to the floor. Stepping over it, she sank herself into the bed, hot cheek on the cool pillow. She saw through the window the glow of the porch light next door go dark, and she lay there clothed only in a bra and cotton petticoat she wore under her sari. Her skin chilled in the open air, but she lay like a stone. She couldn't even weep.

Chapter 17

Jenny

Jenny trudged around her office every day, struggling more to muster the energy to work as her belly got bigger. The muscle strength that her work took was becoming too hard on her, and her back had started giving out. She had to work, though, because Roshan was such a wild card lately, vacillating between depressed mornings drawing messy, drunken sketches before work, and perky mornings, waking up early for work like his old self when he wasn't drinking.

"Mr. Hawkins," she said exhausted. "Amanda will give you a list of aftercare instructions in a minute." She patted the elderly man's rope-veined hand and leaned back into more back pain than she had leaning forward. "You did great. Just follow up with us in a week, and we'll see how you're doing."

The old man nodded and mumbled "thank you" with half of his mouth slack. Jenny stood up, patting his shoulder as she pushed her weight forward in order to slide off of the rolling chair without letting it roll out from under her. She felt like a walrus.

Amanda handed Jenny's cellphone to her as she left the operatory. "Roshan," she whispered.

Amanda was incapable of hiding her feelings, especially her disdain for Roshan. Jenny had learned to quit sharing too much information about the two of them with Amanda over the last few months. Their friendship, though never very close, suffered, but Jenny couldn't stand the judgment that came from other people anymore. In-laws, coworkers. It didn't matter. The details of what went on behind closed doors at her house—not the idyllic things that went on in most newlywed's homes—were not anyone's business anyway. Jenny had to figure things out on her own without anyone else's opinions.

"Hey, baby," she said, putting the phone to her ear and walking into her office.

"Hey." His voice sounded flat, but not slurred.

"You feeling any better today?"

"What's that supposed to mean, Jen?"

"Nothing. I could tell how upset you were when you got off the phone with your mom last night before bed. I may not understand Gujarati, but I understand anger." She swallowed hard to keep down her anger during the long pause.

"I called to remind you that my mum has an outfit for you to wear tonight to the Diwali celebration. She'll bring it by the house after work."

Jenny dreaded seeing his mom. Esha had not called them for weeks after the wedding, and Roshan said to let it lay for a while. Then, when she and Roshan did go visit her at her house, the house Roshan still paid for, because she wouldn't come to the home he and Jenny shared, she was cold and formal, and usually made sure that Monisha and Hema were there to help serve food so that no personal conversation could take place. Although Jenny was two weeks from her due date, Esha had yet to mention the baby at all. No inquiry into the child's sex. No inquiry into Jenny's health. Nothing.

"Okay. Yay. I wish Hema were in town to bring me one. I hate having to take anything from your mother."

"Well, baby, this is what it's going to take. I have to try to make amends. I need to do it for the baby. You think this is easy on me? I have obligations you can never understand."

She didn't answer. Instead, memories rose of heated, drunken rants about how he didn't deserve his family's love, and how he loved her and the baby so much but he didn't deserve any of them. Sometimes, after dinners with Jay and Hema with talk of family get-togethers that Roshan wasn't invited to, he would tuck her into bed and drive around for hours in the dead of the night.

"I want to make it work for the baby too, Roshan. This is not easy for me either."

I never planned on any of this.

His voice softened. "I know. Let's just try to do this, okay? If my mom says anything to you, just let it roll. It won't help matters to snipe back. It's just how Indian mother-in-laws are."

Jenny saw Amanda motioning to her out of the corner of her eye to get back to patients. Jenny had been making a strong effort at patient relations lately and had to hurry back.

"Baby, I have to get back to work. Don't you have any patients waiting on you?"

"Um, actually my morning has been slow. I think I'm going to go for an early lunch."

"Okay, but Roshan," she added in a young girl's voice that she recognized from childhood pleas to her father, "please make it just lunch today. Order water?"

"Yeah. Sure. I'll come home in a respectable state tonight."

It wasn't just tonight she was worried about. It was letters from a malpractice attorney she found under his desk at home that worried her. They must have slipped out of his briefcase. One was dated three months ago, a few days before their wedding. And the other was dated last week. He had never once mentioned them to her, even when she was sure he knew she could overhear his phone conversations with the attorneys from another room.

"I love you," she said soothingly. "I really do."

"Love you too, Babe. See ya tonight."

She hung up the phone and felt pain zing her lower back. She'd been having back pain for the last month as her belly had gotten bigger and the weight put more pressure on her back. After sitting all day working on patients, her back ached so much when she got home that she couldn't find a comfortable position to lie in the bed. Roshan would massage her back, and even when he was less than sober, he gently rubbed until she relaxed and could sleep.

But when she rolled over, she knew he would often leave the bed. In the mornings, she was the first to wake and would find a glass left on the counter with traces of caramel-colored liquid in the bottom. They didn't talk about his drinking, but he never made an effort to cover it up either. And over the past few weeks as her belly grew rounder and she wanted to slow down, he became more defensive about it. And he was going in to work later and later, and he'd be home when she'd get home in the evenings, always sketchbook in hand, dirty socks on the coffee table, with his head bent down, hand scurrying heatedly across the page, creating dark images of faces and places she didn't recognize, and didn't want to either.

As she walked into the hallway toward her next patient, a hot grip suddenly squeezed her lower back, and she had to stop in her tracks. Breathless, she leaned against the wall until it subsided.

"You okay?" Amanda asked as she led a teenage girl toward a chair. She gestured for the girl to sit in the chair and turned toward Jenny. By this time, the pain had subsided, and Jenny stood upright.

"Yeah, I'm good. Just back pain."

"I remember how that was. You're due in two weeks, right?"

"Twelve days, actually. Twelve days left to work and make some money. But who's counting?" She managed a small grin, a person in her peripheral vision catching her eye. It was Wanda standing by the front checkout counter, looking at her, waiting.

"Oh, you'll be fine. Roshan's practice is good, right?"

"Yeah. Yeah, I guess it'll be fine. Yes, Roshan works." She left Amanda to prep the teenage girl and walked slowly over to Wanda. "Hi, Wanda. Long time no see."

"Hey doll. Wow. You sure have grown. Close, huh?"

"Yes, almost there. Where've you been? You dropped off the face of the Earth after the wedding."

"I've been around." Wanda looked around not making eye contact with Jenny. "Things have, um, not been going so good for me for a while." Her eyes looked glassy, and Jenny's stomach sank into a familiar pit.

"Say no more. You're not feeling well."

Wanda grinned sheepishly and looked at Jenny at the sarcasm in her words.

"Yeah. I guess I'm not doin' too good."

Jenny pulled Wanda into her office and shut the door.

"Where's James?"

"He's gone."

"What happened? I thought you guys were both doing so well. You talked like you were happy together..."

"I started not feeling good again and just couldn't help myself. He, ah, found some stuff in the bathroom a couple months ago, and I threw it away. I never used it. I just got it in a moment of weakness. I was clean, I promise you. But, we fought about it, and he left. He said he couldn't trust me. I got no place to live. With him gone, I can't afford the rent."

Jenny knew what Wanda was there for. She did not respond with an offer.

"So, you're not using now?" Jenny didn't think her pupils were dilated, but her hands shook while she wrung them. Her hair was brushed, and she looked good in spite of her predicament. Maybe, just maybe, she was okay. Maybe she wouldn't disappoint again.

"So, I guess, I was wonderin', um, maybe you could borrow me a little cash? Just enough to get into a motel or somethin' 'til I can figure myself out. Maybe enough for a week?"

"I'm not giving you money." Jenny felt her cheeks turn red and suddenly felt dizzy. She had to sit in her desk chair to keep from letting on to how she felt. She had too much to handle.

There was a knock at the door. "Dr. Jenkins. Your 3:30 is prepped. You also have an emergency toothache waiting in the lobby. We really need you."

Jenny pulled out her checkbook from her Louis Vuitton bag, scribbled out a check, and ripped it out of the book. She reached across the desk and deposited it into the woman's open palm. "Who's gonna help you? Why don't you go get yourself a motel room and ask for Jesus to help you. You're supposed to be reborn, right? Go find him." She pushed herself up from the chair, legs spread apart, and finished lifting her weight up with her arms. Despite the hot ache in her pelvis, she forced herself to the door. Before she opened it, she closed her eyes and leaned her forehead against the door frame. Then she said to Wanda, who sat fingering the crisp check over and over in her hand, "Get yourself together in a week. If I see you aren't blowing the money on more junk, I'll help you. Call me with the address of the motel you're at, and I'll come pick you up then."

Amanda still hovered by the door, silent and at a courteous distance.

"Amanda will call around and find a good place for you to stay. I'll take care of the cost…for now."

"Thank you, baby. I won't disappoint you this time. I promise."

"Amanda will show you the back door. You can walk around the building to get to the street."

She left the door open, and her mother shakily put the check in her scuffed up leather purse. When the woman stood to leave, she raised her hand to wave, but Jenny had already turned her back and begun to look at the teenage girl's chart. When she heard the back door shut, she put the chart down and gloved up, feeling her cheeks burn hotter and hotter.

Ignoring the heat that was engulfing her from top to bottom, she smiled reassuringly and warmly at the girl before pulling her mask up to her nose.

With bloody gloves, she focused quickly and precisely on taking away the pain of the young girl in front of her, all the while ignoring her own.

By four thirty, Jenny had packed up her briefcase. Amanda came into the office just as Jenny attempted to sling the shoulder strap on to her shoulder.

"No, don't. I'll do that." She grabbed it from Jenny gently and easily slung it over her own. "You don't look so hot, doc. Do you want to call Roshan to come pick you up?"

"No, I'll make it. I'm just tired. I'll have a few minutes to rest before his mom comes over to the house."

"His mom? What for?"

"She's bringing an Indian outfit for me to wear to an affair tonight. It's Diwali."

"And what is Diwali?"

"Sort of the Hindu Christmas. Festival of lights. It's my first one, but I'm told there's dancing and music and food."

"And lots of Roshan's family?" Amanda asked dryly.

"Yes. Lots of aunties and uncles," Jenny said, rubbing her tight belly absentmindedly.

"Well, that should be fun for you, Miss Popularity." They walked out the backdoor to Jenny's car. Amanda placed the briefcase in the backseat of the gold Mercedes and shut the door, facing Jenny.

"I know this is none of my business, you've made that clear. But I have to ask, why do you put up with this? If my in-laws treated me like the plague, then I'd make sure Robert and I and the kids high-tailed it to somewhere like Montana, leaving no forwarding address."

"That's not an option, Amanda. Roshan will not leave them. It's either all or nothing. And I have a baby to think about."

"But what about you? Don't you care about yourself? Do you like being an outsider? Don't you want a family who loves you?"

"Amanda," she said as she lowered herself gingerly into the driver's seat. "I never had that kind of family. I'm sure you noticed with Wanda's visits. Nothing has changed but the color of skin. But I want my kid to have a family though..." Sitting pushed the baby up into her chest, and she struggled for breath. "...So, I'm going to go home and dress up in Indian clothes, and try to make a family for my kid to live in, even if I have to pretend I'm someone I'm not." She strapped herself in with difficulty, slipping the belt under the squiggling feet and hands that visibly rippled her belly. Even the baby knew she was stressed. "See you tomorrow, Amanda. Thanks for caring."

She drove away, watching Amanda shake her head and walk back into the office to lock it up. Her hope was that Roshan would already be home and at least he could hold her for a private moment before Esha and Monisha got there. She needed his arms around her or she felt she would fall apart. Maybe today would be a good day for them.

Esha's car was already in the driveway when she pulled up to the house. Her hopes of time with her husband sank. Inside, Roshan was in front of the TV watching a car show on cable with a large water bottle beside him. He waved, got up, and came to her at the door. She was so happy to smell only cologne on him.

"Hey, baby." He kissed her neck and wrapped his arms around her lower back gently.

"Hey. You're home early," she said, for once pleased to see him here already.

"Yeah. Got done early." He kissed her lips, stymying any further probing into the subject.

His breath smelled of fresh toothpaste with no sour hint of bourbon.

Peaceful relief settled over her. Though she knew from experience it was temporary, she desperately needed to know he would take care of her now and allowed herself to enjoy the moment.

"She's here." He motioned his head toward the stairs leading up to their bedroom. "Already awaiting your highness's presence in our room."

"How much time do we have before we have to be there?"

"About thirty minutes. You two make nice and hurry, okay?"

"Okay." She swallowed her pride and stepped up the stairs but was stopped in her tracks with a gripping, searing pain in her lower back. She cringed and bent over, unable to stifle a moan. Roshan rushed over to her before she could tilt backward off the step and pulled her weight to him.

"You okay?" he asked, his voice squeaked with concern.

Gritting her teeth, Jenny lied. "I'm fine. Just a back spasm. Give me a second, and I'll be fine."

"You're so close to your due date. Do you think it could be—"

"No. It's not labor." She shut him down quickly and pulled herself upright with the hand railing. It couldn't be labor. She was not ready. It could not happen. Not yet. She forced herself to ascend the stairs carefully, keeping a look of peace on her face as Roshan watched her walk up. She had to keep going. She knew the baby would have to come sometime. But she dreaded it. She needed to maintain control.

Once at the top of the stairs, she heard two women speaking inside the master bedroom. The Gujarati was so fast that she could only make out one of the few words she had learned in the language over the last few months.

Wo. Daughter-in-law.

And the harshness of Esha's voice when she spat out the word, right before Jenny walked through the doorway, lingered in the room with the surprise on Esha's face at the sight of her.

"Oh, Jenny. You early. We not ready yet." Monisha looked up at Jenny with a more welcoming smile while Esha busied herself laying out matching jewelry sets next to outfits spread out on the bed. There were three outfits, all Punjabis with drawstring pants. One was laid flat across the pristine white bassinet that stood beside her side of the bed, and the others were spread out on the bed. There was a brown and black one with gold trim that made Jenny think of mud, and she looked from it to Esha, wondering if she thought that would be flattering on her.

"Jenny, come sit." Monisha pulled her gently to the bedside and sat her down. "You rest while we figure this out. You look exhausted."

You have no idea.

"Okay, try this one on." Esha held up another Punjabi that was a sour green with cheap looking silver leaves printed on the cuffs and sash.

"This one?"

Jenny tried to politely smile, but her disdain for the outfit must have been apparent, because Monisha quickly piped in.

"Nah, Esha. Not that one. I told you not to bring that one. It's old. That's from our time." She shooed it away and touched the sleeve of a vibrant purple one spread out on the pillows at the head of the bed. "This one, Jenny," she asked with a smile, ignoring Esha's glare. "You like this one?"

"It's very pretty. Sure, I can try that one on."

"That one? Monisha. Isn't that one Hema's?"

Monisha nodded. "Yes. She wore it when she was pregnant. It's only 2, 3 years old."

"Well," Esha looked Jenny up and down, "do you really think it will be big enough?"

Jenny sat on the bed as if she were a fly on the wall, watching the exchange. She was in too much pain to move or take the bait thrown at her.

"*Bhabhi*," Monisha retorted defensively for Jenny, "if it fit Hema, it should fit her. I sewed a larger panel in the front of the pants, and of course it's drawstring. It'll fit."

Esha busied herself with arranging a set of gold, silver, and green bangles with a necklace and earring set by the green outfit. "But," she said slowly, "my *wo* here is bigger than our girls. See?" She pointed to Jenny's rib cage and held up her hands spread apart. "See, wider. Hema is small here like Priya—" She caught herself and stopped for a second. "I don't think it will fit. Besides," she turned toward Jenny, who sat silently in the grip of pain, and asked, "this color is bright for your skin color. You don't really want to stand out anyway, do you?"

Really? Did she really say that to me?

Jenny snapped. She was done with all of this nonsense. "Why don't I want to stand out at the *garba*, Esha? So that Priya's friends will not notice me? So that all of the old people will not have a spectacle to stare at as soon as I walk through the door?"

Esha looked at her wide-eyed, fueling Jenny's explosion.

Monisha sat quickly on the bed next to Jenny, blocking the space between her and Esha. She held up two sets of bracelets to Jenny. "Come on, ladies. These or these?"

Jenny looked at the bracelets not seeing them.

Yeah, I'm speaking up. And you're gonna listen.

She tried to stand, had to get out of the room. But, her lower half would no longer lift her. She sank into the grip of a white hot hand squeezing the small of her back. Her head pounded so much suddenly that she could barely see.

"Jenny, you okay?" Monisha asked. When Jenny didn't answer, she took her pulse, then adeptly helped her lay on her left side. "Better?"

Jenny nodded but spat out more to Esha, who was lifting and examining clothes as if she were the only person in the room. "You want to go around with your people and hide me in the shadows, pretending I'm not here? Parade your precious son in front of everyone? Am I interfering with you finding a suitable girl for him again?"

"Jenny, calm down." She saw Monisha glare at Esha and motion her away. "*Bhabhi*, get a moist wash cloth. And go get Roshan." She held Jenny's wrist to take her pulse again and looked concerned. "Have you been having headaches?"

"No," she lied.

"Contractions?"

"No. I'm fine," she barked then glanced at the genuine concern in Monisha's eyes. "Well, maybe some pressure. But just for a couple of hours. I'm fine. Just stressed."

Placing her hand on Jenny's hardening belly, Monisha gently spoke, "Jenny, dear. Try not to let this bother you. You have someone else to worry about now. My *bhabhi* is not bad. She's been through a lot. You have no idea. She's very self-conscious of how people see her. Our people talk."

"Roshan has told me some things about his dad. I know. But, why doesn't she just tell people off? What kind of people treat a woman badly when it was her husband who was the bad guy?"

"Our culture is our culture. Women haven't had much control over their own lives until recent years. When Esha and I were growing up in India, even our little brothers had more say in things than we did."

Jenny heard footsteps coming up the stairs.

"Jenny, Esha has always needed Roshan. She lost so much. He is all she has. She lost Pri—."

"Her suitable daughter-in-law."

"No, not just that. Her husband not only took her dignity. I'm sure Roshan has told you about the unfortunate circumstances of his sisters's passing. About his father. And his mum has had years of pretending she is fine, for Roshan's sake. Give her some room."

Jenny was confused by the dark look that came over Monisha's face. "His dad is dead, right? What happened to Esha's daughter?"

"You don't know? Oh my God. There is so much you need to know about this family. Roshan needs to tell you. But, right now I can tell you this. Roshan's father was a troubled man and abused Esha when she was pregnant...and the baby died."

Shock shuttered through her entire body, and Jenny put both arms protectively across her belly as if the ghost of Roshan's father could harm her baby now.

Roshan led Esha into the room, and both came to her side of the bed. He looked irritated. Esha hovered in the back, running her fingers across the lavender satin trim of the receiving blanket that draped, still creased from its packaging, over the bassinet. She was watching Roshan and Monisha tend to Jenny, but it looked to Jenny that she wasn't really seeing them. Was that worry in her eyes?

"Are you having a baby now?" he asked, his voice was full of forced cheerfulness, but wobbled with a hint of fear, or was it annoyance?

Jenny looked at Monisha for an answer.

"I don't think so," Monisha said. "Her pulse if steady. Some contractions, probably Braxton-Hicks, nothing to worry about." Monisha gave Jenny a motherly scowl then turned to Roshan and Esha. "Let her rest. No more stress for her today or she might really go into labor and she still has another two weeks left."

"What's stressing you?" Roshan asked as he took the wet cloth from Esha. He placed it on her forehead and glanced sideways at Esha, asking her silently if his mom was the problem.

Her head felt like it was full of pebbles, and she wanted nothing else to roll around in there.

Your drinking. Your lawsuit. Esha. Wanda. Loss of control. Fear.

Jenny looked at him and then at Esha, and said, "Oh, just things. Work."

Monisha and Esha excused themselves. Alone with Roshan, Jenny let down her guard. Just a bit.

"Are you ashamed of being with me?"

"What kind of a question is that?" A spark of frustration flickered in his eye, but disappeared. "No, I wouldn't be with you if I were."

"Your mother is."

"Yes. She is. And can you expect her to feel any differently?"

She felt like he'd spit in her face. "What? Are you defending her?"

"No. I'm not." He slapped the comforter beside her. "But, she has every reason to be embarrassed about you. Look at how we handled things from an Indian point of view for a second."

"Okay. You were in a bad marriage. You pursued me. You ended your marriage. You married me. And you are starting a family with me. I thought Indian men can do whatever they want."

"Ha, I wish. You make it sound so clean and neat. Everything I did affected my family, Jen. People talk about my mum now. My aunt is trying to find a girl for my cousin to marry after he graduates from Emory this spring, and no family will touch him with a ten foot poll because of me. It's not you. It's me that did the damage. She's just taking it out on you."

"Why don't we just tell everyone to fuck off and take our baby and live our lives far away?"

"It doesn't work that way for me, babe. And quit trying to change that. The fact is, I have to put on a show. You have to put on a show. And my mum has to put on a show. It doesn't matter what's going on behind our doors or what people are saying about us, we have to put on a smile and go to these Indian functions. It's not just about you anymore, Jen. Get used to it."

She stared in disbelief at his callous words. "You think I don't know that?" She sat up and raised her voice. "I've been working my heavy pregnant butt off to keep us afloat for months. You think I don't know about your lunchtime cocktails? Your water bottles of vodka you take to work?" She stopped herself unsure of how far to go, but she had to go ahead and say it. "And the malpractice suit?"

His face showed no expression. He looked as if he expected her to say it.

"Roshan, I'm also excellent at putting on a smile and pretending, dear."

At that, he stood up and left her in the room, sitting on the bed. Alone. Along with his footsteps on the stairs, there was a loud thud on the wall. Downstairs she heard him talking to Esha and Monisha, she heard the jingling of the car keys, and the rumble of his car engine roaring down the street.

A few moments later, Monisha entered the room again with a glass of water and Jenny's cellphone. "You left this downstairs. Thought you might need it."

"Yeah. I had some tough cases today. I'm expecting at least one of the patients to call tonight for more pain meds. It always happens."

"Jenny, I suggest you put your partner on call tonight. Doctor's orders." She set the water glass on the bedside table and continued. "Your baby needs you to rest. All of this—" she looked around the room "—can't continue." Esha appeared in the doorway again, but stood there quietly leaning against the frame.

"I know, Monisha...thanks. I'll be okay. I promise. I'll chill."

"I'll call your OB for you to make him aware of your condition. He's good. We did our residency together, did I tell you that? He'll take good care of you."

Esha cleared her throat, a request to be let in the room.

"Please. We go ahead and go to the dinner. But, call me too, if you need something. Okay?"

Esha's voice had just a dash of concern but Jenny wasn't buying it. Jenny had to force herself to make eye contact with her mother-in-law.

Sure, I'll call you. But I won't tell anyone. Don't want to embarrass you.

But instead of speaking her mind, she politely responded, "Thank you."

After they left, she went out to survey the damage and saw an all too familiar sight. On the wall by the stairs was a fist-sized hole with drywall dust and crumbles falling out of it. Feeling like she was going to hyperventilate from anger, she grabbed the handrail and gripped it hard, wishing she were strong enough to rip it out of the wall. Beginning to understand Roshan's rages now, she banged her head on the wall next to the gaping hole. The pain drowned out the rocky throbbing inside, and she felt a bruise coming on. She pulled a piece of the chunky drywall off and threw it to the stairs. One by one, she threw pieces at the thought of Roshan, another at Esha, another at Wanda, and another at the hot knife in her back, and at herself for being here right now. The steps were sprinkled with white dust and flecks and chunks of the wall, and her nails were white underneath. Her forehead rested sideways on the wall, and she peered into the hole, letting her anger seethe into the skeleton of the house that had been insulating the magma of emotions that had been roiling around inside it for these past months.

Suffocated in another spasm, she slid to the steps and couldn't move, crying out in pain. No one was there to hear her, and she couldn't even scoot her body up or down the stairs to get to her phone. Alone in the house, she screamed into the carpet without tears until the labor pain subsided this time. No one was there for her, and she was the only one that could protect herself and her baby.

Please baby, please don't come yet.

Chapter 18

Roshan

His buzz was in full swing as he sat in his car parked at the back of the lot facing the building under what in summer was a lush canopy of crepe myrtles but was now a fence of nude branches sporting brown leaves that swayed by tenuous stems in the wind. The BMW's top was up, but he could hear the scratching leaves falling down on the cover and sliding away into the dusk. Luckily, he had managed to get to the hall before most of the *garba* attendees, so he took the secluded corner spot shielded by random shrubs between him and the hall where every celebration planned by the Gujarati Community Association had been held for years. The last time he had been there was for the *Navarthi garba* before he married Jenny, but that was a night he didn't want to remember.

Roshan's vantage point afforded him a view of glittering colors of the *chandiya cholis* and kids dressed in bright colors, bouncing excitedly behind their parents under the dim street lights, and as they approached the brighter lights of the building, their happy faces lit up even more when the doors opened and the interior lights spilled out with the music. Most of the kids were dressed in Indian attire, and Roshan remembered being that age and rebelling against wearing Indian clothes to functions.

When he went to *garbas* as a young kid, he thought getting dressed up was fun at Diwali, but in middle school, he grumbled that he couldn't be at home hanging out with friends from school. Didn't matter; he never got his way. Rarely got to hang out with school friends. So, his rebellion was to refuse to dress like his mum wanted him to. Jeans and Polo shirts were his way of thumbing his nose at them at these festive occasions.

A swig of bourbon went down warmly, and as he continued to watch through fogged glass, the doors to the community center opened and closed, letting out bursts of *bangara* music and light with each swing. Half of him wanted to go in. He watched for his mother and his aunts and cousins to arrive, and the thought of his mother being there kept him in the car. The other half of him wanted to go home to his fragile wife, to his unborn baby whom he wished so much for now. But he couldn't bring himself to do that either.

So he sat, bottle in one hand, cellphone with its ringer turned off in the other. Each time it lit up with a text or alert of a voicemail from Esha or Jenny, he deleted it without a glance before turning it over on his leg until the glow of the screen died and it was blank again. He couldn't. He just couldn't.

Finally, the phone gave up trying to rouse his attention, and he hooked it up to the sound system to cue up *All Apologies.* Nirvana banged into his ears and though he was nearly a middle-aged man sitting in a parking lot drinking himself into oblivion, he felt like a high school kid again, losing himself in his tunes. Like in the song, everything was his fault, indeed, and he leaned his head back and nodded with the beat for a long while, feeling his head raise higher and lighter as the booze kicked in. He barely felt the vibration of the phone again under his hand.

He looked at the screen, expecting to see Jenny's name appear. It was Jay. He hardly ever called him anymore. Usually texted. So he knew he had to answer. He knew he'd be looking for him, and Roshan couldn't lie to him. Jay always saw right through him.

"'Sup?" He tried to sound casual, but his "s" came out slurred.

"Where are you man? I gotta talk to you."

"I'm having myself a little drink. In my car."

"Where's your car?"

"Not at home. That's for damn sure." He laughed but was met with only silence on the other end of the phone.

"*Bhai*. Where *are* you?"

"I'm at the *garba* hall. Thinking about going in. Haven't danced in a few years. Can you believe that? Thought it might be fun. You coming with Hema and the kids?"

"Yeah. We're coming. For God's sake, you sound shitty. Don't go in. Wait for me in the car. We need to talk."

"Yep. Sure man." Roshan laid his head back again and closed his eyes, losing himself in the music. Kurt Cobain railed at him, challenging his identity as he sang the next song, *Come as You Are*, his favorite pity party song of all time.

Pissed off, not wanting to think, he pushed the power button and sat in silence. The *bangara* drums from the hall vibrated his car again as more and more partiers passed through the entrance doors. Another sip, then a big swig, and a blessed numbness melted into him.

Just a few minutes later, he jerked at the knock on the passenger side window. He saw Jay's face peering at him in the dark and unlocked the doors.

I am in trouble.

Jay walked around the car quickly, sliding into the passenger seat and shutting the door, never once looking Roshan in the eye. Hema and the kids were entering the building, and Hema turned their oldest daughter's face away from the car.

"Your wife is in labor."

Roshan turned to look at him, a delayed surprise showing on his face, then faced front again and pounded the dashboard.

"How do you know?"

"My mom called me. Jenny got herself to the hospital and her doctor called Mom while she was at the garba, concerned because Jenny was alone. Apparently, Jenny had texted and called your mom when she couldn't get through to you." Jay looked at Roshan's phone turned face down and narrowed his eyes. "My mom has tried to call yours but still no answer. She said your mom skipped out on the garba and went home after they left your place, so she might have turned her phone off and went to bed."

"Well, Jenny's better off alone. I can't be with her. I'm no good. You're the good husband and great dad. Jenny knows I'm not that guy...and won't be to the baby either." He bit his lip hard.

"You can't leave her alone to have a baby—*your* baby. You have to go to the hospital. She needs you—"

"She doesn't need my shit!" Roshan snapped. He rubbed his face and sighed, pulling his cheeks down, trying to massage some feeling back into them. "When we were kids, I hated those clothes. See that kid over there. The one with the shaggy hair. He's about 14. Looks like a scarecrow, and the white pajamas he's wearing don't do him any favors. Looks just like I used to feel."

Jay nodded and waited.

"But during my senior year, man, I thought they were alright. I liked these functions. Kinda felt like a big man, all the girls trying not to let the parents or old *dohis* see. But they always did. They were everywhere. The parents loved me. You know, we were it. We were the guys. Going to college prime pickings. That pedestal was awesome."

A little girl ran across the lot to her brother, who grabbed her hand. Roshan heard the jingling anklets on her legs jingle-jangle away as her tiny feet pattered. A butterfly fluttered in his chest at the thought of that in his future; he could watch his tiny baby girl toddle around with excitement at one of these things. But he saw himself punch the wall tonight, and then found himself again in the bathroom he shared with Priya covered in the blood of his own anger.

"What happened to me, man?" He picked at his cuticles and didn't look up. "I always did the right thing. When your dad was alive, he taught me that. I did it. Whether I liked it or not. I never meant to marry out. I never meant to be...who...I am...now."

"Who are you now, Roshan?"

"I'm the villain. That's who I am. I betray everything and everybody." He held up his fingers and started counting. "Upbringing. My own mum. And Jenny mostly. I chased her and lied to her so that I could be who she wanted, and I'm not." Roshan held up the wet rimmed bottle to Jay. "Sorry so rude. Want some?"

Jay shook his head in exasperation. "I don't drink anymore. You know, family man?" Jay leaned his head over the seat, surveying the back. "This car smells nasty, man. Have you been pouring that stuff on the carpeting?"

"Nah, there's an empty bottle back there with a little left in it. I think it leaked." He put the bottle to his own lips, then stopped and looked at it, then screwed the lid back on and lay it on the passenger side floor.

"You're going to need to get this detailed." He sat up and asked, "So what do you think Jenny wants?"

"She wants the good guy. Not me." He paused for a moment. "I'm getting sued."

"What for?"

"Malpractice. My attorney's been fighting it for me for months. I kept it from Jenny, but she found a letter that fell out of my briefcase."

"Okay. Look at this rationally. Every doctor gets sued at least once in their career. Even when they do everything right. It's the nature of the beast. You'll be fine because you know what you did was good patient care. Right?"

"I was drunk and pulled the wrong teeth. Five of them."

Jay sat in stunned silence.

Roshan went on. "My assistant tried to stop me, but I barely even heard her talking. I don't even remember looking at the chart. I didn't even remember the patient's name when I got the letter from her attorney."

Jay said nothing for a long time. Roshan's guts felt raw now that Jay knew. His brother in life. His friend. And now he and his wife knew his secret. He lifted the capped bottle to his lips again, but the sloshing of liquid in his stomach suddenly felt nearly explosive. Still, he reflexively opened it and put it to his mouth. The bourbon poured in and dribbled out before he nestled it in his lap, cradling it against his dampened shirt.

"Do you remember Mohan Uncle? How he gambled away everything out from underneath Shalini Auntie?"

Roshan nodded sluggishly and turned to Jay. He starkly remembered the day that Shalini Auntie and her daughters moved into Jay's family's house. He and Roshan were about 10 and 11, and the daughters, their second cousins, were about three and five years old. He and Jay had helped carry in boxes to the two spare rooms, and the girls, Avani and Meena, had annoyingly tailed them the whole time.

"My daddy's gone on a trip," Avani, the older one, had said. "We won't get to see him for a long, long time, Mummy says." Roshan had just set a cardboard box full of pink and blue fuzzy bears on the floor near the window and turned to see the both girls behind him, staring up at him.

"Where'd he go?" Roshan had heard some adult mumbling the night before when Jay's dad came home uncharacteristically late and sat with their mums for dinner. He knew something was wrong, but as usual no one ever talked to kids.

"A trip. Mummy and Monisha Auntie said he will be gone a long time, but he'll bring us lots of presents when he gets back."

Meena turned away from them with her thumb in her mouth and lay her head on the spread at the foot of the twin bed. Annoyed, Roshan tapped her on the arm and asked her what's wrong. He knew from experience that the water works were going to start, and he might need to get out of there fast. He didn't want to get blamed for it.

"I want Daddy." She rubbed her face into the bed and started to whine.

Avani patted her on the head and said, "It's okay. Daddy will bring us presents when he comes. It'll be so much fun."

The younger sister kept her head on the bed and whined through her thumb. "I don't want presents. I. Want. My. Daddy!"

Roshan would never forget the look on Meena's face. Even at 10, he could feel the hurt in her voice. He knew what it was like to not have a dad.

"Remember how he really fucked up his family?" Jay asked, snapping his fingers in the dark now at Roshan, pulling him from his trance. "Remember how Shalini Auntie didn't leave my house for months after they moved in?"

"Yeah, I remember."

"Well, she didn't leave because she didn't want to face people in the community. She couldn't stand that everyone knew that her family was messed up."

"Yeah, I remember. That day when they moved into your house, I got in trouble for making Meena cry because she was talking about her dad. And her mom came and scolded us for talking about him."

"Right. The entire three years they stayed with us, I don't think I ever heard them talk about him. Then one day, he was there, and we were moving their stuff into their brand new house. No one ever talked about why he was gone. Chapter over. Move on."

"Yeah, so what's your point, man?"

"I have 2 points, bro. First is we take care of each other. My parents took care of Shalini Auntie and the girls. And some uncles in California straightened uncle out and got him back on his feet so he could come back and take care of his family."

Roshan nodded. "That's no secret, man."

"Well, my brother, that is what we are gonna do with you. We take care of each other. Sometimes, you gotta ask for help, and fuck the people who don't matter. Fuck 'em. People are going to know. Hell, they already know for God's sake. Let 'em talk! Who cares?"

"My mum…your mum…everyone…" He smoothed his hand across the dashboard. It felt good under his palm. This was his favorite place. The car took him places fast and couldn't tell his secrets.

"Man, remember Meena when she was little? Remember how she wouldn't even look at the uncles for a long time and would cling to her mummy's legs everywhere?"

"Yeah. Damn she was annoying."

They both laughed.

"Well, you have a kid coming. It needs its daddy. What the hell do you think would happen to my daughters if I dumped them? You have to step up and be the daddy, and keeping problems like this to yourself doesn't help."

Roshan looked at Jay through blurred vision and tried to smile. He knew he was right, and relief flooded through him, and he felt his stomach erupting. He fumbled to get the door open, and as soon as it was cracked, everything he'd drank splattered onto the pavement. The cool air felt good, and he wiped his mouth with the back of his hand. The cuticles on his torn fingers burned, and he longed to wash up, feeling scummy as he was becoming more sober.

When he was pulling himself up, a boy of about 12 came running over by the car, catching a small ball. He stopped in his tracks and looked down at Roshan sliding back into the car. He ran quickly back to his friend a few cars down and whispered something to him, pointing.

Though Roshan was so small when he knew his dad, he remembered seeing him like this once at a family dinner at a relative's flat in the city, and one of his cousins, a girl his age with pigtail braids and puffy sleeves, asked him if his dad was sick because he fell down. Burning embarrassment followed. Was his daddy sick? At that age, he thought he was, but he knew it was somehow a different kind of sick the girl had meant. He knew even at that tender age that he didn't want to be "that man" to any kid ever.

He shut the door and leaned back, trying to breathe and settle his stomach.

"Take me to Starbucks. I need a coffee and a bathroom to clean up in."

Chapter 19

Esha

Holding her iPhone up as she walked to the door to speak to Rich, Esha reread the text from Jenny.

Jenny

Are you available to drive me to the hospital?
Roshan won't text me back. Bryan is in China.
Even tried my mom…

The text had gone unnoticed while she had indulged herself in evening time with Rich yet again on the deck.

Evenings had become a regular time for them to chat and drink *chai* together, a secret she kept from everyone. Not even Monisha knew. After dusk, Esha made the *chai* with extra ginger as Rich now liked, and he would settle Evelyn in for the night and join Esha across the patio table where they relaxed to talk, sometimes for hours. Often she brought out her samosas or *kachori* for him to try, and a few times he brought a dessert from the grocery store bakery, which she didn't touch because they contained eggs, saying politely she didn't have a sweet tooth. Eventually in conversation she mentioned that she was vegetarian, and he reprimanded her for not telling him she wouldn't eat foods made with eggs, vowing to make something good that she could eat.

It felt devilishly good for him to care enough to say that.

After Roshan's tantrum, she begged Jay to find him in hopes he would respond to Jay, if no one else. Then she decided to skip the *garba* and go straight home to find Rich, rather than go and pretend miserably that all was well in front of everyone she knew. She could not face a crowd and be sociable today, no matter how scandalous it would be for her to be missing. She knew some people would gossip about how she must be embarrassed of Roshan, about what a selfish auntie she was for missing her young nieces and nephews dance their first *garbas* on stage, but she was to the point that she was caring less and less.

It had been at least two hours when she left Rich on the deck and went inside to deposit their empty cups into the sink. It was time for the katydids to start up and mosquitos to ignore the citronella candles around them and move in for the attack, which meant time for their evening to wrap up. The towel she picked up to dry her hands revealed her forgotten phone underneath, and when she picked it up, she noticed the alert for a new text message.

Please let it be Roshan.

Certainly Roshan would be back home with Jenny by now, cooled off, and apologizing to her. Tantrums aside, he was a good boy. Her son was a good husband to Jenny, and the look in his eyes when he talked about the baby coming told the story of the loving dad he would become. If only the liquor would go away. The text would be letting her know he was home safe.

Instead, she found the desperate text from Jenny.

A girl needed her husband and her mother when having a baby, and Roshan was missing.

Judging by the few times Esha had met Wanda and the way Jenny looked at her mother and avoided the subject when Esha sometimes asked after Wanda, Jenny would not have a mother with her. Esha's guilt over Roshan's absence pushed her to put their differences aside. She took a deep breath and touched Jenny's number on her phone to make the call.

"Esha. Hi..." Jenny's voice trailed off weakly.

"I drive to your house to pick you up."

"No, Esha. It's okay."

"No, not okay. I come to your house now—"

"Esha. Stop. I'm not home. I'm at the hospital."

"Oh. Hospital, my God!" Her high-pitched voice cracked at a peak, then relieved, she stated happily, "Oh. Good. Roshan came back to you."

Jenny was silent, then she gulped and her scratchy voice admitted, "No."

"My...God. You okay? I'm so sorry I didn't see your—"

"Esha, I have to go. The nurse is here. If you talk to Roshan, please tell him I'm here."

"Oh God. I come now, okay?"

"Suit yourself. I'm not going anywhere."

Esha flew out to the back of the house. She hated to drive in the dark and needed someone to take her. Monisha had told her after the *garba* she had go to the hospital for a patient, and there was no way she would call Ashmi to drive so far to pick her up.

Crickets chirped in concert for her when she poked her head out the back door into the darkness. Something scurried around in the shrubs between her and Evelyn's yard, and she took a step back, remembering the snakes they had in India. Branches rustled and snapped a few times and then a calling meow echoed into the night as a cat bolted out and across the deck before her feet.

"Miss me already?" Rich's faceless chuckle floated from the darkness left by blown out candles.

Yes, actually I did.

"I must go to hospital. My daughter in-law is having her baby."

In the dim glow of the kitchen lights from her window, Rich's outline became visible as came closer to her. "So, Roshan came back?"

"No. He's not there. That's the problem."

"Can I drive you? I've heard you are a slow driver from my mom. And if my snail-paced mom says you're slow, then you probably shouldn't be on the road." He smirked at her, and she shook her head, smiling.

"She's right, and I don't see at night. I was hoping you would offer." Strange how comfortable she felt with him and even stranger that she allowed herself to admit it. He was now her friend. That felt good.

They glided in a blur over empty highways in Evelyn's Buick to the women's center entrance at the hospital. Thankful to now be a volunteer, she directed him to park in employee parking where volunteers were allowed to park. She waved at the attendant who knew her, and he let her out of the car before parking.

Inside, Esha greeted her co-worker at the reception desk in the hospital lobby. "Hello Marquita."

"Hey, Esha! How you doing?" The young woman had been sitting behind the counter texting on her cellphone but jumped up to hug Esha. Marquita taught fitness classes when not volunteering at the desk or attending pre-med classes at the local university, and she gripped Esha firmly.

"Good, my dear."

"It been a minute since we seen you 'round here. Where you been?"

"I've taken some time off. October is holiday season for us. Diwali. Our Christmas."

Rich came in the sliding doors behind her, standing behind her at a polite distance.

Marquita asked him, "May I help you, sir?"

"Oh, no, I'm here with her."

Marquita looked him up and down, then looked at Esha with a sly grin as she crossed back over to the other side of the counter.

Esha felt very uncomfortable. It was improper for her to be out somewhere with a man that was not her relative, and a black man at that. Oh, this would be a scandal to top Roshan and Jenny any day. She'd never done anything like this before in her life.

"You look real pretty tonight. Coming from a party or something?"

Esha ignored the question. "My daughter-in-law is here in labor and delivery."

"Your daughter-in-law?" Marquita looked shocked. "I didn't know you had a daughter-in-law. How come you never told me?"

Esha looked around impatiently and felt ashamed to answer. "Oh, it just never came up." She saw Rich hovering behind her, and he shook his head slightly at her words.

"Hmmm. Well, let me look her up. What's her name?"

"Desai. Jenny Desai."

"Mmm. No Desai. Could there be another name?"

"Try Jenkins."

"Oh, here it is. Jenny Jenkins. They married?"

"Yes. A few months now. I guess she hasn't changed her name yet."

"Hmm. Just a few months, huh? I guess her baby premature?" Marquita smirked jokingly.

Esha enjoyed working with Marquita, but now her comments were getting on her nerves. Esha stared stone-faced at her.

Marquita, getting the message, said, "Okay. Sorry. She in 408."

"Thank you, dear."

Esha motioned for Rich to follow her. As they entered the elevator, their arms brushed, and Esha felt needles of embarrassment and excitement. She forced herself to focus on the baby coming and on how to handle Jenny when she got up there.

"You okay?" he asked.

"I...don't think I am."

"Your nephew will find your son. And you can figure out how to talk to Jenny. She is a person too. Just look at her as the mother of your grand-child. And she's probably scared to death right now."

"Yes, you probably right."

They rode up to the delivery floor in silence, and as they approached the room, her stomach squirmed.

"I'll stay in the waiting room while you go see her." He moved to hug her, and she recoiled in surprise, hiding her embarrassment. It was impossible for him to understand that she couldn't have that kind of relationship with him. Americans can't understand that a widow's life is destined to be one of loneliness.

"Okay," she nodded, stepping back quickly.

Counting off the room numbers in her head, the click, flip, click, flip of her *chappals* on the tiled floor echoed too loudly. She knew she should've changed out of these dressy sandals and put on sneakers. But, shamefully admitting her own vanity to herself, she'd wanted to stay in her Indian clothes in front of Rich. Glitter and color made her feel pretty, feel like her young self.

She knocked on the door and a weak voice said, "Come in."

Slowly, Esha peaked around the door. In the bed, Jenny lay on her side facing the door. An IV was taped to her hand with a mound of tape, and it rested on the railing. Her blond hair was pulled behind her in a ponytail, and her head rested on the pillow next to an emesis basin. She held a white washcloth to her lips and didn't lift her head when she saw Esha.

The look in her eyes made Esha's heart sink. This girl who'd just been an outcast in her mind while dominating every thought she'd had about her son was really just a girl in pain, one who now looked very, very alone.

"Hello," she said in the soft voice she'd used for Roshan as a child late at night when he'd been up sick from some virus or another over his childhood. Her instinct was to rush right to the bedside and take the washcloth from Jenny's hand, wet it with cool water, and place it on her forehead, but she held back. She felt like she needed an invitation, that the tense air that had been long between them still hovered.

"Hi." Jenny tried to turn her head, but moaned and turned back to the basin.

"May I come in?"

Jenny silently nodded as she closed her eyes.

Esha walked to the bedside and asked, "Can I get you something?"

"Mmm. A little water. I'm allowed a few sips."

Esha poured some ice water from the plastic pitcher that sat on the wheeled table next to the bed and brought the cup to Jenny's face. The bent straw crunched into the crushed ice at the bottom and splattered a drop onto Jenny's nose. She didn't flinch. Jenny tried to lift her hand to grab the cup, but her eyes slammed shut and she curled in a ball, moaning loudly. Esha instinctively placed her hand on Jenny's shoulder and rubbed gently, the same way her own mother had done for her during Roshan's delivery. Esha remembered that the time her daughter's sad delivery happened, her mum was in the states with her brothers, and her heart still hurt from the void her mum's absence created during that horrible night.

Many moments later, Jenny's face relaxed, and she sunk further in the bed, breathing heavily. Esha put the white straw to her lips and let Jenny sip.

"Thank you."

"Of course. No thank yous to me."

"Is Roshan coming?"

Esha fought back tears. "I've sent Jayesh out to find him. But, so far, nothing."

A trickle of tears streamed in a line down Jenny's cheeks, dripping onto the pillow.

Esha asked, "May I?" as she placed her hands on Jenny's arm and shoulder. Jenny acquiesced, and Esha rubbed and gently kneaded the muscles of her arm, her shoulder and her neck. "Relaxing makes the baby relax. You must relax. Everything you feel, the baby feels. And it stays with the baby always. Think good things." She couldn't let herself look at the poor girl's face, still wet, her eyes staring at nothingness on the wall in front of her.

Oh Roshan, where are you?

"You're mum. Is she here?" She tried to change the subject, tried to find a positive for her daughter-in-law to cling to. Perhaps Wanda being there could be a good thing.

"My mom. No. She won't be here." Her voice was flat. She turned her head away from Esha and tried to turn over on the other side but couldn't move, only ending up burying her head in the pillow.

Confused, Esha asked, "But, how did you get here? If Roshan didn't, who else but your mum?"

"I drove myself."

"What? You drove yourself? How? Oh my...oh Jenny..." She just couldn't say anymore.

"Roshan didn't answer. Bryan and Craig are in China for the adoption. You didn't answer. I had to. The labor was not so bad then." Pausing with a grimace on her face, she added, "I've been a big girl for a long time. I just did it."

Stunned, Esha said nothing. She wondered about Wanda. She didn't know much about Wanda but did not like her look. The last time she'd seen her was at the wedding, and the embarrassment of the woman's language still lingered with her. Whenever Jenny came up in conversations and new people asked what kind of family she comes from, Esha would skirt the issue. Esha just felt something was off with the woman. The problem was Esha was afraid the apple didn't fall from the tree. She hoped she was wrong.

She pulled her hands off of Jenny's arms and got her cellphone out. "I call her for you. What's her number?"

"No," Jenny nearly shouted. "Don't!"

"A girl's mum must be with her when she has baby. It her duty."

"Stop." Jenny's face reddened with anger. "Leave it alone. Do not get involved in this."

Esha stepped back, trying to hide the sensation as if she'd been slapped. Her sympathy was waning.

"Okay. We wait for Roshan, then." She sat on a chair near the window and looked around the room silently. Jenny seized up in pain again, and Esha stepped over to the bedside, only to have Jenny's hand swipe away her touch. When Jenny relaxed again, she pushed the nurse call button and asked the nurse for help going to the bathroom.

The voice crackled over the speaker, "Okay. I'll be there shortly."
Jenny winced in pain.

Feeling hesitant, Esha spoke with her motherly voice. "I help you."

"That's okay...I'll just have the nurse—"

"Sure? Please, let me. You're...family."

The words fell like rocks out of her mouth. It was the first time Esha
had ever said them. But her mother's voice whispered in her ear, an echo
from years past: *We ladies help each other. All we have is each other.*

For a moment, Esha was in the dim light of her marriage bed with eyes
locked on her mother-in-law's, clinging to the comfort of her crooning
words. She felt resentful that her own mother was already in the U.S. with
her brothers, but Esha also felt blessed to have the love her husband's
mother had always given her, especially now as she herself was wracked
with the pain of labor. Her reward for that pain had been Roshan, and her
mother-in-law was there, a stand-in for her mum, to share in that even
before her husband had come in. Esha knew Jenny did not want her, but
she needed someone. Anyone.

"No, it's just, I'm...the nurse...please..." Jenny's voice trailed off, and
she closed her eyes.

"No, I just help you. I get the nurse, and we help you together."

"Stop. Please." Jenny begged. Her fists clenched at her belly, and she
froze again, eyes shutting the world out of her suffering. A moan, like
that of a little girl mumbling in her sleep at a nightmare escaped her but
disappeared with the spasm.

As Esha said she would go help find the nurse, she came into the room.
Esha told the nurse she'd be down the hall if Jenny needed her.

When Esha saw Rich sitting in the waiting area chairs next to Monisha,
tears spilled and she couldn't see. The two were in quiet conversation and
looked up at the same time, hushing suddenly when they saw her. Monisha
knew now, and her kind eyes hugged Esha telling her it was alright.

"Everything okay?" Rich asked.

She wiped her eyes and nodded.

Monisha stood, putting her hands on the backs of Esha's arms. Face to face, she said, "I spoke to the doctor a few minutes ago. Her labor is progressing nicely. She is dilated to five centimeters, almost ready for the epidural." She grabbed Esha's hand and held it firmly in hers. "She needs someone in there with her. Her mother? Roshan?"

"She doesn't want her mum," she said, adding tearfully, "No one knows where Roshan is. I haven't heard from Jayesh."

"Then you need to go back in there. Swallow whatever you want to prick her with at other times. You are her mother-in-law, like it or not, and her husband is nowhere. Go help this girl."

Esha squeezed Monisha's hand back. The squeeze was a thank you, and I love you, and a release of her anger.

"She doesn't want me."

"Go anyway. People don't always know what they need, *bhabhi*. For all of your sakes, go back in there."

"Okay. I'll go."

Monisha pulled out her cellphone, patted Esha on the back, and left the waiting room to call Jay again. Rich reached up from his seat toward Esha's arm and touched her elbow softly.

Surprised, she nearly pulled away, but when she looked down, the warmth in his eyes kept her still, and locked in for just a moment.

"Do you want me to walk you in there? Of course, I'll stay outside the room."

"Yes. I need someone with me to keep me from losing my courage."

Rich stood without removing his tender touch from her elbow, escorting her slowly down the shining white hall to Jenny's room. He nodded his head toward the door, and Esha slid in.

She stood just inside the door, looking at Jenny lying in the bed with her eyes closed. She wanted to cradle her head as she would any woman in pain. She wanted to relieve her pain. She was giving birth to her grand-child. And she was Roshan's love. Her son, with his problems, wasn't here, Jenny's mother was no mother to her own child, and Esha was the only one. But that brick wall of animosity still stood tall between them, and the awkwardness of her presence in the intimate moments of the girl who'd made her blood boil scared her.

What if Jenny softened to her? What if she could fit into the gap for Jenny? Where would Esha put her anger? She wasn't sure she wanted to let go of her anger. It had been her constant companion for so many years, for so many reasons. She didn't know who she could be without it.

"May I come back in?" she breathed.

Jenny opened her eyes and smiled slightly, too exhausted to speak. Esha moved quietly toward the bed.

"Is Roshan coming?" Jenny said weakly.

"I don't know yet. I'm so sorry. Jayesh is still looking." Esha's heart hurt at the look in Jenny's eyes, as she leaned her head back and stared up at the ceiling blankly. She knew the cold void of loneliness during birth. No matter how many mothers or aunties or friends might have surrounded Esha during Roshan and her daughter's birth, the emptiness frozen into her heart by her husband's years of violence and absence still chilled her bones. A child's father should be not only its creator, but should see it into the world. She raged at her son, probably with a bottle in his hand at that very moment.

"Do you think he'll come in time?" Her voice crackled into the tiny pitch of a child. "He was so angry. All of the time now," she whispered. Eyes squeezing tight into her constricting face, she curled up and gave a guttural growl.

As Esha answered, "I don't know," the heavy door glided open slowly. Jay, followed by a wobbly Roshan, stepped inside. Jay stood at the doorway, nodded at Esha, then at Roshan, and backed out. Roshan stared at Jenny as if he were a child who'd been caught breaking a rule and awaited a forgiving word as permission to move in.

His eyes drooped, and his hair was tousled. With one hand, he awkwardly leaned on the wall. With the other, he gripped a disposable coffee cup. When Esha allowed her eyes to meet his, he moved in to hug her and asked into her shoulder, "Mummy. How's she doing?"

Without answering, Esha pulled back, his rancid bourbon, bitter coffee breath turning her stomach. She held his cheeks firmly in her hands and bored her eyes into his as she'd done when he was a child when she was angry with him. Searching for the eager-to-please little boy she hoped still lurked in there, she probed the amber eyes she'd always known had peered out from a sweet soul. There it was, inside the shining hazel-flecked iris that quickly looked to the floor, welling with a sheen of tears. But he was not a child anymore, and she released him, dropping her arms to her side. Stepping aside, she swallowed a shout, saying clearly and slowly in Gujarati, "You see for yourself."

Slowly he stepped to the bedside and looked at Jenny, surveying her with a grief-stricken expression.

"Hi," he whispered, and placed his hand on hers. Without waiting for a response, he leaned into her and placed his forehead to hers. "I'm sorry."

She opened her eyes and moaned softly into him. "You're here." A sudden stream of tears rolled off her cheeks, down her neck and onto the worn cotton gown as his hand moved up to caress her head, brushing back stray strands of hair.

What had repulsed Esha before, the unnatural connection between the two, now touched her.

His hand cupped Jenny's head protectively, Jenny's face looked peaceful for the first time as she relaxed into him. They held still against each other, and Esha looked away, squirming, feeling like a voyeur in this private space. A part of her longed for someone to touch her like that. The someone that came to mind was Rich, and she swatted the image away.

Busying herself with filing the plastic water pitcher from the tap, she kept her back to them, wondering if she should go or not. He was here. He held Jenny. But was his absence forgotten? Or forgiven?

Water fell into the pitcher, turning the crushed ice inside into slush. Behind her, she heard more whispers, but the heavy door opened with a team of voices invading the reverie between her son and his wife. Roshan turned from the bed and Esha looked toward the door at Wanda pushing her way inside, followed by Rich, Monisha, and Jay. Rich and Jay flanked her at the ready to grab her, if necessary.

Monisha quickly stepped in in front of Wanda. "Roshan, Esha, we tried to tell her to wait, but she—"

Esha stepped up next to Monisha forming a line in front of the bed.

Wanda rolled her eyes at the women and spoke through them to Jenny. "I got here as soon as I got your text, baby. I finished up my business and here I am!"

The cloud of smoke that hovered around her stung Esha's nose, and she had to cover her face with her palm to prevent herself from coughing.

Dramatically, Wanda pushed herself through the women to the bedside, nudged Roshan out of the way, and took Jenny's hand in hers. Everyone in the room moved toward her. Esha's instinct to keep Jenny and the baby away from the toxic air guided Esha to the bedside behind Roshan, ready to remove the woman's touch from Jenny. But Roshan moved in toward Wanda and carefully removed her hand from Jenny's.

"Hello, Wanda. How are you?" His voice was a little too loud, and Wanda balked at him, looking at her hand like he had stung her. She stumbled back a step and steadied herself on the sink behind her. She was a shadow of the person who'd been at the wedding just months ago. No longer dressed in what was her better clothes or wearing carefully applied makeup, she wore faded out dungarees and a near threadbare black tee shirt with the name of a rock band on it. Her eyes looked strangely glassy.

"I'm good now, doll baby," she slurred at him, moving again toward the bed. Instead of trying for Jenny's hand, she stepped to the foot of the bed, and placed her hands on the form of Jenny's feet underneath the bleached blanket. Then, she untucked the edge of the blanket from Jenny's toes and flipped it up so she could pat Jenny's feet, but then left her feet exposed and stepped away.

Jenny tried to turn over on her bed to see Wanda down there but grimaced in pain. "Wanda."

Rich moved behind Wanda. Everyone in the room paused, ready to move if necessary.

"I'm here, doll baby. Now I can be here for you…" Wanda looked at everyone staring at her. "…If your gang will back off a little for a girl's mom."

Esha's skin crawled from the way Wanda's hand quickly rubbed and patted Jenny's legs while she steadied herself on the mattress with the other, her hands like poison ivy creeping up the bed eager to spread their toxin.

"How's my baby doll?" She circled over to the side of the bed opposite of Roshan and patted Jenny on her hair.

"You shouldn't'a up and drove yourself. I had to check on you." Wanda involuntarily tugged on Jenny's hair back and forth, back and forth, braiding her ponytail between her calloused fingers as she rambled.

Wanda is a caricature of a mother.

"Wanda, please step over here." Roshan motioned toward the door, his voice calm and concise. Esha, taking a cue from him, went to Wanda's side and placed her hand on Wanda's elbow.

But, Wanda kept speaking to Jenny as if she and her daughter were the only people in the room. "You know I'm here for you now, baby. I'm always gonna be here for you from now on." Tears sprung to her eyes, and she used both hands to wipe the tears but only succeeded in spreading the wetness across her face.

"Wanda, you're using. Leave, please." Jenny sounded weaker, and she shrugged her hair out of the woman's fingers.

Looking around at the faces staring at her, Wanda humphed, incensed. "I am not, young lady. I just had a little something for my back pain. It's prescription." Then she added, "Maybe I shouldn't of had any drinks on top of it, but that was James's fault. His ass up and left me! I told you, and it's been so hard, baby. I miss him so much. I can't go to work 'cause he's there. I ain't got nobody to talk to." More tears spread down the leathered wrinkles of her face, and she turned her back to the room, her face in her hands.

What a selfish excuse for a woman.

"Come, Wanda," Monisha insisted to Esha's relief. "Now things are not about you. This is about Jenny. I'll take you to the waiting room. Come. Now."

"No." Wanda twisted around. She reached her hand to the bedrail and gripped it tightly. "Jenny, baby, I'm your momma. You need me here. How're the contractions?"

"Wanda. Now," Roshan fumed. "She doesn't want you here. Not like this." He reached for Wanda's elbow while Monisha put her hand on the woman's shoulder. Together, they tried to turn Wanda, but Wanda pulled her arm away, shrugging off Monisha's hand.

"I...will...not...leave." Wanda spun around glaring at the crowd around her.

Esha was glad to see Rich and Jay move in closer, but before they grabbed her, Jenny held up her hand and said a flat, definite "Stop." She crunched into the fetal position then, eyes clenched, teeth grinding, whispering "Leave" before she shut down into her inner world of agony. Esha looked to Roshan, and saw red rim his eyes with anger.

"Please control yourself, son," she whispered to him. After a tense, torturously long moment, he nodded and took a deep breath. Esha allowed herself to swallow again.

"Come, Wanda. Come, let's go get some water." Esha tried to lead the woman by the elbow again toward the door. Wanda shrugged Esha's grip from her and began to march in a zigzag toward the two men stationed at the doorway. She stopped and faced Roshan, getting closer to his face with each word.

"I am her momma. You know she needs me now."

"She needed you for a long time." He stepped back still looking down at his mother-in-law's face. Esha could see the lines in his jaw harden, and his words came out thick and slow. "But, she doesn't need an addict. Look at you...you look like you haven't slept for days. Now, go. Go and be the kind of mom you're best at—invisible."

Face up and eyes unmoving from Roshan's, Wanda planted her feet and slapped him. A collective gasp escaped into the room. Immediately, Jay and Rich rushed to Roshan and ushered him backwards, Jay muttering, "Come on, man. Come, let's just go over here." Monisha helped Esha forcefully push Wanda toward the door, and Esha fought the urge to shove her to the floor.

Again Wanda struggled against the hands on her and turned to Roshan. Smoothing her hair back and straightening her shirt, she carefully enunciated ever word that came next.

"Well, ain't you the pot calling the kettle black, sir. You're a whiskey man, I smell. I never been a good mom. I know that. But, at least I own my problems." Esha tried to grab her again, but Wanda was too quick, putting her hand on his arm and squeezed. "But, you…where was you? Where was Prince Charming in the princess's time of need? Tell me, Mr. Kama Sutra, why did she need to go text her junkie momma when she's got you to take care of her? Ya think maybe she don't want to have nothing to do with your kind no more?"

Fury overtook her, and Esha gripped Wanda's shoulders like steel and reeled her around to bring them face to face. "Do not speak to my son. Not like that. Not any other way."

Wanda poked her index finger into Esha's chest and mocked, "Don't speak to my son. Not any way…" She yelled at Jay and Monisha. "Ha. You and your people come to this country and act like yer better than us? Maybe I'll just go out and make a little call to immigration now."

For the first time in her life, Esha wanted to punch a woman right in the face. Everyone in her family was a citizen of this country and had more education in their little finger than this woman, she wanted to say. But someone like this Wanda didn't deserve the breath it would take. Monisha stepped to the door and said, "I'm going to the nurse's station to call security" and disappeared.

Wanda sniffed, turned her nose up, and shuffled to the door with everyone but Roshan trailing her. Out of the corner of her eye, Esha saw him cradle Jenny and wipe her tears with his shirt.

Rich and Jay flanked Wanda as she passed out the door and into the hallway. Esha peeked after them, both hands on the door frame, gripping the molding in the way she wanted to grip the woman's neck.

"Auntie, we'll be right back," Jay called quietly over his shoulder. He and Rich escorted Wanda, who was laughing, to the elevator.

A nurse came straight at them. "Ma'am, security is on their way. You need to leave."

Wanda stepped into the opening elevator and waved goodbye, giving them the finger just as the doors shut in front of her.

Esha joined them in the hall. The nurse continued, "Some of you have to stay in the waiting room. Only two visitors are allowed at a time in the labor and delivery rooms. We've had some complaints from other patients about the noise here. Is there a problem solved now?"

Rich, stepping closer to Esha, placed a palm on her shoulder. "Yes, is everything okay?"

"Yes. All is okay for now," she replied to him. To the nurse, she said, "I'm sorry, nurse. We will have no problems anymore here. I'll make sure of it."

The nurse nodded pointed to the waiting room. When they all sat down, she disappeared into the alcove at the nurses' station again and Monisha excused herself to check on her patients, leaving Esha, Rich, and Jay with the other patients' relatives. Jay went to a corner to take a call.

"Wow, Esha. You okay?" Rich asked.

"Yes. I'm fine. But, not sure about my son or Jenny. The baby…oh God… my grandchild will be caught up in this…this disgusting mess."

"Then, my friend," Rich spoke firmly, "you need to swallow your pride and be there for the baby. Pure and simple. Like you told Wanda, it's not about you anymore. It's about that baby coming into this world."

He was right. Esha's eyes burned with tears. She wrung her fingers in indecision, not seeing the hallway anymore, but seeing little Roshan's eyes that night he'd looked into her swollen, black-and-blue eyes as she lay in her bed with a mushy stomach and empty arms.

My boy has seen so much, and he needs me now more than ever.

All of her hopes and dreams for a perfect life for him, her efforts to mold him into a portrait of perfection that she could display on her mantle, had not been for nothing. This portrait was different, messy, and still in the making. Her son still needed her, and with him came the package of his family. But, how she could do that was still a mystery to her.

God will show me. We have all been put on this path together, and we will see when it is time.

Through blurred vision, she allowed herself to look into Rich's face. "Thank you, my friend. Thank you."

Silently, Esha turned from Rich and went back into Jenny's room. She was going to just put it out there for Jenny and Roshan. She was going to tell them that she was here to help, that they both needed her, that the baby needed her. Maybe she could even bring herself to say that she loves them. All of them.

The door gently glided open. She stepped inside. The lights were dimmed, and Roshan and Jenny were whispering. He sat on a chair, his torso stretched across the head of the bed, arms wrapped around Jenny. Amid the IV tubes and the fetal heart rate monitor beeps, he cradled her like an infant and crooned in her ear.

"Are you going to help me do this? I can't do this alone." Her voice wisped from her, its desperation settling into her own heart.

"I promise you, I will be here with you all the way. I'll never leave you alone again. You and the baby are my world."

"Make the pain stop, Roshan. I'm worn out."

"I'll get the nurse in here. Maybe they can give you the epidural now."

"No." She pulled him to her tighter and buried her head in his neck. "Not the labor pain. That I can tolerate because I know it'll end."

He pulled back to look at her, and she kept her head down. "Then what?"

"It hurts to love you, Roshan."

Before Esha stepped back outside the room, the image of Roshan's drawn face etched into her brain. Chewing his bottom lip, just as his father had done during his few moments of guilt, he lifted his head and stared at the ceiling. His lips moved without sound, and she read his lips.

He was praying.

That was something his father had never done.

Without a sound, she slipped from the room and confirmed with the nurse that security had taken care of Wanda downstairs. A few minutes later, Rich and Jay went home. Esha rested in a chair in the family waiting room, sometimes kept company by Monisha who was in and out of her own work until Monisha left in the early morning hours, leaving Esha alone with her thoughts amongst the low hum of voices from the TV across the room.

She leaned into the firm vinyl back of the chair but had to slump and slide down in order to rest her head on the back. Legs outstretched on the magazine-covered coffee table, toes freed from her *chappels*, she knew she looked a sight. Her coarse hair must be fuzzy and mussed, the silk fabric of her Punjabi hung wrinkled down her side, and she had taken off her sash to place over her eyes in hopes of a moment of rest.

What seemed like just a few moments later, a hand shook her awake. Disoriented, she pulled the sash from her eyes and struggled to clear her vision. Roshan, with rumpled hair, but clear eyes, towered over her with a grin.

"She's here."

"Wanda?" Esha asked, standing to attention with a wobble. She looked around but saw no one.

"No. The baby. She's here."

"She?" Esha asked in wonder. "A girl?" An unexpected rush of joy tickled her spine, and she hugged her son. He felt firmer than he'd felt before to her. Strong. Like a father. She knew it was her imagination, perhaps wishful thinking.

"You want to see her?" he asked like an ecstatic child ready to show off his new toy.

"Of course!"

Roshan led her to the room again. He knocked softly, "Sweetie, I've got Mum."

"Okay. Come in."

Jenny sat up in the bed, covered in a mound of blankets. Her damp hair hung in her face, and she tucked it behind one ear absently, eyes taking in the bundle at her breast. An electricity shot through Esha as she saw the tiny squirming underneath the swaddled blankets. A clenched fist, pink fingers curled up in a soft ball, peaked up from the blanket, introducing herself to Esha. Jenny looked up at Esha and lifted her chin and bobbed her head toward the woman, giving Esha an Indian gesture to "come here."

Esha bobbed her head in return and approached the bed with palms clamped against her cheeks.

"This is Abigail Diya Desai," Jenny whispered more toward the baby than for Esha, and Esha felt the joy of the words rolling from Jenny's mouth.

"Diya? Oh, wonderful name. It means brilliant light. Do you know that?" Esha asked Jenny.

"Of course. We did our research."

"Mummy, what do you think?" he asked. "You're a *ba*. You got what you always wanted."

"Yes." She couldn't take her eyes off of the bundle as she squeezed Roshan and Jenny's hands at the same time. It wasn't how she pictured it would ever be, though. She noticed Jenny looking at Esha's hand touching her own and felt a slight jerk, but Jenny relaxed rather than recoiled. The soft contented breaths drifted in the air as the baby nursed at Jenny's breast, and Esha's own breasts prickled at the memory of nursing Roshan so long ago.

The baby's head reared back from Jenny's breast, and her face was still, lips pursed, sound asleep. Jenny covered herself with her gown and looked up at Roshan. Esha asked, "May I?" as she gestured to caress the baby's head. Jenny nodded and Esha lay her palm on the knit cap that hugged the child's tiny head.

"Does she have much hair?"

Roshan laughed. "Oh yeah. Maybe more than me." He proudly pulled off the cap, exposing a wispy mess of long black curls, still damp, pressed flat.

Esha's granddaughter had puffy eyes, and her full lips, wide nose, and hair were all Roshan's. It was as if he were born all over again. But, her cheeks were delicate and her skin fair, feminine like Jenny's. Her fingers were long, and she tried to remember who in her family had long fingers. Perhaps it was someone from Jenny's family.

"I need some juice, please, Roshan. Take her." Instead of handing the baby to Esha, she motioned for Roshan to step from behind and take the baby.

"Come here, my Abigail," he crooned.

Jenny reached for her juice and sipped while Esha and Roshan gazed at Abigail.

"You call her Abigail? Not Diya?"

"Yes, Mummy. She's an American girl. It'll be much easier in school. But she is also Diya. We won't let her forget that."

"Such a shame. Diya so beautiful name. American names have no meaning, no? Just choose for how sounds?"

"Yes, they have meaning." Jenny answered between sips, looking miffed, making Esha regret the comment.

Roshan added, "Abigail is from the Bible. It means 'father's joy.'"

"Oh, she must be your joy, for sure, Roshan." Esha gestured for him to lay Abigail in her arms. Roshan looked to Jenny. She nodded. Esha took the weight of the child in her arms and supported her head with one hand.

"I hope you celebrate this joy, mummy and daddy." She gently rocked from one foot to the other and kissed Abigail's fuzzy forehead. "She is light in your lives now. Now is your job to keep the flame alive." Placing the baby back into Jenny's arms, she cupped her daughter-in-law's cheek and turned to her son. "Don't mess this up."

Jenny looked up at Esha and to Roshan's eyes for a reaction. Esha braced herself for his temper, but, instead, she was surprised by a hug.

"Thank you, Mummy."

Chapter 20

Roshan

Roshan swatted the chiming alarm away in the dark as if it were a bug, but it got louder and louder. He rubbed his face and eyes against his pillow, but his eyes were dry and the lids felt stuck to his eyeballs. In the dark, they saw nothingness, and he fumbled around the bedside table for the button on the alarm clock, nearly knocking over a baby bottle next to it. Jenny had her back to him, finally in a deep sleep after letting him feed the baby a bottle during the night instead of nursing. Her determination and energy to be supermom since the birth waned over the weeks, and all he wanted to do was help her through this, to show her—and himself—that he was there to take care of her.

He made it to his feet and walked nearly blindly through the dark to her side of the bed. He opened the bathroom door just a crack to see the silhouettes of his ladies, both breathing softly, almost in unison. Wisps of hair draped over Jenny's mouth and forehead, but her face was so relaxed, she couldn't have felt it if she'd tried. Her arm dropped over the side of the bassinet beside her. Her fingers just grazed the edge of Abigail's blanket and twitched a couple of times. If he had the time, he would have sketched them to keep them like this forever. Sobriety was good for his art, and he wanted to capture that too.

It was 5:12 am, time for Roshan to hit the shower and unfortunately only twenty-five minutes since he had laid Abigail down after her last feeding. He'd heard her delicate grumbling and jumped up before it could wake Jenny.

An hour earlier, as silently as he could, he'd lifted her soft form out of the bassinet and cradled her in his left arm on the way to the kitchen. As he warmed a bottle of breast milk in a warm bowl of water, Abigail began to turn her head toward him and bury her face in the softness of his t-shirt. Mouth open, becoming more and more squirmy, she rooted around impatiently at the mercy of the time it was taking to warm her milk. Roshan smiled at her dark gray eyes as she opened them in burgeoning anger, and he kissed her on the forehead, crooning to her, "Daddy's getting your bottle. Be patient, my baby. Daddy's got you."

Finally, when she began to protest loudly for her snack, the milk was warm, and he sat down on the sofa with her. Once the bottle was in her mouth, she'd quieted. He sat in the dark, listening to her gulps and soft noises, and leaned his head on the sofa back, eyes closed, but trying not to sleep with her in his arms. The house was his and Abigail's alone at that moment, peaceful and precious until that voice crept up on him.

Jenny will never know if you get a drink. Just one.

He had been sober since the baby came, and the voice had been easier to ignore than he thought it would be because he was there with his two girls who needed him so much. Tonight, he knew the voice would go away if he ignored it hard enough, and he focused intently on his daughter's sounds with her bottle. It didn't work.

After she was burped, changed, and content in that milk-drugged sleep of newborns' lives, he lay her in the bassinet next to Jenny, making sure Jenny didn't move from the commotion. Then he slunk into the spare bedroom at the end of the hall and shut the door as silently as he could. With the light on, he rummaged behind some blankets on the top shelf of the closet, a place that Jenny couldn't reach without a step stool. With a guilty heart but quickening pulse, he pulled out his last bottle of Jack and cradled it in his arms like he had his daughter. Abigail cried out down the hall, and he slid the bottle under the bed and held his breath. Jenny's groggy voice barely penetrated the bedroom door, but it sounded like she was singing softly for a moment. He cracked the door and leaned his ear out with his breath held, waiting for silence again. A few moments later, all was still.

With bottle in hand again, he went into the adjoining guest bathroom and turned on the light. He couldn't go downstairs to get a coke to mix with the liquor, so he'd drink water from the tap after the shot. And it would only be one this time. The attorneys and Jenny had made it clear they would push for him to go to rehab if he didn't stop as a good faith gesture in front of the judge. Jenny had watched him pour another bottle from the linen closet down the drain, and he couldn't disappoint her about this one, so he would have only one, and no one would know.

Before the rim touched his mouth, the aroma turned his stomach, but his head begged him to drink anyway. He had not drank in over three weeks ago, and his stomach resented him for this as the heat channeled into him with one swig and again with another. He bent forward to drink cold water from the tap and gagged on his way down, making the mistake of looking at himself in the vanity mirror. Here was a sad sack of a man looking at him, heaving over the bathroom sink, drinking water like an animal, sneaking booze while his baby and wife slept in the other room.

Disgusted, Roshan poured what was left of the whiskey down the drain and chased it with half a bottle of Scope to cover the smell. While he watched, tears threatened to surface out of fear that he couldn't make it without alcohol. He was left with only himself and wasn't sure if that was enough. Could that be enough for him to take care of his wife and baby? And his mum? Hands shaking the whole way, he turned off the lights, took the bottle to the recycling bin outside, and then went back in to bed to try to pretend this had not happened. Sleep had hit him hard for that twenty-five minutes, thanks to the swallows he had taken in, but now that he was up and the reality of what lay ahead of him this morning, he stepped into the shower, a little shaky, careful not to let the glass door touch the frame and make noise.

In just a few minutes, he was dried, dressed, and spritzing on cologne from the random assortment he kept on his dresser when he heard Jenny stirring in the bedroom. Not caring where it went like he used to in his meticulous younger days, Roshan plopped the bottle down, letting them cluster randomly. Jenny came padding into the bathroom, hair tangled and eyes puffy. With eyes half closed, she wrapped her arms around him and whispered, "Good luck today. I hope this attorney is as good as everyone says."

"You shouldn't be up, honey. Go back to sleep while you can. It won't be long 'til she's hungry again."

"I know. I just can't sleep anymore. You let me sleep seven hours last night. That's an eternity compared to what I've been getting. I'll be fine."

He lifted her chin and looked her in the eyes. "You sure? Really sure? I can ask my mum to come help you for a while today…"

Love for his mum and how she had loved him as a child filled him, and he desperately wanted that love with Jenny when he couldn't be there, no matter that it could smother. He was so worried about her and his inability to stand up, even when he tried. Why couldn't Jenny let in more help? Doubting himself this morning, he knew she was going to need it, and now that his mum had opened to them, he wanted her mum to be a part of his daughter's life. As long as she didn't bring Rich around them. Roshan was still her son and wanted to give her what she needed now.

If that voice will just go away.

"No," she said firmly. "No. I can do this myself."

"Babe, I know you want to, but you're not really doing so well with not sleeping and all. You said so yourself last night."

She'd collapsed into a puddle on his shoulder last night, a bundle of tears and confessions of anxiety over being a mother. He'd given her a mild sleeping pill and tucked her into bed early, promising he'd stay up all night if he had to just to take care of the baby.

"No." She was still firm. "I'm fine. I'm fine. I'll do it."

"Okay," he said, reluctantly, looking at his watch. He had to leave to get to his deposition on time. "Call my mom if you need help. Okay?"

"Okay. I will." Her eyes told him she was lying.

"And nap when the baby naps. We have the dinner at mum's tonight, and you'll need to be fresh. Mum invited a lot of people, so be prepared, okay? Everyone wants to meet the baby. Even Ashmi Auntie."

"Okay. I'm fine."

She kissed him and waved him away. He didn't believe her.

As he was walking away, she tugged his arm and pulled him to her again. "Thank you."

"For what?"

"For…really being a good father and husband. I know the stress is hard on you, and I'm proud of you for not—"

Suddenly, she was wide awake. The toothpaste apparently had not covered up his secret.

His skin suddenly lit up on edge, and he curtly squeezed her waist and pulled away. "Okay. Listen, I have to go. I'll call you later."

He walked away, leaving her looking after him. The baby was starting to squirm in her bassinet, and he hoped Jenny could deal with the day. But, his mind had to turn to the matter at hand: meeting with this attorney and getting himself out of this hole he had drank himself into.

A very strong cup of coffee on the way sounded like a good idea. The traffic was a beast. Arriving at the attorney's office forty-five minutes late with his life-saving coffee in hand did not bode well for the attorneys' opinions of him, and he worked hard to turn on his charm to fix that.

There were two attorneys: Jason something, a red headed guy about thirty with a rough southern accent, and the other a woman named Julia Garcia who spoke as if she came straight off a plane from Brooklyn. He tried to charm Julia with his smile, but she remained all business during the entire meeting. Jason, on the other hand, was easily talked into a tangent on Falcons' football, and Roshan found out he had been the star quarterback of his Jasper football team during high school before becoming a small fish in a big pond when he left the Georgia mountains for law school in Atlanta. However, after getting all the facts of his side of the story, Jason teamed up with tough talking Julia against him.

"Dr. Desai," Julia tapped her pen on the conference room desk across from him, "you do realize how serious these charges are against you?"

Of course he did, that's why he was there, and that's why he poured that liquor down the drain this morning. No way would that have happened otherwise.

"Yes, I understand."

"We are dealing with malpractice, Roshan. May I call you Roshan?" Jason drawled.

Roshan nodded. He regretted avoiding Beau for the past months and wished now he could be there with him. Reality hit. He really needed an attorney.

"Malpractice can take your license and your practice."

Roshan nodded again. The letters they had been sending him for the last few months already dropped that bomb.

Jason leaned back in his chair and pulled the lapels of his suit tighter. "We have talked the plaintiff out of criminal charges."

Roshan nearly passed out from relief. Pictures of himself in jail away from his family, of the look on his mother's face, of Jenny's face visiting him in jail all faded away. He had really fucked up and gotten a second chance, for sure.

"You pulled the wrong teeth while intoxicated, so count your blessings," Jason stated. "God has thrust his hand down here to save you on that one."

A good ole boy turned lawyer to TV evangelist in one sentence.

His patience was thinning, but he was a captive now to his stupid actions.

Julia added, "But the malpractice case may exceed the limits your malpractice insurance covers, and the court can attach the award to your practice. You will most probably lose it."

He expected that, but his head still felt like it had been crushed with a brick. What would he do? How would he hold his head high around anyone? Around his own wife, who was the epitome of success?

He sat there for what seemed like forever, listening to the duo tell him all they could try to do to help him, asking him to give them a list of colleagues who might vouch for him in a civil trial. That was a long shot. He had not been seen as successful, even competent, among fellow dentists, and he knew none would stick his neck out for someone like him. He wouldn't have either.

With the certainty that he would lose his license, he left the office after more meetings with the state board of dentistry and other people-who-know-people who might be able to help him. As he was walking out the door, Jason-from-the-mountains stepped out with him and confided in him, "You know, my dad was an alcoholic. Now I'm not saying you are. But he did some things he wasn't proud of when he drank, and rehab helped clean him up. He really straightened up well after that, and maybe, just maybe, a judge, even in a civil case, would go easier on you if you consider it yourself."

"That sounds a lot like jail, but thanks for the suggestion, Jason." Roshan shook his hand and went to his car.

The thought of rehab terrified him. People in that place would hold him accountable. He would be there alone with nowhere to run from the mirror. It felt like ants were crawling all over him at the prospect of never having one single drink again in his life. Panic filled him up to the brim, and he desperately tried to think of something to take it away.

Traffic was torture, and he was in hell in the interstate rush hour parking lot of Atlanta's perimeter. Should he—could he—call Jenny? Horns honked and tires screeched all around him pounding his senses, and when he reached down to dial her number, a beat up car with rusty paint and nothing to lose, jumped into the three inches between him and the car in front of him. Roshan slammed his brakes.

"Motherfucker!" he yelled with his windows closed, flipping the long-haired driver the bird. He wanted to stop the car and beat the hell out of the guy, but with an audience of thousands of commuters, he held himself back.

For another hour he stewed on the road, and when traffic finally picked up, he passed the exit toward his home and took one miles down the road.

What am I doing?

Ignoring the shrieking voice of reason, he pulled the car into the parking lot, his fingers locked it up with a chirp of the remote, and his legs walked him into the building.

An hour until he needed to be home and ready for the dinner was more than enough. Jenny would have to be strong and live without him for that much longer. His head hurt from the pressure of faces pushing their way out of his mind: the redheaded quarterback evangelist and the Brooklyn chick with her red lipstick, his mum and her knowing looks, Jay and his advice that he didn't deserve...and Jenny and the baby, waiting at home for him to pave the way for his family into the world and make everything okay. As he passed under the sign that read "Jim's Bar and Grill," all of the phobias melted away at the thought of the pure, relaxing heat that would soon flow down his throat.

Over an hour later, Roshan hit the highway and had a tough time staying in his lane, pulling away from a couple of close calls with tractor trailers beside him. The buzzing of his skin, what had felt so good when leaving the bar, now lit him up with fear, and he took an exit and pulled over in a gas station about half way home. He got out and was shuffling into the convenience store when he noticed a cop parked on the side of the lot. Roshan thought he watched him go in and come out with a bottle of Coke, or was it his imagination?

Concentrate. Focus. One foot in front of the other on the pavement.

He successfully reached the car and almost fell into the driver's seat, spilling his drink. The smart thing to do would have been to sit there for a while and drink the coke in hopes that the caffeine and sugar might tone down his intoxication. But, instead, he got paranoid that the cop would approach him and gingerly put the car in drive and left the lot. In the rearview mirror, his eyes were so focused on the cop whose nose was in his dashboard computer in his squad car that Roshan nearly hit a car down the road and swerved into a dead end road near a neighborhood. To be safe, he took back roads the rest of the way to his old house though he knew it would keep people waiting on him that much longer. But, if he wanted to get there at all, neighborhood roads with low speed limits and no trucks was the only solution.

When he rolled the car carefully beside the curb at the back of the guests' cars lined up outside Esha's house, he counted his blessings and drank a few swallows of soda. Jenny had texted him already that she brought Abigail to Esha's house early to dress for the dinner. It would be weird for Jenny to be in the house he had not so long ago shared with Priya, and he didn't text her back because he didn't want to go into that tonight. There was only so much he could handle after his long day on top of a sleepless night.

Esha, amidst all of the preparation for the big dinner at her house, had found time to shop for an Indian outfit for Jenny and Abigail for the occasion. He was glad Jenny had conceded to wearing clothes that Esha had picked out, as well as found the energy to get herself and Abigail over to the house.

He was very worried. Jenny's usual strength seemed to drain from her after the birth, and he barely knew her. She was three weeks into maternity leave, and he couldn't see her bouncing back enough in three more weeks to return and function in her practice. The kind of patients she treated expected not just a dentist who catered to their every whim while doing top notch work, but they also expected a premier image from her. From the look of things lately, she was far from that point. One evening last week, his mum had brought dinner for them after he had returned from work, and Jenny refused to eat it, instead taking the baby into their room and shutting the door as Roshan used a torn piece of *roti* to scoop lentils that smelled of delicious mustard seeds and cumin into his mouth. Esha gave him a knowing look and shrugged her shoulders and went and asked Jenny if she could bring her anything. Jenny wouldn't answer, and Esha came back to him and sat with him at the table.

"Does she hate me so much?" Esha asked.

"No, Mummy. She doesn't hate you. She doesn't trust anyone to help her anymore. She said she's not letting anyone in again. Me included."

"I tried to help her in the hospital. I'm trying to put aside our differences."

"Mummy, she's been burned. A lot. And it's gonna be a while before she can let go how you treated her before." He only wished she'd accept more help from Esha. Her pride was standing in her way of climbing out of the well of depression.

His mum had nodded, given him a hug, and gathered her things to leave.

"You good?" She put her hand on his shoulder at the doorway. Roshan knew she was asking if he was drinking. He had nodded.

Before stepping inside the house through the door from the garage into the kitchen, he tucked his shirt in and straightened his collar, finally giving his mouth another spritz of breath freshener. The smell of home enveloped him and made his stomach growl.

As a crowd of aunts and uncles and family friends and cousins greeted him, he took in the aroma of *poori* fresh out of the oil and caught a glimpse of a tray of *paturi* rolls slathered in cilantro and mustard seeds ready and waiting for him on the buffet. Most of his aunts were in the kitchen, of course, adding more mounds of food to trays, turning puffed up *rotis* over the stove flame, then deflating them with a tiny ladle of buttery *ghee*. Immediately descending on him were Monisha Auntie and Hema amongst a chorus of voices erupting from the women, "Ah, Roshan! You're here!"

Mummy had invited so many people, he wondered what she was doing. In three weeks, she had turned from sniping at Jenny, pretending she didn't exist around other people, to "Team Roshan and Jenny" wherever she went. Abigail had changed everything for her.

I hope the rest of these people take it all as well, for mum's sake.

Monisha Auntie pulled away from him and gave him a knowing look that reduced him to a child. Her lips stretched thin and tight as he stumbled over to the TV room where the men were gathered, and she swiftly grasped Esha's arm as she emerged from the restroom beside the kitchen. Roshan saw her out of his cloudy peripheral vision whispering in his mum's ear and then both shaking their heads discreetly. He kept walking into the TV room.

Men filled the room, and another chorus of "Hey, Roshan's here!" erupted. He concentrated on walking straight lines and enunciating his words, but his thick tongue mangled too many Gujarati sounds, and it was obvious he was drunk.

The décor of the room was the same as Priya had left it. A framed photograph of his grandparents posing with Roshan's mum and two uncles as children, hung above the sofa next to an expanse of wall on which Priya's family picture used to hang. A silk screened print of a scene from the Ramayana, with Rama's face, a vibrant blue, and Hanuman's monkey face staring bravely at him holding swords, hung over the mantle. On the bookshelves beside the fireplace was another gap in the décor, still wide open where they used to display their wedding picture. He was grateful Esha had finally put it away.

"Hi, Uncle…Hey, *bhai*…I'm good…How are you?…How's mom?…How's dad?…Good…" He meticulously repeated the same meaningless greetings over and over, lauding himself for his acting abilities, seeing that no one raised eyebrows at him. Finally, it occurred to him he had not seen Jenny or the baby. He made his way through the crowd to find his wife and daughter. Out of the corner of his eye, he saw a cluster of ladies chatting in a corner, admiring a vase on a shelf that Priya had bought on their vacation to Tuscany years ago while taking turns looking in the direction of the sofa. His eyes trailed the direction, and there was Jenny sitting with Abigail in her arms. Alone.

Jenny caught his eye and waved with eyes full of gratitude, but her mouth dropped when his foot slipped out from under him for no reason at all and he tripped a couple of steps before catching himself.

She knows.

He cautiously walked in the direction of the ladies on his way to Jenny. There were four of them, all mums of his childhood friends, all plump with middle age with varying degrees of salt and pepper in their hair. With eyes on Jenny, they spoke softly to each other in Gujarati. Roshan had to walk around a couple of guys standing in the middle of the room and calculatedly stopped to talk to Jay while keeping out of the women's view. He shut out what Jay was saying to him and honed in on the women's conversation.

"That's her. Yes, over there."

"Oooh, so that's what she looks like. Since we weren't at the wedding..." Irritation grinded in her voice.

Why would we invite you?

"Well, Esha wouldn't have pictures around either. Of course. I mean why would she? Advertise this...mess?"

That's why you weren't invited to the wedding.

"Poor thing. Esha's been through a lot in her life. First the disaster with her husband, and what a disgrace that was."

All four women shook their heads in unison.

The mum of one of Roshan's friends in high school said, "Shame. She tried so hard to raise Roshan alone. And now, look at how he paid her back."

"Like father, like son, I guess."

Blood rushed to Roshan's face, and he had to resist the urge to ball up his fists. He looked for his mum. Thank God she was nowhere near enough to hear. He hated these women because of their gossip...and because...they were right.

Whiskey-scented words spewed out of him before the women even saw him. He pushed his way past Jay and over to the cluster, revealing himself to them. With wide eyes, they all four stepped backward and looked at each other.

"Excuse me, ladies," he slurred, venom rolling out of his mouth. He nodded sloppily at them. "Auntie, Auntie." Even in his rage, he addressed them as he should. "I hear that you haven't met my wife and daughter yet. Well, let me introduce you. Come, come." He ushered the four women, who looked around the halting crowd in disbelief, before being placed in front of Jenny. In a bellowing voice, Roshan said, "Mummy, come. We need to formally introduce Jenny and Abigail to everyone here. Apparently, there is a little grumbling among my Aunties here that they had been passed over greeting her." His mum rushed over to him and stood blankly, frozen, and Roshan felt Jay stepping up behind him.

"Jenny, let me introduce some special ladies to you. Anita, Bhavini, Bharati, and Jagruti. Anita and Bharati are my mum's longtime friends, and Bhavini and Jagruti are my good friends from way back." Bowing to the ladies, he gestured toward Jenny in a large sweep of his arms. "Ladies, this is my wife and daughter."

Neither the ladies nor Jenny spoke. A wide-eyed crowd formed in doorways and pushed into the room, stunned. The other men were sitting their water glasses down anywhere convenient to them.

Jay's breath warmed the back of Roshan's neck, whispering, "What are you doing, *bhai*?"

Roshan brushed his neck off and went on. "Jenny, I overheard them wondering about you over there, so I thought you all should meet. Ladies, Jenny is a doctor and a new mom, as you can see. She's beautiful, right? Quite a catch for me, wouldn't you say?" Pausing for a moment, he looked around at the audience and then smiled a piercing smile at the ladies. He saw Esha's mouth hanging open but ignored her. His mum then stepped toward them with a plastic smile on her face. Still, Roshan believed she was happy the way the introduction was going.

"Jenny, Anita is a homemaker. Am I right?"

Anita nodded silently.

"She has three daughters, busy lady, right, Anita Auntie?" He looked at her terrified face and went on. "I just don't know how Anita found time all these years to be such a good mum to her girls, what with sneaking over to Maggan Uncle's house to screw when his wife was gone to work."

The collective gasp whooshed out of onlookers' mouths and filled the room.

Roshan stepped back, feeling a little dizzy, the final peak of the liquor high swallowing his brain now. Jenny looked up at him in fear, clutching the baby closer to her chest. His heart was ripping from that look, from what he was doing to her, but he patted her on the shoulder and said, "Honey, don't be upset. I just want you to get to know everyone here, since they are so curious about you."

"Roshan, stop." Jay put his arm around his shoulder like he would a buddy he was whisking away for fun, but Roshan shrugged him off. A couple of uncles spoke up, jeering him to go upstairs, but he laughed inside that Maggan Uncle had slipped away, and Anita flew into the kitchen with several women trailing behind her.

"And Jagruti here, she is a pharmacist. She's married. Has, what? Two kids already? Congratulations, Jagruti. Well, while she is working hard, and raising her kids, her husband is stealing money from his convenience store partner. Am I right, Jagruti?"

She looked at him and turned to walk away. "I'm not staying here for this, Roshan. You have problems."

He called after her, "And I hear you just got a sweet new Lexus. Life is good, huh?"

Jay grabbed him from behind and started pulling him backwards.

He caught a glimpse of Jay with Anita's husband, Chintu, on either side behind him. All of the women save Esha and Jenny had fled to the kitchen, leaving Roshan in a grip, surrounded by the men. Jenny still sat on the sofa with a stunned and terrified look in her eye, and his mum went over to her side and sat down next to her.

Jenny pulled back and clung tight to the baby. "That's enough, Roshan."

"Let's go," Chintu said.

"Out of here."

Roshan pulled away from the grip of his captors and turned to face them, but stumbled backward.

'What's the matter?" he slurred, as they caught him again and dragged him out the garage door. "Uncle, why are you so mad? I just wanted to let everyone get to know each other. After all, since there's so many fun stories going around about me and my family, I thought it was only fair to share some of everyone else's."

In the garage, his uncle spat out, "You're a son of a bitch, just like your father."

"At least I'm not married to a gossiping whore."

Maggan's fist smashed into his eyes in a flash of bright light, and Roshan fell back into a stack of paint cans.

"Okay, I deserved that." He rushed tripping past both men and said, "I'm just going to get my wife and daughter and leave now."

Fighting lose from their grasp, he rushed back in to the den toward Jenny, who was standing up and packing her diaper bag. "Come on, baby, let's get out of here."

She pulled back like his touch was poisoned, turning her back to him to keep the baby from his grasp, as Roshan was forcefully grabbed from behind again, this time by the stronger hands of two other men. Jenny bent over the coffee table, still grasping Abigail tightly in one arm, moving away from his mum's outstretched arms offering to hold the baby, rapidly stuffing everything into the bag as tears poured down her face.

Roshan yanked himself from the men as hard as he could and broke free, but as his arms flung up and away, he lost his balance over the edge of the coffee table. Unable to brace his fall, he slammed into Jenny hard.

The impact of their bodies colliding sent the baby flying from Jenny's arms as his drunken body fell flat on top of Jenny's. In gut-wrenching slow motion, Roshan watched his daughter's tiny head bounce off of the edge of the sofa, twisting her whole body up in the air, before she landed limp as a ragdoll on the carpeted floor at Esha's feet.

Screams from all sides pierced his ears, and instantly he was excruciatingly sober. Immediately jerked up and hauled by the hair, shoulders and legs toward the door, he saw the women gather around Esha and Jenny as they picked up his daughter, silently crying as they caressed her head and gently inspected her tiny frame all over. His baby wailed without breath, her cheeks turning red and then purple.

"Jenny," he called weakly.

Jenny looked up at him vacantly, but Esha moved in front of her, turned toward him and the men, and ordered, "Get him out of here." She turned her back to him, bending over Jenny and the baby as he was dragged into the dark night.

Chapter 21

Esha

"How did this happen?"

The on-call doctor looked up from the patient's chart and directly at Jenny in the children's hospital emergency room.

Esha got nervous. Jenny looked like she would be sick.

This doctor, a woman with very short black hair who looked to be Muslim, maybe Pakistani, was going to think the baby had been abused. Why wouldn't she? Esha looked at the doctor's identification badge. Yes, Massoud. Definitely Pakistani. Okay, they're usually good doctors. As Jenny hugged Abigail's sleeping form to her chest, straightened up her shoulders, and began to answer with a confident voice, Esha held her breath.

"I was holding her, someone tripped into me, and she fell out of my arms. It was a ridiculous accident."

Esha could tell she was trying to keep emotion out of it, to sound light, but a tremor hovered on the edge of her voice like Esha's had so many times before in India. She was in danger of sounding like she was trying too hard.

"Who tripped into you?" Dr. Massoud peered over her glasses at both of them with a pen ready to jot notes on everything they said.

Esha had seen many news reports on TV about how the authorities here handled child abuse. Things weren't settled in the home; no, they were settled by taking a child from their home. She had to do something.

Esha shook her head and piped in. "Me. So embarrassed! I tripped over my sari when I bent down to get something on the floor." She bent over to demonstrate and flipped the flowing fabric pleats at her feet and looked up, "and I took a step and fell! You know saris, no?"

"Okay then." The doctor nodded her head at Esha and added dryly, "No sorry, I don't know saris. I was born here. But it happened to my mom once when I was a kid. At a wedding going up some stairs. She fell hard."

The doctor smiled benignly and jotted down some notes without looking back up at them. After a tense few moments, Abigail began to stir, and the doctor directed Jenny to place her on the bassinet so she could examine her.

As the doctor unwrapped the swaddling blanket, she asked, "When you fell, what happened?"

The image of Roshan being torn out of the room burned Esha's memory, and the sound of her own iron-clad words crunching out of her mouth, ordering the men to get rid of him, echoed in her ears.

Dr. Massoud's long fingers very gently pushed and felt all over Abigail, who went from whimpering to crying, to quickly cheeks turning purple and shuddering with angry wails. The cries were a good sign, Esha presumed. Babies that were not okay did not cry.

"She bounced off the sofa and landed on the carpet. Then I picked her up, and we brought her here immediately after that."

Esha moved closer to Jenny, both hovering over the baby, both ready to scoop her up as soon as possible. She was freezing—hospitals were always kept so cold—and wrapped her *ootni* from her shoulder around her neck for warmth. She wished she could cover the baby up and grew angry as the examination dragged on. Finally, the doctor stated that the baby looked good, and she could be held now. Esha and Jenny both reached out to cover her, but Jenny swiftly had her wrapped with both hands under the baby, pulling her up to her chest. Esha, empty handed, wanted so desperately to comfort her granddaughter, and Jenny avoided her eyes and turned away. Old pain for her own lost baby and new pain for her lost son cut through her, and she hugged her arms tightly around her waist.

The doctor ordered an X-ray just to be safe, and Jenny rocked Abigail for hours while they waited in the exam room to be taken down. Dark circles sunk in her eyes, and Esha thought she would drop soon.

"Give, I hold her. You must sit."

Jenny shook her head and stared at the wall. "Where did they take him?"

Esha didn't want to talk about him, even with Jenny. "My brothers took him to Jayesh's house. Jayesh texted me earlier that they will plan a flight to a rehab in the morning." She tried to touch Jenny's arm under the baby, but Jenny shirked. "Roshan will be gone for a while."

"He's been gone, Esha."

Esha agreed with Jenny. She tried to remember when he had been Roshan, the real Roshan that was her son, and she couldn't. She wondered if he had ever been real with Jenny.

"Did he ever tell you he used to draw when he was a boy? He was very good."

Jenny looked at her strangely. "Yes. He didn't stop when he grew up, Esha. He hates being a dentist but did it for you. When he is depressed, drawing is all he does. I think it's the only thing that makes him happy now."

A hollowness opened up inside her as she shamefully remembered the time when Roshan was in tenth grade and his teacher failed him on his notebook check because he had drawn pictures throughout the entire book instead of writing his chemistry equations. Esha tore into his room with a trash can, throwing away every single sketch pad, drawing, oil pastel, and charcoal pencil she could find. He shoved his feet into his running shoes that afternoon and bolted out the door, not returning until midnight exhausted and drenched in sweat. Esha knew now it was that night Roshan ceased to be himself. And it was her fault.

"I wanted him to be the best back then. He can't draw all day long... goes nowhere." This was true, but another nagging truth clung in her throat still.

"Why nowhere?" Jenny asked. "He is the best at it. He could have made a good career of it."

The truth clinging inside her throat slipped out and into the open air for the first time. As she spoke, she saw the words in the air and examined them as if they weren't real. "His father was an artist. So I couldn't allow it." She stood up and paced, still hugging herself, imagining herself holding the following words in her hands, turning them over and over. "He had to be better."

Neither of them spoke for a long time, and Jenny lay the baby on the bed to change her diaper. While Jenny pulled off the tabs at the baby's waist, Esha got out the new supplies and handed them to Jenny. She accepted them, and the two of them worked together to get the job done.

Once Abigail was dressed and clean again, she was in Jenny's arms. Jenny leaned in to Esha. "Can you hold her? I need to use the restroom."

Esha ecstatically took the baby in her arms. Before she left the room, Esha had to ask Jenny before life got in the way again. "Do you think I'm a bad mother?"

Jenny stopped and looked at her in shock. "You're a mother who did the best she could. Better than my mom did for me. So, no, I don't think you're a bad mother."

"I tried so hard. I think I loved him too much."

"I did too, Esha."

"You done loving him?"

"No, but I don't know if I can be married to a liar and a thief."

"What you mean liar and thief?" Her son lied, yes, and was a lot of things, but he was no thief. How could she?

Jenny breathed heavily and came over and sat down again, cupping her daughter's head as she lay in Esha's arms. The weight felt good against Esha, and Abigail started to squirm.

"He's a liar because he promised he would take care of me. And he's a thief because he stole my trust in people. In everyone."

They both stared at Abigail's lips pursing and when her fist pushed around, opening and closing, and finally reaching her mouth where she slurped happily on it, they smiled at each other for the first time that Esha could remember.

Jenny stood back up and left the room, leaving Esha alone with the baby. With every moment that passed while Jenny was gone, a wave of strength overcame her from God, and she promised herself and God that she would take care of her children, all of them, no matter what happened. She closed her eyes and began to whisper the mantra to the room, not stopping or letting go of the baby when Jenny returned and sat next to her. She didn't need to be in front of her Ganesha at home or light her *diyas* to make *arti* with her hand over the flames. She had her Diya right there in her arms and knew that the greatest God over them all would find a way to bless them when it was time.

Oṃ bhūr bhuvaḥ svaḥ
tát savitúr váreṇ(i)yaṃ
bhárgo devásya dhīmahi
dhíyo yó naḥ pracodáyāt

Oh God! Thou art the Giver of Life,
Remover of pain and sorrow.
The Bestower of happiness
Oh! Creator of the Universe,
May we receive thy supreme sin-destroying light,
May thou guide our intellect in the right direction.

The door swung open, and Jenny reentered the room. Esha opened her eyes, still mouthing the words silently. Jenny paused at the door and said, "Go on." Esha closed her eyes again, and Jenny sat down in the chair next to her.

When Esha handed Abigail to her, Jenny leaned back in the chair and said, "Thanks. For the prayer, I mean. That was nice."

Early the next morning when Esha pulled the car into Jenny and Roshan's driveway with both Jenny and the baby asleep in the back seat, she felt a rush of relief over her. Jay and Hema were already there waiting in their car for them. Jenny had agreed to let Esha stay at the house with her for a night or two to help out with the baby since she was so exhausted from the ordeal. She had hesitated for a long time in the hospital, then when Abigail had cried loudly and Jenny looked as if she would unravel at every edge, she acquiesced. Esha had called Monisha who went to her house, put together a suitcase for her, and sent it with Jay and Hema.

Her family was the best she could ever ask for.

Rich had texted her as they were leaving the hospital, a short "good morning to you," which made her feel naughty. Since the night in the hospital when Abigail was born, they had spent time together not only in the evenings, but during the days too. Esha had tried to stay out of Roshan and Jenny's space for those first few weeks, and most of her time ended up being spent with Rich and Evelyn at doctor visits, or Esha fixing them a bland version of her lunch when they returned home, which Rich ate heartily, but Evelyn couldn't touch anymore. She had even stopped drinking the tea, and Esha, saddened, knew things were not good.

Esha didn't text him back and made sure she deleted the text from Rich so no one would see it by accident. She put the phone in her purse, fearing their flirtation had gone way beyond what she could handle. A relationship with him—oh God, she couldn't believe she was even thinking those words—would never happen. Some lines were so old that they weren't made to be crossed. Yet her heart ached for it.

She got out of the car and greeted Jay and Hema, who pulled out a suitcase and two cardboard boxes full of food dishes.

"Good morning, Auntie." Hema hugged her, and Jay gave her a half hug while holding a big box.

"Good morning." The sunrise was beginning to burn off the mist around her favorite magnolia tree in her yard but still had yet to warm the air enough. Winter was coming, and she still only had her *ootni* to cover with.

Jay peered into the backseat of the car. Jenny's head lay back on the headrest, and her arm rested across the baby's rear-facing car seat. Both girls' eyes were shut.

Hema asked quietly, as if her voice could wake them through the car door. "How are they? Abigail will be okay?"

"Yes, thank God. They both just need rest. That's why I'll stay for a while." Her skin was getting chill bumps, and her teeth began to chatter a bit.

Hema picked up a box and told Jay, "Come on, honey, let's get them in. It's freezing."

Jay nodded, "Yes, ma'am."

Esha and Hema woke Jenny and helped her get the baby seat into the house while they all carried something. Jenny walked next to Hema up the front steps, and Hema offered to help carry the baby seat.

"No, thanks, I've got her," Jenny replied, groggy and heavy voiced. Her arm drooped a little, and Hema helped her lift the seat again without saying anything. Jenny smiled at her gratefully.

Once inside, Jay and Hema unloaded the food supplies.

"Come, Auntie. Jenny, come see. My mum will have my hide if I don't tell you exactly what she sent."

Jenny smiled politely as she and Esha watched Jay and Hema pull out containers portioned for sailors.

"I hope you two plan on eating twenty-four hours a day, Jenny. Auntie, take inventory, here goes..."

No one said the obvious that these were the leftovers from the dinner all of the women had made last night that didn't get touched because of Roshan. But, food was food and had to be eaten. It would save Esha trouble too, because cooking her food at Jenny's house without her proper Indian spices and ingredients would be impossible. She knew Jenny and Roshan ate meat and wasn't thrilled with even eating on their plates, much less trying to find food in their kitchen. Who knows what she would come across? Certainly no *masala*, she guessed. Maybe some barbeque sauce or Heinz 57 steak sauce like she had seen in Kroger before.

Starving for breakfast, Esha's stomach rumbled over each container. A large jar of *daal* soup sloshed around and was placed next to a bowl of crispy on the outside, soft on the inside potatoes skillet fried with mustard seeds and cumin. Next was a foil packet of fresh *rotis* stacked together, still smelling of warm *ghee*, and a small jar of mango *achar*, tipping over abruptly, threatening to spill its thick red oil out the top and onto the plastic bag that covered it. Next came a bowl of puff pastries filled with a mixture of corn and spices, and Esha could already feel the flakes falling from her mouth.

Jenny picked up the baby who was getting restless now that she was no longer in the steady motion of the car, rocking her as she looked on, curious, and swallowing out of hunger too.

"What's that?" Jenny pointed at a foil pan covered with a sheet of plastic wrap.

Esha was surprised at Jenny's interest because the few times she had dined with her, Jenny had turned her nose up at most of their food, and when she did eat anything, it was with a spoon and cold looks at the others at the table who were comfortable using their fingers and pieces of *naan* and *roti* to scoop up their food.

"A corn dish. Best with coriander chutney on top," Esha said. "It looks like my bhabhi made us my favorite breakfast food, not just sent us leftovers. You like corn?"

Jenny nodded.

"Then you like this. Put some coriander chutney and these crunchy things on top." She held up a full bag. "Mix it up, and God, so good."

Jenny absently said, "Mmmm" as she started to walk away with the baby.

"Hema," Esha said, "would you help Jenny with the baby? I think the diaper bag is by the door."

"No, Esha, Hema, I'm fine. I'm just going to sit down with her. I don't need anything."

Hema walked with her, and said, "Okay, well, can I keep you company? I didn't meet Abigail before last night—" She paused as if she'd swallowed a fly. "Uh, tell me all about her." Hema walked with Jenny into the living room, and Esha thought she saw Jenny smile but couldn't be sure with the all of the tired hair hanging in her face. She heard them sit down and start talking and was so happy to hear Jenny say, after a few minutes, "I'd love to change out of this outfit into some sweatpants. Can you hold her while I go upstairs?" Esha turned to Jay while he helped put away dishes.

"So, *bhai*. How's he doing?"

Jay stopped and put his hands on the counter next to Esha. His hair stuck up too, showing his own lack of sleep. "Well, we kept him at our house last night, and dad is making arrangements this morning. We should have him in a place by tonight."

"No, I mean, how is he doing?"

Jay looked at her. "Not good, Auntie. He stayed in the guest room and cried himself to sleep. It was…really hard to see."

Esha imagined Roshan as a little boy going to bed in tears, being punished with no TV for something he did. Her heart would break back then when his little body would shudder in sobs, and she would always end up going into his room and sitting on the edge of the mattress and rubbing his back until he calmed down. But that was then, and now she couldn't—wouldn't—do that.

"Okay, then. Okay." She hugged Jay and said, "Thank you for being a good brother to him." She wanted to talk about him, but she also wanted someone else to worry about him for a while. Right now, she was numb to her son. She shooed Jay to the side and then busied herself with putting every jar, every bowl, and every foil tray in just the right place in the refrigerator and pantry. Jay stepped back when he saw she was going into her organization mode and knew from his childhood experiences to give her space to do her work. The work soothed her mind, and when everything was in its place in Jenny's kitchen, she felt relaxed. At least she could have control over some things.

She opened a cabinet and found a plastic container of her special *chevro* mix that she had sent for Roshan months ago. He had told her not to send it because he was not eating fattening foods anymore, but she had insisted. If he had at least one food she could give him, she would feel a little better that her son was being taken care of.

What was left in the container made her smile wider than she thought possible that morning. When she had mixed the trail mix, it had included roasted peanuts, crispy rice, crunchy lentils, dry cereal, dried fried onions, and was sprinkled in a hot spicy sugary coating, but all that was left in the container was fried onions sticks and crispy rice pieces. Roshan had gone through and picked out his favorite parts from the mix, just like he had as a kid. She had shouted at him back then because she spent so much time making all of the ingredients that went into the mix, but this time, she wanted to hug him.

Somewhere deep inside, he was still her boy. Now, he just had to find a way himself to keep that little boy afloat without drowning him in drink.

Jenny came in. "Oh, that stuff is really good. Do you make it yourself? Roshan and I would snack on it before bed every night when I was pregnant. We both picked out the same stuff too." Jenny got a glass of water, tucked a stringy strand of hair behind her ear and went back into the living room to Hema, who was waiting to hand the baby back to her and leave. Esha put the container facing squarely ahead back in its spot in the cabinet, and with a peaceful calm, went out of the kitchen to see them out the door. Jay promised that his mum would be by later to check on them, and Hema told Jenny to call her if she needed anything. Jenny looked surprised by the offer, and then announced she was going to take the baby upstairs.

"I take the baby while you rest?"

Jenny responded with no energy in her voice. "No, I can do it. I'll be fine."

Esha responded, "But, I'm here to help."

"No. I'm okay. I've got this. Really." She took the baby upstairs and shut her bedroom door behind her. Esha stood at the bottom of the teakwood stairs and tried to put all of this together in her mind. Her family was surrounding them, Hema was reaching out to Jenny, Esha was more comfortable in Jenny and Roshan's house than she thought she would be where a tiny lingering shred of her son had revealed itself, and yet Jenny wanted to be alone.

"Auntie, she's been under a lot of stress. Let her be for now. She'll come around," Jay told her.

"You've all had a tough time." Hema told Esha, hugging her goodbye. "When the kids are in school, I can come help if you need me. Or, bring you more things, whatever you need. Okay?" Hema paused and added, "Ashmi Auntie has said she will come with more food later. Just ask what Jenny likes. She'll even make Italian or something if Jenny doesn't like Indian."

The look of shock in Esha's eyes must have amused Jay because he playfully slapped her on the shoulder. "Poor Jenny, couldn't get anyone to talk to her. Now she'll never get rid of us. If Ashmi Auntie is on board, Lord help us. We'll need to tape her mouth shut to keep her from reporting to the Guju news."

Hema frowned. "I think she's sincere, Jay. After last night, I think a lot of people have changed their thinking."

Esha retorted, "Oh, *dikra*, I'm sure. There are some who I can never show my face around again." The horror of Roshan's words, and the people's faces as he spoke pierced her again, but the way the men surrounded him and how the women who mattered most surrounded her and Jenny made her feel like things could be okay still. "But Ashmibhabhi must be on board. She stuck with us." Then she snickered, "I'll go buy the tape."

Esha hugged and kissed them both on the cheek and waved goodbye as they pulled away. Yes, family had to stick together. And Esha knew from experience that we don't choose our family, but we're connected somehow with them until the end.

When she shut the front door in front of her, she wanted to go up there and push her way in and take charge of the baby. At the same time, Esha fought the urge to slip on her *chappals* and leave the house to get away from all of this. Then she thought about that tiny little girl upstairs who she knew was going to need her, and she decided to rest on the sofa for a just a few minutes instead before making any rash decisions. She lay her head on the arm of the sofa and didn't wake up until the doorbell rang and the midmorning sun scorched her legs from the exposed window in the living room. Disoriented, she sat up and looked around, trying to figure out what the sound was. It took her a moment to realize she was in Roshan's house and that the ringing was the doorbell, but she had no idea who would be ringing it.

She smoothed her flyaway hair from her face and wished she had brushed her teeth.

Where did Jayesh put my overnight bag?

Running her tongue across her teeth as she walked to the door, she hoped it was no one she would know on the other side. Surely it would just be a sales person.

Rich was on the doorstep when she opened the door.

"Hello?" she asked surprised.

"Hello." His sunglasses and shaved head gleamed in the morning sun. He wore a white shirt and blazer, much more dressed up than usual.

"What are you doing?"

"I hadn't heard from you in a while. I wanted to stop by. And talk to you about something."

Esha instinctively looked both behind and outside. No one was around.

"I don't think anyone around here is going to rat you out to your people that I'm here. Relax."

That's what you think. You just missed them.

"Why? How? Where did you get this address?"

"Jay gave it to me. He gave me his card at the wedding, and I texted him that I needed to talk to you about my mom, so he gave me the address.

May I come in?" He held up a small box wrapped in pastel teddy bear paper. "I'm bearing a gift."

She smelled cologne wafting from him. Esha felt so self-conscious in her unwashed state and wanted to say no, absolutely not, but instead, she said, "Oh, I'm sorry. Come in. I'm sorry."

He stepped in and handed the box to Esha. "For Jenny and…Roshan." His eyes were sympathetic as he said Roshan's name.

"Thank you." She stared at him and smiled, not moving.

"May I sit down?"

He gestured for her to go first, and they sat on opposite ends of the large leather sofa, and Esha lay the box on the cocktail table, picking up a burp cloth and twisting it around in her hands. The few feet between them was not enough for her to ignore the energy she felt from his body seated close but so far away.

"You haven't been returning my calls or texts. I was worried about you."

"I'm okay. Just busy. And…sorting things out."

"What exactly happened with Roshan? Do you want to talk about it?"

"Oh, no. No more talking. Please."

"Okay, sure. Whenever you're ready." Rich paused and then scooted closer to Esha. He touched her knee, but Esha jerked away like she'd been touched by a live wire. She tried to shrug it off, but her embarrassment shown in her face, and she looked away.

"I'm flying back up to New York."

At that, Esha looked him boldly in the eye, questioning. This changed everything. She no longer had eyes around her or in her conscience spying on her behavior.

"Why?"

"I have to get back to my work, my life. Mother is not getting better. I've found a nursing facility near my home. I'm bringing her with me."

Esha smiled. "Why didn't you tell me all this time?"

"I didn't want to let go before it was time."

The baby cried from behind the shut door upstairs, and Esha looked up there nervously when she heard footsteps. She had been so ready to push him away, to end these inappropriate feelings she was allowing herself to have, and now she was so sad to lose him and Evelyn.

"I will miss your Mum. She became my dear friend."

"I know. She's down about leaving. The house. She's been there since Dad died, a long time. And about leaving you. But, I have to get back to work. And you have your own life now. You can't be next door with her all the time anymore. Maybe you could fly up to visit her…and me… sometime?"

"I don't know. I have Jenny, the baby…Roshan. Maybe, soon, I can visit…her. Or, maybe you could fly down here some time for a visit. To keep me posted on Evelyn."

They looked at each other quietly, Esha conscious, nervous, of the increasing footsteps upstairs. He extended his hand to hers, and she let it stay on her lap and be covered by his.

Jenny appeared at the top of the stairs and called softly, "Um, Esha, could you bring me the burp cloth. I forgot it down there."

Esha froze when she saw her, and Jenny smiled a big, knowing grin.

"Hi," she said to Rich from above. "We met at my wedding. Nice to see you."

"Nice to see you too." He stood and waved, looking at Esha out of the corner of his eye. Esha was speechless and confounded on what to do next, still seated. Rich rescued her.

"Congratulations on your new baby, by the way. My mom sent a baby gift for you." He pointed to the box on the cocktail table.

Jenny kept smiling, looking back and forth between Esha and Rich. "Thank you so much."

Rich stepped even farther away from Esha, who was feeling a little bolder because of Jenny's expression, and she herself stood, moving closer to him. Jenny was not judging, she was sure. She actually looked happy for her.

"I came by to bring the gift and was telling Esha here that my mom and I are moving back to New York. So, just saying a quick goodbye."

Suddenly aware she was still holding the burp cloth, Esha walked up the stairs and handed it to Jenny. "Here, take. I wash more for you soon." Jenny thanked her, and Esha avoided her eyes.

"Okay," Jenny said to both of them and turned back to the upstairs hallway. "I'll let you get back to talking. Thank you for the gift, Rich. Safe travels."

Rich looked at Esha when Jenny was gone. "The cat's out of the bag now. Sorry."

"She won't say nothing. I saw in her face."

"Well, I'm going to go now."

They walked together to the door and stopped to look at each other.

"You didn't answer me," Esha said, looking up at him, "about visiting."

"Yeah. Maybe I can work it work out."

His face felt dangerously close to hers, but she didn't look down. She felt his breath between them and held his gaze.

"I need to get going, and I see that you're very busy," he said gently. "Give my regards to Roshan when you see him." He opened the door and put a foot out on the stone stoop. "Take care of yourself. And text me sometime. Let me know how you're doing."

"Okay. Goodbye Rich. Travel safe." Her skin still tingled went he shut the door, and she felt more alive than she had in over a week. Her life was a different one now, and he was going, but she was good.

As she watched his car pull out of the driveway, she reached for her iPhone. Tapping quickly, she tapped send before she could let herself regret it.

Esha
I'm good. You say you wanted to know.

She saw his car stop down the street. A reply chirped on her phone.

Rich
Wow. You're quick. See you soon. Very.

The car pulled forward again and disappeared, but Esha's smile stayed on her face.

Thanks to Jay and Hema bringing her things from home, Esha did not need to leave the house. Monisha called one morning on her way to the store.

"I'm coming with Ashmibhabhi now with groceries. Have some things from home to make your food. I'm sure Jenny's kitchen doesn't have rice flour or fresh ginger."

"Ashmibhabhi is with you?" Esha's tried to convey her consternation through the phone. She knew her other sister-in-law was sitting right next to Monishabhabi in the car.

"Yes, all is well." Esha could tell Monisha was trying to sound benign, and Esha had to take her word for it. "What kinds of things does Jenny like to eat?"

Esha thought about that. She wasn't really sure. In the pantry were boxes of steel cut oatmeal and a few cans of organic chicken noodle soup, and she had thrown out some spoiled deli turkey just this morning from the refrigerator. But Jenny had eaten none of that and had picked at the Indian food Esha had warmed. She was spending most of her time upstairs sleeping, and lately, on the phone with her office staff talking about work. She was due to go back to work in two weeks, and it was plain that she was having a hard time with the stress.

"I'm not sure, bhabhi. Bring me some things to make *biryani*, and I can make that for her. That is maybe more her taste than some other things we've had."

When they arrived with arms full of grocery bags, Jenny was napping, and Esha had the baby in her arms. Ashmi had her hair pulled back in a ponytail and wore yoga pants and a sweatshirt with a *bhindi* on her forehead. Esha had never seen her so casual outside of the home, and

Monisha was dressed in slacks and a blouse for work. Ashmi leaned to hug Esha balancing bags in her arms, oohing over the baby. She rushed to sit down her load and wash her hands quickly.

"Come, give," she told Esha.

Esha reluctantly handed over her bundle and told Ashmi to sit. She knew Ashmi was a mother, of course, but was hesitant to let anyone else hold Abigail as if she were her own baby. This was worse at night when a gnawing feeling pained her. She would never let anyone hurt this baby girl. Perhaps it was God giving her a chance for redemption.

"So, things good here?" Monisha asked, looking over her shoulder at Ashmi on the sofa.

"Yes, okay." Esha peered at Ashmi as well, careful to choose her words around her. Ashmi was focused on looking at Abigail, though, who lay on her lap, chewing on her fist. "I'm worried about her though. Jenny is not eating and crying a lot. Very depressed."

"Try to get her to eat. She needs to for the baby. Her milk will dry up if she doesn't."

"Yes, I know. I'll take breakfast to her room."

"I went through this when I had Raj and Nikhil," Ashmi said from the sofa. Her face was soft. "I was in India at my parents. Remember? My mom got me through it." She bounced the fussing baby. "You need to stay with her."

Monisha and Esha looked at each other. They had no idea about this.

"Don't look like that. You think I have no feelings?"

Esha boldly said, "Honestly bhabhi, I'm surprised. That's all. You haven't been exactly friendly with Jenny, so I just didn't expect—"

"You weren't exactly friendly to her either, bhabhi," Ashmi retorted. She put the baby on her shoulder and rubbed her back, clucking her tongue. Abigail quieted. Esha's cheeks burned, but she realized that Ashmi was right.

"Ashmi, bhabhi, come on." Monisha admonished. "Let's not—"

"Not what? Look at this little girl. We all have this baby to take care of. Our Roshan is gone. Am I going to be cold? So, I'm learning there's no shame in some change. Okay?"

Ashmi stood and came over to the Esha and Monisha. "My friend, well, who I thought was my friend, called this morning to gossip about Roshan and Jenny. I…just…had to hang up." She kissed the baby's head and added, "She is our little Roshan's. And Jenny is…her mom. I get it."

Esha thought she would burst into tears. Who was this bhabhi in front of her? She was behind them? A glimmer of hope shined in her eyes.

"Yeah, of course, there's a lot going around about all of this," Ashmi continued. "It will die down but not be forgotten. Roshan has made sure things will change. For all of us."

Not such a bad thing, maybe.

Monisha took the baby from Ashmi and bounced her. The women looked at each other, then Esha, still not one to show feelings, said, "Okay, then. Let me get back to work. I have washing to do, need to check on Jenny." She thanked them for the groceries and went back in to start breakfast. She wondered what kind of food Roshan was getting for breakfast in his hospital.

She woke Jenny up to nurse the baby, who was fussing and sucking on her fingers. Jenny took her and absently shut the door without a word.

Esha started sautéing some day-old *Idara* squares to soften them but turned off the stove and hood fan. She thought she heard something from upstairs

Jenny's door was closed, but there was no mistaking the sounds of racking sobs through the walls. Esha had kept her distance so far but was going to follow Ashmi's advice.

Stranger things have happened.

She ascended the steps to the master bedroom and stood outside the door.

The baby was wailing, and Jenny was sobbing.

"Jenny. You okay?"

The sobs were stifled, and Jenny replied with a rattled voice, "Mmm, I'm fine. I'm okay. I'll be out in a few minutes."

The baby began to wail louder.

"You sure? I can take the baby. Let me take her."

"No, no. I'm okay. I'm trying to feed her. She'll settle down."

Esha stood at the door without answering and listened. She heard Jenny crooning softly through a teary voice, "Mommy's got you. Shhh, shhh. Please eat. Please settle down." Her pleading voice melted into sobbing again, and the shudders and wails from both of them hit Esha to the bone.

"Jenny, I'm coming in." She waited a second in case she protested, but there was none.

The curtains were drawn and the bathroom light was on, casting a sickly glow on them on the bed. Jenny sat up, hugging herself, rocking back and forth. The baby lay next to her, red in the face, fists tight in the air, legs shaking out straight in anger. Jenny did not look up when Esha swept up the baby and cuddled her in one arm. Cluck, clucking her tongue at the baby, she patted her back and propped her up on her shoulder, so the baby's head wobbled above it. The wailing softened.

Esha sat on the edge of the bed, careful to kept up the rhythm of pats to the back

Jenny looked at her outstretched legs, and hugged herself around the chest tighter. "I can't do this."

"What? Take care of her?" Esha smiled at the tiny bobbing face rubbing against her shoulder. "Yes. You can."

"No. I can't. I can't do this alone. I'm alone." She started crying again, then sucked in air and said, "I'd never depended on anyone before Roshan came along, never pictured my life with him like that. But I let myself, and now he's gone and I'm here with this baby who I can't even get to stop crying."

"Jenny, you are not alone."

Jenny scoffed. "Do you see your son anywhere in this picture? No. He's in rehab. He's not here for me. For us." She touched the baby's hand. "I don't even know how to be a mother. Look at who I came from. I'm on my own, and I cannot do it."

Esha stood up and looked down at her. "Pretend you Roshan making sketch of this now. See who is holding your baby right now in this picture in your head?" she asked softly.

Jenny gasped for air and looked up at Esha. Esha cradled the baby in the crook of her arm and swayed swiftly. Abigail's eyes were closed, and her fist was in her mouth. The only sound from her was the slurping of her fingers.

"You."

"So, there is another person in this room with you, no?"

Jenny looked her in the eye and gulped. "Yes."

"Okay then. You not alone."

"Yes, but Roshan should be here. I need him." Jenny's eyes squeezed away the tears and she rubbed her face. The skin on her cheeks and around her eyes was raw and red.

Esha looked at her compassionately, yet stern at the same time. "Yes, my son should be here. But he's not. He can't be. And won't be for a while. But, I am here." Esha sat on the side of the bed and lay the baby next to her, gently massaging her belly in a circular motion. Every morning she would do this with Roshan as a baby. All babies need massage; it helped to get all of the air out of their bellies and calm them. Abigail's face relaxed, and her eyes looked around the room toward her mother's voice.

"Why? Why are you here? After all that happened? After how he humiliated you in your own home? You never wanted me around. And I'm the reason he's done this." Tears rolled out of her swollen eyes, and she heaved a heavy sigh. "Everyone hates you now because of Roshan and me."

"Jenny. We don't make the picture we in. God's hand draws us how he see, not how we see. I here because I want to be here. Everyone I love does not hate me. Or you. Matter of fact, my two bhabhis just here asking after you." She stood and grabbed a tissue from the night stand, handing it to Jenny. "Nobody else matters." She swatted the air as if the people were hovering there. "I love my son. I love my baby here." She bent over and smiled into Abigail's face, and the baby's mouth almost mimicked her smile in return. "You my daughter-in-law now. My *wo*. Okay? I can't be nowhere else. I have no daughter. My son not here now. With his own mad hand he erase himself, maybe just for now." She looked toward the closed drapes and got lost in the past for the moment and whispered, "I know how it is, no husband. You should not suffer because yours gone, too. I here with you. You not alone." She pulled Jenny's hand to try to get her to stand. "Now, come. We get gripe water for baby's stomach. Magic medicine."

Jenny smiled weakly and rubbed her eyes. "What is that?"

"Is for what you call...colic. Baby drinks small drops, calms down gas. We get at Indian store. We use on our babies, safe. Now, up," Esha commanded. "You eat breakfast and feed your baby." She pulled her and this time, Jenny stood, and took the baby.

"Okay, yeah. I feel dizzy. I am a little hungry."

"What you like to eat, then? No more spicy food for you. Baby don't like, I think. You want some that steel cut oatmeal thing in the cupboard?"

Jenny shook her head and said, "No, that is Roshan's. I don't like that. I'm actually craving some grits. And maybe a scrambled egg."

Esha cringed and ushered Jenny and the baby out the door and down the stairs. "Oh, you asking a lot from this vegetarian. But I do my best."

In the kitchen, Jenny held the baby while Esha dripped some gripe water into her mouth, and they fumbled around the stove with eggs and a skillet. Jenny watched her for a few seconds and without words took the egg carton from her and handed her the baby. "It's okay. I'll do it. I know this grosses you out."

"Okay, but I watch. I need to know how for next time. I get used to it. Maybe my granddaughter will eat these things someday. Who knows?"

Jenny said, "We'll see. Or maybe we'll go vegetarian. I've been reading some bad things on Facebook about meat processing scandals lately. Maybe you all have been right all along."

Esha bounced the baby and watched as Jenny milled around the kitchen, disheveled but with new energy, cracking eggs into a bowl, whipping them with a fork, adding just a dash of milk and salt and pepper. To Esha's dismay, the runny eggs were naked, would have no flavor. If Esha ate this, she would have to add some chopped green chili to it, but of course, that would never happen.

"Is that all you put in eggs? No spice?"

"Nope. I want to be able to taste the eggs."

Esha kept quiet.

Soon the eggs were solid in the skillet and Jenny said, "Oh yeah. The grits." She rummaged through the pantry looking.

Esha felt dumb asking, but she had to. The question had burned inside her ever since she moved to Georgia so long ago but never knew anyone who ate them.

"By the way, what grit?"

Jenny turned and laughed out loud. "We have a lot to teach each other."

"Whatever it is, I hope you make more *tikku* than your bland eggs."

"*Tikku* means hot, right?"

Esha nodded.

"We'll see what we can do with grits then. *Tikku* grits might be worth trying."

Chapter 22

Jenny

The traffic on the way home was light for a Friday. She had been driving Roshan's car lately just to feel close to him. He had been gone for six weeks now, and her anger had waned to more of a dull ache of missing him. Not the him that he was when he left, but the him she knew before all of this happened, the him she knew always hovered just under the surface, popping up enough times to keep her hooked into his love.

The tires glided along the interstate, and she turned on the stereo. Roshan had forgotten one CD in the deck, having uploaded his music onto his iPhone since buying the car, and Jenny discovered it by accident while playing with buttons the first time she took it out. It was the soundtrack to the Bollywood movie *Salaam Namaste.* She didn't even know he listened to Indian music anymore, so she had googled it out of curiosity, finding out it was a movie soundtrack from 2002 released when the two of them met their first year in dental school. She listened to it now sometimes on her way home because, though it was something he never shared with her, just hearing the same songs he loved from that time brought her back to the new love feeling they had for each other back then and gave her a shred of hope that they might find that again.

Her phone rang as she was changing lanes. It must be Bryan, she thought. He and Craig were bringing Sophie, their new daughter over tonight to meet Jenny for the very first time. Jenny couldn't be more excited. Feeling good now, back at work, coming home to a happy baby taken care of by Esha everyday...and now getting to see her best friend for the first time since Roshan left.

The name on the screen made her catch her breath. It was Roshan.

She had spoken to him often since he went to rehab, though most times conversations were short and tear-filled on both sides. She had made three trips there for some family therapy sessions.

"Hello," she said welcomingly, trying not to expose her surprise. What was she supposed to say to him these days?

"Hey, honey. How are you?"

"Really good, Roshan. How are you?" His voice, deep and stronger now, sent goosebumps up her back as she remembered what it was like to hear him whisper into her ear. But, she stopped the thought and focused on the road.

"I'm doing really well too. Really well."

She had to ask the million dollar question now. No more beating around the bush with him or anyone else these days. Life was too short.

"Why are you calling me now? I thought you weren't allowed to until the weekend."

"I'm coming home."

Jenny's foot nearly slammed the brake hard as she slowed down for a turn off her exit, and she had to steer tight to keep from skidding.

"When? Honey, that's great." Her steady voice didn't match the excited words.

"Next week. Jay is flying here to get me. I'm done with everything I needed to do here. Plus, I have to get home and handle some things with the attorneys. They've waited long enough."

"Wow. I'll be honest, I don't know if this is good or bad. Do you think you're ready?"

She didn't want to hurt him, but honesty was her policy now. No matter what. She turned onto her neighborhood's street and pulled over to a park to talk privately before she got home and had prepare for Bryan's visit.

"Yeah. I think I'm ready. I'm stronger. And I have to figure out what I'm doing from here. My career is shot. And I have a family I have to fix."

You cannot fix us. We are fixing ourselves.

"How's my baby?"

She could hear him smile and smiled herself. "She's great. So big. She smiles all the time now."

"I can't wait to see her. I miss you two very much."

There was an uncomfortable pause, and he continued.

"It's okay. You don't have to say it back. I know."

I don't know if I miss you, so how could you know?

The call waiting beeped. She was glad to see that it was Bryan.

"Roshan, I have to go now. I'm glad you're coming home. Really. I've got a call now. But keep me posted, okay?"

"Okay." His voice sounded hurt. "Bye."

She ended the call and had missed Bryan's call too. Before she could take a deep breath, two texts pinged simultaneously.

Bryan
Where ARE you? We're here with your MIL!

Roshan
Would you please send me some pics of Abigail?
Any with the two of you together?

Oh no! The picture would have to wait. She put the car in gear and sped to her house, pulling up in her driveway next to Bryan and Craig's Range Rover. She pulled her things from the car and glanced inside their SUV as she passed. There was a car seat inside! She was so excited, she ran in through the open garage.

When she got inside, her arms flew open when she found Bryan standing at the kitchen counter next to Craig, grabbing them both in a hug. "You guys are a sight for sore eyes!"

"Missed you, Jen," Bryan said, his hard arms squeezing her like a vice.

Craig's more gentle hands rubbed her shoulder softly. "Good to see you."

They pulled apart, and Jenny looked at Bryan, then Craig, then Bryan. "Okay. Stop looking at me and tell me…where she is!" Bryan pointed over his shoulder toward the living room off the kitchen and raised his eyebrows. Jenny's eyes followed the trajectory, and there in the living room was Esha on the floor, sitting Indian style holding Abigail on one side with a short-haired Asian toddler dressed in purple leggings and a frilly top on the other.

"Sophie?" Jenny asked the guys.

"Um, dumb question, Jen. Duh." Bryan laughed at her.

"She's so beautiful, guys." Jenny excitedly started for the living room, but Craig stopped her.

"Wait. She's so shy. It's only been a week since we brought her home. This is the first person she has gone to. Give them a minute."

Jenny consented begrudgingly and watched Esha talk to Sophie and tell her all about the baby. Sophie was pointing to Abigail's ears, and Esha pointed to Abigail's ear and then Sophie's ear, and saying the word "ear" in English and then Gujarati. Sophie said nothing, but seemed to be concentrating hard. They did the same with eyes and nose, before Sophie got bored and ran in to her daddies, where Bryan scooped her up and bounced her around.

Jenny couldn't help herself and gave Sophie a kiss and said, "Welcome to the family, little girl! Nice to meet you."

Sophie buried her little face in Bryan's shoulder. "This is tough for her right now."

Craig patted her on the back and said, "She doesn't understand any English, and there are so many new people around."

Before Esha reached the kitchen with Abigail, Jenny retorted, "Hey, I know how that feels." To Esha, she said louder, "Sorry I left you to entertain my company. I got stuck in traffic." She lied.

"No problem." Esha waved her hand in front of her face. "I was just introducing our girl to small Sophie."

Esha handed Abigail to Jenny, and all of Jenny's daily stresses melted away when she kissed her daughter's cheek and got a smile back from her. She was swaddled in a faded marigold-yellow satin-trimmed blanket she didn't recognize. The frayed edges were folded and tucked like a cocoon around her daughter.

Where did that come from?

Esha walked around the island and started pulling snacks from the refrigerator. Bryan and Craig both protested her getting food out for them. "We're not staying. We came to take Jenny out to dinner. Would you like to join us?" Craig offered as he came around the island to see what she was getting out.

Esha gave him a confused look and kept her distance a bit. This was only the second time she had met Bryan and Craig, and Jenny was pretty sure this must be the first time she had been in this close quarters with homosexuals. Jenny couldn't think of any gay Indian guys Roshan had introduced her to before, though he had mentioned once that he had a lesbian aunt or distant cousin somewhere, but no one ever talked about her.

Esha continued to get out snacks. She always had some on hand. She opened a container of samosas and got out small plates and a bottle of ketchup to dip them in. Craig and Jenny exchanged looks when he stepped a little closer to her to reach for a samosa and Esha stepped back again, using the excuse she needed to get something else out of a cabinet. Bryan mouthed to him, "Leave her alone," and Craig winked at Jenny and stepped back a little.

"Miss Esha, really. We're not staying," Craig said. "Thank you so much, but we have reservations."

Esha, who never took no for an answer on her food, insisted, "Come, take one. Jenny, you must be hungry too from work. Take one. I make hot, hot."

Bryan politely shook his head, but Craig took a bite of one cold. "Mmmm. This is delicious, Miss Esha."

Esha beamed. "See, your....friend likes it. Try."

After a few more futile protests, Jenny picked one up and handed it to him. "Eat it." They all watched as Bryan bit half of the samosa and chewed as if he had straw in his mouth.

"Mmmm. You're right. It is delicious. A bit hot, though" He cleared his throat as he chewed and got down the chunk and added, "Thank you Esha. I'm more of a meat and olive oil and vegetable kind of guy, but Craig here, my friend. He's a good cook and loves making fusion recipes. Don't you?"

Craig jumped on the chance and put his arm around Esha, who didn't pull away this time. Jenny knew how much she loved to talk about her cooking. "Can you tell me what is in this? I'm getting a hint of ginger and something else I can't pinpoint. Is it—?"

"Cardamom. My specialty." Esha started on a roll and ordered Craig, "You like to see my jar? I only get the best quality spices from the Indian grocer."

Jenny looked at Craig with gratitude.

While Esha took Craig to the space she held in Jenny's pantry to show him her spice jars, Bryan and Jenny took their kids to the living room to talk.

"She's big for eighteen months old," Jenny remarked as Sophie sat on Bryan's lap playing with a ball from the diaper bag.

"Yeah. We waited so long to get over there, we were so glad to see she was being taken care of so well. She's great, isn't she?"

"Yeah. I'm really happy for you guys."

Bryan looked around the house and then at Jenny's face. "You look good. Better than I expected. I'm happy you're holding up through all of this."

Pots started clanging, and the refrigerator opened. Craig called from the kitchen, "Honey, um, Bryan. Miss Esha is going to fix us some *chai*, you want some?"

"Looks like we may not make our reservation, huh?" he whispered to Jenny.

"No, probably not," Jenny said.

Bryan called back. "Sure, that sounds really good. Let's try it."

Abigail started to root toward Jenny's chest and work up a hungry cry as they talked and waited for their tea. She needed to nurse her, especially after being away from her all day with only a little time in between patients to pump her milk, so she threw a blanket over her shoulder and lifted her shirt discreetly. She leaned back and relaxed her head, looking at Bryan.

"Have you heard from Wanda?"

Her throat closed up at the question. "She texted me for a couple weeks after Abigail was born, but I blocked her number. Not a peep since then."

Bryan carefully said, "The only reason I bring it up is that my mom said she's been calling her and asking her about me trying to get information on you. Mom says she sounds clean though."

"Tell your mom not to give her my address." Jenny gritted her teeth. That woman was one problem she wanted no part of right now. Or ever. "And on to more cheerful news. Roshan is coming home next week."

"You ready?"

"Hell no," her southern accent reared its head momentarily, "but I will be."

"You going to take him back? Like 'back, back?'"

She laughed. "You mean, do I 'like, like' him enough to take him 'back, back' or just 'back?'"

"You sarcastic woman, you. Yes. 'Back, back?'"

Jenny thought for a minute before she answered. "I don't know. I 'like, like' him. I do. But he needs to figure himself out completely before I let him too far into Abigail's life. Esha and I have a good thing here with her, and I don't want to mess that up. Ya know?"

"Yeah. I know. I see now that kids aren't an experiment. We can't use trial and error with them. You have to be sure when it comes to your kid."

Sophie started crawling off of Bryan's lap and playing with Abigail's squirming feet that were lying across Jenny's lap. Abigail, with her head under the blanket, pulled her feet away each time Sophie grabbed one, and Sophie started cackling. Too distracted to nurse, the baby pulled away from Jenny, so she covered herself up again and held the baby upright with one hand on her belly to burp her, facing Sophie. When she saw Sophie, her face exploded in a smile.

"Craig and I have really had to let go of a lot of our past to get to this point. He wasn't exactly the best dad to his older kids. But, we've even been to counseling. We have to stand up for ourselves when we need to and forgive when we need to."

Jenny watched the girls and asked Bryan with a full heart, "They are going to be good friends, aren't they?"

"Oh, yes. We need to make sure to keep them together. Family is all we have, right?"

Jenny nodded and tears threatened her eyes. "We're not related, you dufus." She had to keep the tears at bay.

"Shut up, Mrs. Obvious. But," he reverted to his small town accent, "If we ain't family, I cain't figure out who is. Family ain't all about them genes they done taught us about in the schoolhouse out yonder."

"You're an idiot, Bryan. And I love you." She put her head on his shoulder again and sat there for a minute until Sophie got jealous.

Esha looked conflicted as she and Craig came in with cups of *chai* for everyone. Recovering, she sat and they all chatted.

Jenny told Esha and Craig stories—only the good ones—from their days growing up together as they forgot all about dinner and ended up letting Esha cook for them after all. With full bellies, they managed to take pictures of each other with the babies before saying their goodbyes.

"Your Bryan is good boy. And his friend Craig. He's good too," Esha stated as she put away dishes.

Jenny couldn't stand it. "Esha, Craig is not his friend. They're married."

Esha kept drying dishes with the towel she had on her shoulder. Jenny waited for a reaction, a few words, anything. But nothing came. Jenny decided not to push the issue. "I'm going to try to put the baby to bed. I'll be back down as soon as she is asleep."

"Okay." Esha stopped the dishes and added, "I know that about your friends, okay? They good boys. Just let me think they friends. Okay for now?"

"Of course." There was a limit to how much change a person could take at a time, and Esha must be at her limit right now. Jenny understood completely. She was at that point too.

After Jenny took the baby upstairs, gave her a bath, and put her to bed, she selected a picture of Abigail smiling and another of her with Esha, and then she sent them to Roshan. She scrolled through the remaining pictures, feeling warmth at the camaraderie amongst the varied group over dinner, and picked one of her with the baby, Bryan by her side, and sent it too.

A little while later after the house was picked up and the kitchen was clean, Jenny decided now was the time to talk to Esha about Roshan coming home. Esha still had a towel over her shoulder and answered a text with a smile on her face when Jenny turned around from the refrigerator. She was dying to ask Esha about Rich but didn't dare to. Esha looked up, unaware she was being watched, embarrassment burning on her face. Jenny couldn't stand it.

"Will you ever see him again?"

Esha put her phone in her slacks pocket and shook her head and waved her hand in front of her face.

"Who you talking about?"

She turned her back on Jenny, and Jenny knew it was to hide her face. "Rich."

"I'm a widow. In ours, we stay that way."

Jenny knew she was treading on untested ice with Esha and might push her too far, but she continued to try and understand her way of thinking. "You don't have to marry him."

Esha turned around while smiling and bobbing her head Indian style.

"Can't you get on a plane and just go for a visit? No harm in that. You're not the one that's dead."

"No means no. Okay. I can't do that. End of discussion, okay?" The phone chirped with a text again, and she pulled it out, looked at the screen, looked up at Jenny, and silenced it, putting it away again.

"Okay, I'll back off." Jenny hugged Esha and added nervously, "but before we go to bed, I have news." Esha waited in silence, wide-eyed. "Roshan is coming home on the weekend. For good."

"I know," Esha said softly. "Roshan called me today."

Leaning against the counter, tired from the long day, Jenny added very carefully, "I don't know if I will take him back. I can't let him hurt my baby again. Or hurt me again."

Growing angry, Esha looked her straight in the eye. "You married him. In ours that means for life. You know what he gave up because he couldn't live without you? And now you going to leave him?"

Jenny was shocked.

Was Esha faking her support all this time?

"Esha, he hurt our baby. I don't know if I can trust he will stay sober. Look at my mom. She couldn't. I'm not going to jeopardize my child." Her fingers gripped the edge of the counter as Esha moved toward her, bracing herself for Esha's inevitable rejection. She should have known it would come. To her surprise, Esha put one hand on Jenny's arm and ran her other hand down Jenny's cheek, the way she had seen her do with Roshan.

"You not alone now, remember? You part of this family now. You and Roshan had a path together, I had no say, you had no say, only God has a say." She looked her hard in the eyes, and Jenny didn't know how to process what came next. "I will not let anything happen to our baby.

Okay? We family. I stand by you, Roshan, Abigail. He comes back to us. We take him, and we take care of him too. Come. We sit down. I have things to tell you."

Jenny's eyes blurred with tears. Confusion overwhelmed her. She had no idea how she felt about Roshan. She loved him. But could she keep him? But this woman wants her to stay part of her family regardless. That was a foreign concept to her. And it felt strangely good. They sat on the couch, and Jenny turned the volume up on the baby monitor.

"You know why me and Roshan came to America?"

"He never talked about it much. He told me his dad died and your brother came to take care of you." She had heard the story years ago and remembered the part about his uncle killing his dad, but felt it best to pretend she didn't know.

"I don't beat around bush. You need to know. His daddy was a good man when we got married. We had arranged marriage, of course, but when I saw him at the wedding, oh, he was handsome, and he good to me. At first. Then he start drinking, like Roshan. He beat me. He beat me when I'm pregnant. Roshan was very young. The baby girl, she died."

Jenny's head swam as pieces of the puzzle fit together, and she imagined now what demons must swarm around in her husband's mind every day.

"I'm so sorry, Esha."

"Okay, no sorries. I tell you so you understand family. My parents and brothers all live far away from us, and I beg for help. My brother come to help me divorce."

Esha started wringing her hands, and it looked to Jenny that she was having a hard time forming the words. She wanted to tell her not to go on, but had to know the whole story from her.

"My husband will not let us leave. He fight my brother, and my brother hit him very hard to stop him. Killed him. In front of my Roshan."

Jenny wanted to grab Esha's hands, but she was far away as she talked, as if confessing to God and not to Jenny.

"He try to hold his daddy, but we take Roshan away on next flight here. We never look back."

Roshan feels guilty.

Esha's confession continued to spill out. "I can't protect my daughter those days. No more daughter. All I have is baby blanket. But my family take care of us, no matter what people say. I try hard to make Roshan better, give him chance. And he will be better. I know he will. He has us, you, me, and the rest of family, together." Esha choked and stared at Jenny. "I have daughter now. And granddaughter. Second chance….maybe you have second chance too."

Jenny felt naked. All of the layers she had built up over her life, like callouses, were stripped away, and the vulnerability she had inside was out there. The woman who had called her trash in the beginning was her mother now.

"Esha, I have no idea what to say." She held her face in her hands and looked at Esha.

Esha replied, "Nothing to say." Esha stood, straightened her clothes, and stretched. "Time for bed now. Done."

"Done," Jenny replied.

We have a deal.

Without speaking, they turned in for the night.

Jenny had just settled onto her pillowcase in hopes of at least four hours of sleep before Abigail woke up again when there was a knock at the front door. It frightened her because it was past midnight, and though the house was in an upscale area, the neighborhood was also often the target of crime. With no man in the house, she decided to grab a knife and her phone, 911 already up on the screen, and go downstairs to the door. She heard Esha's footsteps upstairs in the guest room as she looked through the peephole.

Wanda was on her stoop.

Do I open this door or go back upstairs?

Through the peephole, a bulging image of Wanda's wet-look curly hair loomed up, glowing by the always lit porch light. Her back was to the door, and her head bobbed up and down, side to side, as if she were frantically shifting from foot to foot.

"Who's there?" Esha called from the top of the steps in her nightgown and bare feet.

Jenny walked back up the stairs and quietly said, "I think some kid's ringing doorbells. We can go back to bed."

Esha's eyes narrowed in disbelief. "You sure?"

"I'm sure," Jenny said, holding up the knife and her phone. "Besides, I'm prepared if there're any problems." Her voice came out silly rather than movie action hero confident like she had intended.

Please go away, Wanda. Go. Away.

Esha nodded and turned back to her room. The bell rang. They looked at each other confused, and Esha took Jenny's phone. "You saw no one out there? I call police. We two women with a baby. This is not okay."

Jenny took the phone back. "Don't call." She led her by the arm downstairs toward the foyer. "It's Wanda."

Esha's eyes grew wide, and she immediately shook her head. "No. No. Can't be. Oh, God."

"Should I answer it?" Jenny asked like a child.

The bell rang again, three times in a row. Abigail started to cry upstairs.

Esha widened her stance and put her hands on her hips. "No," she commanded, head shaking almost violently. "I answer. You get baby. I take care of this."

Jenny was so surprised by Esha's strong reaction that she did as she was told. With the baby in her arms, she came downstairs to find Wanda and Esha sitting on the stoop together with the front door half open. Moths flew inside as she got near the door.

"You must go. I give you money and then you go. You hear me?" Esha's voice commanded, the same voice she used when they first met in Roshan's apartment and months ago before the *garba* when Roshan had left the room. Jenny was glad it was not directed at her anymore.

"I ain't goin' anywhere 'til I see my baby girl. I'm clean, and I have a right now to see my daughter and my granddaughter." Wanda looked when Jenny rustled behind her and jumped up. "Oh, baby doll. You're here!" She moved in to hug Jenny, and Jenny put up her hand. "Okay, I understand. I have a lot to make up for. I get it. No hugs."

"Wanda, what do you need?" Jenny demanded, surprising herself with no anger, just pity.

"I need to see you. I'm catching a bus out of town tonight and wanted to say bye. And your mother-in-law here," her words came out as if she were spitting out slugs, "thinks she has the authority to keep me from you."

Jenny didn't ask where she was going or why. She motioned for Esha to come inside the house and told Wanda, "No, Wanda, she doesn't have authority. But, she is my family, and it's understood that family looks out for each other." She made sure her face stayed still as stone.

Wanda got red in the face and puffed her cheeks. "Well, I'm your family. She ain't. I'm your mother. I got a right….oh look at the baby!" She moved toward Abigail with her hand extended, but Jenny pulled back.

"You gave up your rights a long time ago, Wanda. Family is more than sharing blood. I hope you learn that someday."

She started to shut the door, but Wanda stuck her foot in the way. "I tried so hard, baby girl. You gotta know that."

"I know, Wanda. And if you need money, I'll help you now. I wish you well, but you can't come around here anymore."

Wanda, irate, pushed and tried to step inside. "Ooh, look at your house. So pretty. I see why you don't want some redneck momma you ashamed of in this neighborhood. I get it. Come on, just let me come in for a minute. Please…"

Wanda shoved even more, and Jenny twisted to shield the baby, stumbling backward, fear filling her. She felt Esha's firm hand stabilize her, saw her determined eyes as she heaved the door back hard, knocking Wanda off balance, and in one swift motion, she slammed it shut and bolted it.

With her cellphone in her hand, ready to dial 911, Esha stated, "One minute. She leaves, okay. We go sleep. She stays, we call."

Jenny bounced the baby up and down to calm her, but she howled to the point her cries became silent shudders. Not again, she thought. She asked Esha, "Is she still out there?"

Peering through the peephole, she nodded her head. "She sitting there lighting a cigarette."

"Call now," Jenny demanded.

Esha tapped the red dial square on her phone screen and told the operator they needed police to take away a threatening person at their door.

When Wanda was inside the police car and the officer was finished asking them questions, she prayed silently this would be the last time she had to deal with her mother but caught herself. This ordeal was not caused by her mother. That woman was Wanda and only Wanda.

The next five days moved fast. Jenny's heart was in her throat as she showered and got ready for the big day. After deciding on not-too-eager skinny jeans and a loose fitting lavender cashmere cardigan that Roshan had bought her last winter, multiple outfits lay strewn across her bed. Some pieces needed to be placed on hangers in the closet while others needed to be folded and put away, but her hands shook too much to do it right then. She kept looking in the mirror and smoothing the sweater with her damp palms, arranging it as straight and flattering as she could, but she gave up forcing it into place because the fabric's ripples always draped back to where they wanted to hang. She hadn't been this nervous in, well, she didn't know if she'd ever been this nervous.

Roshan comes home today.

Abigail slept in her car seat in the back of the car, and Jenny drove carefully to Esha's house. It was strange driving to Esha's house now because Esha had been staying with her for so long, she felt like she lived with her. Esha told her the day after Wanda's visit that she would go back home, that Jenny and Roshan needed space to decide how to be a family again without her interference. She felt surrounded by hope even though her belly gurgled with nerves as she rounded the corner to Esha's house.

She had pondered about how she wanted things to go on this day. She decided she wanted to be settled inside before they got there, but the driveway was already full of cars and she was nervous about the expectant eyes that would meet her when she walked in the door. Over the past couple months, with Roshan gone, Monisha, Hema, and Ashmi had reached out to her so much, she knew it would feel like home, but she felt self-conscious about meeting Roshan with all eyes on them. There seemed to be no other way though. Not ready to take him back into their home completely and not prepared to take on full responsibility for him yet, Jenny felt the need for family support when the moment came.

The words tumbled around inside her with a soft unfamiliarity.

I have family support.

It was a cold January. Colder than usual for Georgia. She could see her breath when she got out of the car and, tying her black leather coat tightly around her, quickly covered Abigail in her infant seat with the frayed marigold blanket. And it was so hard for her to believe that so much time had already passed since that night at Esha's in November. Christmas and New Year's over with little celebration. Her heart was torn; she longed to see him hold his daughter, but cringed at the thought as well.

Hema greeted her at the door and helped her with the diaper bag.

"Jenny," she hugged her tightly. "Come in. Get the baby warm."

She ushered Jenny inside the foyer and cooed over Abigail as Jenny slipped off her shoes at the door where the other guests had lined theirs up already. She took the infant carrier into the kitchen where the women—Esha, Monisha, and Ashmi—all dressed in saris for the occasion, scurried around between sink, stove, oven, and table, dishes in hand, ladling curries, and frying up samosas for appetizers. When they heard Hema's cooing, they all turned to Jenny and the baby and rushed toward them.

Swallowed in hugs, Jenny tried to answer everyone's greetings and questions.

Esha, swiping the purple and gold embroidered sari pleats on her shoulder to the side, took the carrier from Jenny after hugging her, and lifted the little girl up for all to admire. Abigail lay nestled in her carrier, her bow-topped cap had crept over her eyes and her chin lay tucked into her chest, surrounded by the fluffy faux fur collar of her blue leopard print sweater. The ladies hovered between Jenny and Esha, patting Jenny on the arm and passing Abigail around.

Feeling smashed by a wall of emotion, Jenny fought back tears in the midst of the crowd. She'd not expected this. Esha held Abigail proudly and cooed at her, and the women gazed at the baby as Abigail cooed back. Jenny shed her coat and asked Esha where to put it. Esha handed the baby to Monisha and took her to her first floor master bedroom to lay the coat there. They walked through the TV room, full of husbands, and all greeted her with cheery hellos.

"You ready?" Esha asked, shutting the door to the bedroom.

Yes?

"After the therapy sessions we've all been to, as ready as I'll ever be." Jenny shrugged. "You?"

"Same. The past…done. We move on." Esha rubbed her hands together like she was brushing off dirt, and then pulled Jenny into a hug. The tension in Jenny's chest loosened for just a moment. Esha pulled back and cupped her cheek in her hand, "Remember, we here for him too. What those doctors say to do, right? We help our Roshan go forward."

Jenny wondered how this woman could have lived the kind of life she had been dealt and still be so positive. And she wondered what she had herself done in a previous life that had brought her to this point.

Previous life? Wow. These people are really rubbing off on me.

Back in the kitchen after the excitement died down and Abigail was awake enough to be hungry again, Jenny excused herself back to Esha's bedroom to nurse her. She settled in with the baby on the bed and looked at the minutes ticking by on the bedside alarm clock. It amused her that Esha would still have an old fashioned clock in a carved wood case. Must be like something she'd had in India, she figured, it was so old. But, she was also now a texting wiz on her iPhone. Old and new meet.

Careful to not jostle Abigail while she nursed contentedly in the crook of her arm, Jenny fished her iPhone out of her purse and pulled up Facebook to distract her pulsating nerves for a while. There at the beginning of her newsfeed was a picture posted by BryanCraig, the account the couple shared, for Throwback Thursday, and she was tagged in it. In it, he stood behind her with his arms wrapped around her waist. She wore a shiny teal prom dress, and he had on a black tuxedo over a satin teal vest and bow tie, his hair gelled in a suave messy wave. She remembered him squeezing her with his arms and her eyes darted up with a grin right as the picture was snapped.

Their faces were slim, smooth, and, because they were together, glowing with happiness. The caption read, "Throwback Thursday treat for my girl, Jenny Jenkins. Today, remember I was then and always will be behind you...Bryan." Heart filling with love, she gave the post a thumbs up and put the phone down quickly.

Her breath shortened when she heard the front door open and the male voices that followed. She was close enough to hear almost everything going on. Heavy footsteps thudded into the foyer, and she heard the muffled deep voices of uncles greeting her husband. There were welcoming voices and then footsteps leading to the kitchen where she heard the women greet him too.

Jenny's heart raced. How would he look today? Different from the gaunt man she'd seen on the few weekends she'd been able to fly out to the facility to visit him? It had been a while since the last time. Her heart leaped, despite her struggle with reservations, at the thought of seeing his amber eyes on her. But she pulled that feeling back inside, looking at the baby asleep in her arms now with one hand open relaxed against her cheek. She squeezed her gently, her protective instincts keeping her close. Jenny was strong. She could take care of her daughter. No matter what. The footsteps came toward the bedroom door. Her heart became a lump in her throat. She couldn't swallow.

The door to the room opened slightly, and Esha poked her head inside. "He's here. Okay to come in?"

Jenny swallowed and nodded. Esha backed up to let Roshan pass her into the room, and started to leave, but before she even looked at him, Jenny said, "No. Esha, stay."

Esha nodded and slid behind Roshan's tall figure as he entered the room slowly. He hovered by the door, looking at Jenny, then at the baby, and then at his feet. His black hair was longer than before, and waves drooped down over his forehead, touching his eyebrows, just like he wore it when they met. In a navy V-neck sweater and jeans, his face was a healthy color. Her stomach fluttered, despite her anger, at the sight of his healthy weight and the shape of arm muscles beneath his sweater.

"Hi," he softly uttered without looking at her or Esha.

No one moved or said anything else for a few moments.

Jenny wanted to jump up into his arms but wasn't sure if she wanted to kiss him or slap him. Both would feel good. The scent of his cologne hovered lightly in the air between them, so she tried not to breathe. She had to be rational. She had to be strong.

"May I come over?" he asked tentatively, venturing to look at her face. He swallowed hard, and she felt his trepidation hang solidly in the air.

She nodded and allowed herself to look him in the eye but only for a split second.

While he stepped over to the bed and dropped a satchel gently to the floor, Abigail whined and squirmed, eyes opening after her short nap. Esha, stepping in protectively, said, "I'll change her." She picked up the baby as Roshan sat down on the side of the bed, and Esha ran her hand over Roshan's cheek. He looked at her, and with a small voice said, "See you in a few minutes, Mummy."

Moments later, the bathroom door shut, and her soft voice changed octaves as she and Abigail exchanged baby conversation in happy sounds. Roshan gave a crooked smile and bit his lip before turning to Jenny.

Her legs lay outstretched, and she pulled them up to her chest away from him, scared by his proximity to her. Her eyes darted to his and away fast, and she sat up, turned, and dangled her legs to the floor, so they both sat side by side, looking straight ahead.

"You look good, Roshan." She couldn't resist turning to see him, and he sat straight, already staring at her face. The whites of his eyes, those almond-shaped eyes she had gazed into so many times when they fell in love, those eyes that had turned bloodshot and dull so long ago, were clear and white, and the circles underneath gone.

"Thanks. I feel really good." He gave her an embarrassed grin and looked at his mom's dresser. There was a picture frame face down, and he squinted at it quizzically for a few moments, then turned his head toward her.

They sat in silence for a few moments. She felt mute, so many things running through her mind, but none coherent enough to speak out loud. He reached his hand out to touch her fingers. She stared at his hand, not moving, but allowed his finger tips to touch hers, then slid them away from his. Hints of blue and yellow streaked across the tops of his fingers.

"I'm happy to see you, Jenny. I hope you can feel that way about me someday soon."

Her mouth went dry. He was back in her world now, not a controlled environment that he could be safe in. She wanted to yell at him, she wanted to squeeze his hand, and she wanted to tell him she was glad to be next to him, smelling his warmth next to her. But she did none of those things. Finally, as he was pulling his hand away, she lifted his fingers tentatively, turning them over in examination, seeing smears of color in the folds of his knuckles, and blurted, "Have you been painting?"

He nodded and held up the other hand for her to see proudly. "Yeah. A lot. Brought some of my work to show you."

The sound of dishes clattering vibrated through the walls, and the warm fragrance of something with cheese and green onions mingling with cinnamon and cumin wafted through the cracked door. His stomach growled.

"Hungry?"

"Starving. Missed my mum's cooking."

She blinked at him, and her mouth curled up in a smile. "Wow, that's surprising to hear. She'll be happy." She looked at their feet next to each other all in a perfect row, then glancing back to his face, she said, "I'm really glad to see you looking so good. That makes me happy."

"Thanks." He paused and said, "Of course, you look beautiful. As always. You have more life in your eyes now too. You look happy."

"I am." Without thinking, she reached over to his hand and pulled it to her, gripping it tightly between both of hers. She looked at his face, and his eyes met hers then fell back to the floor again. She squeezed tighter, before asking, "Roshan, do you have a plan for your life now? I have buckled down, moved forward with my work since you've been gone, plan to expand to another location now…been offered a part time faculty position at the dental school too." She lifted his chin and turned his face to her. "I love my job, and your mom and I are making sure our daughter has everything she'll ever need. What will make you love your life?"

"I'm not a dentist. I'm happy when I create. I need to find a way to make that work for me." He chuckled nervously. "I was going to wait until later, but I can show you now." He pulled a letter from his pocket and put it in her hand. "I got admitted to an art education program. At Emory. Nice and close to home." He swallowed. "…if our home is still my home, that is."

Bittersweet breath flowed out of her, and she glanced at the words "congratulations" in the subject line.

"You're going to be an art teacher? She was stumped, but the confidence in his eyes reassured her, and it felt right for him.

"Yeah. I've gone over and over this with my therapist and realized I want to, I need to reach kids early and give them the gift of following their dreams." He looked like he was holding his breath.

"Will that make you whole?"

It was his turn to sigh with relief. "No. I won't be whole until I make things whole with you, Mum, and Abigail. But," he bit his lip again, "I think it'll be the beginning for me."

Esha opened the door and came out of the bathroom with Abigail propped up on the pleated *ootni* pinned to her shoulder. The baby's black fuzz-covered head perched up, her sparkling amber eyes grew wide, taking in the room around her. She sucked on her fingers and smiled when she saw Jenny.

Roshan's face lifted, and he looked as if he'd seen a movie star.

"Wow. She's so big. I cannot believe it."

"Two months makes a huge difference in the life of an infant. She's a whole different person now." Jenny smiled and cooed at Abigail as she bobbed her head around on Esha's shoulder.

"*Dikra*, she like you as a baby. Strong. Never sleeps. But happy. So happy," Esha said joyfully, but went on softly, "And her hair…is like your sister." She paused for a moment then added, "More hair than you had. I shave your head twice when baby to grow thick." She bounced around for a moment, pacifying Abigail, then started to walk to the door. "I give you two more time for talk."

Looking fearfully between Esha and Jenny, Roshan asked, "Did she try to shave Abigail's head while I was gone?"

"Oh, no," Jenny laughed and looked at Esha, who smirked slyly. "This is actually the first I heard of it!" To Esha she added, "I wondered why he was so bald in baby pictures."

Esha shrugged. "It's what we do."

Abigail grunted, trying to move her head up as she lay in Esha's arms. Esha said, "She thinks she ready to sit up. Strong girl."

Jenny added, "I think she'll be a handful later." It felt odd telling this to her husband, who was nothing more than a stranger to her baby, but she wanted him to share in this with her, wanted him to know.

"Please," Roshan quickly asked, a tinge of desperation in his voice, "can I hold her?"

Esha paused mid-step at the door and didn't turn.

Jenny looked at Roshan's face, and the fear in his eyes stabbed her in the stomach. She knew he was afraid he'd lost his daughter forever. He was afraid he'd never hold her again.

Esha turned around slowly and looked at Jenny questioningly. Jenny tilted her head and scooted away from Roshan, making room for Esha to sit between them. Esha handed the baby to Jenny, then smoothed her sari's pleats as she sat. Jenny lay Abigail across both her and Esha's legs, so that the baby's head rested on her mother and her bottom rested on her *Ba*, with her little chubby legs squirming in the air, mussing the folds of the sari again. Roshan got the hint and took her tiny fingers in his and let her fingers grasp his. Abigail cooed and gurgled a toothless smile at her father. He leaned over and brushed his lips on her cheek and the baby cooed more, turning her face toward him. Esha and Jenny both watched him, smiling, as he hovered momentarily over his wife's and mother's laps and inhaled the tiny girl in front of him. Without a word, he stood up and rifled through the satchel he'd set on the floor, pulling out a small sketch pad and pencil.

"May I?" He gestured with his tools.

Touched, Jenny nodded and Esha moved to give her the baby and stand up.

"No, Mummy. Stay." His hand now lay like a feather on Abigail's head, as if to hold them both down. Esha uttered a nervous "Okay, then" and stayed put, primping her bangs with a quick brush and straightening the blanket that surrounded the baby. Roshan tickled the baby's toes and was rewarded with a huge grin. Jenny couldn't hide her joy at the sight and blushed as she smiled herself.

Within a magical few seconds, the outline of three faces bloomed black and gray out of the white void. Roshan's face took on a glow like Jenny had not seen before, and the faster his hand moved, the more he began to talk.

"So, I am going to an AA meeting tonight. I have already spoken to a new sponsor here. His name is Amir, American Pakistani guy, musician." Roshan paused, brushed Abigail's toes again to get another smile, tilted his head, and studied his subjects for a moment.

Jenny was speechless at his chattiness, and listened.

"I met a kid in rehab," Roshan went on. "Don't know if I told you, Jen..." His eyes met hers for a split second, and Jenny shook her head no and waited. His hand stopped abruptly, and his eyes gleamed as he reached into his bag and pulled out of pack of oil pastels. With the giddiness of a child, he nodded as if answering his own internal question, chose a soft pink pastel, and continued his story. "He's 19. Got kicked out of college for drinking and smoking weed on campus, and on his trip of shame home with all his stuff piled in the back of his Dodge Charger—his parents raise horses in Kentucky—he poured himself a few shots of Jaeger and blacked out just as he pulled into his parents' driveway. Took out part of the fence in their pasture...and their dog." He inhaled and shook his head, his hand momentarily pausing the burgeoning of colors. "Kid was almost gone inside when we met. I got him interested in painting and drawing, and he found hope again."

Jenny's throat held back a surge of love at the sight of the hope in Roshan's face.

"Art feeds the soul when a person allows it. As a teacher, I'm going to catch kids with it before their souls wither."

Like his did.

He squeezed Abigail's foot and held it tenderly and all three adults sat in silence until the full flower of faces shown in perfect bloom on the page where just charcoal lines had been.

The curved lines of grandmother, mother, and child's face melted between each other and their skin, though shaded in different flesh colored hues, spread open like pastel petals. Their bodies, though clothed in folds of colliding worlds and generations, sat as one on the bed, with the baby's plump feet protruded from her marigold blanket, and next to them lay the faint outline of a tan hand, tips of its fingers barely touching the pads of her toes.

"It's beautiful, Roshan." Jenny didn't just mean the the portrait he held up humbly.

"Yes," Esha said, then took a quick glance at Jenny before adding, "So nice, son."

The crisp English sounds Esha worked at and the sight of Esha's wet eyes made Jenny's eye threaten to do the same as the urge to grasp Roshan around the neck and bury her face in his warmth overwhelmed her until anxiety slipped a phantom scent of alcohol into her nose as a blur of the faces of her father, Wanda, and Roshan flashed through her mind out of the blue. Her skinned tightened, and she stood up, stepping away from the bed instead.

The baby turned her head toward her mother and leaned toward her, and Jenny scooped her up from Esha's lap.

Roshan, his face showing he was aware why she moved, couldn't hide his emotion. Esha placed her hand on his head and rubbed his hair, and he sat there like a little boy, tears slipping down his cheeks. Jenny rocked her daughter from foot to foot as she handed Esha the letter, inviting her to read it. She glanced over it and gave Roshan a kind look.

"You brought this?" Esha asked him.

"Yes," he said, watching her face. "I'm sorry I've disappointed you. I know you won't approve."

Esha stomped her foot and smacked him softly. "Stop. No more of this. You love art, no?"

He nodded.

"You love your family?"

He nodded again.

"You love yourself now?"

"Yeah, Mummy. I do."

"Then you go be art teacher."

The way Roshan smiled at his mom made Jenny imagine that his father's ghost fled the room for good.

Esha patted him on the head and beckoned toward Jenny, "*Chaal*, then, let's eat. I smell lunch. Lots of food out there, and don't want no leftovers." She stepped out of the room, leaving the door half open.

"Let's go eat," Jenny said, and led the way into the kitchen with Roshan and their baby.

Roshan paused at his mother's's dresser where the picture frame lay. He picked it up with his free hand and looked at the face of his father briefly, then lay it back down the way he had found it. Before turning to follow Jenny out to be with the rest of his family, he lay his drawing on top of the frame.

Monisha handed him a plate in the kitchen. "Hungry for some home cooking? You're favorite foods—spinach paneer, mug lentils, lots of roti and mango achar—a whole buffet for our guest of honor."

Ashmi stepped over and took the plate from him. "Okay, *bhai*. I'll fix for you. Tell me what you want."

Jenny faded back and let Roshan's aunts baby him, catching Esha's eye as she pulled a hot pan from the oven.

Bobbing her head at Jenny, Esha called, "Come, I made Indian-style lasagna, too."

"Oh, good. Did you put in green chilis?"

"Of course. Must be hot, no?"

"Well, if it's not *tikku*—"

"—Not worth eating."

Roshan turned, noticing as Esha and Jenny shared a giggle. His grin was instantaneous.

Esha declared, "Oh no, I forgot to put the garlic bread in the oven."

Jenny touched her upper arm reassuringly. "I got it."

Jenny handed off the baby to Jay, who waited patiently with his daughter at the serving line behind the doting women surrounding Roshan. His outstretched arms expertly enveloped the baby, and he stooped down slightly to let his daughter tickle her cousin's cheek. Jenny entered the cooking zone and did as she was told, listening to the other women chat in Gujarati with one another. She could tell by their manner they weren't talking about her, and they always switched to their best English when speaking to her.

When all the food was finally set out, Jenny asked Jay for the baby again, needing to feel the closeness of her daughter's soft skin for comfort. He reached past Roshan to pass Abigail back to her, and Jenny tried not to look at Roshan in the corner of her eye.

Esha started to make Jenny's plate, but Roshan took it and did it for her. Toting Abigail, Jenny sat at the dining room table where men and women joined together, so unlike the way her first dinners with them had been. Roshan placed their plates on the table, sat next to her, and then touched Abigail's leg as it rested on Jenny's. He gestured for his mum to sit on the empty chair beside him, but Esha bobbed her head and ladled a helping of *mug*, Indian lentils, and saffron rice onto his plate before she moved on to the next person. With his right hand, he scooped up a mash of lentils and rice with his fingers wrapped around a torn piece of *roti* bread, and with his left, he gently tickled his daughter's toes.

"Mmmm," Roshan breathed in. "The taste of home."

Jenny scanned the faces of his family—their family—who watched him. Even Ashmi, who was still standing and serving, stopped in her tracks and touched her mouth with her finger tips and shook her head slightly, obviously fighting back tears. She glanced at Jenny and gave her a crooked smile and then went back to spooning food onto people's plates. Jay squeezed Hema's hand, smiled, and began to ask Roshan about his flight from Phoenix.

Conversation flowed in and out of English and Gujarati, bouncing between family stories of then and now, and Jenny shifted the baby's weight on her lap from her right to her left and back again.

Esha looked at Jenny and outstretched her hands, gently commanding, "Give to Ba. You eat."

As Jenny lifted Abigail across Roshan's shoulder up to Esha, he reached his hand to touch his daughter's tiny closed fist, but Esha pulled the fist to herself and cuddled the baby's hand to her lips nonchalantly, kissing the tiny fist. He bit his lip and looked at the others around the table self-consciously until Esha released the baby's hand, kissed her own fingers, and touched them tenderly to Roshan's cheek before turning to walk the baby around the dining room.

Roshan cleared his throat and set to eating again, subtly dropping his hand as if to adjust the napkin on his lap, but sliding it over to Jenny's left knee under the table. She discreetly patted the top of his hand and then pulled her leg slightly away, tapping his arm to distract from the feelings warming her side.

"Look, Roshan." She motioned to a plate of flaky poori in the center of the table. "I made some of those." Jokingly, she added as she reached out to grab one for him, "Don't let your surprise choke you when you taste it. They're not half bad."

His teeth sank into the puffy pastry and flakes fell onto his plate. "Mmmm, nice. You turn Indian on me while I was gone?"

A murmur of laughter rose around the table.

Jenny looked him in the eyes, lifting the corners of her mouth into a hint of a smile while slightly nodding her head.

No, but I've turned into someone else without you. And I like her.

"Wait until you see what your mum and I do with breakfast."

Acknowledgments

This book is the result of years of hard work that was made possible by so many people in my life.

First and foremost, I thank the love of my life, Dharmesh Parbhoo. From the very moment we met, our connection swept us into a world of mixed cultures that provided the backdrop for this story, and no matter what life pitched at us—and believe me, life has a powerful arm!—Dharmesh's unshakable faith in me and my destiny to finish this book pushed me to the finish line when I thought I couldn't keep going.

I also thank my children—Nicholas, Alyssa, William, Adam, and Chase—who put up with me locking myself in my office many times when I probably should have been spending time with them. I love them with all of my heart.

I thank my father, Fred Bryant, whose constant faith in my ability to do anything I set my mind to helped me grow into a woman who wouldn't give up on herself. Though he is gone, memories of his faith in me fill me always.

I thank my mother, Jean Bryant, who taught me to be a reader, which in turn inspired my writing. She has always been there me for through every victory and failure in my life, and continues to be one of my biggest cheerleaders.

I thank my mother- and father-in-law, Sarlaben and Balventrai Parbhoo, for accepting me into their family as a daughter and always keeping me close.

I thank my sister-in-law, Leena, for being my cultural consultant for the book. Even after 28 years of semi-immersion in Indian culture, my understanding only scratches the surface. She exemplifies a woman steeped in love for her family and her culture, and I admire her strength through adversity that would wither most people.

I thank Wayne South Smith for the inspiring motivation he has given me over the years, and the expert coaching and editing he has provided on this project. I struggled for years with the confidence to write this story, and that all changed when I met him. His talents as a motivational presence and editor are the reasons I finally fleshed out my dreams onto the page and made them into something I can share with others.

I thank Valerie Hudgins for creating my website, *Southern Life Indian Wife*, which helped me build an audience for my story, and for being an early reader of my manuscript. Her favorable response gave me confidence in its audience appeal.

I would also like to thank the women who generously gave their time to read and critique this book when I prematurely thought it was finished: Kim Chamberlain, Miriam Feder, Karen Kroeger, Hana Njau Okolo, Robyn Rubin, and Ann J. Temkin. Their positive comments and words of constructive criticism helped me shape the story into what it is now.

I also thank the people who have come and gone in my life, those who shunned me or Dharmesh from either Indian circles or white American circles. Their attitudes served to instill more appreciation in me for my family, both by blood and by marriage, and realize that true love can really transcend cultural and racial boundaries.

About The Author

Sheryl Parbhoo is an author, blogger, educator, and mother of five. A native southerner, her interest in the intricacies of human culture led to a BA in Anthropology from the University of Memphis. Her longing for the spice of life culminated when she married her high school sweetheart, a South African Indian immigrant, and became a stay-at-home mom to their five children for over 20 years. After diligent, dedicated PTA and Room Mom duties, she earned a BS in Education from Kennesaw State University, becoming an ESOL teacher, focusing on immigrant students from Mexico and Guatemala.

Sheryl is known worldwide for her blog, Southern Life Indian Wife, where for four years she has shared stories from her spicy masala/southern cornbread way of life raising her large multicultural family and navigating the quirks of Southern and Indian in-law relationships. These, along with the responses received from readers, are the real-life inspirations for her novel, *The Unexpected Daughter*.

On sherylparbhoo.com, Sheryl shares her love of writing and personal experiences as a writer. She has been a featured contributor for Masalamommas.com, Twins Magazine, among others. She and her family's blended cultural traditions have been highlighted on PBSNewshour.com, as well as on various online sites.

For more on Sheryl, including social media and contact information, visit sherylparbhoo.com.

65335881R00214

Made in the USA
Charleston, SC
22 December 2016